Praise for the novels of

SHARON
SALA

"Veteran author Sala crafts two exciting leads
bound by their love of animals and reluctance
to trust people."
—*Publishers Weekly* on *The Healer*

"Sharon Sala is not only a top romance novelist,
she is an inspiration for people everywhere who wish
to live their dreams. Her work has a higher purpose
and she takes readers with her on an incredible
journey of overcoming adversity and increased
self-awareness in every book."
—John St. Augustine, host, Power!Talk Radio
WDBC-AM, Michigan

"Sala's characters are vivid and engaging."
—*Publishers Weekly* on *Cut Throat*

Sharon Sala has a "rare ability to bring powerful
and emotionally wrenching stories to life."
—*Romantic Times BOOKreviews*

"A compelling page-turner and a reading experience
I won't soon forget!"
—*Reader to Reader* on *Sweet Baby*

SHARON SALA

THE
WARRIOR

MIRA

ISBN-13: 978-0-7783-2633-5
ISBN-10:   0-7783-2633-0

Recycling programs
for this product may
not exist in your area.

THE WARRIOR

Copyright © 2009 by Sharon Sala.

All rights reserved. Except for use in any review, the reproduction or
utilization of this work in whole or in part in any form by any electronic,
mechanical or other means, now known or hereafter invented, including
xerography, photocopying and recording, or in any information storage or
retrieval system, is forbidden without the written permission of the publisher,
MIRA Books, 225 Duncan Mill Road, Don Mills, Ontario, Canada M3B 3K9.

This is a work of fiction. Names, characters, places and incidents are
either the product of the author's imagination or are used fictitiously, and
any resemblance to actual persons, living or dead, business establishments,
events or locales is entirely coincidental.

MIRA and the Star Colophon are trademarks used under license and registered
in Australia, New Zealand, Philippines, United States Patent and Trademark
Office and in other countries.

www.MIRABooks.com

Printed in U.S.A.

The older I get, the more I have begun to understand the words of my elders.

When my grandfather died, my grandmother was devastated. I remember hearing her say in a tiny, broken voice, "I thought I would go first. I didn't want to be left behind."

When my father, then my sister, died within two months of each other, our whole family was broken. Grocery lists they'd written the week before were still there, but they were not. I remember my mother's shattered words. "No parent should outlive their child."

Long before my fiancé, Bobby, ever began to get sick, he told me out of the blue one day, "If anything ever happens to me, you will be all right."

Then, when he died, I wailed in a lost, hopeless cry, "I wish I could go with him."

In the ensuing weeks after his death, I remembered his prophetic words and I was certain that he was wrong.

I know he laughs now, because time has proved that he was right.

Despite the tragedies and sorrows life hands us, there is always one undeniable truth.

As long as we draw breath, we owe it to the ones we loved and lost to live out our lives without wasting them on regrets.

So...just to set the record straight, you were right, my love.

In honor of those we've loved and lost,

I am dedicating this book to the ones who get left behind.

Prologue

North American Continent—early 1500s

Night Walker, second chief of the Turtle Clan of the Ah-ni-yv-wi-ya, stood on a promontory overlooking the bay of great water near his village. He was a warrior of twenty-nine summers, with a face that was a study in planes and angles. He was also something of an oddity in the tribe, standing head and shoulders above every other warrior. His shoulders were broad, his muscles as hard as the line of his jaw, which, today, was clenched against the angry slap of the wind blowing against his skin. With each fierce gust, his hair—thick, black and straight as the arrows in his quiver—would lift from his shoulders to billow out behind him like the wings of a soaring eagle. As he stood, wearing nothing but a piece of tanned deer hide tied at his waist and hanging to just above his knees, his nostrils flared, savoring the scent of oncoming rain mixing with the ever-present tang of salty air.

For days he'd been having visions that troubled his sleep—bloody visions always ending with death. Troubled by what he believed to be a dark omen of things to come, he'd taken to standing guard on the highest point above the village. Today, when the storm had come in without warning, churning the great water into massive waves higher than Night Walker's head, he'd felt a foreboding similar to that in his dreams.

Now he stood with his feet apart, his body braced against the storm front as he looked out across the bay, watching the dark underbelly of the angry clouds covering the face of the sun. As he watched, a long spear of fire shot out of the clouds and into the water with a loud, angry hiss, sending water flying into the air. Night Walker flinched, and the skin on his face began to tighten. Every instinct signaled that danger was upon them.

A second shaft of fire pierced the clouds, stabbing into the heart of the great water and yanking his gaze from the sky to the horizon. As he watched, a shape began to emerge from the far side of the rocky finger of land pointing out into the water. It was floating on the water like the canoes of his people, but much, much larger, and with big white wings filled with the angry wind. It was unlike anything he'd ever seen, and the sight left him stunned. The unsettled waters were rolling the big canoe from side to side, and he could see men running about on its floor, scrambling like tiny insects trying to outrun a flood as waves washed over the sides. His heart jumped; then his gut knotted as his sense of foreboding grew.

He turned and looked down at the village. His people were as yet unaware of anything more than the oncoming storm. As he watched, he saw his woman, White Fawn, come out of their tepee and go to the woodpile just beyond. She staggered once from a hard buffeting wind, then regained her footing and went about her task. He knew what she was doing—gathering dry wood before the storm got it wet, which made it difficult to burn. She was a good woman, always thinking of his comfort. The mere sight of her always made his pulse quicken. She was his heart, the other half of his soul, and even though the Great Spirit had not blessed them with children, he loved her no less. It wasn't until she went back inside their dwelling that he turned back to the water. When he did, a jolt of fear shot through him. The great canoe was now inside the bay, and three smaller canoes filled with strange-looking men were in the water and coming toward shore.

Their presence was a threat to the Ah-ni-yv-wi-ya, even though he had no words to explain how he knew that. He turned and began scrambling down the steep slope of the bluff, desperate to get back to the village and warn his people.

Antonio Vargas was a pirate with an eye always on the prize just out of his reach. For months he'd heard rumors from Spain that a man named Colombo had found a new route to the West Indies and, in the process, found a land rich in wealth guarded only by a race of savages. In other words, a treasure ripe for the taking.

Before he could act on the notion, an unexpected raid in the night by an English privateer had decimated his crew. They'd managed to escape by sailing into a fog bank. A week later, he'd put into the nearest port and taken on more crew, and for more than a month now, they'd roamed the seas without encountering another vessel or coming within sight of any kind of land. Desperate to recoup his losses as well as his self-esteem, he'd decided to follow Colombo's path and claim some of those easy riches for himself. Only it hadn't been as easy as he'd hoped.

They'd been on the water for more than two months, and Vargas had been beginning to fear his decision had been a bad one when land was finally sighted. It was none too soon. His men were weak, some suffering dysentery. He needed fresh water and fresh food. Sighting land was a godsend, but the upcoming squall at their backs was pushing them in toward shore far faster than he would have liked. As he prayed that they would not founder on a hidden reef, they'd done the best that they could to navigate into the bay. Between the swiftly approaching storm and the sheet of rain that they could see coming across the ocean, he was relieved to drop anchor. Giving orders as fast as he could shout them, Vargas watched as his crew scrambled to obey.

It wasn't until the ship was secure that he took the time to scan the shoreline. Just beyond the shore, nestled up against a backdrop of trees that appeared to be the beginning of a forest beyond, was a village. He couldn't tell much, but it appeared small, composed of no more than thirty dwellings. A slow smile broke across his face. He'd done it! He'd found Colombo's famous new land, too. When he returned, he would also be lauded as a daring explorer. All he needed was proof, like some of the gold he heard Colombo had found. Uncertain as to which would be wisest—ride out the storm before it hit, then go ashore, or go ashore now and take the residents by surprise—Vargas let his greed settle the debate. If he waited, whoever lived there might hide or even run, taking their treasure with them.

Barking another set of orders for boats to be lowered, Vargas watched the village through his spyglass while he waited. When he saw movement and then savages gathering and pointing, he realized that they'd been spotted.

"Make haste!" he yelled, pointing toward shore. "They've seen us!"

Three smaller boats were lowered, manned by six men apiece. Vargas's boat took the lead. About halfway to shore, he looked through his spyglass again, and as he did, his heart jumped. Four of the savages were heading toward the water, while the rest of the villagers had begun to gather in the background, obviously as curious about him and his men as he was about them. The wind was still high, churning the waves. The threatening rain seemed imminent, and yet the villagers didn't seem worried. In response, Vargas's concern over the storm dropped, too. If they thought nothing of it, then neither would he.

Within minutes, the boats were beached. Vargas vaulted out and strode forcefully through the raging surf, ignoring the rising wind and the sea slapping at his legs. Three of his men followed closely. He could hear them cursing and muttering among themselves about the storm and the cold, angry sea. Although more than half of them were weakened from dysentery, he was beyond caring about creature comfort. Greed rose like gorge within him as he watched the approaching savages.

Their skin was dark, but not as dark as a Moor's.

Their hair was long and straight, and seemed to be woven through with bits of feathers and what appeared to be strips of animal skin. They came without care for the wind whipping about their faces and necks, impervious to the impending storm as they stared at him and his men in fascination.

He didn't know or care that they'd never seen men with light skin or hair on their faces, or seen people wear clothing, even in warm weather, that covered their entire bodies. He fingered the scimitar at his waist, then slid the palm of his hand from its hilt to the dirk he'd shoved beneath his wide leather belt. He looked past their crude weapons and animal skins to the bright bits of what he took to be gold, mingled with the strange gemstones and shells they were wearing around their necks. His gaze focused on a small pouch hanging from a leather strip around the neck of one of the savages and he imagined it filled with gold, as well. His imagination swelled as he pictured pots of the jewel-like stones within their huts, maybe even lying about on the ground.

When the first savage stepped up to him and lifted his hand in greeting, Vargas reached for his necklace.

Chief Two Crows, principal chief of the tribe, had been as stunned by the appearance of these men as had Night Walker. With no reason to suspect danger, he'd willingly gone down to greet them. But when the tall stranger with the hairy face suddenly grabbed at his medicine bag and sky stones, he grunted and knocked the man's hand away.

Vargas grinned, then pointed at the chief as he spoke to his men. "So, *amigos,* the savage does not want to share."

Someone chuckled behind him as the first drops of rain began to fall. He reached for the pouch, yanking it from around the old man's neck before he could react, palmed his dirk and slit the savage's throat.

The old chief's shock died with him as his blood spurted onto Vargas's chest.

"Now!" Vargas screamed, then pulled the scimitar from his waist and waved it above his head.

His men swarmed from the boats. With the rain hammering down upon them and the wind pushing against their backs, they raced toward the village, firing their small handguns and hacking at the savages, without care even for woman or child, as they began to run in terror toward the village that would provide no safety now.

Night Walker was halfway down the cliff when he heard the first screams and what sounded like short claps of thunder. But it wasn't until he heard an answering war cry that he knew they were being attacked. He flashed on the visions he'd been having. Fear increased his speed.

He ran without thought for himself while the thunder of his own heart drowned out the screams of his people. The storm was on top of him now, yet he felt none of it. The fear in his belly lent speed to his strides. Tree limbs slapped at his face and against his chest, marking the smooth brown flesh with long, angry streaks, bringing blood that was quickly washed away by the torrent of rain. Night Walker was unaware of all of it—not the sharp, burning pain from the thorny limbs ripping at his flesh, nor the blood and rain pouring down his body. Even though he couldn't hear her, White Fawn's face was before him, her name echoing within his heart. He felt her panic, knew something terrible was happening to her—and that he was not going to be fast enough to save her.

When he finally burst out of the forest into the clearing, it was to a scene of horror. What he saw was worse than his nightmares, bloodier than his visions.

The enemy had come, and the enemy had killed.

Everyone.

The only signs of life were the strangers, ripping clothing from the People's bodies, yanking totems and medicine bags from around their necks. Laughing as if their greatest joy in life was desecration.

When Night Walker saw a tall man with a hairy face reach down and rip the sky stone from around White Fawn's neck, shock rolled through him. Her head lolled lifelessly as the man shoved her limp body aside with his foot. Night Walker saw the rain pouring down into her dark, unseeing eyes, flooding her nostrils, washing the blood from her face.

He screamed—first in horror, then in rage.

With the bodies of his people strewn about like maize husks tossed by the wind, he pulled the first arrow from his quiver, notched it and took aim. The arrow cut through the downpour in a blur, piercing the throat of the nearest man, who dropped the booty he'd been carrying and grabbed at both sides of the shaft. His eyes bulged as a bubble of blood popped on his lips. He was dead before he hit the ground.

Night Walker notched another arrow, took aim and let fly, watching with grim satisfaction as, one by one, the unsuspecting invaders dropped where they stood. Their cries of pain or shock went unnoticed by the others, drowned out by the sound of the storm. He fired off another arrow, then another and another, until he'd emptied his quiver, leaving them with a band of far fewer men than when they'd landed.

It wasn't until he grabbed a club and a spear from a nearby hut and began running toward them, screaming an endless war cry, that the others realized he was there.

A man named Miguelito Colon saw the crazed savage coming toward them and shouted at Vargas over the storm.

Vargas spun just in time to see the attacker run Colon through with a spear. Even though he was accustomed to hand-to-hand combat, he flinched as Colon's guts spilled out on the ground, the spear still quivering in his belly.

Vargas roared in anger, surprised by both the savage's sudden appearance as well as the shocking number of his crew who now lay dead. As the rain blurred his vision, a cold wind whipped through the village, suddenly chilling him to the bone.

At that moment, it crossed his mind that he should have waited until the storm passed before coming ashore. But nothing could change what was, and the savage was only one man—little more than a lingering nuisance.

"Get him!" he shouted, waving his men toward the tall, nearly naked man coming at them on the run.

Arturo Medajine grabbed for his handgun, took aim and fired. But the powder was soaked, and by the time he dropped the gun to reach for his sword, the savage was upon him.

The savage swung his wooden club as he passed, cracking Medajine's skull. The man never knew what hit him.

* * *

Night Walker's gaze was still fixed on the man who'd killed White Fawn. As he passed her grandfather's corpse, he grabbed the spear from Brown Owl's lifeless hands then leaped a small child's body.

The next man to come at him did so with a broadsword. Night Walker dodged, then speared him in the gut. The man was still screaming as Night Walker took the sword out of his hands and decapitated him where he stood.

Vargas was shocked. The savage was still alive and downing his men one after the other. Compared to the others they'd encountered, this one was extremely tall— as tall as Vargas himself. Before he could react, thunder rattled the ground on which they stood. The lightning bolt that followed struck nearby, so close that they were all momentarily blinded. By the time Vargas could see clearly again, the savage was less than a hundred feet away and another of his men was dead.

His fingers tightened around the hasp of his scimitar as a storm gust staggered him.

"Damnation," he cursed, and then swung his blade in the air. "Peron! The savage! Stop him!"

Luis Peron was at home on the deck of a ship, but, weakened from dysentery and slogging around in the mud with the armload of furs he'd just dragged out of a hut, he was at a huge disadvantage. Still, Vargas was his captain, and orders were to be obeyed. He dropped the furs and was reaching for the knife in his belt when a blow from the savage's broadsword split his breastbone.

He dropped where he stood.

Vargas's heart ricocheted against his rib cage. This

wasn't happening. He'd fought the most heinous of men—in seaports, on the sea, in the dark, beneath the subtle glow of a full moon, even in the alleyways of London, England, in full daylight. So why had killing one savage become such a difficult feat?

Nervous now that his men were too few, and knowing he was dangerously out of his element, Vargas began to retreat, taking the remaining men with him.

"Back to the boats!" he yelled, and then, without waiting to see who followed, he started running, now facing the full fury of the storm.

The few surviving sailors gladly obeyed and headed for the boats, following Vargas's retreat. But for every two steps Vargas took, the storm slowed him by one. Afraid to look over his shoulder—afraid to slow down—all he could do was keep putting one foot in front of the other.

Even though the intruders were falling one by one beneath Night Walker's hand, he felt no satisfaction. Revenge would not be done until he had spilled the blood of the man who'd cut White Fawn's throat and ripped away her medicine pouch. Not until he watched the tall, hairy-faced thief draw his last breath would the fire in his gut cease to burn.

When the invaders suddenly turned away and began running back to their canoes, Night Walker panicked. They couldn't escape! They had to pay for what they'd done.

He caught up with the slowest of them within seconds, grabbed him by the hair hanging out from under his water-sodden hat and yanked.

The man's white-rimmed eyes had one last glance of

the sky before Night Walker's flint knife sliced across his jugular and an arterial spray of red shot across his line of vision and everything went dark.

Night Walker only grunted as the body fell at his feet. He was nothing but one less man between him and the one who'd killed White Fawn.

Another flash of lightning shot out of the clouds, striking the bluff on which Night Walker had been standing only a short time ago, momentarily blinding him. Even as he kept running, there was a subconscious part of him that wished he'd still been on that bluff when the fire had come down. Then he wouldn't be feeling this horrible, rending pain. Then he wouldn't have to face burying every person he'd ever known and loved.

By the time his vision cleared, the strangers were at the edge of the great water and pushing off from shore, piling into one canoe as fast as they could climb, leaving the other canoes behind. Rage surged as he lengthened his stride. He couldn't let them get away. Not now. Not when he was so close.

Then he saw the tall one—the leader—grab the oars and begin to paddle against the surge. Still too far from shore to reach them in time, Night Walker knew that revenge was slipping away. When the other men began to row, as well, he knew his chance had flown.

By the time he reached the water, they were as good as gone, but his rage and fury were not. He ran out into the surf until the backwash from the storm reached his knees. He lifted his arms above his head, screaming into the storm—cursing the man with White Fawn's sky stones, calling for the Old Ones, pleading with the

Great Spirit, offering his soul for the right to avenge the deaths of White Fawn and the dead Ah-ni-yv-wi-ya.

As the canoe moved farther and farther away, he stood there in the water, and screamed and shouted, pointing toward the canoe, then slapping his chest and opening his arms as if embracing the storm.

He was daring them to come back, to face him man-to-man—to give him a chance to avenge his people in an honorable way. But it was obvious these men had no honor, because they kept rowing in the opposite direction.

Vargas couldn't believe it. The bastard was still daring them—slapping at his chest as if offering the broad expanse as a target. After the humiliation of turning tail and running, he couldn't resist the offer, but he was too far away to throw a knife, and his pistol was empty. He wasn't sure if he could load his gun again in this downpour, but he was damn sure going to try. He crouched down in the boat, then pulled his jacket up and over his head. Using it as a cover, he began trying to load his gun. The boat was rocking so hard he kept spilling his powder. Twice he dropped the lead shot. His hands were shaking from exertion, but his determination won out. Rising from the bottom of the boat like Neptune coming up from the bottom of the sea, he threw off his jacket, stepped up onto a seat, bracing himself against the rock and roll of the boat. The savage was still there, holding his arms out at his sides and shouting words Vargas could not understand, although their meaning was clear.

He took aim and fired.

The sound of the shot rang in his own ears. Even through the downpour, he could smell the burning powder. In his mind, he could almost see the shot spanning the distance between himself and the savage.

He held his breath—waiting to see the savage drop, just as the others had done. Only then would the whole sorry sortie be behind him.

Night Walker had screamed until his voice was nearly gone. He'd prayed and begged and cursed the Old Ones, demanding to know why he alone had been spared. The muscles in his body were starting to tremble. His gut was a knot of pain. He'd pulled at his hair and ripped his own flesh with his fingernails, needing satisfaction—wanting to die.

Then he saw the leader suddenly stand up in the canoe and point at him.

He screamed into the wind and slapped his own chest over and over, daring the man to come back and fight, but the invaders were still moving toward their winged canoe.

There was a loud noise, and then everything, including time, seemed to slow down. It was still raining, but suddenly it was as if he were seeing each raindrop as it fell, hearing his own heartbeat over the roll of thunder, feeling the exhalation of his own breath more sharply than the wind hitting him in the face. In the midst of that reality, he saw something fly from the hand of the man who'd killed White Fawn, coming at him, cutting through the rain, pushing aside the air with a high-pitched whistle.

He stopped, his arms dropping at his sides as he watched it come, accepting that this was death. The Old Ones had heard his prayer. Whatever this was, it would end his life in battle in an honorable way. He would join

White Fawn and the others. He would not walk this land alone.

He waited. Unblinking. Barely breathing. Watching as death came for him.

Then it hit.

He waited to feel pain.

Expected to see his own blood pouring down his chest.

Instead, it bounced off the broad expanse of his chest and fell into the water.

He grabbed his chest in disbelief.

"No!" he screamed, then spun toward the village, striding to the shore, staring at the bodies, willing them to rise up and walk. This couldn't be happening.

He'd tried to avenge them, but the enemy was escaping.

He'd tried to die, to go with them, but he'd failed at that, too.

He looked over his shoulder. The man in the canoe was staring at him in disbelief. Night Walker's misery was complete. He didn't notice that the wind had died and the rain had quit falling. All he could think about was everything he had lost.

Then the clouds parted, and a single ray of light poured down onto the shore, bathing him in what felt like fire.

So…now I will die.

He arched his back, lifted his arms above his head, closed his eyes and waited to be consumed. Instead, he heard drums, then voices, and even though he couldn't see them, he knew he was in the presence of the Old Ones. When their chants turned into words, he fell to his knees.

"Night Walker—son of the Ah-ni-yv-wi-ya, son of the Turtle Clan—we hear you. Brave son of the Ah-ni-yv-wi-ya, you have fought well. You have honored us in life as you honor us in death. Look now to the great waters. Look upon the face of your enemy and know that whatever face he wears, you will always feel his heartbeat. Son of the Ah-ni-yv-wi-ya, we have heard your prayer. Son of the Ah-ni-yv-wi-ya, listen to our words. You will live until the blood of your enemy is spilled upon your feet. You will live until you feel his last breath on your face. Then and only then, will you be as all men. Then and only then, will you suffer and grow old. Then and only then, will you live until you die. But for now it as you have asked. You will live."

The light disappeared. The clouds blew away. Night Walker swayed, then staggered where he stood. The Old Ones were silent. The fire was gone, and he was not consumed. He looked to the water. The enemy was climbing aboard the great canoe and scrambling about as if they were crazed.

He saw the tall bearded man standing at the front of the canoe, staring toward shore. He felt the man's blood pulsing through his body in an urgent, panicked gush, though he did not know why.

Vargas was in shock. He had witnessed the savage's baptism in fire, expected to see him incinerated, been shocked to see him standing safely on the sand. The men around him began talking in hushed tones, attributing magical powers to the fact that though the savage had been shot, the bullet had bounced off his flesh like a single drop of rain. That he'd been struck by lightning and walked away unharmed.

Vargas was afraid. He didn't know what had just happened, but when it came to the supernatural, he was out of his element. Yet what other explanation could there be? The savage had killed more than twelve of his men single-handedly, been shot without suffering a wound and been struck by lightning without being burned. The man should be dead, and yet they were the ones on the run and the savage was standing alone on shore, watching them go.

He knew his crew was scared. They'd all been through something they didn't understand. But it was over. It was over, and he was still alive to tell the tale. He wanted to turn his back on the whole thing and pretend it had never happened. But there was the matter of all those dead men, and the still-pressing need for food and fresh water.

He felt the eyes of his men on him, waiting to see what would happen next. He'd lost face when he'd let one single man—and a savage, at that—put him on the run. He turned his back to shore and faced the crew.

"Hoist the anchor!" he shouted.

Even though two men ran to do his bidding, no one would look at him. A shiver of fear ran through him. Sailors were a superstitious lot. If they lost trust in him, his own life was in danger.

He shoved one of the crewmen who was running past him. "Weakling! Make haste, or I'll feed you to the fishes."

The sailor staggered, quickly righting himself before hurrying to do what he'd been told. The captain was angry, and they all knew him well enough to know that he would take his anger out on whoever was closest.

But the ones who'd been on shore with Vargas weren't afraid of him—not anymore. They'd seen him panic. They'd seen him turn tail from only one savage and run like a woman toward safety. They were sick and hungry, and someone needed to be blamed for their situation. Vargas was the logical target.

By the time the moon rose that night, Vargas was standing at the end of the plank, begging for his life. It never struck him that the savages he'd killed that morning had been doing the same thing. He didn't feel remorse for what he'd done to them—only that his life was going to end in such a humiliating fashion.

A shot rang out.

Unlike the shot he'd fired at the savage that morning, this bullet quickly found its mark. He felt a fire in his chest, and then he was falling, falling.

Water closed over his face, then washed up his nose, choking off the curses he was heaping on the heads of his mutinous crew. The last image that swept through his mind before he died was of the savage pointing at him from shore.

One

Georgia—Present Day

Despite the hundreds of years that John Nightwalker had been on this earth, he had yet to feel completely comfortable wearing clothes. And from the look the female bank teller was giving him as he stood in line at the First Savannah Savings and Loan to cash a check, she would have been perfectly happy to help him strip.

John felt her gaze but was ignoring all the signals. Not only was he not in the mood for dallying with a stranger, she was wearing a wedding ring—a big no-no for him. He shifted from one foot to the other, then looked down at the two little boys clinging to the legs of the woman in front of him and grinned. The oldest one smiled back, while the younger one continued the exploration of his right nostril with his index finger.

"Hi," the older one said. "My name is Brandon Doggett." He pointed toward the little guy. "That's Trevor Doggett. He's my little brother." Then he pointed at his mother's backside, which John had already noticed was quite shapely. "That's my mama. Her name is Doggett, too."

When Mama Doggett realized her name was being bandied about, she glanced over her shoulder to see who her son was talking to. Her eyes widened slightly as she saw John Nightwalker's face. The smooth coffee skin, high cheekbones, strong chin and nose were telling of his Native American heritage, but it was the sexy smile and glint in his eyes that stopped her breath. She might be married, but she wasn't dead and the man was stunning.

"I hope the boys aren't bothering you," she said.

John grinned. "No, ma'am."

"Daddy calls her Lisa," Brandon offered.

Lisa Doggett rolled her eyes as John chuckled.

The low, husky rumble of his laugh made the female teller lose count of the cash she'd been dispensing. With pink cheeks and a muttered apology to her customer, she began again.

Lisa Doggett, being next in line, finally reached the teller and proceeded with her business. When they were done, the teller handed each little boy a lollipop, which they promptly peeled and popped into their mouths. Lisa flashed John a shy goodbye smile and started toward the front door with her sons in tow.

Being next in line, John moved up to the window, patiently waiting as the teller keyed in some data from her previous customer. There was a moment of silence—a soft, peaceful sound of shuffling feet and the distant murmurs between loan officers and their clients—then John felt the atmosphere change. To him, the room was suddenly stifling and charged with an anger he didn't understand.

"Sir. How can I help you?" the teller asked, but John didn't respond.

His gaze went from Lisa Doggett and her boys, who were on their way toward the exit, to the surrounding customers waiting in line. Suddenly one of the two boys cried out, then turned around and ran. John noticed a toy car in the middle of the lobby and figured it had fallen out of a pocket. He saw the mother's irked expression turn to one of quiet patience as she waited for her son's return.

His attention moved from them to the rest of the crowd. At first glance, no one stood out, and then his gaze fell on a tall, heavyset man standing in line on the other side of the lobby. He was wearing a pair of faded Levi's and a heavy denim jacket. The jacket seemed out of place, considering the outside temperature was in the high eighties. That alone immediately set him apart. The man's lower jaw jutted from his face like a bull-dog's—a strong protruding lower jaw that extended beyond the tip of a nose that had obviously been broken more than once. His skin was ruddy, his hair a brittle yellow color. John could feel the tension emanating from him. He didn't know what was going to happen but sensed it wouldn't be good.

As he continued to watch, the big man headed toward a teller, walked up to the window and slid what appeared to be a white cotton bag across the counter. It looked like an ordinary deposit bag, but when the teller's face turned pale and her eyes widened in shock, John tensed.

He could see the man's lips moving, but he was too

far away to hear what was being said. All of a sudden the teller's eyes rolled back in her head as she dropped to the floor in a faint. Everyone heard the thud as her head collided with the hard marble floor. The teller next to her screamed out for help as everything ground to a halt.

Wallace Deeds cursed beneath his breath, unable to believe what had just happened. In all the years he'd been doing this, he'd never had anyone faint on him before. He was a criminal, but he wasn't stupid. At this point, his best bet was to retrieve the note he'd handed to the teller and calmly walk out of the building. To his dismay, the note was no longer on the counter. It was on the floor beside the unconscious woman.

"Crap," Wallace muttered, and slid his hand in his pocket, taking comfort from the gun he could feel inside. He glanced up and around, quickly sizing up the number of people inside the bank against his need for dough. He opted for a hasty exit.

But his plan was screwed by a secretary who'd come to the unconscious teller's aid. She was on her knees beside the woman and feeling for a pulse when she discovered the note.

I have a gun. Put all your money in the bag and keep quiet or you're a dead woman.

Unaware that he'd been made, Deeds was already heading toward the door when the secretary stood up and screamed.

"Stop him! He has a gun!"

Wallace cursed and turned. The bank guard was pulling out his pistol and coming toward him on the run. Without thinking, Wallace grabbed the nearest customer by the arm and put her in a choke hold as he pulled out his own gun and fired a shot into the ceiling.

"Everyone on the floor! Now!" he screamed.

The bank guard stood his ground, still aiming his weapon and shouting, "Drop the gun! Drop it! Drop it and let her go!"

John groaned. The hostage was none other than Lisa Doggett, the young woman with the two little boys who'd been in line in front of him.

Bad move. Bad, bad move.

The young mother's panic was evident as she cast a frantic, wild-eyed gaze at her little boys. Trevor, the youngest, began to cry and started toward her.

"Don't anybody move!" Wallace roared, waving the gun at the guard, then at the kids and back again.

John knew the man was a hair's breadth away from shooting someone, whether he meant to or not, and Trevor Doggett's determination to get to his mother was putting him in harm's way. There was no time for John to think about the wisdom of his actions.

In one swift move, he pulled a knife from his boot and leaped forward, desperate to draw the gunman's attention away from the boys, his hostage and the guard with the gun, knowing full well that he was going to get shot. Knowing full well it was going to hurt like hell— but it wasn't going to kill him.

That was the edge he had over everyone else in the room. He'd faced death and cheated it countless times over the last five hundred years and had every confidence in the world that he was going to cheat it again.

When Wallace Deeds saw the movement from the corner of his eye, he swung his pistol. A man was coming at him on the run.

"Son of a bitch!" he screamed, then fired.

The shot went straight into John's chest. He felt the impact and a sharp, searing pain, but he didn't go down.

When Deeds' hostage fainted and went limp, she became a liability instead of a shield. Disgusted, he shoved her aside and squeezed off another shot. But it was the knife suddenly protruding from his chest that sent his second shot into the ceiling next to the first.

A collective gasp rose from inside the bank, followed by a silence so stark that everyone froze.

Lisa Doggett had come to and was on her knees, shielding her children with her body.

The tellers had ducked behind the counter.

The people who'd dropped to their bellies when the shooting started were staring but not moving.

No one ran.

No one spoke.

But the ones who could see were staring in disbelief at the two giants standing in the middle of the lobby—both bleeding profusely—waiting to see who dropped first.

The pistol slipped out of Deeds' hand as he reached toward the bone handle of the knife stuck in his chest. But the moment he touched it, he shuddered. Had someone poured hot oil into his chest? He looked up. People's faces were blurring.

"How…" He sighed, then staggered backward.

John groaned as he put a hand to his own chest. The warm gush of his blood was already slowing as he watched the gunman fall. Wallace's head hit the tile with a sickening crack, but he never felt it. He was already dead.

The bank guard holstered his weapon and started toward John.

Lisa Doggett was shaking, but she was alive and her children were safe.

People were getting up and yanking out their cell phones, anxious to tell their loved ones what had just happened. While on his belly, one customer had videoed the whole thing with his cell phone, and now he was in the act of forwarding it to his brother. The image of what had transpired would be all over the Internet before nightfall.

Horace Miles, the bank president, was moving through the crowd, making sure everyone was okay. When he saw the blood on the front and back of John's shirt, he gasped and yelled for someone to call 911.

John was anxious to be gone before he had to explain why the bullet hole in his chest was already nearly closed. He pulled his knife out of the robber's chest, then wiped the blood off the blade onto the man's jacket before slipping it back into the sheath inside his boot.

The bank guard reached John and took him by the elbow.

"You need to sit down, son," he said. "You've been shot."

"I'm okay," John said.

"The police are coming!" someone said.

Sirens could be heard in the distance. John sighed. He needed to leave—now. He started toward the door, but Horace Miles cut him off. Like the guard, he took John by the elbow and tried to usher him to a chair.

"Please," Miles said. "You're bleeding. Let us help you."

"I'm all right...really."

But the bank president would have none of it.

Lisa Doggett came toward him, hugging her little boys to her legs as she stared at him in disbelief.

"You saved my life. You saved all of us," she whispered. "Thank you. *Thank you.*"

"Yeah...sure," he said, then gave in to the inevitable. He was caught now, and there was no way out of it.

The two little boys stared at him—silent now in the face of what they'd witnessed.

"Mama's okay, boys," John said softly.

Brandon nodded. "You stopped the bad man," he said.

John just winked and nodded. The pain in his chest was fading swiftly, but the sirens were also getting closer. Moments later, a half-dozen police cars were on the scene, followed by two ambulances. A paramedic team followed the police inside, then, at the guard's direction, headed for John.

He sighed. How the hell was he going to explain his way out of this?

"I'm okay," he said as the paramedics dropped their bags and began to cut off his shirt. "I said...I'm okay," he repeated, and to prove he was right, he pulled up his shirt, revealing the wound that was almost closed.

Both paramedics rocked back on their heels, staring at John and then at each other.

"Mister...how in—"

"Er...uh...I studied with the Dalai Lama," John said.

"Learned how to control bleeding and heal myself with my mind. Ever hear of it?"

They looked at each other, shrugged, and then began packing up their gear while sneaking curious looks at him.

But they weren't the only ones staring. The bank president was in shock. He'd seen the bullet pierce John's chest, seen the blood spurting, yet now the wound was nearly closed. He'd seen the other scars on John's chest, too, and was staggered by what this man had suffered and lived through.

Just when John was getting ready to leave, a skinny man in a suit followed several uniformed officers into the bank, paused long enough to question the guard, then headed straight for John, who recognized the type, as well as the badge clipped to the man's belt.

Great. A detective. Naturally nosy, disinclined to believe anything he was told. This ought to be good.

John saw him pause to look at the dead man; then he looked straight at John, who stared back without flinching.

Horace Miles stepped into the silent breach by introducing himself as the cop approached.

"I'm Horace Miles, president of the bank. I saw everything."

"Detective Robert Lee," the newcomer said, then put his hands on his hips and gave John the once-over, eyeing the bloody shirt as well as the blood on John's jeans. "So, hero, what's your name?"

Sarcasm was the last thing John expected. It made him angry. He stood abruptly, well aware that he was now towering over the skinny man's head.

"Considering the fact that right now, my chest hurts

like hell, I don't appreciate your sarcasm," he drawled. "My name is John Nightwalker, and I'm not a hero. I was just in the wrong place at the right time."

Lee wanted to be pissed, but the man was right. "Sorry," he said. "That came out wrong. Let's back up and do this all over again. So, Mr. Nightwalker, could you tell me what happened?"

John pointed to the walls where a half-dozen cameras were mounted. "I could…but it appears that Mr. Miles here will be able to provide several different angles on the incident for your viewing pleasure. Suffice it to say, the man tried to rob the bank, took a woman hostage and was pointing his gun at one of her kids. I distracted him. He shot me instead of the kid. I put a knife in his chest."

Believing John had already been tended by paramedics, Lee's next thought was the weapon in question. "May I see that knife?"

John winced as he leaned over, pulled up the leg of his jeans, then pulled the knife back out of its scabbard.

The detective's eyes widened and his mouth dropped as he eyed the wicked blade. It was almost ten inches in length, with its widest point no less than three inches across. The handle appeared to be some kind of bone— maybe ivory. He frowned.

"Hell, mister, that thing's big enough to fight bears with."

"Yes."

Startled by the easy answer, Lee gave John a cool look. "Don't tell me you fight bears, too?"

"Okay," John said, well aware he was pissing the man off. But he didn't care. The detective's attitude was anything but cordial, and John would have liked a couple of painkillers for his trouble.

Lee's mouth dropped. "You fought a bear?"

John grinned slightly. "You don't fight bears, detective. You either outrun them or kill them. I've done both."

Lee snapped his mouth shut and glared.

"Do you have a permit to carry a concealed weapon?"

"Yes, actually, I do." John pulled out his wallet and produced the license.

Lee eyed it without comment, then handed it back.

The bank president was surprised by the detective's attitude.

"I'm sorry for interrupting, Detective Lee, but you don't seem to understand. This man averted what could have been a long, drawn-out hostage situation. He saved a woman's life and, most likely, the lives of everyone in here. There's no way of knowing who that bastard would have shot next. Mr. Nightwalker did nothing but defend himself. The robber shot first. Ask anyone here."

"Oh, I will," Lee said.

"Am I free to go?" John asked.

"I'm going to need you to come down to headquarters and—"

"Why?" John asked. "Your case is closed."

"Because you put a knife in a man's chest, that's why," Lee argued, then realized people were staring and pulled back his emotions.

"He shot me first," John said. "Don't I get to defend myself?"

"Yes, but—"

"I have a permit for the knife."

"I'm the one doing the questioning," Lee snapped.

"Then ask me some questions," John said.

Lee glared, then remembered that this man had supposedly been shot. "If you're shot, why aren't you on your way to the hospital?"

John sighed, resisted the urge to roll his eyes and yanked his shirt off over his head.

"That's where it went in." He turned around. "And that's where it came out. I heal fast."

The raw edges of burned flesh were obvious, but the wound was almost closed. Lee didn't believe a damned word of what he was being told but couldn't figure out the man's angle.

"No one heals that fast," he said. "Those are old wounds. You might have been shot, but not today. You and that dead man were in cahoots, and for some reason you backed out and killed him to keep from being brought down with him."

"Bullshit," John said, and pointed to the cameras again. "Watch the fucking movie, Detective. I've banked here for years. Mr. Miles has my address and phone number if you're interested. Now…if you're not going to arrest me, I'm leaving. I need to rest."

John held out his hand, waiting for the cop to give back his knife.

The silence stretched between them, but John wouldn't budge. Finally Lee handed back the knife and watched John return it to the scabbard, then pick up his bloody shirt and walk out of the bank without looking back.

Lee was angry and distrustful but had no reason to hold him. Instead, he pointed to all the cameras.

"I want that security footage. Now."

Horace Miles waved a teller over. "Go to the back and get all the security tapes from today and bring them here, please."

* * *

Savannah was far behind him as John neared the turnoff leading toward his home. Glad the two-hour trip was nearly over, he began to slow down. Moments later, he turned off the main highway and began the long winding drive up the bluff to his house. Owning the land where his village once stood had taken several hundred years to make happen, but once it had, he found an odd sort of peace in living here again.

He'd dodged civil wars, fought through world wars, and had long since gotten over the shock of watching the unsullied beauty of the country go to hell in a hand-basket while trying to find the reincarnation of his enemy. It pained him to see refuse washing down once-pristine mountain streams. The clean air he'd taken for granted as a child was now a luxury. Landfills were a scourge on Mother Earth. The Ah-ni-yv-wi-ya would be shocked by what time and people had done.

He owned three other homes in separate parts of the country, and every few years he switched residences to keep from having to explain to neighbors why he never aged. It was simple. He would just change his hairstyle and choice of clothing, then present himself as a relative of the previous owner. So far, the system had proven to be fool-proof, but he never took anything for granted. Caution—and finding the soul of the man who'd murdered his people—was always at the forefront of his mind.

For the past three years, he'd been back in Georgia. From his bedroom window he could see the place where he'd laid the bodies of his people to rest. Although their bones had long since turned to dust, his memory of the day was as vivid as if it had happened yesterday.

Usually he took pleasure in the drive up the bluff to his house, but not this time. He was heartily glad it was over. This morning had been unexpected and exhausting. He breathed a sigh of relief as he pulled into the garage, closing the doors behind him. His chest still hurt, but it was no longer open or bleeding. Within a couple of days there would be nothing left but another scar to add to the collection already on his body.

He got out of the Jeep, grabbed the groceries he'd bought earlier and headed for the kitchen. It was a long drive from Savannah, so his only purchases had been nonperishables. When he needed fresh vegetables or anything dairy, he bought it down in Justice, a little town only a few miles away. Justice boasted a population of almost five hundred people and was little more than a spot on the map. Down there, people referred to him as Big John. They knew nothing of the wealth he'd accumulated over the centuries, his skill in the stock market or the goods he imported and exported to different countries. He kept his acquaintances at a friendly arm's length. The less he shared of himself, the better.

As soon as the groceries were put away, he headed for the utility room, stripping off his clothes as he went. The shirt was a bust. Even if the blood washed out, there was the small matter of the bullet holes. He tossed it in the trash, treated the blood spots on his jeans with stain remover, then tossed everything into the washer and turned it on. When he left the room, he was wearing his favorite outfit—the skin in which he'd been born.

His body was toned, his legs long and lean. His shoulders were wide, and bore the weight of centuries of despair with equanimity. His hair, which had once hung all the way to his waist, was now short and spiked. Instead of the occasional feather he'd once worn in it, there was a tiny silver earring in the shape of a feather hanging from his left ear, his only outward claim to his past.

Even though the wood floors were bare of rugs, he moved silently. The windows he'd left open earlier in the day were now funneling a cool ocean breeze against his skin, which he much preferred to air-conditioning.

On his way through the living room, his gaze automatically went to a small scraping knife decoratively framed and hanging on the wall between a stone ax and a dream catcher. That small piece of flint was all he had left of White Fawn. Regret tugged at his heart as he remembered her—bent over the task of scraping meat from pelts and skins with that very knife— remembered the soft, warm clothing she made for them after the skins had cured. If fate had been kind, he would have died with the others. But he hadn't died. He'd asked the Old Ones for the impossible, and it had been given, even though he had yet to fulfill his side of the bargain. Angry with himself and what he considered his failure for being unable to find the enemy, he turned off the memories and headed for his room to shower.

Later, washed clean of blood and wearing a pair of old gray sweats, John went about the solitary business of preparing a meal for himself. His life was what it was—but by choice. Yes, there were times when he was so lonely he couldn't think, when the memory of White Fawn's laugh was so strong he wanted to weep. Yes, there had been other women in his life through the ensuing centuries, but none that had ever replaced her in his heart.

Living in his skin while the world grew up and old around him had not been easy. He'd been an "uncivilized" man to the hordes who'd invaded, when in his eyes, they'd been the ones with no heart and no civility. They recognized nothing of the indigenous people's rights, but he'd soon learned the need to be able to communicate with the interlopers, and had become a guide and an interpreter for the explorers and trappers later on.

Throughout the ages, he'd watched the natural beauty of the land on which he'd been born become glutted with people with no conscience, no interest save their own wishes and desires. They'd come on ships by the hundreds, then the thousands. They'd cut down the trees, and built houses and dams; they'd made roads and cities, and fouled the water and the air so many times over the centuries that he'd lost count. When their numbers had been too many and their greed had been too great, then had come the wars. Fighting over religion and countries and the color of skin. It was enough to make a man go crazy, but he'd been raised in the old ways, and warriors didn't cry. They endured.

After so much time of being a "lesser" member of society because of the color of his skin, the irony that it was now fashionable to be able to claim Native American heritage was not lost on John Nightwalker.

When his food was ready, he filled a plate and took it out onto the patio overlooking the ocean. It was the same place he'd been standing when he'd first seen the devil ship sail out of the storm and into their lives. He cut a piece from the steak that he'd cooked and put it in his mouth, chewing slowly while watching the horizon with a dark, steady gaze. Even though centuries had come and gone since the massacre, old instincts die hard. The need to still stand watch was strong. And even though he didn't believe fate would be so kind as to send his enemy back to him that way again, he had learned long ago not to trust anyone or anything—not even fate.

What he did know, and had known for at least sixty years, was that the soul he sought had once again been reborn. And he knew this because of the signs that came with it.

The first was always the dream of the massacre, after which he would wake up shaking and sick to his stomach, drenched in sweat. He'd learned, too, that the closer he got to the reincarnated soul, the more rapidly his heart would beat. He'd followed those feelings all over the world so many times he'd lost count, but he had never been able to find his nemesis. When the feelings disappeared, he could only assume that his enemy was dead and once again his soul was no longer earthbound.

He finished his meal in silence, watched the sea until the sun had set behind him, then got up and went inside. He turned on the television in the kitchen as he cleaned up, only to find that the botched bank robbery was the topic of the national news. He watched the film clip without moving, wincing slightly when he heard his name come out of the newscaster's mouth. Still, it was done, and he wouldn't have changed anything in any way. When the newscast was over, he turned off the TV and went to bed.

Another day had passed.

One more night alone.

Detective Robert Lee hit Rewind on the bank security tape, then Stop. Then Play. Once again he saw the botched bank robbery in progress, from the moment the teller fainted to the point where the perp headed for the door. He saw the guard grab his pistol as the perp took a hostage. It wasn't pretty, but it was, in the realm of law and order, what constituted an ordinary screwup, not unlike a dozen other scenarios he'd seen in his eighteen-year career on the force. It was what came next that didn't make sense. And if he hadn't been watching it over and over for the last few hours, he wouldn't have believed it had happened.

When he got to the point where the perp, who they now knew was a man named Wallace Deeds, had taken a hostage, his attention shifted into high gear. First the hostage's two little boys began to cry. When the smallest boy started toward his mother, Lee began to tense, waiting for that damned Indian to make his move. And even though he knew what was going to happen, it was still shocking to witness. All of a sudden, Nightwalker was in full camera range, running at the gunman and his hostage with a knife in his hand.

Lee watched Deeds spin and fire. He saw the bullet hit the Indian. He saw blood spurt out the back of his shoulder and his shirt instantly turn red. Then Lisa Doggett went limp and Deeds shoved her away. He watched her come to and run to her boys, shielding them with her body. Deeds seemed to be about to fire a second shot, but it never happened. One moment the knife was in Nightwalker's hand and the next it was in Wallace Deeds' chest.

Deeds went down, but the Indian didn't. That was what kept freaking Lee out.

When the Indian bent over and pulled the knife out of Deeds' chest without staggering or showing any pain, Lee simply couldn't wrap his mind around it. He wanted to have a reason to go after Nightwalker, but there wasn't one, and considering the half-dozen new cases on his desk, he knew it was time to let this one go, however reluctantly.

Two days later—Justice, Georgia

Alicia Ponte's life was one of wealth and privilege. She was the daughter of a rich man, the type of woman who headed committees and organized charity functions. She wore the right clothes, knew the right people and always made the society pages. She had friends, but none were close. She'd had one boyfriend in college and a brief relationship with another man over three years ago, and nothing that mattered since.

At twenty-seven years old, she had always thought of herself as confident and self-assured, but the last twenty-two hours had proved her wrong. She was scared—as scared as she'd ever been—and of someone who was supposed to love her. The irony that she'd waited until now to run away from home was lost in the gut-wrenching fear that kept her moving. But her flight was about to be sidetracked by the need for fuel.

She glanced down at the gas gauge. It was too close to empty to dare trying to make it to Savannah, but according to a road sign she'd seen a mile back, Marv's Gas and Guzzle should be able to take care of that.

A short while later, she came upon the city limit sign of Justice, Georgia, population: 488. Alicia didn't care how many people lived here. She just wanted some of Marv's gas—and maybe a cold drink and a snack— then she was back on the road. Only, running wasn't going to solve her problem. She couldn't run forever. She needed a place to hide. That she was hiding from her father was nothing short of horrifying, but there was no denying what she'd accidentally overheard.

Her father—Richard Ponte, the largest arms manufacturer in the western hemisphere—was selling weapons to the enemy in Iraq, as well as to the American soldiers who were fighting them. Profiting from the war in the most hideous manner and arming both sides with the same most up-to-date munitions money could buy.

Her father had been overseas for almost a year, opening a new recycling plant in Taiwan, overseeing the closing of a tire factory in India. She'd visited him a couple of times but had opted to go back to Miami. It made her uncomfortable to know that he was taking advantage of the poverty and strife in those countries by paying the workers only a fraction of what he would have had to pay American employees. Once he was back, she was excited to have company for dinner again.

She'd been on her way into his office to see if he would be staying home for lunch when she realized he wasn't alone. She heard her father and his old friend Jacob Carruthers talking, and she smiled to herself, thinking she would get to share a meal with Uncle Jake, as well. Just as she started to knock, she heard her father curse, which shocked her. He didn't behave like that in her presence, and she knew if she went in now, he would know that she'd heard him. So she hesitated, and as she did, she heard something far worse.

The phrase "shipment of arms" was common in her father's world, and she normally thought nothing of it. It wasn't until she heard the name Osama bin Laden that she knew something wasn't right. Then, as she listened, for the first time in her life, she knew the true meaning of the phrase "her blood ran cold."

Osama bin Laden was happy with the goods.

She put a hand to her lips to keep from gasping aloud. There had to be some mistake. Then she heard her father mention a delivery in Afghanistan to al Qaeda. Then the Kurds and Mohammed al-Kazir. The nail in her father's coffin was when she heard Jacob say that bin Laden would double his offer if they could deliver before the end of the month, and something about the thirteenth being a problem, because it was some kind of holiday.

She heard her father chuckle, then comment with something to the effect that he would make them pay out the ass if they wanted the good stuff.

She felt sick. This couldn't be happening. The last comment she heard was the one that sealed their fate.

"You know," Jacob said, "U.S. Customs might start getting wise. There are only so many plows and tractors that one company can import."

Her father snorted. "I pay enough money under the table to smuggle any damn thing I choose."

Alicia had no memory of how she'd gotten out of the hall and back up the stairs to her room. The next thing she remembered was being on her hands and knees in her bathroom, throwing up in the toilet. She threw up until her belly hurt and her jaws ached. By the time she managed to drag herself to bed, she was in a cold sweat. The maid had come in to clean, but Alicia had sent her away, claiming she was coming down with the flu.

By the time the maid made it back downstairs, Jacob Carruthers was gone and Richard was on to the next big thing. The maid hesitated in the hallway, then knocked at Richard's office door.

"Yes," he muttered, irked at being disturbed.

The maid opened the door just enough to pass on her message.

"Sir…Miss Ponte has taken ill…the flu, she thinks, and said to pass on her excuses because she's going to skip lunch."

"Yes, thank you," Richard said.

Her father had too many irons in the fire to worry about a flu bug unless he was the one getting ill, Alicia knew, so for now she had some time to regroup. She'd never been able to lie and get away with it, and she'd never been able to hide her feelings. One look at her face and her father would have known something was wrong. It wouldn't have taken him long to get it out of her, so she'd done the only thing she could think of to do: she'd packed a bag and run.

And she was still running. She needed to tell someone what she knew, but her father's power was great and his reach was long. He had strong ties to almost every arm of the government. She didn't yet know who to tell or who to trust. Maybe he could live with the blood of innocent soldiers on his conscience, but she couldn't— wouldn't. And she wasn't going to let him get away with it, either. The next day, after he'd left for the office, she left him a note that she was feeling better and was going to take off for a few days at a spa. Then she'd emptied one of her sizeable bank accounts and left Miami in the middle of a thunderstorm—perfect weather to match her mood.

The spa excuse had worked for only one day. When she'd failed to check in, Richard began making calls. When she didn't return the first call within the hour, he'd called a second time, then a third. By noon, Alicia had a half-dozen unanswered messages on her cell, including a text message from him hinting at concern. After that, she'd stopped keeping track. It was inevitable that she would have to answer, but she wasn't ready. She was so angry with him that she could hardly think, and at the same time she was afraid. She knew her father's reputation. He was ruthless when it came to getting his way. He wouldn't take kindly to having someone mess in his nest, which was exactly what she planned to do. She had to be far enough away—and safely concealed—before she trusted herself enough to call back. And most of all, she had to be certain of her own ability to avoid giving herself away and figure out a way to keep him from tracking her via her phone. There was a part of her that felt like a traitor to him, but she kept reminding herself that at least she wouldn't be a traitor to her own country.

The fact that her father was in bed with the terrorists responsible for the tragic events of September 11, 2001,
was chilling.

Unbeknownst to his daughter, Richard Ponte had in-
stalled GPS locator systems on every vehicle in his
empire, and he already knew her whereabouts. In fact,
he had sent Dieter Bahn, his right-hand man, to bring
her back. Ponte had no idea what was going on with her,
but he was beginning to realize it was serious. He knew
she'd emptied one of her bank accounts and that she was
running. He just didn't know why. But he was determined to find out. And when Richard Ponte was determined to make something happen, it happened.

Alicia was focused on the needs at hand, which were
food and fuel, both of them less than a quarter mile
ahead. She was debating between something sweet or
salty for a snack when her cell phone began to ring. She
glanced down at caller ID, and her heart skipped a beat.
It was her father. Again.

She'd lost count of how many times he'd called. As
nervous as she was about it, she knew that communi-
cating would help keep him off her back. She just didn't
know if she could trust herself to stay calm. As the
phone continued to ring, she finally made a decision.
She pulled over to the side of the road, put the car in
Park, then answered. Her heart was pounding. All she
could think was, *God help me.*

"Hello?"

"Thank God!" Richard bellowed. "Alicia! What the

hell are you up to? Why haven't you been answering your phone?"

"I'm not up to anything," Alicia said, hating herself for the quaver she heard in her voice. "I left you a note telling you where I was going. I just wanted a little getaway. I certainly didn't expect a constant barrage of phone calls, trying to check up on me as if I'm some teenager. For pity's sake, Dad, get a grip."

"Don't start that crap with me!" Richard yelled. "You emptied your bank account and you're not returning my calls. What am I supposed to think?"

Alicia swallowed past the knot in her throat. "That I'm twenty-seven years old and that it's my money?"

Richard was so angry he was shaking. He didn't like to be thwarted, and he didn't like to be reminded that it was his deceased wife's money that had set him up for life and left their daughter independently wealthy.

"Is it some man? If it is, I can tell you right now, he doesn't love you. He's just after your money."

Alicia felt as if she'd been slapped. That her own father would deem her unworthy of a man's love without the money that came with her was, at the least, humiliating. Her voice was shaking when she asked, "Why, Daddy? Why wouldn't some man love me? Why would you say something like that?"

Richard couldn't have cared less that he'd hurt her feelings. "I was right," he crowed. "It *is* a man. Now listen to me. Quit acting like a child and get yourself back to Miami before you get into something you can't get out of. You're too trusting. You're too naive. Is he there with you now?"

"There is no man," she muttered, suddenly wishing

there was. It would be a far simpler dilemma than the one she was in.

"I don't believe you," he said. "You went sneaking out of this house like some bitch in heat. You must have had a reason."

It was the "bitch in heat" reference that did it. Suddenly the past few days of being sick at heart and scared half out of her mind bubbled up and over. She started talking, and the more she talked, the louder she got, until she was screaming at him just as he'd screamed at her moments earlier.

"The only man in my life that made me leave home was you!"

Taken aback by her sudden rage, Richard had to struggle to answer. "Me? You're not making sense."

It was as if someone had opened a festering wound, and now that the pressure was gone, the poison was spilling out of Alicia without a thought for caution.

"I know what you've been doing…you and Uncle Jacob. I heard you two talking. You're selling weapons to the enemy."

Richard felt the floor tilt beneath his feet. Jesus, Mary and Joseph. "You're wrong," he insisted. "I don't know what you think you heard, but you're wrong."

"No. I'm not wrong. You're the one who's doing something wrong…horribly wrong. What I don't get is why, Daddy? Why? We have more money than we could spend in two lifetimes. Why would you betray your country for more?"

Richard felt as if someone had just punched him in the gut. He sat down on the side of his desk before he fell. Son of a bitch…she knew!

"You don't know what you're talking about," he said. "You misunderstood what was being said. You need to come back now and I'll explain… I'll—"

"I don't believe you. I don't want to ever see your face again."

"What are you going to do?" he asked.

Alicia didn't know she was crying until she tasted the salt of her own tears. Angrily, she swiped at them with the back of her hand. "What I do is no longer any of your concern."

There was a long, uncomfortable silence, then one last question. "Alicia."

"What?"

"Are you going to tell?"

Alicia disconnected, threw the phone down in the seat and pulled back out onto the highway, still heading for Justice.

Richard's heart was hammering so hard he couldn't catch his breath. How had this happened? They'd always been so careful. He shoved a hand through his hair and then covered his face with both hands as his mind began to race through the possibilities of what might happen next.

She wouldn't tell. She was his daughter—his own flesh and blood. Surely she wouldn't turn in her own father? But he couldn't be sure. She'd sounded so angry. He'd never heard her like that before. So…what next? Sit here and wait for the hammer to fall on his carefully balanced empire—or take back control?

Shock was soon replaced with anger. There had been dozens of times throughout his life when he'd felt as if he'd been here before, in another time and place. faced with ruin through the behavior of others. The longer he thought about it, the more he realized he wasn't going to sit back and let her destroy everything he'd built. He would get her back first, then figure out what came next.

He reached for the phone and quickly dialed Dieter Bahn's number. By the time the other man answered, Richard was completely calm.

"It's me," Richard said. "How close are you to Alicia's location?"

"Less than five miles, I think," Dieter said.

"When you find her, bring her back…even if you have to tie her up to do it. Do you understand?"

Dieter was the kind of man whose loyalty to the man who paid his salary ran bone-deep.

"Yes, sir," he answered.

"And, Dieter…"

"Yes, sir?"

"Let me know when you have her in the car."

"Yes, sir. I will, sir."

Without even bothering to say goodbye, Richard ended the call. Then he stood up and moved to the windows overlooking his estate, the seat of his empire. If things went wrong, he could lose all of this tomorrow. But that wasn't going to happen. Things wouldn't go wrong. Dieter would get Alicia, and then…

He paused, jangling the change in his pocket without thinking. What was he going to do with his daughter when he got her back? How could he keep her quiet? What assurance did he have that she would keep his secret? He sighed.

He had no assurance. None.

He caught a glimpse of his own reflection in the window, then yanked his hands out of his pockets and quickly looked away. He'd worked too hard and too long to be brought down by anyone—even his own daughter. If she didn't comply…

A muscle suddenly jerked at his temple as the thought slid through his mind. Then it would be too damned bad for her. Accidents happen.

John Nightwalker was in his Jeep and heading out of Justice. The sun was warm on his face, even though his eyes were well-hidden behind dark aviator sunglasses as he drove down Main Street. Someone yelled out his name, and he waved before he looked.

It was Mildred, the pharmacy clerk. She'd tried to hook him up with her daughter for the last two years until, thankfully, her daughter had eloped with one of the Samson brothers, who had a roofing business in a nearby town. When Mildred figured out that having a son-in-law who owned his own business was better than a man with secrets, she'd let him be.

He braked for a red light while the wind whipping through the open windows tugged at his hair like the fingers of a jealous lover. His hands, brown and strong, curled around the steering wheel as they'd once curled around the shaft of a spear. Time had not taken the warrior out of the man—only increased it. As he neared the city limits, he glanced down at the gas gauge. Better fuel up now and get it over with, even though the day was hot. He had milk and eggs in the backseat, as well as some fresh vegetables, but a quick fuel stop shouldn't hurt anything.

He pulled up to an empty pump at Marv's Gas and Guzzle, waved at a local who was pulling away and got out. He swiped his credit card at the pump just as he'd done countless times before, then began to refuel. It was a slow time of day. There was only one other vehicle in sight, and it had two flats, which told John it had been there for a while.

A flock of gulls circled overhead, probably checking out the fish heads behind the bait-and-tackle area of Marv's store. He thought about the ocean and decided that when he got home, he would go for a swim. Water was always a source of renewal for him.

The pump kicked off, breaking into his musing. He was replacing the hose when a white BMW wheeled off the highway, coming toward the pumps at a high rate of speed. He stepped back in reflex, even though the car was going to be stopping on the opposite side from where he'd parked.

All of a sudden his heart started beating erratically and his stomach knotted in pain. The air around him felt charged with an electricity that, in the last five hundred years, he'd experienced only a handful of times before.

Whoever was in that car was either the reincarnated soul of the pirate he'd learned was named Antonio Vargas or someone close to him. His fingers curled into fists as a dark, bloody rage swept through his mind. Suddenly he was seeing the village all over again— puddles of blood beneath rain-soaked bodies, children's bodies burned and broken, clothing ripped and ornaments cut from the corpses of his people.

The need for revenge swept through his mind so fast that he staggered. Then he caught a glimpse of a tall, shapely body, the silhouette of a beautiful face, hair as black as midnight, and knew a moment of regret. What an irony, that the soul he sought had come back in such a form.

Then their gazes met, and within the space of a heartbeat, all the warning signs John had come to recognize were gone and he knew this wasn't the person he sought, although there had to be a connection.

Her face was heart-shaped, her features strong but perfectly proportioned. Full lips marked a wide, expressive mouth that was, at the moment, twisted in some sort of grief. When his gaze moved back to her eyes, he felt himself drowning in the tears blurring her vision.

Pain shot through his gut so fast it left him momentarily breathless. He hated to see a woman cry. They stared at each other, eye to eye, separated by less than a yard. Finally John found his voice.

"Are you hurt?" he asked.

Alicia shuddered. His voice sifted through her wounded spirit like cold water on a burn, easing the shock and pain of what she was feeling, if only for a moment.

"No…I, uh…" She swiped at the tears on her cheeks and then threw back her head, unaware that the simple lift of her chin had given her the look of an able opponent, not a victim. "Crap," she mumbled, her fingers shaking as she tried to pull the nozzle away from the pump. "I need gas."

Not wanting to lose the connection with her, John moved a step closer.

"Swipe your card. I'll pump it for you," he offered.

But Alicia knew that credit card transactions could be traced, and since the last thing she wanted was to let her father know where she was, she hadn't even brought a card with her.

"Uh…I'm going to pay cash."

John pointed toward the sign at the pumps. "Then thank the economy for the problem, but they won't turn on the pump until you've prepaid."

"Yes…of course," Alicia said, and tried to put the nozzle back on the pump. But her vision was still blurred from tears, and she kept missing the slot.

"Here, let me," he said softly, then swiped his own card, waited for the approval to come up, then stuck the nozzle in her gas tank.

Alicia took a deep breath. When the stranger moved between her and her car, she suddenly shuddered. In spite of the mess she was in, she didn't understand the urge she felt to put her hand on the back of his neck. Instead, she began digging through her purse, pulled out a handful of bills and then found herself fixated by a single bead of sweat that had escaped his hairline and was sliding down the jut of his jaw.

Her nostrils flared as the thought of being naked under this man flashed through her mind.

God. Where had that come from?

When the man turned around, Alicia thought that from the look in his eyes, he was on the same page.

"Thank you for your help," she said, and thrust the handful of bills into his hand.

Before John could respond, another car pulled off the highway and up to the pumps, coming to a stop right behind the woman. He saw her eyes widen and her pupils dilated in shock.

"Oh no. Oh God… He found me."

Two

John didn't know who the man was, other than a big bald bodybuilder, but the woman was obviously afraid of him. He made a point of never involving himself in marital discord, but there was no way he was going to lose track of her until he figured out how she fit into the puzzle of the soul he sought. He replaced the nozzle and stepped back to watch from between the pumps as the man continued to approach.

"Get away from me, Dieter," Alicia warned.

Dieter paused, smiling openly as if to say this was out of his hands.

"Come, come, Alicia, your father wants you to come home."

"How did you find me?" she asked.

Dieter shrugged. "GPS."

Alicia's lips went slack. "You're not serious. Dad has a tracking device on my car?"

"They're on all his cars," Dieter said. "I would have thought you'd known that."

"It's obvious I don't know him nearly as well as I thought I did," she muttered.

Dieter took a step closer. "So you'll come with me now?"

Alicia's pulse skipped as she took a nervous step back. "I'm not going anywhere with you."

"Oh, but you are," Dieter said, and lunged, only to find himself suddenly face-to-face with a man who'd come out of nowhere.

Dieter frowned, then looked at Alicia. "Who is this? Is he with you?"

John answered, "Who I am is not what you should be worrying about. I heard the lady tell you to back off at least twice, and you're not paying attention."

Dieter jabbed a finger at John, poking him in the chest. "You aren't part of the equation," he said. "I take my orders from her father, and he wants her home."

When John grabbed the finger and twisted it backward, it sent a shooting pain up Dieter's arm all the way to the back of his jaw. Even worse, it somehow rendered him immobile, and he didn't know why.

"Ow! Shit! Let me go. Let me *go!*" he yelled.

But John continued to maintain pressure as he addressed Alicia. "I take it this man isn't your husband?"

Alicia's voice was shaking. "No, he works for my father."

"Did you do something illegal?" John asked.

Alicia rolled her eyes. "No."

"You're not wanted by the police?"

"No. Lord, no."

"I'm assuming you're of legal age."

Alicia stifled a snort, which John interpreted as a yes.

"Then I'd say you're free to do what you want."

Alicia's eyes filled with tears all over again.

"I'll never be free again," she said, more to herself than to John, but he heard it and knew her peril was working to his advantage.

John looked back at Dieter, whose face was turning paler by the minute.

"Are you going to keep following her?"

"It's my job," Dieter moaned, still trying to figure out why he felt numb all over.

"Then I guess she'll need a head start," John said, then grabbed Dieter's neck with his other hand and squeezed. Dieter dropped between the car and the gas pump like a stone.

Alicia shuddered. What had just happened? "I need to hide," she mumbled, still staring at Dieter's body.

"Why are you afraid of your father?"

She wiped her hands across her face. "This is a nightmare. Please…I need to get another car and get to a place where he can't find me until I can figure all this out."

John exhaled softly. Bingo. Right into his lap.

"I can help."

Alicia swayed where she stood, then looked up. His eyes were so dark that she couldn't see the pupils. She shivered. She didn't know this man from Adam. He could be a serial killer, a sadist—anything. Then she asked herself: Was her father any different? Should she trust the devil she knew or the devil she didn't?

John felt her pulling away. He had to act fast.

"My name is John Nightwalker. I live about fifteen miles from here, and as you can see, I have a car. You'll have to leave your car here anyway, and I'll help you all I can. Just tell me what you need."

Alicia saw his lips moving, but she'd lost track of his words as soon as he'd said his name. The skin was still crawling on the back of her neck, and she had the strangest urge to cry.

"So…what do you say?" John asked.

Alicia blinked. "Um…I, uh…"

"You can trust me," he said.

Somehow she knew he was telling the truth.

"Yes, okay."

John's pulse skittered, then settled. Was this it? Was this the beginning of the end of his search?

"Better get your things out of your car," he said.

"What about him?" she asked, pointing to Dieter.

"I'll take care of that," he said.

She hurried to get her suitcase. When she turned around, John was pulling a six-pack of beer out of his Jeep. He popped the top of a can and forced Dieter's lips far enough apart to pour the tepid amber liquid down his throat. At that point Dieter coughed and came to, hacking and spitting. John helped him up, opened the door to Dieter's car, then squeezed the same nerve on his neck that he'd squeezed before and once again rendered him unconscious.

John grunted softly as he maneuvered the other man into the driver's seat. Once he had Dieter behind the wheel, he poured the contents of two more cans of beer onto his clothes and then onto the seat, tossed the rest of the six-pack onto the floorboard, then stepped back and shut the door. To the observer, Dieter would now appear to be drunk and passed out in his car.

John turned toward Alicia. "Get in," he said as he took the suitcase out of her hands and put it in the backseat.

Alicia took a deep breath and looked back down the road on which she'd been traveling. She knew what was behind her. Time to take a chance on what was ahead. Then she looked at John, exhaled slowly and scooted into the passenger seat as John slid behind the wheel.

"Buckle up," he said, and pulled out onto the highway.

She began fumbling with the seat belt as he picked up his cell phone and punched in a number.

"Police. Whatcha need?"

"Hi, Carl, it's John Nightwalker. I want to report a situation at Marv's Gas and Guzzle. There's an abandoned car at one pump and a drunk passed out in the car behind it. Someone needs to get those two cars towed out of the way so people can get gas when they need it."

"Is the drunk a local?" Carl asked.

"Nope. Out-of-state license. Don't know anything more."

"Figures," Carl said. "I'll get someone down there right now. Thanks for calling."

"No problem," John said. There was a glint in his eye as he disconnected.

"Thank you," Alicia said.

John nodded.

At that point, the silence inside the Jeep became uncomfortable. What on earth had she just done? Alicia wondered, realizing how completely she'd given herself over to this man. All she could do was pray she hadn't put herself into a more dire situation than the one she'd been running from.

"I won't hurt you," John said, then turned and caught her staring. Once again, he looked straight into her eyes.

It was a fleeting look, but there was something in it that Alicia found comforting. A second or so later, he turned his attention back to the road, but it was enough for her to relax.

She shivered slightly, then leaned back against the seat as the wind whipped through the windows, putting her long dark hair in disarray. But her appearance was the last thing on her mind. For the first time since she'd starting running, she felt as if she was at least partially in control. Maybe this nightmare was going to have a positive outcome after all.

Richard waited for the phone call from Dieter telling him that he had Alicia and was on the way home, but it never came. He left a scathing message on Dieter's cell, then left to attend a business dinner, confident that everything was under control and his subordinate was just off the radar for some reason.

Dieter, however, was not as certain. Waking up in jail was the single biggest shock of his life. He'd been in jail before, but he'd always seen it coming. This time, he had no idea how or when—or why—it had happened. He swung his legs off the bunk, swiped his hands across his face, then stumbled to the bars, rattling them to emphasize his demand.

"Hey!" he yelled, then winced. Yelling made his head ache. "Jailer! Jailer! I need to make a phone call. It's my right. I get to make a call."

A few moments later, the door across the aisle opened and a tall scrawny man in a khaki uniform sauntered in. Dieter stared. The man was rail-thin with a hawk nose and a big bushy mustache.

"What?" the man drawled.

"I get to make a call! Bring me my cell phone."

The jailer shrugged. "You use our phone and reverse the charges…understand?"

"I don't understand anything," Dieter muttered. "How did I get here?"

"Hauled your drunk ass in, that's how."

Dieter frowned. He hadn't been drinking. He'd been— "Oh hell," he muttered. Alicia. The big Indian. Richard was going to kill him.

"Here's the phone," the jailer said as he thrust a cordless headset through the bars. "Make it quick."

"Where am I?" Dieter asked, realizing he didn't even know the address of the jail.

"You're in jail, mister," the jailer said dryly.

Dieter cursed beneath his breath. "Very funny. What's the *name* of this godforsaken place?"

"You're in Justice, Georgia, and I hope the irony of that is not lost on you."

Dieter glared. "I need privacy."

"Tough shit. You get one call, and I'm not going anywhere."

As Dieter punched in the number, it occurred to him that he was probably safer in jail. At least here, Richard would have a harder time killing him. However, Richard didn't answer the call, and Dieter was forced to leave a message.

"Mr. Ponte, it's Dieter. I'm in Justice, Georgia…in jail. I caught up with Alicia at a gas station, but she wasn't alone. She had someone with her who knocked me out. I'm not sure how I got from there to jail, but I need someone to bail me out."

As soon as he'd disconnected, he handed the phone back through the bars. The jailer took it, smirked and slammed the door behind him when he left.

Dieter dropped back down on the bunk, then put his head in his hands and groaned. This wasn't good. It wasn't good at all.

Alicia was accustomed to the best. The best cars. The best clothes. The best of everything money could buy. So when John Nightwalker said he was taking her to his place, she didn't expect to find much of a house at the end of this road through nowhere, but to say this exceeded her expectations was an epic understatement. His home was a magnificent edifice of wood, rock and glass that appeared to have grown from the very bluff on which it was sitting.

The front of the house faced the driveway, which left the back to overlook the ocean. She could see all the way through the soaring front windows to two stories of glass at the back that seemed to go on forever—disappearing up and into the startling blue of the sky overhead. The panorama they would reveal up close had to be amazing.

Her breath caught in the back of her throat. The beauty of it was obvious, but it was the loneliness she sensed along with that beauty that brought tears to her eyes.

She got out without speaking and walked toward the rim of the bluff, mesmerized by the view beyond. But the longer she stood there, the more she felt he hadn't built here for the view. As she looked around the area, she realized that from where she stood, it would be impossible for anyone to get to him without being seen. She couldn't help but wonder what demons John Nightwalker watched for when he looked through those windows.

"Welcome to my home," John said.

Alicia couldn't find the words to answer. She just nodded, then turned around and followed him back to the car, picking up her suitcase as he took the groceries and led the way inside.

John was so wired he could hardly focus. After centuries of waiting for this day, it was the closest he'd ever been. Only once before had he been so near. But that had been ages ago, on a train running through Central Europe. That day he'd known, as surely as he knew his own name, that the man he sought was only a few cars away. He'd felt the rhythm of his heartbeat as the pain of recognition spilled through him. He'd been running through the cars, searching for the person who held the key to all he sought, when a hard jolt sent everyone flying out of their seats, followed by the sounds of buckling metal and steam spewing into the air as the train derailed violently. He woke up some time later to the sound of people screaming and a horrible emptiness that meant one thing: the gut-wrenching knowledge that whoever it was he'd been after was dead, but not by John's hand.

Nothing had been resolved.

Now his mind refocused on the woman at hand as he stepped aside to let her in. The way he figured it, playing things cool and easy was the best way to alleviate her fears, although staying calm around her was almost impossible. He'd waited so long for revenge. He needed to find out if her father was the man he sought. He guessed that he was, but couldn't be sure—wouldn't be sure until they were standing face-to-face.

He didn't know what was going to happen after this quest was over, but right now he didn't care. If he turned to dust, so be it. Revenge was a cold mistress, and he was tired—tired of it all.

"The kitchen is through here," John said, leading the way.

But Alicia was so enthralled by this place that she kept lagging behind. The walls were a pale blue. The floor tiles were oblong, rather than square, and in an off-white color with gold veins scattered throughout. The furnishings were different shades of gold and blue, with snow-white throw pillows of every size. She could see a huge library off to the left, containing what appeared to be a well-organized office. The walls were covered with art and artifacts, most of which appeared to be of Native American theme or origin. The ocean breeze funneling through the open windows billowed the sheer white drapes hanging from ceiling to floor like earthbound kites. The faint scent of salty air permeated the rooms, along with another pleasant but less distinctive scent. It took her a few moments to locate the source, and when she did, she was once again surprised. A huge vase of wisteria sat on a waist-high table in the hall, giving every room access to the sweet, sweet smell of the blooms.

"The flowers…"

John paused and turned. "Yes?"

"They're lovely," she said softly.

For the first time John felt a sense of guilt. This woman was obviously in dire straits, or at least she thought she was. She was also stunning to look at. He needed to remember that her well-being was just as vital for him, albeit for different reasons, as it was for her.

"They were White…uh…my wife's favorite," he said, glancing toward the vase of white and lavender flowers, the slender stalks drooping from their weight. "They used to grow wild where we lived."

Alicia's eyes widened. Past tense. "She died?"

John flashed on White Fawn's sightless gaze and the blood spilling from the gash in her chest, then stifled the anger he still felt. "Many years ago," he said shortly, and changed the subject. "Let me put the perishables up, and then I'll show you to a room. You'll be comfortable here until you figure out what you need to do, okay?"

"Yes, and, John…thank you," she said.

He nodded, well aware that she wouldn't be all that grateful if she knew of his ulterior motives.

"Yeah, sure," he said, stifling another twinge of guilt.

Alicia was standing on the balcony off John's bedroom, overlooking the ocean, watching the light fading from the sky. She'd asked permission to see the view, and he'd made himself absent to let her enjoy it. Now a faint sliver of moon hung awkwardly against a growing darkness as a few wispy clouds passed in front of it. Night birds were beginning to call. A stiff breeze lifted the hair from Alicia's neck, chilling her all the way through. She wrapped her arms around herself as a shudder ripped through her.

From behind, she heard a footstep, then felt the weight of something soft and warm settling on her shoulders. The gesture was both thoughtful and unexpected. As she pulled the edges of the sweater close around her, the scent of musk and a fainter scent of cigar smoke wafted toward her.

She hadn't seen John smoke, yet she recognized the singular scent of fine cigars.

"Thank you," she said softly, then looked back toward the water. "This is all so beautiful, but I'm sure you already know that."

John knew she was referring to the view, but for the first time since she'd walked into his house, he was looking at her and seeing her as the beautiful woman she was, not just as a means to an end.

"Yes...very beautiful," he said.

Alicia looked up, caught his gaze on her and lost her train of thought.

"Talk to me," John said suddenly.

"I...uh..."

"Where do you live?"

"Most of the time in Miami."

"Is that where your father is?"

She nodded.

He stifled a smile. Now he knew where to go. His suitcase was already packed. He was willing to leave her here on her own if she chose, or she could keep on running. But tomorrow morning, he was going to Miami.

Even though he'd gotten the information from her that he needed, he decided to keep her talking. The more he knew, the more likely his success would be, and he was long overdue for success.

"Why are you running from your father?"

Alicia pulled the sweater up beneath her chin and looked back across the water.

"It's an ugly story."

"I've heard ugly before."

She was startled by the undisguised anger in his voice, reminding her that she was about to spend the night with a stranger. Still, he'd taken a chance for her. He deserved to know that what he'd done might put him in danger.

"A few days ago I overheard my father and an old friend of his discussing an impending business deal. It had to do with selling weapons to terrorists…the same people our soldiers are fighting in Iraq."

John was stunned. It was the last thing he'd expected to hear. "Are you sure? I mean…is there a possibility you misunderstood?"

Alicia pivoted, her voice rising as she answered. "To my knowledge, there is only one Osama bin Laden, only one group called al Qaeda. Do the words 'delivery in Afghanistan, money transfers to Geneva,' suggest anything to you?"

John flinched as if he'd been kicked in the belly, then walked past her in the darkness, bracing his hands against the balcony rail as he stared off into the night. He'd waited an eternity for justice, but did his personal justice supersede the safety of thousands of young servicemen and women?

He turned abruptly, a looming silhouette against the sky.

"His name… What's your father's name? How would he have access to those kinds of people?"

"His name is Richard Ponte. He's the largest arms and munitions manufacturer in the western hemisphere."

Darkness hid the shock on John's face. It seemed that the soul of the man who'd killed his people had not learned much during the ensuing centuries. Then another thought surfaced. Alicia Ponte was clearly afraid of her father's wrath, so…what did she think he would do to her?

"Does he know you overheard that conversation?"

Alicia's shoulders slumped. "As of this afternoon, yes."

A chill ran through John's body that had nothing to do with the temperature outside.

"You fear him because…"

"Because when I figure out who in Washington, D.C., I can trust, I'm going to turn him in."

John couldn't believe it. The Old Ones must be cackling among themselves over the twist they'd just delivered. If Richard Ponte was indeed the man he sought, he was going to have to stand in line to get to him.

"What lengths do you think he'll go to, to stop you?"

Bile rose in the back of Alicia's throat. This was the question that had been hanging at the back of her mind ever since she'd left Miami. Saying aloud what she feared was only going to give life and power to the fear, but she had no choice. By going with John Nightwalker, she'd put him in the same tenuous position in which she'd put herself.

"Whatever it takes to silence me."

Even as John asked, he couldn't wrap his mind around what kind of man could commit such a heinous act. "You think your own father would have you killed?"

"In a heartbeat."

There was a long, uncomfortable silence, which Alicia finally broke.

"So…about now I'm guessing you wish you'd left me standing back at Marv's Gas and Guzzle."

She didn't know there were tears on her face, but John saw them. Damn it…he didn't want to feel sorry for her. Then she took a deep breath that sounded suspiciously like a sob.

"Well, hell," he muttered.

Alicia saw a tiny flicker of moonlight catch on the tiny silver feather hanging from his ear as he moved toward her. Before she knew it, she was in his arms, with her nose pressed against his chest.

"What I wish is that you didn't think your father is capable of killing you. That's too much for anyone to bear," he said quietly.

The rumble of his voice lulled her into a false sense of security. He was big and strong, and he'd come to her rescue. Lord knew she needed help. But she couldn't continue this way without pointing out the obvious. She lingered one last moment longer, then stepped back.

"John…you have to know that by helping me, you're putting yourself in danger."

"You don't need to worry about me."

"But—"

John shook his head. He'd made his decision. He would help her get her story to the appropriate people first, then go after his own revenge. It was the right thing to do. The *only* thing.

"Seriously, I can take care of myself—and you—if you'll let me."

"I've already involved you too far."

"Then the discussion is over," John said. "I'm in. So how are you going to handle this?"

Alicia shrugged. "Carefully, that's for sure. My father has friends in high places. I've got to make sure that I tell someone who won't give me up to Dad."

John stuffed his hands in his pockets and turned around, gazing back out across the water. As he wrestled with his conscience, he could hear the waves hitting the rocks that jutted out from the beach into the black, bottomless depths. Decency was winning out over revenge, and it wasn't making him happy.

"I might know someone," he finally said.

"In D.C.?" Alicia asked.

He nodded.

"And you trust him?"

John turned. "As much as I trust anyone."

Alicia frowned. There was a tone in John's voice that she didn't recognize. It felt like sarcasm, but that didn't make sense. Still, she wasn't in any position to be picky.

"Then I thank you," she said. "But it needs to be soon. If Dad believes I'll give him up, he'll run. He has the whole world in which to hide, and if he does, you know what that makes me? A sitting duck, that's what."

"I'll make some calls tomorrow. But for now, you need to get some sleep."

Alicia nodded, then lifted her chin. With a quiet grace, she took off the sweater he'd put around her shoulders, handed it to him with a slight nod, then turned around and walked back through his bedroom, then across the hall to her own.

John's fingers curled into a fist as he clutched the sweater. It was still warm from her body. Muttering a soft, unintelligible curse, he followed her inside, locking the doors behind him. By the time he'd set the security alarms, the light was out in her room. He paused in the hallway by her door, then turned and entered his own suite.

It was time to rest, and to hope that tonight would be a night without dreams. But after the excitement of the day and the fresh hope that his quest would soon be over, it was too much to ask.

She looked up from the cooking fire, smiling at his approach. Her smile widened when she saw the haunch of deer meat he carried on his shoulder.

"I have made your favorite," White Fawn said.

Night Walker inhaled appreciatively as he laid the deer haunch aside and squatted down beside his woman to peer into the cooking pot. The ground maize had been cooked to a thick porridge consistency, and flavored with strips of pemmican and fresh berries.

Night Walker dipped the stirring stick into the pot, then tasted it.

"More berries," he said.

White Fawn laughed out loud. "You always say that," she said as she thrust her hand into a basket beside the fire and scattered another handful of small black berries into the pot.

When Night Walker cupped the back of her head, she leaned into his touch.

"I would lie with you," he said softly.

An ache spread through White Fawn's belly as she saw the look in Night Walker's eyes.

"And I with you," she answered.

Night Walker set the pot beside the fire and threw a blanket over the meat to keep off the flies, then followed his woman into their hut. He pulled the flap over the doorway, shutting them in and the rest of the village out.

With one pull, the skins he wore tied around his waist fell at his feet.

White Fawn was already naked. Without taking her eyes from his face, she lay down on the furs that were their bed and waited for him to join her.

When he did, he made no pretense as to his intentions.

He lay beside her, then rose up on one elbow and slid his hand between her thighs, gently nudging her legs apart.

White Fawn's heart was already beating fast, anticipating the pleasure that was to come.

In one swoop, he was inside her. She wrapped her legs around his waist and pulled him down, burying him deep. When he began to move, she met him thrust for thrust, and for a while, time stood still.

The scent of woodsmoke mingled with the passion-induced sweat from White Fawn's body. Her tight, wet heat pulled at Night Walker with every thrust. She was everything beautiful to him, his own personal aphrodisiac. He would never get enough—could never get enough—of the woman who held his heart.

Slowly, slowly, the rhythm of their lovemaking became less steady, more frantic, harder and harder, until it burst within. White Fawn held him as he spilled his seed into her so-far-fruitless womb, then wept quiet, happy tears as he collapsed on top of her with a soft, satisfied moan.

John jerked, then sat up abruptly, searching the shadowed corners of his room for the woman he'd been making love to. His shoulders slumped as he wiped a shaky hand across his face and crawled out of bed.

He didn't think about his guest as he walked naked through the house, quietly disarmed the security system and strode outside. The cool air felt good against his heated skin as he made his way down the backside of the bluff to the water below.

The steady ebb and flow of the ocean pulled at his senses like a drug as he walked into the surf. The water was cold—so cold—but he didn't care. He needed the shock of it to wash away the dream—which was, if he'd ever stopped to analyze himself, ironic. While remembering their love and what he'd lost was often too painful, it was the memory of what had happened to her that kept him focused and sane.

When he was knee-deep in the ocean, he dove headfirst into the next wave and began to swim, fighting the current because it was the only enemy at hand. He swam until his muscles burned and his legs felt like jelly. Only then did he stop. Treading water, he turned to look toward shore. From this distance, his house was barely the size of a child's building block, but the anger was gone. All that was left was a bone-deep weariness.

Without thinking, he began the long journey back, one stroke at a time.

Dawn was imminent on the horizon as he came out of the surf, his head down, his shoulders slumped. His steps dragged as he began the climb up the bluff.

Alicia woke up suddenly, her heart thumping, her eyes wide with fright. For a second she couldn't remember where she was or how she'd gotten there. Then her gaze centered on a dream catcher hanging on the wall opposite her bed, and a face slid into her mind.

John Nightwalker.

She rubbed her face with her hands, then swung her

legs off the bed and stood, stretching slowly as she made her way to the bathroom. A few minutes later, she came out just as the digital readout on the clock flicked over to ten minutes after six. The bed looked inviting, but there were too many unknowns in her life for her to be able to go back to sleep.

She needed to get to the authorities as soon as possible. The quicker she put a stop to her father's dealings with terrorists, the sooner she would be safe. Once everyone knew, it would serve no purpose to keep her quiet. Nothing else would stop him. She'd grown up seeing his ruthlessness firsthand. Her mother had been the one who'd taught her what it meant to love. Her father's lessons in life consisted of disappointments and lies. But her mother had been dead for years now, and Alicia was a woman long grown and strong. And she swore that determination—the one trait she'd inherited from her father—was going to prove to be the one that took him down.

Her suitcase was open on the floor. She thought about getting dressed, but it was nearing daybreak, and the idea of watching the sun come up on the horizon to signal the beginning of a new day was too enticing to miss. She noticed that the alarm system had been turned off, so she felt no concern as she hurried downstairs, then out the French doors to the terrace beyond. She walked to the edge, then out onto the grass and headed to the edge of the bluff.

A sea breeze instantly caught the hem of her nightgown and threaded it between her legs as she braced herself against the railing. The view was everything she'd expected and more. Already the line between dark and dawn was fading fast. In the east, there was an aura of pink and orange playing at visibility. Just another minute or two, and the sun in all its glory would be evident.

Alicia found herself watching intently, trying to guess the exact moment of its appearance, and because she was so focused on the sky, she didn't see the man swimming in the water below. But then the sun broke, and all of a sudden the day was there. She smiled slowly in appreciation and was about to turn back when she saw him, waist deep and emerging from the ocean as steadily as the sun had appeared from below the horizon.

The first thought that crossed her mind was awe. The second was lust.

He'd been a commanding figure in clothes. Naked, he was magnificent. Even from this distance, the copper perfection of his body was impossible to ignore. Muscles everywhere they should be, wet and glistening in the new light of a new day. Then she looked past the obvious to the way his head was hanging, and the slight but weary slump of his body. He walked across the sand as if he was carrying the weight of the world on his shoulders, and something told her that had nothing to do with a strenuous workout.

A lump rose in her throat. Then he paused. When she saw him cover his face with his hands, her vision blurred. She could feel his sadness from here. But why? She thought of the way he'd spoken about his wife, and her heart ached. She'd never known love like that.

It wasn't until John dropped his hands and looked up the bluff toward his house that Alicia realized he could see her. Now she was stuck. If she moved suddenly, he would think she was ashamed to be caught spying on him. So she did the only other thing she could; she waved and called down, "The sunrise was beautiful!" Then she waved once more and walked back into the house and up to her room.

She swiped angrily at the tears in her eyes as she dug through her suitcase for a clean change of clothes. He could think what he wanted. It was his own fault for walking around naked. Ignoring him would have been a whole lot easier if he had a potbelly and thinning hair.

A few minutes later she was dressed in a pair of blue shorts and a loose white blouse. She walked barefoot down the hall to the kitchen, hoping for a cup of coffee. But she got way more than she hoped for when John came in the back door.

"Good morning," he said, and strode through the kitchen, leaving sandy footprints on the wood floor.

Alicia nodded, but the answer she might have given was stuck in the back of her throat. He was still unashamedly naked, but that wasn't what had caused her heart to skip.

It was the scars.

Small ones.

Large ones.

All over his body.

All she could think was, what in God's sweet name has happened to this man?

Three

Dieter was heartily glad that there were several states between him and Richard Ponte as he listened to his boss berate him up one side and down the other. He shifted the phone from one ear to the other while walking to the impound yard, confident that whatever it was he'd missed hearing wasn't going to kill him, although Richard might.

"Do you have any idea where she's gone?" Richard snapped.

Dust puffed up on Dieter's pant legs as he walked, but he didn't have the luxury of caring. "Not yet. I just got out of jail, and I'm on my way to get my car out of impound."

Richard's voice was quiet, steady—the antithesis of what he was feeling.

"You'd better be in a hurry. You'd better be running, boy," Richard said. "You'd better finish what I sent you to do or don't bother coming back, because if you come back without my daughter, I'll kill you myself."

Dieter picked up his step, telling himself it was just

a figure of speech, that Ponte didn't really mean it. Then Ponte's voice got even quieter.

"Do we understand each other?" Richard asked.

Dieter changed his mind. Ponte's threat was more than serious.

"Yes, sir. I understand. I'll call you as soon as I have her located again."

"Make it quick."

"Yes, sir," Dieter said, praying for the disconnect. When it clicked in his ear, he breathed a sigh of relief, dropped his phone in his pocket and lengthened his stride.

A short while later he had his car out of impound, heartily thankful that, if this had to happen, it had occurred in such a backwater place as Justice. He'd checked the trunk of his car to find everything he'd had with him was still in place. The black duffel bag was still lying at the back of the trunk, behind a spare tire and tools. He pulled it out, grunting with satisfaction as he checked through the contents, making sure everything was still there.

Two handguns with a fairly large supply of ammunition. A nice set of lockpicks, along with a couple of small hand drills—tools any burglar would want. A first-aid kit with two different vials of drugs meant to render someone unconscious, along with the necessary supply of syringes. Any cop worth his salt would have searched and confiscated all this. He thought of the skinny, smart-ass jailer who'd smirked at him, and snorted. The laugh was on them, and they didn't even know it.

Satisfied that all was in place once again, he zipped up the bag, shoved it back behind the spare tire and slammed the trunk lid shut. As he got back in the car, he already knew his next destination would be the last place he'd seen Alicia Ponte. At a place called Marv's Gas and Guzzle.

Daisy Broyles had come to work for Marv Spaulding on her sixteenth birthday and had been here ever since. Job security had been assured after she'd turned nineteen and married Marv. Now they lived in the little brick house behind the store, which suited Daisy just fine. She liked small-town living, and Justice, Georgia, was small-town personified.

This morning was passing much like every morning did. Herbert and Hubert Cooper, two old bachelors who happened to be identical twins, had come in around seven o'clock, downed their usual three cups of coffee and two of Daisy's fresh-baked cinnamon rolls apiece and then left with a wave and a promise to be back tomorrow.

Marshall Walters' daughter, Sue, had stopped by for gas to mow their lawn.

Three little boys came in with a dollar apiece and spent fifteen minutes arguing between themselves before settling on pop and candy. And the morning went on, with a steady flow of locals stopping by.

The morning scent of cinnamon rolls was slowly being replaced by the food Daisy was preparing for the lunch rush. She already had a dozen burritos fried up, a pan of crusty chicken strips, a big bowl of potato salad and a bowl of slaw. She was wrapping her chocolate-chip cookies in clear plastic for individual sale when she saw a car pull off the highway and park near the door.

She frowned, recognizing the car. No one had ever

pulled a stunt like that here. Passing out drunk at one of
her gas pumps was ridiculous. He could have killed
someone driving drunk. Yesterday, it was all anybody
had wanted to talk about when they'd come in. She was
tired of the subject, and tired of the jackass who'd done
it. Marv had reminded her last night that they'd been
lucky the sorry sucker had stopped before he'd passed
out. Like Marv told her, if the drunk had still been
driving when he'd conked out, they might have had a
mess on their hands. What if he'd hit the pumps? What
if he'd run into another customer? Finally Daisy had
relented, admitting Marv had a point.

But seeing the man walking toward the door didn't
mean she was ready to sell him some more booze so he
could get behind the wheel and drive again. With that
thought in mind, she braced herself against the counter,
crossed her arms over her ample bosom and set her jaw.
Southern women had their ways. If he argued with her, she
would show him what a real steel magnolia was all about.

Dieter didn't know he'd already been made, but it
wouldn't have mattered. Finding Alicia's car parked
right beside his in the impound yard hadn't made him
feel any better about the situation. It was his own fault
for giving away the GPS business. He'd just assumed
she would have known. Now she was running again, but
in what—and with whom? He needed to find out who
that big Indian was she'd been with yesterday. He was
the only lead he had.

The bell over the door jingled, then played a short
burst of "Dixie" as the door swung shut. Surprised by
the unexpected tune, he was actually grinning as he

spied the clerk. But from the way she was glaring, she didn't look happy to see him.

He shifted his attitude to all-business as he moved toward the counter.

"Uh…ma'am…I was wondering if you were working here yesterday?"

Daisy glared. "I work here every day. You buying gas?"

Dieter stuttered. "Uh…no, I was wondering if—"

"Cokes are on sale. Ninety-nine cents for a 16 ounce."

"No thanks, I was just—"

"Goes good with the cinnamon rolls. Dollar apiece, but they're homemade and worth every penny."

Dieter was slow, but he finally caught on. Nothing came free, not even information. He grabbed a Coke and pointed toward the bakery case. "I'll take two," he said as he dug in his pocket for money to pay.

Daisy sacked up two cinnamon rolls, added a napkin and took his money. Only after she'd realized he wasn't in the market for booze and had done some fair trading— money for goods received—was she ready to listen.

Dieter stood, waiting for her to nail him again while the condensation on his cold pop ran between his fingers and dripped on the floor. The smell of cinnamon was enticing. He wished he smelled as good, and thought about taking time to find a motel for a shower and shave. But dealing with body odor was going to have to come second to the task at hand.

"Uh…"

Daisy frowned. "Speak your piece, mister. I ain't got all day."

Dieter nodded. "Yesterday, I, uh…"

"Oh, I know all about yesterday. You passed out

drunk in your car right out there at my pumps. I don't take kindly to drunk drivers."

Dieter didn't intend to go into details. He just needed answers, and the way he figured it, an apology would get him further than an explanation.

"I'm real sorry about all that," he said. "I hope you weren't put out in any way."

Daisy sniffed. "I might have missed a customer or two, seeing as how you were blocking one side of the pumps."

Dieter nodded. "Yes, well…like I said. I'm sorry."

Daisy frowned. "So what's your problem today?"

"Yesterday, before I…uh, I mean…there was a man at the other pump when I arrived. I was wondering if you noticed who it was…or if you knew him?"

"I didn't even see *you* until they came to haul you and your car away. Unless they come in, I don't pay them much mind. Lots of people come and go here, and most pay at the pump with credit cards these days. Pumps won't work unless they come in and pay me first, or use a credit card," Daisy stated. "What did he look like?"

"He was a little above average height. Native American, with short dark hair and a silver earring in on ear."

"Oh. That sounds like Big John," Daisy said.

Dieter's pulse kicked. She knew him. Maybe things were going to work out after all.

"John. Yes, yes, that's the name he gave. Do you know where I can find him?"

Daisy's eyes narrowed suspiciously. "Why?"

"Uh, well…we were talking, and he mentioned he had a car for sale. I thought I'd drive by and take a look at it, since I'm still in the area."

Daisy frowned. "I don't know exactly where he lives. All I know is it's that way."

She pointed north.

"I seem to have forgotten his last name," Dieter added.

"Nightwalker," Daisy said. "His name is John Night-walker."

Dieter smiled. "Thanks so much," he said, and headed out the door. He opened the Coke and took a big bite of a cinnamon roll before he put the car in gear and drove away. Things were already looking up.

Richard Ponte was alternating between panic and pure unadulterated rage. This was a nightmare. His carefully balanced empire was in danger of toppling, and all because of his own blood. A part of him knew it was his own fault. He'd been so confident of the power he wielded that he'd gotten careless, doing business at home. He knew better. But he hadn't *done* better.

He glanced at his watch. It had only been an hour since he'd last talked to Dieter. He palmed his cell phone, resisting the urge to call Alicia again—to try to talk her into coming home on her own. After the fight they'd had, he knew that wasn't going to happen. She hadn't seemed to care about where the money came from that had afforded her the luxurious lifestyle she'd enjoyed. Who knew she could turn into a flag-waving bleeding heart? The truth was, he didn't really know her at all, and this incident was proof of that. And learning she was no longer alone had been shocking. Where had the man Dieter described come from? How and when had she met him? It was all a mystery—and a mess.

The phone began to ring, jarring him out of his reverie. He glanced at the caller ID and then relaxed, shifted into business mode and answered with his usual voice of authority, and the morning continued.

Alicia was pouring herself a refill from the coffee-pot when John came back into the kitchen. This time he was dressed, thank God. She didn't think she could take another reality jolt like that without making a fool of herself.

"Did you find everything you needed?" John asked as he got a cup down from the cabinet and filled it.

Alicia lifted her cup. "Coffee was enough."

John's eyes narrowed thoughtfully as he raked her body with a slow, assessing gaze. Then he reached back in the cabinet, got down two bowls and pointed to a door behind her.

"There are a couple of kinds of dry cereal in the pantry. Pick one for yourself. I want Cocoa Puffs. Would you mind passing them over?"

"But coffee is—"

"You're too thin."

Alicia's mouth dropped. In the world of high fashion, there was no such thing. She reached for the Cocoa Puffs and handed them to him, and as she did, she began to smile. The cartoonlike characters on the cereal box were such opposites of the persona this man projected. She eyed the other box of cereal, touting health and bran, then opted for Cocoa Puffs, as well.

"I don't think I've ever had chocolate anything for breakfast before."

He arched an eyebrow. "Why not?"

Alicia paused with the bowl in her hand, and even as

the words were coming out of her mouth, she knew how ridiculous they were going to sound.

"I guess because no one ever offered it."

John's eyes widened as he turned, staring at her as if she were a curiosity.

"Haven't you ever made a meal for yourself?"

She felt heat on her face and an odd sense of guilt, as if she'd been examined and found lacking.

"No."

He thought of White Fawn, down on her knees scraping bits of flesh and tallow from the insides of skins, hanging slivers of deer meat over small fires to smoke and dry. Picking berries to add to his meals, the tips of her fingers stained blue from their juice.

Then he took a slow breath and nodded. Judging her wasn't any of his business, although he couldn't resist a small dig.

"Sounds to me like you should have run away from home a long time ago."

"You're probably right," she shot back. "Pass me the cereal when you're through, please."

He grinned and handed over the box.

Alicia felt its weight in her hand, but at that moment, she couldn't have moved to save her soul. That smile... Sweet mercy. Thankfully, he turned his back on her to retrieve the milk from the refrigerator. By the time he came back, she had pulled herself together and had filled her bowl.

"Don't float it," she muttered, when he began to pour milk on her cereal.

He paused, eyeing the intent expression on her face

as she watched the little chocolate puffs rising with the milk. He didn't want to admit it, but she intrigued him.

"Then pour it yourself and consider it your first stab at cooking."

Alicia's face burned even more. She'd been rude, but not intentionally.

"I'm so sorry," she said. "That came out as a demand, and I didn't mean for it to."

John shrugged. "You're not running for Miss Congeniality…but we need to remember that you *are* running. So sit down and eat. When we've finished, we need to make a plan to get you to the proper authorities."

Alicia wanted to be angry. She wasn't used to being talked to this way, but her own sense of justice made her admit she'd asked for it.

"Yes. Thank you," she said, then took the spoon he offered and followed him to the kitchen table.

They ate in silence. Every now and then, Alicia would sneak a peek at his face to see if he was still irked with her, but he seemed to have let it all go, which was fine. She thought about the scars on his body and wanted to ask, but she'd already been rude once. Adding to her list of transgressions didn't seem like a good idea, not when he was helping her like this. So she dug into her cereal, enjoying the sugar-loaded treat more than she would have imagined.

Once John looked up and caught her in the act of staring. Instead of looking away, he surprised her by staring back.

Before she could move, he reached over and swiped his thumb across the corner of her mouth. "Chocolate milk." When he licked the milk off his thumb in a slow, studied motion, an ache shot through her belly so fast she groaned.

"You okay?" he asked.

Hell no. "Other than the fact that you've discovered my ineptitude at feeding myself, my inability to take care of myself and the fact that I can't keep all my food in my mouth, I'm just peachy."

It was the sarcasm that got him. He grinned.

"Point taken." He got up and put his dirty dishes in the sink. "Don't rush on my account. I'm going to the office to check my e-mail and make a few calls."

Alicia nodded, while another concern suddenly surfaced. She didn't know a thing about what he did or how he got the money to live this way.

"What do you do for a living?" she asked.

He paused, his eyes narrowing thoughtfully, then shrugged. "These days, I mostly buy and sell stuff."

"Oh...you play the stock market?"

"I don't play at anything. One facet of my life is importing and exporting things, some of which are antiquities."

"Really? Like what I saw hanging on your walls?"

"No, most of those are family relics. Feel free to look around. I won't be long." He turned and left.

Alicia nodded, then eyed his purposeful stride, along with his backside, with honest female appreciation.

Once she finished eating, she set her dishes in the sink as he'd done, then glanced out the windows. The wind was up. Whitecaps rode the waves all the way in to shore and then out again, while the waves crashed against the rocks. Not a good morning for a stroll on the beach, although it mirrored the turmoil in her life.

She needed to think. She knew senators, congress-men—all kinds of Washington, D.C., bigwigs…but they were also her father's contemporaries. His cohorts. They were people who'd been to dinner at their Miami home, who'd vacationed with them at their villa in Italy. Which ones—if any—could she trust with her information? She'd grown up watching her father buy loyalty the way other people bought groceries. If she told the wrong person, she would be signing her own death warrant.

She wandered past the library, then down the hall into the living room, where Native American artifacts had been hung in tasteful abandon. But she wasn't really seeing them for the worries and thoughts going through her mind. Then her gaze landed on some photos, and she moved a little closer.

They were obviously old—tintypes, sepia-colored daguerreotypes, even an old panorama-style photo taken on the rim of some mountain that overlooked a great chasm with a river far below.

She squinted her eyes to read the tiny label affixed to the bottom of the frame, noting that it was of a portion of the Grand Canyon and the river was the mighty Colorado. The photo to the right was of a single figure, a Native American man with hair hanging almost to his waist. His face was painted and his chest was bare. He was wearing a breechclout made of skins, with some kind of leggings. It was hard to make out details, consid-ering the picture was an old sepia print, and faded at that.

But Alicia hadn't been raised in her father's business without some of it rubbing off, because it was the rifle he was cradling in his arms that caught her attention. It looked like a long rifle. One of the old single-shots that required patches and powder and lead balls. She glanced at his face again, partially hidden by the long fall of hair on either side, then started to move on when something caught her eye.

She leaned closer, peering intently at the man's bare chest. There was a crescent-shaped scar right below his collarbone on the left side of his chest, just like one of the scars she'd seen on John's chest this morning, when he'd walked into the house naked. She glanced up at the face in the photo, studying the features beneath the paint. Something about them...

"Fierce-looking creature, isn't he?"

She jumped. The deep rasp of John's voice in her ear was unexpected.

She nodded, then glanced at the collar of John's T-shirt, curious about the similar scar, but the shirt concealed it.

"Do you know who he is? There's no name on the photo."

John glanced down at her, then shoved his hands in his pockets and shrugged.

"A distant relative."

"Oh...that explains why I thought he looked a little like you."

John's mouth twitched at the corner as he pretended to study the photo a little closer. It wouldn't do to tell her flat out that it was him, and that he not only remembered the day the picture had been taken, but that he still had the rifle he was holding.

"I guess, to the whites, all Indians look alike," he said, and then changed the subject. "Regarding your situation...have you figured out how you're going to inform the authorities of what your father is doing?"

Alicia frowned. She didn't think of herself as ethnically prejudiced and didn't like him attributing that bias to her.

"I didn't say that," she replied, ignoring his question. "I said he looks a little like you. In fact, you even share a similar scar. Right there," she added, pointing to the photo.

Without thinking, John's hand moved to his chest, feeling the scar beneath the soft fabric of his shirt. He started to ask her how she knew about his scars, then remembered he'd walked bare-assed through the house right in front of her this morning, and sighed. It served him right.

"Hmm, I guess we do," he said. "I never noticed."

"You have a lot of scars," she said.

"Yes."

Alicia thought he would elaborate, but when he didn't, she didn't have the guts to ask him why.

"Now, about those phone calls," John said. "What's your plan?"

Alicia could tell the discussion about his ancestry was, for the time being, over. And he was right. There were things that needed to be set in motion so justice could be served.

"There are a lot of powerful people who are friends with my father, but this isn't information that a regular police department would even deal with. Maybe the FBI…only Dad went to college with the deputy director. Don't misunderstand me. I'm not accusing him of being in cahoots with Dad, but I'm also not certain if he'd believe me. I have this image in my head of trying to convince people of the truth while Dad finds a way to make me out to be crazy…claiming I'm trying to ruin him because he disowned me, or something. And I don't want to wind up in some loony bin, drugged out of my mind to keep me quiet, or six feet under because I was nothing but collateral damage on his path to his personal goals."

John was listening, but he was also distracted by the fact that from where she was standing, he could tell she wasn't wearing a bra. It irked him that he'd even noticed, and he chalked it up to the fact that it had been a while since he'd been with a woman. Maybe all he needed was to take another drive down to Savannah, although the last time he was there, he'd gotten mixed up in a bank robbery and shot for his troubles.

"So what do you think?" she prodded.

That you're not as skinny as I thought. "Uh…that it's your call."

She groaned, then turned away and strode to the windows.

John followed.

"Look…if you really don't trust the powers that be, there's always the media," he said.

Alicia's frustration shifted. "What do you mean?" she asked as she turned to face him.

"You know the newspapers…always ready for the next big scoop. I know a journalist who works out of D.C.—Corbin Woodliff."

"The Corbin Woodliff who won a Pulitzer a couple of years ago?"

"Yes."

Alicia's pulse skipped. That might be the answer. "Can you get me in to see him?"

"If he's in the country," John said, watching the play of emotions on her face.

Alicia's voice rose an octave, evidence of her excitement. "If he broke the news, then the authorities would *have* to follow through. They couldn't ignore it. They couldn't be bought off if there was a huge public outcry."

John nodded.

A smile began in her eyes, then spread to her lips as she impulsively threw her arms around his neck and hugged him.

"Oh, John…I think you've just saved my life…again."

The first thought that crossed his mind was that he'd been right. She wasn't wearing a bra. The second was that he'd managed to keep himself involved in her business by being the go-between for her source, which was good. He would do whatever it took to get to Richard Ponte. He wouldn't let himself care that he was using her. His agenda had been going on too long for him to care about anything or anyone but the end result.

Before Alicia had a chance to register what she'd done, an alarm began going off. She jumped back, startled, as she looked around for the source of the sound.

"What's that?" she cried.

John's eyes narrowed. "A security alarm. Someone just came through the gate at the end of the driveway."

"Was it locked?"

"Yes." He didn't add that he had additional security in place, in case anyone tried to bypass that lock.

"It's not possible that it's just a delivery…or a visitor?"

"I don't get visitors."

Alicia looked at him strangely. "Ever?"

"Ever," John muttered as he headed for his office to check the security cameras, with Alicia right behind him.

Within seconds of getting to the security screen, he recognized who had triggered the alarm—and so did Alicia.

"It's Dieter! Oh God…he's found me! That means Dad knows where I am again." Panic set in as the ramifications began to unfold. "That means you're in danger, too. I shouldn't have—"

John grabbed her by the shoulders. "Stop it! Stay here. I'll deal with this."

"But—"

He gave her a slight shake. "No buts. Just sit here and calm down. I'll be back."

That was easier said than done, but she did sit down, her gaze glued to the security screen as she listened to John's receding footsteps.

It hadn't taken Dieter long to find where John Nightwalker lived. Ironically, his success in locating the man was entirely due to the friendliness of Southerners. After a few wrong turns, he'd come upon a farmer fixing a fence on the shoulder of the road and stopped to ask him if he knew where an Indian called Big John lived.

The man swiped at the sweat on his face with the back of his sleeve, then pointed north. "About two miles on down the road. Got two big iron gates right across the drive. Can't miss it," he said, and went back to his fence.

Dieter quickly located the place. But the gates he'd been expecting were something similar to what he'd seen out in the farmer's pasture to separate one field from another, not these. Not only were they every bit of fourteen, maybe even sixteen, feet high, they locked electronically. They were made of massive iron bars and very similar to the gates at the Ponte estate in

Miami. It made him wonder who John Nightwalker was, and what he was doing up in those trees that he didn't want anyone to see. Those gates told him that further security measures were no doubt also in place, but he was too afraid of his boss to listen to common sense and take a chance of failing him a second time.

There was a call button on the gate that was meant to be used, allowing whoever was at the other end to furnish access. But Dieter didn't intend to announce his arrival.

He popped the trunk lid, then got out. Moments later, he headed toward the gate with his duffel bag in hand. He worked his way into the wiring, bypassed the electronic switch and disarmed it. When he heard it click, he grunted with satisfaction.

Within minutes, he was most of the way up the drive, running a mental checklist of his weapons and what he might need to get Alicia Ponte into his car.

When he turned a curve and saw Nightwalker's black Jeep coming at him at full speed from the house in the background, his mind went into a tailspin. How the hell had the man known? No time for that. He switched into operations mode. He could ram the Jeep, but if the impact disabled his own vehicle, then he couldn't get away. He was grabbing for his handgun as he stomped the brake and jammed the gearshift into Park.

He jumped out, keeping the open door between him and the vehicle coming at him, then hunkered down and fired.

The first shot hit a tire; the second went into the radiator, sending a spew of steam into the air. He expected the man to get out, but he thought the man would run for cover, not come at him with his bare fists. He hadn't planned on leaving a body behind, but Ponte's orders had been plain: Bring Alicia back at all costs. And now that order was about to cost this big Indian his life.

He stood up from behind the car door and took aim.

"Stop right there or I'll shoot," he yelled.

But John didn't stop.

Seeing the gun was proof enough to him that Alicia had been right about her father. He wanted her back bad, and he was willing to do anything to shut her up. When Dieter yelled, John knew what was coming. He dreaded the first burst of pain, even while knowing it wouldn't last.

"You're trespassing on private property," he called as he continued to approach.

Dieter's finger tightened on the trigger. "I came to get Alicia. Turn her over to me now and I'll let you live."

"No," John said coldly. "Get off my property now and *I'll* let *you* live."

Dieter's heart skipped a beat. Why would an unarmed man make such a futile threat? Was there something here he was missing? He glanced nervously from side to side, searching the perimeter of the roadside for the possibility of guards he hadn't taken into account, but no one showed. Convinced he was still in control of the situation, he pointed the gun straight at John's chest.

"I'm warning you," Dieter said. "Get back. All I want is the girl."

"Not in this lifetime," John said, and made a lunge toward the door.

Dieter fired and ducked just as the door slammed into his belly, face and shins. He was so blinded by the blood and pain he didn't see his shot hit John in the shoulder, didn't see the ensuing stain of red that began to spread across the front of John's shirt.

The shot spun John around, landing him flat on his back in the dirt.

From her chair in the library, Alicia saw it all. The shock of realizing Dieter was willing to kill to get to her was confirmation of how desperate her situation was. When she saw Dieter fire and John fall back into the dirt, she ran out of the house and down the driveway, screaming Dieter's name, begging him to stop and praying the shot wasn't a mortal one.

Dieter staggered out from behind the door with the gun in his hand and his face streaming blood. His nose was broken. His lips had been crushed against his teeth so sharply that the insides felt like raw meat. There was a cut on his cheek and another on his chin, and he was cursing at the top of his voice, nearly blind with pain.

"You sorry bastard! You broke my face! All you had to do was back off, but you didn't!"

He pulled the trigger again, sending a shot into John's leg. The wound in John's shoulder was already closing, and he was halfway to his feet when the next shot dropped him again. In the distance, he thought he could hear Alicia screaming. That meant she hadn't stayed put. It also meant he needed to gain control of the situation before Dieter grabbed her and took off.

He rolled over onto his belly, grabbed a handful of dirt and then gritted his teeth as he pushed himself upright. Before Dieter could register the fact that the man he'd put two bullets in was up, John threw the dirt in his face.

Dieter ducked, but not soon enough. Dirt hit him square

in the face, filling both eyes with painful grit and sand. He clawed at his face as John grabbed him, knocked the gun out of his hand with a hard chop to his wrist, then hit him in the chin with his fist. Dieter went down like a felled oak.

Once John had the man down and out, he gave in to the pain, leaning across the hood of the assailant's car, bent double with the suffering.

That was how Alicia found him. The horror in her voice was evident as she arrived, out of breath and screaming.

"Oh my God, oh my God… You're shot. He shot you. You need to sit down." She started rifling through Dieter's car, looking for his cell phone. She found it on the console and ran back to John's side. "I'll call for an ambulance. Oh…wait…I don't know this address. What do I say?"

The pain in John's leg had subsided to a dull throb. He pushed himself up from the car, took the phone from her hand and laid it on the hood, then grabbed her by the shoulders. "Stop. Look at me. I'm okay, see?"

"You're not okay. You're bleeding." She yanked at his shirt, pulling it back so she could see the wound more clearly.

John gritted his teeth. Now it would come. He pulled away from her grasp, but she was still staring, her mouth agape.

Alicia could see where the bullet had gone in. Although the flesh looked red and swollen, the tear was almost shut. It didn't make sense. She kept looking from the wound to John's face and back to the wound again. Then he moved, and as he did, he put himself directly between her and the sun. Within seconds, Alicia's view of him changed. All she could see was a dark silhouette, backlit by a halo of light. The skin on the back of her neck began to crawl as the thought went through her mind that John Nightwalker wasn't human.

It was the only thing that made sense of what she had seen. He'd been shot. She'd seen him fall. The coppery scent of his blood was still strong in her nose, but the hole in his shoulder was almost closed. She looked down at his leg. The bloodstain on his jeans had quit spreading, too.

"How…?"

"It's complicated."

She wrapped her arms around herself and then took an unsteady step backward, staring at him in disbelief.

John had been there before, watching the looks on people's faces, seeing the doubt, then the fear. Sometimes it bothered him. Sometimes it didn't. Today was one of those didn't-bother-him days, and besides, there were things yet to be done. He glanced down at Dieter's unconscious body, then pulled his cell phone out of his pocket.

"Who are you calling?" Alicia asked, then got her answer when he began to talk.

"Hi, Carl, this is John Nightwalker again."

"Hey, John. How you doin'?"

"Oh…okay, I guess—although I've had better days. Someone just broke into my property and took a couple of shots at me. Shot out a tire and my radiator, too."

"For the love of Pete! You don't say. Hang on. I'll dispatch some help right out to you."

John winced, then shifted the weight from his right leg to his left. "Thanks. I've got it under control, but I want to press charges. Could you send someone out to pick him up? Oh…you'll also need a wrecker for his vehicle. I'll be needing a wrecker, too, but I'll call Shelby's Garage down in Justice."

"Consider it done," Carl said, and then added, "You sure seem to be havin' yourself a run of interesting moments."

"I guess you could say that," John said, and then hung up.

As soon as he disconnected, he dialed Information and was quickly connected to Shelby's Garage. After a quick conversation he hung up, then dropped the phone back in his pocket. He spoke without looking at Alicia.

"I need to change clothes before the police arrive, and you need to go back to the house. Keeping you out of the equation means keeping your location secret a little while longer."

Alicia hadn't moved. She couldn't quit staring at John, and for some strange reason, she felt a horrible sense of loss. This time yesterday, she hadn't known this man existed, but now he'd managed to become an integral part of her safety, which made no sense. Why was he willing to involve himself to this degree in a stranger's plight?

"John…"

He paused, sighed, then turned to face her.

"Yes?"

"Who are you?"

"I'm just a man," he said, but the weariness in his voice told a different tale.

"No…that's not what I mean," she said. "Let me put this a different way. Why are you willing to put your life in danger for a total stranger?"

Now it was John's turn to feel a little off center.

Whatever he said next would have to be a lie. He couldn't let it matter.

"Let's just say I live my life the way I do for a reason."

He didn't elaborate, but Alicia wasn't willing to let it go. She thought of all the scars on his body and wondered if they had anything to do with his lifestyle.

"Like what? What in God's name happened to you, and how does your body do what it does?"

For this, he didn't have to lie. "Life is what happened to me. As for your other question, the honest truth is…I have no idea. Now let it go."

At that point, Dieter groaned.

"He's waking up!" Alicia cried, her fear obvious.

"He's not going anywhere," John said, then turned away and headed for his Jeep. He came back carrying a length of rope, bent over, grunting slightly as the muscles flexed in his shoulder, and quickly tied Dieter up.

When he stepped back and realized Alicia was still standing there, watching, he pointed up the road.

"The house. Hustle. I'll be right behind you."

Before she could move, John began taking off his shirt. She turned on her heel and started walking. When she heard the sound of his footsteps close behind her, she began moving faster, then faster again, until she was running. She didn't look back until she reached the house, only to discover that John was no longer following her. She stood in the doorway, trying to figure out where he'd gone, when he suddenly appeared in the front yard in clean clothes and began jogging back down the driveway. He'd obviously taken a different route and gone in the back way.

As she watched, she heard the sound of sirens in the

distance. She remembered John's warning and stepped inside, quickly closing the door behind her.

The quiet inside the house was balm to her shaken senses. She turned, taking in the serenity of what she saw and felt, but her thoughts wouldn't turn off.

God in heaven, what did I just see? She put her hands over her face, stifling the urge to scream. *What is John Nightwalker? Is he real, or is he an angel who appeared in my life to help me out of this mess?*

The sirens were louder; then suddenly they stopped, shifting reality to the here and now. John Nightwalker was not an angel, and she was out of her mind. Curious as to what was going on down the drive, she moved to the window, pushed a curtain aside and peered out.

A police car was there, and Dieter was on his feet and in handcuffs. She felt a spurt of satisfaction in watching him climbing into the back of the cruiser. John was still talking to the police when a wrecker arrived, soon followed by a second. She watched both cars being towed away; then the police car followed, leaving John alone in the middle of the drive.

Then he turned around and looked toward the house.

Alicia shivered. Now what?

When he started walking back, she knew she wouldn't have long to wait.

Four

John told the authorities the truth, up to a point. Yes, Dieter Bahn was a stranger to him. No, he didn't know why the man was on his property other than to take stuff that didn't belong to him. All true, in a way. What had surprised John was that when Dieter came to, he didn't explain himself or deny anything John said.

To John, that said a lot about Richard Ponte's power. A flunky working for some average businessman would want to clear his name quickly and would claim he was only following orders. But Dieter not only took the blame for being on John's property unlawfully, he didn't deny trying to kill him.

And neither man mentioned Alicia Ponte's name, even though she was the only reason he'd been there at all.

John's attitude toward his enemy was taking on new ramifications. Richard Ponte had to be a fearsome man in his own right to demand and obtain such total allegiance. Dieter's behavior also gave further credence to Alicia's fear that her father would be willing to kill her to shut her up. It remained to be seen if Ponte's power reached far enough to get Dieter out of jail. The law didn't take kindly to attempted murder.

John watched the wreckers leave, then headed back toward the house. He needed to get some tools and repair the lock at the gates. And then there was Alicia. She'd seen his "abilities" firsthand. Would she let it go as he'd asked, or would he have to face another round of questions? He wasn't all that optimistic, but telling her the truth was not an option.

He was less than a hundred yards from the house when the cell phone in his pocket began to ring. He was about to answer it when he realized it was Dieter's cell, not his own.

His first instinct was to ignore it, and then he saw the caller ID. The opportunity to talk to his nemesis was almost irresistible, even though it would alert Ponte to the fact that, once again, his plans to take care of his daughter had failed. But John would know when he heard the voice if this was the man he sought, and the urge to confirm his beliefs was strong.

The phone kept ringing.

If he answered it, he would reveal the fact that Alicia was still in motion, still able to turn on her father, not to mention where she was.

The phone rang again.

He flashed on White Fawn's throat, gaping wider than her mouth, itself frozen in a death scream.

The next ring broke him.

His instinct to protect lost out to his need for revenge. "Yes?"

The deep, angry voice was not the subservient tone

Richard Ponte expected from Dieter, but the thought that someone else might have answered the phone never entered his mind.

"With a tone like that, you better have a positive report to turn in," he growled.

The moment John heard the voice, his ears began to roar, as if he were standing in the middle of a hurricane. He felt the blood draining from his face, leaving him disoriented and light-headed. Afraid he was going to be sick where he stood, he bent double, trying frantically to clear his mind.

"Answer me!" Ponte shouted. "By God…I need to know. Do you have Alicia?"

It was the shout that brought John out of his fugue. He straightened slowly, battling the weakness with all his strength. His fingers clenched around the phone as the muscles in his jaw tensed. The same fury was in him now that he'd felt the day he stood in his village amid the carnage of all those he knew and loved. His voice was dark, loud, angry.

"Yes, I have Alicia," he said. "And your flunky is on his way to jail for attempted murder."

Ponte gasped. "What do you mean…you have Alicia? Who are you? A kidnapper? Name your ransom. I want my daughter back."

"You aren't listening to me," John said. "Dieter is on his way to jail for trying to kill me. The authorities are already getting involved in your business, as am I."

"Where? What do you want? Name your price and—"

John interrupted, his voice softening to a frightening whisper. "You want answers? Then shut up and listen.

I know who you are. I know what you did. And I've waited more than five hundred years to make you pay."

Something floated in and out of Ponte's mind so fast it didn't have time to register. It wasn't anything tangible—just a feeling that he'd heard this voice before. But the timeline was a joke.

"I don't know who you are, but you're obviously a lunatic. Five hundred years? I wasn't alive five hundred years ago, so whatever you think I did, I didn't. Got it?"

"Richard Ponte might not have been there, but you have a soul, and it was there. It's been recycling for centuries, and I've been chasing it for just as long. Now I've found you, and I intend to make you pay."

Richard was staggered by the venom in the other man's voice, and a little frightened of the crazy talk. Insanity was impossible to fight.

"Pay how? By claiming my soul? Who do you fancy yourself to be? The devil?"

"The devil wouldn't want you—but I do. Look over your shoulder, woman killer. I'm coming for you."

Ponte's belly rolled. Woman killer? This must have to do with the guns he was running. "Who are you? Some loony Afghan? Some pissed-off Iraqi? If so, don't blame me. Blame your crazy leaders and your ancient religions. This is the twenty-first century. Get with the program."

By now John was shouting. "The twenty-first century, the seventeenth century, the thirteenth century…they're all the same to men like you. You take what you want without thought for anyone else and leave death in your wake. You brought your men to my land in your ship, looking for gold. When you didn't find it, you killed them. You killed all my people. You killed my *wife*. You cut her throat as she screamed for mercy. You took her necklace. When I found you, you were clutching it like a trophy. You tried to kill me, but I didn't die. I *can't* die—not until I watch you take your last fucking breath."

When the man began to shout at Ponte in some foreign language, the skin on Ponte's face began to tighten and burn, and though he had no idea what he was hearing, he wanted to throw up.

John was out of control. Almost six hundred years of frustration—of waiting—were boiling up in him. Richard Ponte had been a killer then, and from what John could tell, his enemy was repeating the cycle again and again. John kept reciting the curse in his native language, the same one he'd invoked centuries earlier, cursing his enemy's soul through eternity until his demand for retribution had been met.

Richard Ponte could hear the stranger screaming at him, although he still didn't understand what the man was saying. The longer he stood with the phone frozen to his ear, the more certain he became that he was experiencing something entirely outside his frame of reference.

There was a sick feeling in the pit of his stomach, and his muscles were beginning to give way. He staggered across the room, then dropped into the chair behind his desk to keep from falling. All the while, the stranger's words drummed through his mind, accusing him of something he didn't understand but couldn't find the words to deny.

He felt his throat tightening—closing—as if he were being choked, then a burning sensation in his chest. He tried to turn loose of the phone, but he couldn't feel his fingers. He didn't know how long he'd been sitting there before he realized the line was dead.

He stared at the phone, then dropped it suddenly, as if he'd been holding a snake, and jumped up from his chair. He strode to the window, desperate to center himself. The view was the same view he'd had of Miami ever since he'd set up offices here. The skyline was familiar. Outside, the traffic in the streets was no better and no worse than usual.

So why did he feel like a stranger in his own skin?

Why this overwhelming sense of despair?

Was it because Alicia had eluded his capture and was about to bring him down, or was there another older—darker—sin that was about to do him in?

He shuddered. Impossible. This whole scenario was ridiculous. Why had he let the ravings of a lunatic bother him for even a moment? He had to put a spin on Alicia's disappearance, and he thought he knew how. If he let it leak that she'd had a mental breakdown and had been kidnapped on the way to treatment, then Dieter's transgressions could be explained. Shooting at a kidnaper to get the boss's daughter back was definitely justified. A satisfied smile broke across his face just as there was a knock on the door.

He turned, grateful for the interruption, just as Charlotte, his secretary, walked in with an armful of mail.

"It's sorted as usual, Mr. Ponte. The small stack on top is your personal mail, and remember, you have an early lunch appointment with Mr. Carruthers at eleven before his flight back to D.C. this afternoon."

Something inside Richard shifted again as his composure strengthened.

"Thank you, Charlotte," he said, then strode to his desk and began to go through the mail. "Before you leave, would you please bring me a fresh cup of coffee...and some painkillers. I have the beginnings of a headache."

"Yes, sir...right away, sir."

By the time Charlotte shut the door, Richard's emotions were completely under control again. The longer he sat, the more he convinced himself that what he'd experienced was a momentary panic resulting from Dieter's failure. It was time to implement the backup plan.

First thing was to leak a story to the media that his daughter had suffered a mental breakdown and that he'd received a ransom demand. He knew she had no proof for what she'd heard, and maybe, if he destroyed her plausibility before she spilled her guts, he could effect some successful damage control. It would also put an end to whoever it was he'd just talked to on the phone. If the man was identified as a kidnaper, then he, too, would be neutralized.

Ponte grinned, pleased with his plan, and began flipping through his Rolodex as his secretary returned with the requested painkillers and a fresh cup of coffee. By the time his call was answered, he had his story in place.

"Federal Bureau of Investigation. How may I direct your call?"

"This is Richard Ponte. I want to report a kidnapping."

Once Alicia saw the sheriff driving away with Dieter Bahn in handcuffs, she began to relax. She was still watching John's approach when she saw him pause, then take a phone out of his pocket to answer a call. That in itself was of no consequence. Cell phones were a part of everyday existence. It meant nothing—until she witnessed what came next.

He was some distance from the house, but close enough that she could see his expression change from calm to enraged. She couldn't hear anything he was saying, but she could see that he was shouting. She ran to the door and out onto the landing, not sure what she could do, but fearing the trouble might involve her.

Once outside, she heard him shouting. The tone of his voice was frightening—filled with a rage she'd never seen. But it was when he shifted from English to a language she didn't understand that she saw something in him that made her afraid. Afraid of him. Afraid for her life.

She watched until he suddenly disconnected in anger, dropped the phone onto the ground and stomped it to pieces. When he looked up, she panicked. What if she was next?

His body language alone was frightening. His hands were curled into fists. His shoulders stiff with tension. When he threw his head back and screamed, she bolted. Going back into the house would be like shutting herself in with a mad dog. She headed for the bluff.

John didn't know Alicia was anywhere around until he saw her leap from the landing and realized she must have seen everything, or at least enough to scare her. He could only imagine what she was thinking, seeing him lose control as he'd just done. He would like nothing better than to be rid of her, but he needed her. She was bait—bait he needed to get to Ponte. Ponte had to want her silenced, and he wouldn't stop until she was, which meant he, or some of his minions, would come after her, and when they did, then John's quest would be over. He knew how to get information out of an unwilling man. He'd had an eternity to learn from the best. Someone would tell him where Ponte was. At that point, Alicia Ponte would be on her own. Until that happened, he couldn't let her go.

When he started after her, his healing muscles protested. She was all the way down the bluff and on the shore, running for all she was worth, when he caught her.

The pounding rhythm of Alicia's heartbeat was so loud in her ears that she didn't hear anything, not the roar of the surf, not the jarring thud of her own footsteps as she ran. She didn't know John Nightwalker was right behind her until he grabbed her arm and yanked her off her feet, then hauled her against his chest.

At the moment of contact, she screamed, then began pummeling him with her fists.

Instead of fighting her, John just held on, letting her fear run its course until she was weak from fighting. Only after she collapsed against him, weak and weeping, did he begin to talk. The tone of his voice revealed his anger, as well as confusion.

"What the hell is the matter with you? Why were you running from me? I'm the one who's been helping you, damn it. I took two bullets to keep you from winding up back in your father's grasp, and this is how you behave? Explain that to me, lady…because I can promise you, I have a lot better things I could be doing."

Alicia pulled away, and the moment she did, her legs gave way. She sank to her knees, aware of the wet sand and the lapping surf washing at her feet and legs. She reached for the water, then cupped her hands to catch the inflow and sluiced her face over and over until her long dark hair was stuck to the sides of her cheeks and she could feel sanity returning.

John stood by, his expression inscrutable. A part of him felt sorry for her, but not enough to stop using her. She wasn't anything to him other than a means to an end. Then she looked up, and for a fraction of a second the water droplets on her face looked like tears.

He flinched, then gritted his teeth.

"I'm sorry," she whispered. "It's just…I saw you…screaming…shouting, and I didn't understand. I thought…" She shrugged. "I don't know what I thought. You just scared me. That's all."

John exhaled slowly. That he could understand. He squatted in front of her, watching the play of light against the water droplets on her face, seeing the color of the ocean echoed in the stark expression in her eyes.

"I'm sorry," he said, his voice quiet once again. "It's complicated."

Alicia rocked back on her heels, braced her hands on her knees and stared at his face, unable to read his expression. She was in one hell of a fix. She had to trust someone, and right now, he was all she had.

"I'm sorry, too," she said. "I just… I panicked, that's all."

He nodded. "After all you've endured, I can understand that. But we need to focus on the business at hand. That phone call…the one you saw me take…"

"Yes?"

"It was your father. He knows Dieter is in custody. He doesn't know who I am, but he knows you're with me."

Alicia shivered, both from the chill setting in and from what he was saying. She couldn't rationalize the way he'd reacted after talking to a virtual stranger.

"He knows. How?" she asked.

This was where it got tricky. Did he tell her the truth or…? The words came out of his mouth before he could stop himself.

"He knows because I told him."

Alicia shivered again. This time from fear.

"Why? Why would you do that?"

He shrugged. "I'm not sure. It was an impulse. It's done."

Alicia began to get up. John reached down to help her, but she pushed his hands away and dragged herself to her feet.

"Then tell me something," she said. "And don't lie to me. I'll know if you do."

"What do you want to know?"

"I watched you. You were screaming into the phone. You were shouting and screaming and…then you started talking to him in another language. You don't react like that to a total stranger. So explain this to me…. Why did you behave like that to a man you've never met?"

John thought about a lie for less than a second, then let it go. He had nothing to lose by telling her a partial truth. She still needed him as much as he needed her.

"Your father might want you dead…but not nearly as much as *I* want to kill *him*. He butchered my family…everyone I ever knew. I've been looking for him forever, and when I find him, I'm going to make him sorry he was ever born."

Alicia knew she was staring, but she couldn't bring

herself to move. This was a nightmare. All of it. First her father—now this. She couldn't take it all in.

Her voice softened to the point that John had to strain to hear her, and when he did, he felt the first hint of regret.

"Were you following me, too? Are you using me to get to him?"

"I didn't even know you existed, but I won't deny meeting you was a godsend. Ultimately, meeting you will lead me to him."

Alicia's mouth went slack. She heard what he was saying but kept telling herself she'd misunderstood. With every word she spoke, her voice continued to rise, until by the time she was done, she was screaming.

"You're trying to make me believe that you've been looking for my father for years…that I just happened to show up in the place where you live—by accident—and that I'm now the key you need for revenge?" She thought back to that moment at the station where he'd stepped in to "save her" from Dieter. "You didn't really care what Dieter was going to do to me, did you? If I'd been the daughter of someone else, you would have left me dangling, wouldn't you?"

"I wouldn't have let him hurt anyone," he said.

"You lie." Alicia doubled up her fist and slugged him in the chest. "To hell with you and your agenda. I don't believe a word you've been saying. You said you'd help me, but you're just helping yourself. You don't care what happens to me. I'm only a means to an end. You don't even care that tens of thousands of American soldiers have been put at risk, are being betrayed every day they stand on foreign soil, by one of their own. I trusted you." She shuddered, then combed her fingers through her hair, shoving it away from her face. "Damn you, John Nightwalker. Damn you and my father and all men straight to hell."

John's belly knotted. For the first time in centuries, he felt guilt. Even more, he felt shame. He watched her striding back up the beach toward the steps, then lifted his chin and followed. What was done was done. Now they had to find a way to work together or one of them would die, and he knew damn well it wouldn't be him. But there were things to put in place, like damage control. He needed to get her to safety so she could tell her story before anything else happened.

He pulled out his cell phone and punched in some numbers. When the call was answered, he began issuing orders with little more than a brief hello to preface them. By the time he got to the house, the next leg of their journey was in place. They couldn't stay here any longer. It had been a year since he'd been to his home in Arizona, but it was out in the middle of nowhere, with no neighbors. He'd already called the caretaker, and sent him out to turn on the utilities and stock the place with food. As soon as he took her to D.C. and she finished telling her story, they were going to Sedona.

By the time he got back to his house, the front door was standing ajar. He sighed. He could only guess at how pissed Alicia must be. This whole stupid mess was his fault. He'd thought of nothing but his own agenda, and she was right. As badly as he wanted revenge, first Richard Ponte needed to be outed as a traitor and the flow of illegal weapons into Iraq stopped.

"Alicia!" he called.

She didn't appear. She didn't even answer.

"Shit," he muttered, and headed for her bedroom. He found her there with an armful of her clothing and her suitcase open on the bed.

"What are you doing?" he asked.

"Don't treat me like a fool, and don't act like one," she snapped. "You can see what I'm doing. Where are we going?"

John stood for a moment, taking in her defiance, and he had to admit, she wore it well.

"I have a place in Arizona. After we do what we have to in D.C., we're going to Sedona."

"How do we get there?"

"Chopper."

"Are you the pilot?"

He nodded.

"Then pack your jammies, Tonto, because if I know my daddy…he'll be all over this place before dark."

John flinched but forced himself to ignore the ethnic slur. He'd had it coming. He left without comment and headed for his room. Within the hour, he'd emptied his safe, packed his suitcase and was outside tying it on the back of a big black Harley he'd wheeled out of the garage.

Alicia walked outside, then paused on the doorstep. "Want me to lock the door?"

"I've got a remote," he said. "It will arm the alarm and lock everything down. Hop on," he said, and handed her a helmet. "Although I have a helipad here, I keep the chopper at a hangar on the other side of Justice. With the Jeep out of commission, this is the only ride. Have you ever been on a motorcycle?"

"Considering the fact that I've never made my own

breakfast before this morning, what do you think the odds are that I went through a biker-babe phase?"

He arched an eyebrow but refused to spar with her. "I'll take that as a no," he said, and handed her a helmet.

She put it on, then straddled the bike, wishing she had jeans instead of dress slacks as he tied her suitcase on behind his. But it was too late to worry about fashion as John swung his leg over in front of her and sat down on the bike.

"Wrap your arms around me and hold on," he said.

She nodded, although he didn't see her acquiesce. He'd already fired up the engine.

She wrapped her arms around his waist just as he put the bike in gear. It fishtailed once in the loose gravel as they took off down the driveway, but he quickly got it under control.

Alicia's heart was thumping wildly. She wanted off, but she wanted away from her father's reach worse, and thanks to Dieter, this seemed to be their only out.

As they drove through the open gates, John realized he hadn't gone back to repair the lock Dieter had sabotaged. Now there was no time to fix it himself. He would call Smith Electric when they got to the hangar. The few things from his past that he'd managed to hold on to were too precious to him to lose them to some burglar.

When they hit the highway, he accelerated, taking a measure of satisfaction in the way Alicia Ponte's arms tightened around his stomach. But he had to give her credit. She was meeting this latest twist without complaint. Despite her complete disillusionment with him, she seemed equal to what lay ahead.

"You okay?" he yelled.

"I'm not talking to you!" she yelled back, then closed her eyes and rested her helmet against the middle of his back so she didn't have to watch the trees blurring into a solid line on either side of the road.

He grinned and took the curve low and fast, just for the satisfaction of feeling her flinch.

All too soon, they were back in Justice. He decided to stop at Smith Electric instead of calling, giving the repairman instructions while Alicia kept her head down and her face concealed behind the visor of the helmet. After that, they were off to the hangar.

Alicia stood nearby, watching as the shiny black chopper was moved outside. It looked to her like a big dragonfly. While she'd been all over the world in all sorts of planes, she'd never flown in anything like this. The very size of it was intimidating. There wasn't nearly enough bulk between her and the heavens for her peace of mind, but a quick getaway was paramount.

She had to find someone who would listen to her, who would start an investigation into her father's business dealings overseas. Fate had dumped her in this man's lap. So be it. But she'd already made up her mind that she would puke up her guts and hope they landed on his shoes before asking him for another damned thing, including meds for motion sickness or blinders so she wouldn't have to see the sky all around her.

John was all-business as he went through the pre-flight checklist while the chopper was being fueled. Being thorough and careful was part of being a pilot. It was like riding a horse. You never wanted to start out on a long journey without knowing your mount was well-rested, and had been watered and fed. The same applied to horsepower, especially when you were several thousand feet up in the air. He sensed Alicia's eyes on him, but he didn't give in to the urge to look. He wasn't in the mood for any more crap, which was what he figured she was still dishing up.

When he finally waved her over, Alicia was more than ready. She picked up her suitcase and started walking, her bag bumping against her leg with every step. When she reached the chopper, John reached down to take her suitcase, but she pushed past him and swung it up into the cabin on her own, then crawled into the passenger seat and began fumbling with the buckle, leaving him under no misapprehension as to how truly pissed she was.

He resisted the urge to roll his eyes as he tossed his bag in beside hers, then crawled up into the cabin and buckled himself in, as well.

"Do you get airsick?" he asked.

"No."

"Pity," he drawled. Seconds later, they were airborne.

It wasn't until Justice was nothing but a spot far below that Alicia began to relax. Dealing with John Nightwalker and his two-faced lies was less of a problem for her than the fact that, for the time being, she was out of her father's reach.

About fifteen minutes into the flight, she looked over at John.

He felt her gaze and turned.

"What?" he asked.

She hated herself for admiring even one hair on his head, but he *was* stunning. His profile was pure in every sense of the word: high cheekbones, strong chin, proud nose with a hint of a hook that went with his ethnicity. And that damn little feather dangling from one ear. When he looked at her, his brown eyes darkened to the point of appearing black. She felt his impatience with her, but damn it, he'd started this ride and she wasn't about to let go. Right now, she needed him as much as he seemed to need her. So they would use each other, and if hate was the result, she didn't care. Not if he kept her alive.

John wasn't used to being scrutinized to such a degree, or being around a woman who was at ease with being silent.

"If there's something you need to say, spit it out."

There was a hint of the imp in her voice. "Are we there yet?"

The familiar question all traveling children were prone to ask surprised him. He laughed before he thought, then shook his head and turned away. He was using her for bait, and now that she knew it and hadn't offered to slit his throat, he didn't want to like her.

Satisfied that she'd gotten under his skin, if only for a moment, she settled back into the seat and began concentrating on how she was going to be able to convince Corbin Woodliff that her father was a traitor. If only she had proof, something more than just an overheard conversation. Then she sighed. It wasn't up to her to play detective. That was for someone else to do. It was her responsibility to reveal what she'd heard so she would not be guilty by omission.

The trip felt as if it would never end. The farther they flew, the worse she felt. Every now and then, she knew John was looking at her, but she refused to look back, and the silence between them continued until the crack and static of radio traffic startled them both and John returned to the business of piloting.

They set down once to refuel and get some food. John ate without care or consideration for the tumult her stomach was in, even though she was sure he suspected it when she refused the sandwich he brought her. The scent of the barbecue he was downing was up her nose and in her clothes. She wanted to slap him. When he offered her the extra sandwich again, she snapped. She took it out of his hand, took a great big bite out of the middle, chewed and chewed until she thought she was going to spew, then finally swallowed it.

"Yum," she said, and handed it back, reached for her cold soda and added insult to injury to her already rolling stomach by downing a big drink.

Then she slumped down in the seat, closed her eyes and promised God that she would give her first child to the priesthood if He would keep her from throwing up. The fact that she wasn't Catholic didn't work into the prayerful equation. She just didn't want to see another smirk on John Nightwalker's face and hoped, if and when the time ever came, that her firstborn would understand. She would rather fail in God's eyes than have John Nightwalker see her weaknesses.

To her undying relief, she finally fell asleep once they were back in the air. She didn't know how long she'd been out when she suddenly felt a shift in motion, which woke her instantly.

She straightened up in the seat, then looked down. The view below was a giant grid of streets and houses, outlined in green from thousands of trees. A long, winding river was a muddy blue ribbon slipping through it all. When she recognized the giant obelisk that was the Washington Monument, she knew they'd arrived.

John's focus was on landing, as he communicated with the tower at Dulles International. He knew she was awake and was once again surprised when she didn't begin talking or plying him with questions. Besides the fact that she was furious with him, he'd figured out that she tended to keep her own counsel and didn't feel the need to talk when there was a lull in conversation. The irony of it was, she was more like him than he wanted to admit.

When they were finally cleared for landing, John competently set the chopper down. Once they were on the ground, he took off his headphones, then turned toward Alicia.

She looked back, waiting for him to make the next move.

"We're taking a cab from here to the hotel," he said.

"When do I get to talk to Woodliff?"

"Tomorrow morning. I told him we needed privacy. He offered his home."

Alicia took a deep breath, then exhaled slowly. "The sooner I get this off my chest, the better. I just hope he believes me."

John could tell she was nervous. With that kind of information, who wouldn't be? And even if she wasn't close to her father, as she'd claimed, having to give him up still had to be tough.

"He's a journalist. He'll have his own contacts to verify information. What will happen is that the report alone will ignite its own investigation. If there *is* someone in power in D.C. who might have been inclined to bury the info, the fact that the public knows will keep that from happening."

She nodded, then unbuckled her seat belt and reached behind the seat for her suitcase.

"Let me," John said.

Instead of arguing, she shrugged and got out, leaving him to get the luggage, then followed him inside and through the airport itself until they got to a place where they could hail a cab. Alicia immediately felt better with her feet back on solid ground. By the time they reached the hotel, she was almost giddy with relief. When they went to sign in, John pulled her aside.

"I already made a reservation for us while you were asleep. It's under my company name and will be more difficult to trace if your father is so inclined."

"Thank you," Alicia said. "I have money. I can pay my own way."

"We'll deal with that later," he said. "Let's just get up to the suite first."

"You reserved a suite? As in…more than one bedroom, right?"

He arched an eyebrow. "Unless you're ready to move our loving relationship to the next level."

"You are such an egotistical ass," Alicia mumbled.

"You don't have to like me. But you do have to trust me."

Alicia couldn't believe what he'd just said. "No, John Nightwalker, I don't have to trust you. Not for one minute. But I'll use you, just like you're using me, and you'd better trust me when I tell you, if it comes down to you or me winding up in my father's gunsight, I choose you. We already know you're invincible. I, on the other hand, am not."

John's eyes narrowed angrily, but he couldn't fault her reasoning or her mood. He'd set himself up for this whole damn mess, and he was willing to do whatever it took to get the soul he sought and bring some sense of peace to what was left of his life.

He shrugged. "Whether we like it or not, for the time being we're stuck with each other. Please wait here," he said. "I'll be right back."

Alicia stood with the bags as he checked them in, then quietly followed him to the elevator, then up to their suite.

"Take your pick," John said, pointing to the bedrooms on opposite sides of the sitting room.

As far as she was concerned, it didn't matter. She took her bag and headed for the one on the right, shutting the door firmly behind her as she entered.

"We'll order dinner from room service," John called.

She didn't respond.

"I'm having steak. If you want something different, speak now or forever hold your peace," he added.

Alicia opened the door long enough to put in her order.

"Rib eye, medium well. Steamed vegetables, and cheesecake. No wine. No salad. No potato. Iced tea. I don't care what kind of cheesecake as long as it's a big piece. Thank you very much. I'm going to take a bath now—with bubbles, if they have some. Knock when the food arrives."

She closed the door, leaving John to deal with the knowledge that she was going to be naked in bubbles and he was going to be ordering room service. Something was wrong with that picture, but he didn't want to explore the possibilities.

He carried his suitcase into the other bedroom, tossed it on the bed, then sat down. The quiet was comforting, something he was used to. Then he heard the sound of running water from across the suite.

He didn't have to like her to get what he wanted. He didn't *want* to like her—but she did have her moments. Then he heard something strange, and stood up and walked all the way across the suite to stand outside her bedroom door.

She was singing. They were on the run from her father, who wanted her dead, and she was *singing*.

He leaned forward, trying to make out the words, and when he recognized the song, a slow smile spread across his face.

"Bridge over troubled waters."

That was the understatement of the month.

He stood for a moment longer, listening as she hit a high note, then impulsively reached out and put the flat of his hand on the door and made himself a silent promise.

Anyone who could still sing after the kind of day they'd had was worth whatever trouble it took to save her.

He would make sure that Alicia Ponte stayed safe.

No matter what.

Five

Richard sat across the table from Jacob Carruthers, his old friend and partner in crime, watching the play of sunshine on the man's face and thinking to himself how old Jacob was starting to look. It didn't occur to him that he was suffering the same fate. Richard felt as young today as he had on his thirty-first birthday, which was the day he'd made his first million, and as invincible.

"Want some more wine?" Jacob asked as he refilled his own glass.

Richard nodded. With everything that had happened in the past few days and what he was about to do, Jacob needed to be forewarned. As soon as his wineglass had been topped up, Richard offered a toast.

"To business," he said.

Jacob smiled. "To business," he echoed, then took a sip.

"We need to talk," Richard said.

Jacob waved an approaching waiter away. As soon as they were assured of privacy, Jacob leaned back in his chair.

"About what?"

"We have a small problem," Richard said, and then added a wry smile, intending to make sure Jacob knew it was no big deal. His old friend had a tendency to panic, and Richard didn't need the added stress. Not when he had everything under control. So he began.

"Last week, when you were at the house…"

"Yes, what about it?"

"Alicia overheard us."

Jacob's nostrils flared as he divested himself of the wineglass, then leaned forward, his voice barely above a whisper.

"Are you talking about—"

"Yes."

"Fucking A."

"It's our fault. We shouldn't have discussed that outside the office."

"But we did. Now what? What did she say? Is she upset?" Jacob grabbed Richard's arm, his fingers digging through the suit fabric and into the flesh. "Are we okay?"

Richard frowned. This reaction was what he'd expected. Jacob always saw the negative first.

"Hell yes, we're okay. Stop worrying."

"Don't tell me to stop worrying. We're at war with another country, and what we're doing… Crap. We execute traitors here. These are our lives we're talking about. I want to talk to her. I need to look her in the face and hear her say we're okay."

Richard glanced away, afraid some of his concern might show. "She's not in Miami at the moment."

Jacob inhaled sharply. He'd seen that look on Richard's face before and knew he was hiding something. "Then where is she?"

Richard shrugged, then took another sip of his wine. "She panicked. But I have it under control."

"She panicked? Panicked how? Like I'm panicking now, or panicking as in…hit the ceiling?"

Jacob set his glass down abruptly, sloshing some of it over onto the tablecloth. The stain spread rapidly, a dark ruby stain—like blood.

"I said, I'm handling it. I'm holding a press conference this afternoon. Harold will be there."

Jacob's eyes widened, and his voice rose in opposition. "Harold as in Harold Parsons, Deputy Director of the FBI? You've involved the FBI? Are you out of your fucking mind?"

"Shut up!" Richard snapped. "This is the way it's going to be. I will be issuing a statement that Alicia suffered a nervous breakdown a few days ago, and that on the way to a hospital, she was kidnapped. That way the man she's with will be—"

"She's *with* someone? Who? Is he a cop? I can't believe we're sitting here waiting for lunch to arrive and drinking wine like idiots when our world is falling down around us. I'm out of here."

Richard looked around nervously. People were beginning to stare. "Sit down and listen, damn it! I don't know who the man is. I don't know where they hooked up, but announcing her nervous breakdown will negate anything she might say to the wrong people, and saying she's been kidnapped will put the man she's with on the defensive."

"This is a nightmare," Jacob said, swiping his face

with his hands. He downed his wine in one inelegant gulp. "Where's Dieter? Why isn't he on top of this?"

"He's following orders," Richard said, refusing to reveal that, at the moment, his cleanup man was sitting in jail, accused of attempted murder. The news conference this afternoon and Richard's team of lawyers would take care of that.

"You'd better make this go away," Jacob said. "I'm not going down for this just because your daughter got religion. If you need me, I'll be back in Boston by tonight." Then he stormed out of the restaurant.

Richard was worried. Jacob's behavior was erratic— too erratic to be trustworthy. If he found out Dieter was in jail and that Richard had no idea where his daughter was or what she was doing, there was no telling what he would do.

Richard needed to regain control. He glanced at his watch. No need to eat a meal he wouldn't be able to swallow. He called to tell his driver that he was on the way out, signaled the waiter and canceled their order, then left a handful of bills on the table as he hurried out of the restaurant. There were a few details he needed to deal with before the press conference. Now was not the time for any more slipups. The Miami sun was warm on his face as his driver pulled up to the curb. He got in, barking orders even before he was seated.

"Take me back to the office, and make it quick. I need to pick up a file before we head to the courthouse for the press conference."

"Yes, Mr. Ponte," the driver said, and put the car in gear.

Richard took a deep breath as he leaned back in the seat, too bothered to appreciate the ebb and flow of the ocean, which he usually enjoyed, or the sun-drenched palms lining the streets. His mind was racing, trying not to let Jacob's panic derail his carefully laid plans. Although Dieter was, for the moment, out of pocket, he wasn't the only shark in Ponte's food chain. He took a cell phone out of his briefcase, along with a scrap of paper with a phone number scribbled on it. The cell was a disposable—one he would toss once this call was made. And this was a number he would never put on speed dial—a number he would never want to be traced back to him.

He punched in the numbers, then waited. The man who answered was rude and abrupt, which didn't matter, because Richard wasn't in the market for manners.

"What do you want?"

The growl sounded feral. Richard hesitated as an image flashed into his mind of his daughter when she was five, running toward him, crying. He'd picked her up and kissed the finger she'd just mashed. He remembered the feel of her little arms around his neck, and her tears, wet against his cheek. Could he do this?

"Talk, damn it, or hang up. I don't have all day."

"I have a job for you," Richard said, the decision made.

Alicia was still in the tub when she heard a knock on her door.

"Food's here," John called.

"Don't wait on me," she said, then flipped the drain with her toe before getting out of the water.

Suddenly hungry, she toweled off quickly, then chose to wear what she normally wore to work out in, instead of street clothes. Her hair was still damp and her feet were bare when she came out of her room in a pair of gray sweat pants and a blue cotton T-shirt.

She noticed John had showered. His short, spiky hair was seal-black and still damp, and he'd changed into jeans and a polo shirt. Silently admiring the copper tone of his skin against the pure white of the shirt, she slid into the other chair at the table and lifted the dome from her plate, sniffing appreciatively at the perfectly done steak. She poked at the steamed broccoli and carrots with her finger, then took the dab of whipped cream from the top of her cheesecake and ate it first.

"Umm," she said.

John removed the cover from his food, as well, without commenting on her inspection of her dinner. At this point, he figured the less he said to her, the better off they both would be. But to his surprise, she initiated a conversation soon after taking her first bite of steak.

"This is very good. Thank you for ordering. I want you to know that I have money and will be paying my own way."

"That's not necessary," he said.

Alicia pointed her fork at him. "I didn't say it was necessary. I just said I'll be doing it. Would you pass the salt, please?"

"It's right in front of you," he fired back as he cut another piece of steak and popped it in his mouth, then reached for the remote. If this was the way it was going to be, he wasn't in the mood to fight about it. He flipped through the channels until he found CNN, then returned to his meal.

Alicia frowned when the TV came on but didn't say anything, and so they continued, listening to the news rather than each other. She was in the middle of dessert when an announcer broke in with a news flash. She didn't pay much attention until she heard the name Ponte. At that point she dropped her fork and spun her chair around to face the screen.

"Turn it up!" she said, but it was an unnecessary request. John was already reaching for the remote.

They sat in silence, their food forgotten, as the anchor kept speaking.

"As you can see, Deputy Director Harold Parsons of the FBI is, at this moment, at the courthouse in Miami, Florida, awaiting the arrival of world-renowned armament and munitions magnate Richard Ponte. Rumor has it that Ponte's daughter, twenty-seven-year-old Alicia Ponte, has been kidnapped, and that he is about to make a public plea for her safe return."

Alicia jumped up from her chair. "You bastard. You sorry bastard." She looked at John, trying to gauge his reaction. "Don't you have anything to say?" When he didn't answer, she rolled her eyes and dropped back into her chair. "Oh God…why did I think I could get away with this?"

John felt Alicia's fear, and a part of him acknowledged her concern. Hell, he'd just been branded a kidnapper, but he couldn't think past the fact that he was about to see the face of his enemy. He knew the face would not look the same, but it was impossible to hide the truth of a human soul, and this soul was dark—and had continued to choose darkness over and over each time it had been reborn. He would know his enemy at last. He would *feel* his presence.

The pitch of the news anchor's voice deepened in

accordance with the seriousness of the moment as he continued to narrate over the live shots being broadcast.

"Richard Ponte is arriving now. That's him in the white linen suit and yellow shirt, coming down the steps. He and Deputy Director Parsons have been friends since college, so the deputy director's presence at the podium obviously goes beyond what his position demands. Ponte is coming forward. It appears that he's going to speak first. We're now going live to the courthouse—"

Richard felt as if he were on roller skates. He strode down the steps toward the bank of microphones with what he hoped was a serious expression and not one of panic. He accepted Harold's handshake, then impulsively gave him a brief, manly hug, setting the stage for what he hoped was an "in your face" to his daughter, reminding her that, with his connections, how dare she threaten to bring him down? Then he turned to face the cameras.

"Ladies and gentlemen, thank you for coming. And I must thank my old friend, Deputy Director Parsons, for standing with me on this difficult day. I've been putting this off, hoping against hope that I would not have to make this announcement, but I can't wait any longer. The safety—even the life—of my daughter, Alicia, is at stake. Several days ago, Alicia suffered a nervous breakdown. After an unsuccessful attempt to treat her within the safety of our home, I was forced to seek care for her at a private institution. On the way there, she was kidnapped."

He paused, reveling in the collective gasp he heard from the reporters, and felt a returning sense of power before he continued.

"There has not been a ransom demand, which, in itself, is even more frightening. All we know is that she was last seen in Georgia in the company of a man named John Nightwalker, who is believed to be of Native American heritage. I am offering a million-dollar reward for information leading to the safe recovery of my daughter."

"Oh, perfect," Alicia muttered. She was so wrapped up in her own disbelief that she missed the fact that John's breathing had sped up, and that he was standing with his fists doubled and a look on his face that, had she seen it, would have sent her running.

John was so full of rage that hearing his name being broadcast across the world in such a way—and by a mortal enemy—didn't even faze him. After the phone conversation they'd had, he read it as an out-and-out dare.

Alicia's hands were shaking. "John, John, I'm so sorry. I didn't expect him to—"

"*I* did," he said. "Let it go."

"People saw us in the lobby. It won't take long for someone to put two and two together. Corbin Woodliff won't talk to us now, and with the deputy director of the FBI standing beside my father, going to the authorities is impossible. They wouldn't believe a thing I said. Not when I've just been branded a cuckoo. God…oh God…we're dead."

There was a sudden knock on the door.

Alicia stifled a scream, clapping her hands over her mouth as John motioned for her to get back. She ran toward her bedroom, then stood in the doorway, just out of sight of the entry.

John looked through the peephole, saw a bellman's uniform and relaxed.

"It's just a bellman," he said, and opened the door.

"Good evening, sir. I've come to pick up your food cart."

John frowned. "I didn't ring for a bellman. We're not even through with our food."

"I am," Alicia offered, then knew she should have kept her mouth shut when the bellman's focus suddenly shifted to her. Before she could say *I'm sorry,* he reached behind his back and came out with a gun.

She screamed and dived toward the floor as John went for the bellman. The gun popped. She screamed again, glimpsing a tangle of arms and legs just before crawling into her bedroom and locking the door. Seconds later she was scrambling, trying to find something to use as a weapon.

Suddenly she heard a deep moan, another pop, then silence. She staggered back against the wall with her hands over her mouth, her gaze fixed on the doorknob. A faucet dripped in the bathroom behind her. Outside, the distant sound of sirens could be heard. She wondered if they were coming here—if someone had already notified the authorities. Obviously the bellman had recognized them and wanted the reward money for himself. This was a nightmare that kept getting worse.

Then she heard John's voice.

"It's me. Open the door."

Muttering a swift prayer of thanksgiving, Alicia leaped forward and unlocked the door. When she saw John still in one piece, she threw her arms around his neck and hugged him fiercely.

"Thank God you're all right," she said, then saw blood on the front of his shirt. "Oh no! Are you…?"

"It's not mine," he said gruffly, trying not to think of how right it felt to be holding her close, and gently pushed her aside. "Get some towels and wipe up what you can of this blood. I've got to get rid of the body."

John had moved all the food trays off the cart. The bellman was lying belly down across it. He wasn't moving.

She shuddered. "At least it's him and not us," she said, then grabbed a handful of hand towels and some wet washcloths, and began scrubbing at the blood splatter, only to realize she was making it worse. "He recognized us, didn't he? He must have been after the reward money."

"The reward hinges upon your safe recovery, remember? So why point a gun at you and not me, the accused kidnapper?"

"I don't know…. Maybe—"

"There are no maybes. He's not a bellman. That gun had a silencer. He was a pro. Someone knew we were here, all right. Someone who wanted you dead."

Understanding dawned. "Daddy?"

"That would be my call."

"Son of a bitch!" she said, and threw down the towels.

Anger was the last thing he'd expected. Maybe panic, surely fear, definitely tears. But anger? There was more of the warrior in this woman of wealth than he would ever have imagined.

"This blood isn't going to come up," Alicia said. "But we have to hide it. If only…" Her gaze fell on the complimentary bottle of wine that had been in their suite upon arrival. "You get that out of here," she snapped, pointing to the dead man. "I'll handle the blood."

Yet another side of Alicia Ponte was revealed. She couldn't fix her own breakfast, but she sure knew how to deliver orders. And she had a point. They needed to get the body out of the suite. Thanks to the silencer, the gunshots would have gone unnoticed, but John was guessing there was a dead bellman somewhere in the hotel who was missing his uniform. When that body was found, the manager would lock the place down. They needed to be out before that happened. So much for their best-laid plans.

He went into his room and pulled back the bedcovers, then pulled off the top sheet, folding it until it fit over the body, sort of like a tablecloth. They weren't too far from the stairwell. If he didn't come up with a better plan on the way, he would push the cart out onto the landing and leave it there.

"I'll be right back," he said. "I'll knock once so you'll know it's me."

Alicia was in the act of removing the cork from the wine bottle as John opened the door. He paused long enough to make sure the hall was empty, then shoved the cart forward. Blood was beginning to drip from beneath the sheet. He had to hurry.

The exit to the stairwell was four doors down. He passed the first two without a hitch, but when he heard the ding of an approaching elevator down the hall behind him, his heart skipped a beat.

"Shit," he muttered, and kept on pushing, afraid to stop, afraid to look back.

He passed another doorway. The exit sign was in sight,

but now he heard voices. Any second, the people who'd been on that elevator would turn the corner and see him.

It was the sign, Employees Only, that altered his course. Taking a chance that the doors would be unlocked, he turned the knob. It gave. Without a wasted second, he pushed the cart inside, shoving it all the way in to rest by a bank of electrical boxes and two wooden worktables. The door swung shut behind him as he stood inside, waiting until the hall was clear. He glanced around, seeing mop buckets and vacuum cleaners, and breathed a sigh of relief. No witnesses in here, either.

The voices quickly faded. They were going up the hall instead of down this way. He'd been lucky. He glanced down at the blood on his shirt, then frowned and pulled it over his head. He knew enough about DNA not to leave it behind, but he didn't want to be caught wearing it, either. His skin cells would be on it, along with the gunman's blood. A deadly combination. Then he grabbed a cleaning rag from a shelf and went about wiping his fingerprints off the doorknobs, the walls, the cart and the buttons on the dead man's uniform. Anywhere a print might stick, he scrubbed.

As soon as the hall was empty, he slipped out of the storage room and hurried up the hall with his shirt wadded in his hands, thumped once on the door and when it swung inward instantly, realized Alicia had been waiting.

He strode in, then froze as the door swung shut behind him.

"What in hell did you do?" he asked.

Alicia was a bit startled by the fact that he'd left the room dressed and come back half-naked. She was trying to focus beyond the bronze six-pack on his belly and the myriad scars.

"Umm…we had a drunken orgy, and we are very sorry for the mess," she said. "I left a note of apology and asked them to charge the cleaning costs to the credit card."

"Looks like we had fun," John muttered as he eyed the carefully placed wine spills now concealing the blood, and the empty glasses and the overturned bottle. It was genius. Once again, he was forced to view her in a different light.

Alicia was still rattled from the sequence of events but was doing her best to stay calm. "It's all a bit fuzzy to me, but then, I can't hold my liquor, you know."

John rolled his shirt in the hotel's plastic laundry bag, to keep the blood off everything else, tossed it into his open suitcase, then turned and looked—really looked—at her.

She was pale and shaken, but her head was up and her eyes were clear. Her actions showed someone with the ability to stay calm in the face of danger. Someone who would always have her partner's back. It was a whole new way of thinking about her.

"So I guess my plan to ply you with drink to have my way with you is out now?" he said.

Alicia blinked. Then she realized he wasn't angry with her.

"So you do you have sense of humor," she said.

John grinned slightly as he dug through his suitcase for another shirt.

"I have my moments," he said. "Pack your stuff. We've got to get out of here."

"I'm already packed, although I don't believe there's a place on earth that we can get to where my father won't find us."

"He probably traced the chopper by my flight plans.

It would be simple enough to do. I can't hazard a guess as to how he located our hotel so quickly, but a lot of money can turn the best of intentions into a crime."

"Where are we going?" she asked.

"Give me a couple of minutes, then I'll tell you," he said.

He pulled the clean shirt over his head, then sat down on the mattress and took out his phone. He punched in the numbers, then waited, wondering if, when the man he was calling saw his name on the caller ID, he would still answer. To his relief, he did.

"John?"

"Corbin. I wasn't sure you'd still talk to me."

"What's going on?"

"I take it you saw the big press conference."

"Yes. Listen…if you're in trouble, maybe I can—"

"It's a cover-up, Corbin. And when you hear what Alicia Ponte has to say about her father, you'll know why he said what he did."

"She's with you? Now?"

"Yes, but by choice. We came across each other by accident, but I'm with her now to the end."

Alicia stood silently by, listening to John weave his tale, knowing he was leaving out his own agenda, but it no longer mattered. A few minutes ago he'd saved her life. She owed him a little leeway.

"So what's the scoop on her mental status?"

"Damn sharp, and right now? Mad as hell."

"Are you referring to the press conference?"

"Not entirely. We had a visitor in our hotel room a bit ago. He was a pro. Silencer and all. Her old man doesn't want her back alive. He wants her stopped before she can get to the authorities with what she knows."

"What happened to your...visitor?"

"You don't want to know."

Corbin's silence worried John, but only for a moment. Within seconds, he was right back to asking questions.

"So what's the big scoop?" he asked.

"It's her story to tell, but because of the recent turn of events, there's no way we'll still be around tomorrow to keep our appointment with you. So what I'm asking is, will you take my word for it that she has something vital to tell involving national security? Look at this from Alicia's standpoint. You saw the press conference, so you also saw the man standing beside Ponte. If the deputy director of the FBI is her father's college buddy, he's not going to believe anything negative she has to say about her old man. She doesn't know who to trust. That's why I suggested you."

"Ah...I get it. A journalist would be interested in the scoop rather than the cover-up, or something to that effect."

"Exactly."

"Okay. If you can get here without being seen, I'll talk to her. What I would suggest is that you effect some kind of disguise, especially for her. Her face is being plastered all over the television."

"Really?"

"Yes, really."

"We'll be there within the hour."

"I'll be waiting."

"Corbin?"

"Yes?"

"Thank you."

"No. If she brings me a big story, it's *me* who'll be thanking *you*. Take care."

John disconnected, pocketed his cell, then finished throwing the rest of his stuff in the suitcase.

"You need a disguise," he said. "Corbin said they're broadcasting your picture."

"I hope it's a good one," Alicia said, and opened her suitcase back up. She stared at the contents for a couple of seconds, then pulled her sweater over her head and dropped her slacks around her ankles.

"I'll just be—"

"Oh, get over it," she snapped. "You paraded in front of me in your freaking birthday suit and dared me to care. My lingerie is as modest as a two-piece swimsuit." Then she added, "As long as we don't get anything wet."

Once again, his perception of her underwent a change. He watched as she put the sweatpants back on, as well as the blue T-shirt, then put on the only pair of high heels she had with her. She took the hem of the T-shirt, twisted it around and around until it was tight against her body, then tied it in a knot beneath her breasts, leaving her midriff bare. Then she grabbed a comb and a hank of her hair and began back combing it like crazy, until she had a passable imitation of a rocker's mohawk. She sprayed it stiff with hair spray, then grabbed her makeup bag and dashed into the bathroom.

Past curious, John followed, intrigued by the ongoing transformation. He watched her draw huge black eyebrows over her own delicate arches. After that she added layer after layer of mascara, then painted an enormous red pout onto her lips.

"How do I look?" she asked as she turned to face him.

"Like I should be asking what you charge."

"Depends on what you want," she fired back, and tossed everything back into her suitcase. "I'm ready when you are."

John made a mental note to delve further into that statement later and grabbed both their suitcases, then added one last comment.

"We're going down in the elevator together, but do not look at me or talk to me. For all intents and purposes, we don't know each other. When we get off the elevator, you go through the lobby first. I'll be right behind you. I'll get a cab. When you see me loading the suitcases, start walking toward the corner. I'll pick you up there. As long as no one sees us together, we shouldn't ring any bells."

Alicia nodded, but as they started toward the elevator, she heard voices behind them.

"Don't look and don't stop walking," John said quietly.

"God in heaven," Alicia mumbled. Then, when she heard a man's low chuckle behind them, she put an extra swing in her step and lengthened her stride. By the time she got to the elevator, her flushed cheeks were a nice match to her red lips.

To their relief, the men who were behind them didn't get on the elevator. When the door closed and they were finally alone, she started to shake. John put a hand on her shoulder.

"Hang in there, baby," he said softly. "You're pulling this off like a pro."

The minute the endearment came out of his mouth, he wished he could take it back, but it was too late. The longer they were together, the more of an affinity he was feeling with her.

There was a roaring in Alicia's ears. She kept praying to God she wouldn't faint. She was vaguely aware that John had said something but hardly even noticed when he touched her out of concern. All she could think of was getting across the hotel lobby. She knew people would look at her, but hopefully without recognition.

Then the doors opened.

"Here we go," John said softly.

Alicia nodded, stepped out in front of him and started across the lobby toward the front doors. A bellman on the way to the elevators did a double take, then whistled beneath his breath.

A tall, leggy blonde actually smirked at her as Alicia caught her eye. But it was the older woman who sniffed in complete disapproval that made her relax. They really thought she was a whore. Hot damn, she was pulling this off. By the time she walked past the doorman, she was strutting.

John, on the other hand, felt almost naked. He was an Indian. Although they hadn't shown his picture, there was no way around his appearance. But he hadn't signed in under his name, only the name of his company, and lots of people couldn't tell the difference between Native Americans, Mexicans and East Indians. Hell, this was Washington, D.C. He could be any one of a dozen nationalities without looking out of place.

Alicia, on the other hand, might be missing her calling. The stage was almost visibly beckoning. If they weren't in such a damn mess, he would be enjoying this.

Finally he, too, was across the lobby and out the door.

A bellman followed. "Do you need a cab, sir?" he asked.

John nodded and set down the suitcases as the bellman

stepped forward and blew a whistle, then motioned toward the next cab waiting in line. Within moments John was in the backseat and heading out the drive.

"Take a right at the corner," John said. "And…see that woman in the blue shirt and high heels?"

"Yeah, man, I see her just fine," the cab driver said.

"When you get to her, stop."

The cab driver glanced up in the rearview mirror, grinned and nodded. "Sure thing."

John didn't give a damn about what the man thought was happening. He just needed Alicia back under his wing. Then, the moment he thought that, it startled him. When had she become something other than a means to an end or a simple responsibility?

Moments later, the driver pulled to a stop. John opened the door. He didn't even have to say anything. In seconds, Alicia was in the seat beside him. She took a deep breath, folded her arms across her knees and rested her forehead on them.

John put his hand in the middle of her back. The thud of her heartbeat was rapid and strong against his palm. Then he slid his hand upward, cupping the back of her neck, then urging her up. She came without arguing and buried her face against his chest.

They rode all the way to Corbin Woodliff's house without speaking a word.

When the driver let them out, Alicia had pulled herself together and John was trying to forget how it had felt to hold her close against his heart.

Six

After the tension-packed exit they'd made from the hotel, arriving at Corbin Woodliff's house was anticlimactic. It was nearing nightfall. Lights were already lit inside the houses they were passing, emitting a warm orange glow from behind the sheer curtains. She imagined families inside those houses, going about their lives without drama, and wished she belonged to one of them instead of being her father's daughter.

The cab driver pointed to a house a few lots up.

"You said 3100, right?"

"Yes."

The neighborhood was made up of homes from a bygone era, many architectural masterpieces. The Woodliff home itself was an unassuming two story Tudor, with tall, stately trees making their own statement along the avenue. Rosy pink azalea and lavender crape myrtle bushes bordered the long driveway leading to the house, like flowers along the brim of a woman's hat. Abundant and lush, their pastel colors softened the dark stucco and darker beams. Normally Alicia might have appreciated both the architecture and the landscaping, but right now, there wasn't anything normal about her life or reactions.

"We're here," John said.

As the driver parked and got out to retrieve their suitcases, she shivered from a sudden attack of nerves and automatically reached up to smooth down her hair when she felt the stiff, back-combed mess, and remembered she was still in disguise. She knew what she looked like. Lord only knew what Corbin Woodliff would think.

"No one is going to take me seriously looking like this," she muttered.

John knew she was nervous, but he was afraid that too much sympathy would push her over the edge. It made sense that anger—or at the least aggravation—would be an easier emotion for her to handle.

"One man's hooker is another man's eye candy," he drawled. "Relax. Corbin is an all right guy. I'm thinking he's going to admire your disguise."

Unaware that he'd intentionally pushed her insult button, she gave him a cool glare. "Such a sweet-talking man. Be still my heart."

Relieved to see the fire back in her eyes, he stifled a smile. "I meant no disrespect. Just stating a fact."

Speaking of facts, she wondered if they were still alone. She turned in the seat and looked back at the way they'd come.

"Do you think we were followed?" she asked.

"No."

"You're sure?"

"I'm Cherokee. My people have been known as excellent trackers for centuries, and I've been paying attention. Yes, I'm sure."

Since he'd been the one to bring up the subject of ethnicity, she made herself face him.

"Um...about that... I'm sorry I called you Tonto the other day."

John grinned. "I just called you a hooker. Consider us even."

At that point, the cab driver knocked on the window and gestured that he'd finished removing their suitcases from the trunk, so John and Alicia exited the cab. As the driver set Alicia's bag in front of her, he gave her an appreciative look. When she stuffed a wad of money in his hand, he winked.

"If you need a ride later, give me a call," he said, and handed her his card.

Her nostrils flared in anger.

John grabbed her elbow before she could fly off the handle and turned her toward the door.

"I was going to pay," he said as the cab disappeared back down the driveway.

"I've already told you. I pay my own way." Then she pointed toward the cab. "Did you hear what he said to me?" she asked as John picked up their bags.

"Give him a break, lady. The disguise was your choice. You did a good job, okay?"

"It's easy for you to say. I've been labeled a nutcase by my own father—who wants to kill me, by the way. I look like a whore, and you hate my guts. All in all, these last few days have been something of a revelation."

"I don't hate your guts," he muttered.

"Could have fooled me," she said, then turned her back and rang the doorbell.

John sighed. Her spurt of attitude was gone. He knew she'd led a privileged life. This was not only hard *on* her, it was hard *for* her. He couldn't imagine what must be going through her mind, knowing her father was willing to kill her to shut her up.

"Look, Alicia, I—"

Before he could finish, the door opened inward and Corbin Woodliff was standing there, eyeing both of them with something akin to shock.

It had been at least fifteen years since John and Corbin had seen each other face-to-face, although they had kept in touch, but Corbin was at least twenty-five pounds heavier. His hairline had receded noticeably, and the hair that was left was almost entirely gray. And, as was the way of many men who begin going bald, he was growing facial hair. His beard was a grayish red, clipped in a neat Van Dyke style. He was wearing dark slacks and a white polo shirt, untucked over his burgeoning belly.

John braced himself for the comment he got most often, which was, "You haven't aged a bit," set down the suitcases and held out his hand.

"Corbin, it's been a while."

"That it has, my friend," Corbin said. "A very long time since that coup in Venezuela."

The two men shook hands, then hugged briefly before stepping apart, and John's looks were never even mentioned, though at that point Corbin allowed himself a good look at the tall, wild-haired woman standing behind John. Her belly was bare. Her face needed to be. She was almost as tall as John and had a glint in her eye that mirrored his. Oddly enough, and despite their situation, they were rather well-matched.

"Miss Ponte, I presume. Please come in...come in."

"This is a disguise," Alicia offered as they paused in the foyer.

Corbin grinned. "It's a doozy."

Alicia sighed. "Considering the circumstances, thank you for seeing me."

Corbin glanced at John. "I owe John a favor. Come on. I think we should go into the library, where it's more comfortable. I'm assuming you two weren't followed," he added as he peered out before quickly closing the door.

"We're good," John said.

"He's Cherokee," Alicia snapped.

John grinned and shook his head at Corbin, indicating it would be wise not to follow up on that remark.

Corbin stifled a smile as he led them into the room across the foyer.

The faint scent of cigar smoke and that smell familiar only to rooms that house old books was pervasive. But Alicia was past being bothered by off-putting aromas. Weary to the core, she sank into an overstuffed chair. The oxblood leather was butter-soft beneath her palms as she scooted back in the seat, watching the two men as they spoke quickly in tones too low for her to hear. She knew they were talking about her—or, at the least, John's dilemma after becoming associated with her. She could have argued the point that he was in this as deep as she was, and for his own reasons, but right now, she just wanted the secret out and the burden off her shoulders.

"Can I offer either of you something to drink?" Corbin asked as John took a seat in the chair beside Alicia.

"Not for me, thanks," John said.

Alicia shook her head.

Corbin eased himself down on the matching sofa on the other side of the coffee table, then leaned back and crossed his legs, leaving his big arms loosely folded in his lap.

Alicia felt like a bug pinned to a mat as she waited for him to speak. He waited too long.

Nervously, she scooted to the edge of her chair. "I understand you've heard the bullshit my father put out about me."

John shifted in his seat. Good. At least her attitude was back. The last thing he wanted was for her to start crying. It was the single chink in his stoic countenance that neither age nor time had changed. He couldn't withstand a crying woman.

Corbin nodded. "I did, and I have to say, he seemed sincere."

Alicia's eyes glittered angrily. "Hell yes, he seemed sincere. He wants me back in the worst possible way, and preferably in a body bag."

Corbin's position shifted from one of nonchalance to intensity as he glanced at John, as if trying to read his expression, then back to Alicia.

"Pardon me, Miss Ponte, but—"

"Call me Alicia."

He nodded. "Alicia…you have to understand. It's difficult for me to think a man would put out a hit on his own daughter. You're going to have a tough sell trying to make that stick."

"Someone's already made an attempt on her life," John reminded him.

"You sure it wasn't a bid for the million-dollar reward, instead?"

John answered sharply. "He shot at her. The gun had a silencer. The reward was for her safe return. You figure it out."

Corbin nodded thoughtfully, then shifted his focus to Alicia.

"What do you know that your father is afraid you'll tell?"

"I overheard a conversation between my father and his business associate, Jacob Carruthers, that I wasn't meant to hear."

"Are you referring to Jacob Carruthers of the Boston Carruthers?"

"Yes, although he's just Uncle Jacob to me. I've known him all my life."

"So what did you overhear?"

"My father and Jacob are selling munitions to al Qaeda."

"Christ Almighty!" Corbin said, then stood abruptly and grabbed a digital recorder from the desk behind him. He turned it on as he sat back down. "Are you sure you didn't misunderstand what was being said?"

"How many Osama bin Ladens can you think of who are associated with al Qaeda and would be needing fresh munitions for Fallujah?"

Corbin appeared to be in shock. Alicia knew how he felt. For a few moments, he just sat, staring at the floor. She didn't know if he was gathering his thoughts or still doubting what she'd said. Then he looked up.

"If this is true… Don't get me wrong…. I'm not saying you're lying, I'm just trying to wrap my head around the vastness of these ramifications—not the least of which is that this would make him a traitor to his country. And in a time of war. Dear God."

Alicia didn't know how pale she'd become, but she was all too aware that she was shaking from the inside out. Even though she believed her father was trying to kill her, she didn't have the same darkness in her heart. Just saying the words that would guarantee his death felt sickening.

"Can you prove any of this?" Corbin asked.

"No. I just heard what I heard."

"Does he know your intentions were to tell the authorities, or is he just guessing and trying to cover his ass?"

"Oh, he knows," Alicia said. "It wasn't my wisest or finest moment. I'd been dodging his phone calls for three days when I finally answered. I didn't start out intending to tell him, but…well…it just happened."

"Since he's been forewarned of your intentions, this could be near impossible to prove. And making the authorities believe you enough to even start an investigation will be difficult now, considering the announcement he made about your mental state."

"I know. I wasn't thinking. The three days I wasted running, I could have used to start the ball rolling, but my father's reach is long and deep within the government. He's been furnishing munitions to our armies for years, as well as to many European countries. I had no way of knowing who to trust."

"I see what you mean," Corbin said. "Can you remember anything else? Did he mention names…dates…money transfers?"

"Only that the delivery would fall on the thirteenth, which seemed to be a problem because it was some religious holiday, but he didn't say what month. I also heard another name, although I don't know if it was a go-between or the person to whom delivery was going to be made."

"Do you remember it?" Corbin asked.

Alicia sighed. "I remember all of it. I've thought of nothing else since the moment I realized my father and Uncle Jacob were betraying our country and our soldiers. The name he mentioned was in conjunction with a place in Afghanistan. He mentioned the Kurds, then a man…Mohammed al-Kazir."

Corbin's eyes suddenly widened. "Are you sure that's the name?"

She nodded. "Why?"

"According to the latest intel, the present leader of al Qaeda is reported to be a man named Mohammed al-Kazir. They think he's embedded somewhere within the mountains of Afghanistan, although I heard a bit of gossip regarding Turkey. I do know there hasn't been a sighting in months."

Alicia felt sick. The reality of what she'd heard suddenly solidified. Her stomach lurched. "Bathroom. I need to use your bathroom," she said, and put her hand over her mouth.

John jumped up. "I saw one off the foyer," he said, and grabbed her by the hand.

Alicia ran with him, too afraid she was going to embarrass herself to argue. The contents of her stomach were at the back of her throat as John slid to a halt and all but shoved her into the room on her right. She leaned over the toilet and threw up her guts as the door swung shut behind her.

John stood outside the bathroom, wincing with every

retching sound she made, but not from disgust. Once again, the torment of her life had been brought home to him in a blatant and physical way. His desire for revenge was centuries old and in every pore of his skin. He breathed it, ate with it, lived with it—unable to escape it even in sleep, because, more often than not, his dreams were littered with flashes of White Fawn and his people bathed in blood. But it was also familiar.

But this was all new to Alicia Ponte, and she was in shock. Her life as she knew it was over. Everything she had known and trusted was a lie. Her father was no longer her father—he was her enemy. Now the woman she'd considered herself to be was gone, leaving her an unknown. As his quest for justice was finally coming to fruition, Alicia's world was coming to an end.

"Is she all right?"

John looked over his shoulder. Corbin was standing in the hall behind him.

"No, but she will be," he said.

"That's a hell of a thing to find out about your father."

"So you believe her?"

Corbin shrugged. "*You* believe her. I believe *you*—even though I'm starting to think you've been keeping secrets from me."

John's heartbeat stuttered. His life was nothing but secrets, but he hadn't expected Corbin to call him on it.

"What do you mean?" he asked.

Corbin let his gaze slide from the perfect structure of John's coffee-brown face to the silver feather earring, his wide shoulders and flat belly.

"I'm thinking you've found the secret to eternal youth. You look damned good, my friend."

"It's all in the DNA, white man."

Corbin grinned. "Maybe in my next life I'll get to come back as a Native American."

"Be careful what you ask for," John said.

Corbin laughed, unaware that reincarnation was not only possible but probable. However, John wasn't going to debate the quirks of living and dying with a man who operated on nothing but finding and proving the facts.

A few moments later, the door opened. Alicia walked out with her chin up and her shoulders back.

"Sorry. I think it was something I swallowed…probably my pride." Then she added, "Thank you," to John without looking at him.

Oh hell. She'd been crying. However, the jut of her chin was clue enough that she didn't want it mentioned. And she also needed another dose of attitude to keep her emotions in check. Considering the fact that everything he did aggravated her, it was easy to piss her off.

"Consider it selfishness on my part. I didn't want to have to mop up after you."

Corbin's lips parted slightly, shocked that John was being so rude. But when he saw the fire in Alicia Ponte's eyes reappear, he realized that the tension between them might be more than anger. He smiled to himself, thinking he would like to be a fly on the wall if they ever gave in to what was simmering between them.

Alicia glared at John but refused to spar, then turned her attention to Corbin.

"There's one other thing I should probably mention."

Corbin's interest spiked. "Yes?"

"Uncle Jacob…Jacob Carruthers."

"What about him?"

"My father likes him, but I've often heard him refer to Uncle Jacob as weak-kneed. If that's the case, you might be able to make him talk. If he was promised life instead of hanging—or whatever it is they do to traitors these days—he might turn. Knowing him as I do, I'm guessing he's been in panic mode ever since he learned I was running."

Now she really had Corbin's attention. "I have some friends in the Bureau." When he saw Alicia getting ready to argue, he held up his hands. "I know, I know...I saw the deputy director standing beside your father. I know all about their college days together. But Richard Ponte isn't the only one with ties to the big shots. I've been in D.C. going on twenty-five years now. I have some connections of my own. I'm thinking if I can round up a couple of *my* buddies and show up on Jacob Carruthers' doorstep, your suggestion might produce some usable facts."

"That would be great!" Alicia cried. "Would you...I mean...if he talks...would you be able to let me know?"

"Oh, you'll know. If he talks, the Bureau will most likely launch a full-scale investigation. It will be the biggest news to hit the country since Saddam Hussein's capture."

Alicia's smile was bittersweet. Stopping the flow of illegal weapons to the enemy was not only necessary but was the honorable thing to do. Knowing she'd done what was right was one thing. Knowing she'd just signed her father's death warrant was another.

"That's good," she said.

John saw her chin tremble. He felt her pain and wished he wasn't beginning to care. But like Alicia, he was driven to do what was right at all costs. Now that they'd done what she wanted to do, it was his turn. But how to use her without getting her hurt was going to be a problem.

"About Carruthers…does he still live in Boston?" Corbin asked.

"Yes."

Corbin grinned. "Fabulous. I have a favorite pub there that serves the best corned beef on rye I've ever eaten. Do you like corned beef on rye?" he asked.

For Alicia, the mere mention of food brought the threat of another round of nausea. John saw her pale, then swallow several times in rapid succession. Once again, he chose sarcasm to give her the breathing space she needed.

"Personally, I don't eat anything I can't shoot with my trusty bow and arrow," he drawled.

Corbin laughed, and thumped John on the shoulder. "You are such a wise-ass. That's only one of the reasons I like you."

"I'm old. I've heard it all before," John fired back, and then cupped Alicia's elbow. "We need to get to the airport, and I don't want to call another cab."

"I'll drive you," Corbin offered.

"You're a very recognizable face. It would be best if we weren't seen together," John said.

"True, true," Corbin said, then snapped his fingers. "How about you drive yourselves in my car? Call me and tell me later where it's parked, and I'll take a cab and retrieve it."

Alicia was touched by the trouble this man was willing to go to. "I want to say this again, I really appreciate everything you're doing on my behalf."

"It's not just for you, Miss Ponte. If all this is true, our soldiers and our country have been betrayed. And…there's also the fact that you may have just handed me the story of the decade."

Alicia felt as if she'd been slapped. "*If?* Are you saying you still don't believe me?"

"No, that's not what I'm saying. I'm a journalist. Everything for me has to be fact, and what you've told me has yet to be proved. What I am saying is…John Nightwalker believes you, and I believe in John Nightwalker."

Alicia eyes filled with tears, but there was a set to her jaw that dared both men to keep their distance.

"I wish I could say the same," she said bitterly.

John looked at Alicia, then at Corbin, his mouth twisting with regret. "It's a long story."

Corbin seemed flustered. "Uh…can I make you two some sandwiches or something before you leave?"

John nodded. "That's nice of you, Corbin. Maybe a—"

"It's best I don't eat before I fly," Alicia said.

John sighed. "Yeah, me, too. Besides, we had a big dinner earlier."

Alicia stifled a gasp of disbelief. Was that John Nightwalker being considerate on her behalf?

"Then I'll be right back with the keys," Corbin said, and hurried off.

John shoved his hands into his pockets and turned his back on Alicia. *Don't say it, woman. Don't be nice to me. Don't you dare. I need to keep all the distance I can between us to do what I have to do.*

He heard her footsteps. She was right behind him.

"John."

Shit. "Yeah?"

"How much do I owe you for our hotel room?"

He grinned. Way to go, lady. When he turned around, the smile was gone. "We didn't even get to sleep in it."

"They'll still charge you for the night."

"You are the most aggravating woman I think I've ever known," he complained.

"Will a hundred and fifty cover it?" she asked.

"Perfectly," John said, and held out his hand.

She dug in her purse, pulled out a wad of bills big enough to choke a horse and counted the money out in tens and twenties, then handed it to him. She knew John was irked. There was a muscle jerking in the side of his jaw, and his eyes were so dark they looked black.

He watched her flash the roll and knew she'd done it to back up her claim of being able to pay her way.

He pulled out a roll half the size of hers, but made up of nothing but hundred-dollar bills. He calmly folded what she'd given him into his roll before putting it back in his pocket.

Alicia's eyes widened at the sight. Then she grinned. She'd showed him hers. He'd shown her his. She sighed.

"You win," she said.

"What?" John asked.

"Yours is bigger," she said.

"And don't you forget it."

They wouldn't look at each other, but the anger between them was gone. Somewhere between the tears and the double entendre, John had given up the fight. He didn't have to hate her to get what he wanted. Trouble was, she was the first woman in centuries who'd intrigued him enough to want anything beyond a casual relationship. He could like her. He might even allow himself to enjoy her company—if she would let him. He just needed to remember not to fall in love.

The chopper flew west through the darkness. The night sky was clear and cloudless, and while John's path was guided partly by the gauges on the flight panel in front of him, he also knew where he was from the location of the stars. For centuries, on foot, then by horse, then in a variety of wheeled vehicles, he'd used the heavenly constellations as a road map. After he'd gotten a pilot's license, nighttime had become his favorite time to be in the air—giving him the illusion that he was almost close enough to touch those same stars that had forever guided him.

Outside the chopper, everything was inky-black. Inside, the array of lights on the panel was a mixture of red, green, yellow and white. The gauges glittered like the strings of lights on a Christmas tree, only to be reflected on the faces of John and his weary, airsick copilot, who'd fallen asleep more than two hours ago, after their last refueling stop.

There was a sense of peace, being so high, knowing that, for the time being, they were out of reach of evil. And there was another idea that kept pushing at the boundaries of John's world, the sense that this woman could become important to him in a permanent and personal way. But that notion was in complete opposition to his agenda. How could he have any kind of a relationship with her—how would she ever trust him— knowing the only reason he'd linked himself to her was to get to her father? Would she believe his feelings had changed?

He sighed, weary to the core. So many years—so much time—and all of it spent searching for revenge. He couldn't help but wonder if the final irony was going to be visited upon him. What if he found and dispatched his enemy just as he was falling in love, then died as his enemy died? What irony. He'd had over five hundred years to get loving right, and he'd wasted it all chasing a ghost. He was damn sure the Old Ones weren't going to give him a few hundred years more to spend with a woman. He'd made his choice when he'd asked for the impossible. Whatever ensued when his fight was over, it would be what it would be.

Beside him, Alicia stirred. He glanced over, allowing himself the freedom to study her at leisure. Once they'd gotten airborne, she'd wiped off the makeup and managed to run a brush through her hair, although the T-shirt was still tied beneath her breasts, leaving her flat midriff bare.

She was too thin, and it had been ages since she'd eaten. As soon as they got to his place outside Sedona, he would get some food in her. Then they could rest for as long as they wanted. The property was listed as belonging to one of his companies. His name did not appear on any company rosters. It would take considerable skill to search through the maze of paperwork he'd laid down before anyone would know it was his.

He glanced down at the flight panel, then out the windows, and rocked his head from side to side, trying to loosen up stiff muscles. They were less than an hour away from their destination. He would be heartily glad to get out of this chopper and into a bed. The way he felt now, he could sleep the clock around, although, with Alicia along, that wasn't going to happen.

"Are we there yet?"

John flinched. The sound of Alicia's voice was startling. The question wasn't.

"Almost. Less than an hour out."

"Thank God," she said, and stretched as best she could without dislodging something important. "Is there any water left?"

John handed her what was left in his bottle. "If you don't mind drinking after me."

She twisted the cap off without answering and tilted the bottle to her lips, emptying it in three gulps. It was refreshing, despite the tepid temperature.

"Umm, good. Thanks," she said, and put the cap back on before laying the bottle on the floor at her feet.

The moment John saw those supple, sensuous lips encircle the opening where his mouth had been, every muscle in his body tightened. Imagination quickly put her mouth on his body, and then things went from bad to worse. He looked away, caught a glimpse of his own reflection in the windows and frowned.

Hell in a handbasket. He was just horny.

"You're welcome," he said, and just to focus his energy on something else, took the chopper down a thousand feet.

The dip in elevation did a number on Alicia's stomach, but not being able to see land below kept her from being sick.

"What was that all about?" she muttered as the chopper leveled off.

"Turbulence." It wasn't a lie. His gut felt as if it had gone through a blender.

Alicia peered out and down, marveling at the lack of lights below.

"Is your place inside the Sedona city limits?"

"No. About thirty minutes out, as the crow flies."

"So you're out in the desert."

"Smack-dab," he said.

Alicia nodded, and as she did, she felt herself suddenly go light-headed. She attributed it to a lack of food.

"Hope you have a can of soup or something around when we land. I think I need to eat."

John gave her a quick glance. It wasn't like her to complain. "Are you okay? There are some peanut-butter crackers over there."

"Don't want to mess up a good thing. I think I'd better wait, but thanks."

And she was being nice? Now he knew something was wrong.

He looked up at the sky, judging how long they had left, and guessed it was no more than fifteen, maybe twenty minutes to his place.

"We'll be there before you know it."

Alicia nodded, then pulled her knees up to her chin and put her head down.

Now John was getting worried, but the chopper was going as fast as a chopper could go. There was nothing to do but fly it and hope by the time they landed, she would be back on track.

Finally he saw Orion, the Hunter, as always guiding him to his destination. When he was a thousand feet off the ground, he could turn on every outside light on the property by remote control, including the lights around his landing pad, and that was what he did.

"Here we go," he said, and took the bird down, controlling the power and their lives with just a touch of his hand.

Alicia lifted her head and put her feet back on the floor. She tightened her seat belt and gripped her seat with both hands. The burst of light where there had been only darkness was startling.

"Ooh!" she gasped.

"Welcome home," John said softly. Minutes later, they were down.

The rotors were still winding down as they exited the cabin. John had left the suitcases behind so both hands were free to get Alicia safely inside. As they came out of the chopper, her first step was a stagger.

"Woo. Don't have my land legs yet."

"Hold on to me," John said, and offered her his elbow.

Alicia clasped it—and him—as if he were her life raft and let him guide her. It wasn't lost upon her that, once again, she had put herself at this man's mercy. At first she'd felt betrayed that he was using her to get to her father. But she couldn't overlook the fact that he kept pulling her proverbial bacon out of the fire. He'd put Dieter on his ass twice and been shot twice for the trouble. He'd stopped a hit man from taking her out and was keeping her in style. If this house was anywhere near as spectacular as the one on the bluff in Georgia, it would be the perfect place to hide out.

She watched him unlock the door, then step inside and disarm the security system. She was beginning to realize that, in his own way, John Nightwalker was as much an enigma as her father. He seemed indecently wealthy and lived without companionship behind massive amounts of security. Once again, she reminded herself to ask him exactly what it was he imported and exported, and—even more important—the details of what her father had done to his family. All she knew was that they were dead and John blamed her father. She had just assumed it must have happened during some kind of explosion relating to the manufacture of Ponte munitions. Well, her father understood revenge. That was something he and John had in common.

"How are you feeling?" John asked as he led her to a chair in the kitchen.

"Weird," she said, and shrugged. "Maybe a glass of milk…some crackers…nothing big. I think it's just because I threw up the only thing I'd eaten today."

Without thinking, John brushed the back of her head with his hand. It was a gentle stroke, meant as a gesture of comfort, but when she leaned into the touch, he felt her yield. Whether she knew it or not, it was a telling moment between them. A sign of trust that hadn't been there before.

He quickly moved to the refrigerator, and made a mental note to call the caretaker tomorrow and thank him personally for cleaning and stocking the house. Everything he could have wanted was there, in duplicate.

He poured her a small glass of milk, then sliced a couple of pieces of farmer's cheese from a brick, put them between buttery crackers and gave them to her on a plate.

"Eat this," he said. "I'm going out for the bags."

Alicia sighed, then reached for the milk. She was finishing her first cheese and cracker sandwich when John came back inside. He reset the alarm, then gave her a quick glance before disappearing with the luggage. When he returned, the crackers were gone and she was finishing off the milk.

"Feeling better?" he asked.

"I hope so. At least not so empty."

"Good. Maybe all you need is some peace and quiet, and I can guarantee there's plenty of that out here."

Alicia stood and started to carry her dishes to the sink when John stopped her.

"Leave it," he said. "I'm going to take you to your room. Now that we're here, your only job is to leave the worrying to me."

She looked over her shoulder to the back door. "We're safe here, right?"

John realized the panic was still there. He needed to relieve her mind, but wasn't sure what it would take. All he could do was his best. He looked at her then, a mishmash of the disguise that she'd left D.C. with, along with her own natural grace. A mixture of she-wolf and princess. Sometimes he couldn't tell them apart.

"Woman."

Alicia turned abruptly, not only startled by what he'd called her but by the serious tone of his voice.

"What?"

"I promise you—with my life—that I will not let you be hurt. Even more, I will not use you to get to your father. My fight is not with you, and it was wrong of me to think that I could use you."

Alicia's chin quivered. Her vision blurred. This was the last thing she'd expected. His capitulation threw her even more off center than she already was. If she was no longer able to hate him, then how was she going to maintain emotional distance from him? Hating him was all she'd had to keep her attraction to him at bay. Now, like the damnable man that he was, he was promising to turn himself into some heroic hunk of masculinity.

John saw the tears. Damn it.

"Don't cry…don't you dare go and cry on me, woman."

"I'm not crying," she muttered. "It was probably the cheese. I think the cheese was too spicy."

"Like hell," John said. "The only thing blander than farmer's cheese is butter." He yanked a paper towel from the roll on the counter and handed it to her. "Blow your nose and follow me."

Alicia took it and blew as she followed him out of the kitchen. She was too weary and too light-headed to take note of the furnishings and decorations. All she wanted was a bathroom and a bed.

John stopped halfway down the hall, then opened a door and turned on the light.

"This is yours. It has an adjoining bathroom. The bed is turned back. Anything you might need in the way of toiletries is in the bathroom. If you need me, my room is directly across the hall. Just knock once. I'll hear you."

She nodded without looking up and moved past him.

John sighed. "Are you sure you're feeling better?"

She turned then to face him, looking first at his eyes, seeing the gentleness in them that belied the tone of his voice. Then her gaze moved to that small silver feather dangling from his ear. It was as motionless as the man wearing it, giving her the impression of a wild animal poised to attack. Then finally to his lips—full, sensual, carved in perfect proportion to the rest of his face. She wondered if they would yield as he'd just done, if they would be soft and warm, coaxing things from her that she was already willing to give. She wondered, but she knew that knowledge wouldn't come tonight, or tomorrow, or maybe ever.

Finally she looked away, then shrugged.

"Right now, John Nightwalker, I'm not sure of anything."

Seven

For John, being in Sedona was always healing. Here, reality blurred and his anger dimmed. There was always a feeling of being a thought away from an unseen world. He kept more of his collection of Native American religious relics here than in Georgia and had built a sweat lodge a short distance away from the back of his house. Practicing the old ways always gave him a new sense of purpose, similar, he supposed, to those who gained inner peace and insight from meditation.

Even though he was travel-weary, he made certain all was secure in the house before retiring. He checked in on Alicia, heard her slow, steady breathing, and was satisfied that whatever had been upsetting her had passed. When he finally got to his room, he stripped in the dark, showered by the yellow glow of a night-light and crawled into bed. Naked and exhausted, he pulled up the covers and fell fast asleep.

White Fawn's breasts filled Night Walker's hands as he lay behind her, spooned one to the other and warm beneath the fur robes. Outside, rain blew in a wild, scattered blur, running down the sides of their hut like a waterfall. Even though he was deeply asleep, his subconscious recognized the feminine curves, as well as the musky scent of her body, causing his own body to grow hard with longing.

White Fawn roused slightly, smiled to herself as she felt the thrust of her man's member between her legs, and shifted just enough to accommodate his desires.

Night Walker woke up inside his woman and quickly became lost in the tight, wet heat. Thrust followed thrust until the pressure built to bursting.

John woke abruptly. Emotionally, he knew where he was. Alone and more than five hundred years lonely. Physically, his body ached for release, but it wasn't going to happen now. He glanced toward the windows. The sun was long since up. He swung his legs over the side of the bed and strode into the bathroom. A cold shower later, he came out and moved to the closet, quickly dressed in running shorts and running shoes and left his room.

The door to Alicia's room was still closed, and the house was quiet. He started to leave, then remembered how pale she'd been last night. He wouldn't be satisfied to leave until he knew she was okay.

The knob turned noiselessly, and he pushed the door inward just enough that he could peer in. The moment he did, he knew he'd made a mistake. She was flat on her back with one arm over her head, the other thrown out beside her. The top sheet was between her legs and draped over one shoulder. The rest of her was bare to the world and as naked as the day she'd been born.

He stared too long, then gritted his teeth as he backed out and closed the door. He stood with his head down, his hands curled into fists as he struggled to gain control of his emotions. Damn. Damn, damn, damn. Now he was going to have to live with the reality of knowing how long her legs were, and how the curve of her hips and breasts accentuated her flat belly and narrow waist. And her skin. Alabaster. He hit his fists on the sides of his legs and then strode toward the kitchen.

Without wasted motion, he put a pot of coffee on to brew, left Alicia a message and disarmed the security system. He didn't know if he could do it, but he was going to try to outrun the lust with which he'd awakened, as well as the newfound hunger for the woman asleep so close by.

He stepped outside, quickly scanned the area for signs of intrusion and saw nothing but a lone buzzard circling high up in the sky. The chopper was the only thing that seemed out of place. He went back into the house, picked up a remote from inside a drawer, stepped back out on the terrace, aimed and triggered it. Within moments, a framework arose around the pad and chopper like a portable gazebo draped in a sand-colored fabric. He watched until it had unfolded completely, then punched another button that added a sand-colored roof to the structure. Now the chopper was no longer visible from the air. At that point, he replaced the remote and pulled the door shut behind him, taking a moment to pause on the terrace.

The sun was as hot on his face as the blood that pulsed through his body. Running was going to make him hotter, but it might also save his sanity. He took a slow, deep breath, stretched a couple of times, then jogged off the terrace, aiming for a giant saguaro about a half mile away—the first marker for his run.

Each stride of foot to earth was a body-jolting collision with the unyielding land of the desert. But as time passed, he moved deeper and deeper into the runner's zone. At his passing, tiny sand lizards went scurrying into their burrows. A huge tarantula on the hunt felt the unfamiliar quake of John's footsteps and dropped its prey before scuttling away on thick, hairy legs. The buzzard that had been high overhead dipped lower, checking out the arrival of new meat on the hoof before opting out. It flew away, for the time being leaving the visible sky bare of life.

By the time John passed the giant saguaro and then the rusted-out chassis of a 1957 Ford that was a half mile farther on, his body was beaded in sweat. But his mind was clear. He was no longer running away from desire, he was running for the joy of it. By the time he reached his turning point, which was a pair of large, pillow-shaped rocks lying side by side that he thought of as the breasts of Mother Earth, he was ready to head home.

Even though he was almost two miles away, the land was so flat that he could still make out the roofline of his home. Beneath it, an innocent woman had given herself into his care. For now, he'd outrun the urge to betray that trust. He began the run home with a lighter heart, enjoying the workout his body was getting.

When he was about a quarter of a mile away, he saw a flash of red on the terrace, remembered seeing a shirt of that color on the chair in Alicia's room and knew she was awake.

Even though they were together by necessity, it had been a long, long time since he'd had anybody to come home to. Instinctively, he lengthened his stride.

Alicia had gone to sleep without remembering ever getting into bed. Sometime during her sleep, she'd begun to dream.

In the dream she was running, screaming out Nightwalker's name. The air was filled with smoke, and even though she couldn't see it, she knew her home was burning and people were after her. The thunder of their footsteps was so close behind her that she could hear the sounds of their breathing, heavy from the exertion. The flesh on her face was stinging, as if she'd gotten too close to a flame, and her clothing felt wet. She knew it was blood—her blood—although she was too afraid to look.

Suddenly someone grabbed her by the hair. She threw up her arms and shrieked in desperation as she was yanked backward and thrown to the ground. Her attacker was on her now, riding her waist as he pinned her arms to the dirt. In her dream, she knew she was screaming and pleading for her life when suddenly a gust of wind blew away the smoke and she saw him. His features immediately blurred, but her gaze locked onto his eyes—green and bulging, with short, stubby lashes.

It was then that her subconscious could no longer

protect her from the identity of the man who'd been chasing her, who'd thrown her to the ground and who now held her pinned with his fingers around her neck.

It was her father.

The man who'd given her life was now about to take it. Richard Ponte was like a madman. He kept pushing at her, pummeling her with his fists and trying to throttle the life from her body. The next thing she knew, he was coming at her with a knife.

She screamed one last time—calling Nightwalker's name.

Then everything began moving in slow motion. Her focus shifted from her father's face to the thin stiletto blade coming toward her. Sound faded until there was nothing but the thunder of her own heartbeat and the whoosh of her blood as it pulsed through her body. The knife was at her throat now, burning her flesh as he sliced the blade across her neck. Her body arced, as if a jolt of lightning had gone through it, riding the pain and ebbing life force in desperate denial. She didn't want to die.

Suddenly a man with dark skin and black hair was pulling the stranger from her body, breaking him like a bundle of sticks and tossing him aside like dross on the crest of a tidal wave.

She knew him. Nightwalker. The man who'd promised to keep her safe.

Then he was on his knees beside her, his face taut with agony. He was pleading with her, begging her not to die. She kept hearing him say he was sorry, over and over and over, and then everything stopped.

One second she was with him, and then she was

watching the scene from afar. John Nightwalker was clutching her lifeless body to his chest as he rocked in mute despair, and she knew that she was dead.

She woke abruptly, her heart thundering in a panic she wouldn't soon forget. She crawled out of bed on her hands and knees, and then staggered until she was standing, clutching the bedpost at the foot of the bed to keep from falling. Her body was bathed in sweat, and she kept running her fingers all along her throat, unable to believe it had just been a dream. It had seemed so real. She could have sworn she'd felt the pain of the knife slicing through her flesh, smelled the coppery scent of her blood spilling out onto the ground and known with a certainty that she was dead.

"God in heaven," Alicia whispered, and then swiped the hair from her face. She stared about the room, re-orienting herself, remembering where she was and how she'd gotten there, then sighed.

Sedona.

She and John had flown to Sedona last night.

She glanced toward the windows. Sunlight was pouring through the cracks around the shades. She moved toward them on shaky legs and then pulled a cord, letting in the light to chase away the remnants of the dream.

She didn't know what time it was and didn't care. For now, time had no meaning in her life other than that it had to pass. She thought of Corbin Woodliff and wondered if he was making good on his promise. She hoped so. If not, she'd put her life on the line for nothing.

Her belly growled, reminding her that she'd had little to nothing to eat yesterday. Suddenly nervous about facing John Nightwalker, she headed for the shower. A

short while later, she left her room in search of her host
and some breakfast, wearing a red cotton shirt and a pair
of white shorts. Her face was devoid of makeup, and her
legs and feet were bare. Her freshly shampooed hair was
dry and shiny and hanging loose against her neck. The
heavy weight of it matched the weight in her heart.

Her life was in tatters, and the man who'd promised
to help her was a jumble of contradictions. What more
could go wrong?

She found his note in the kitchen, as well as the
freshly brewed coffee, and gratefully poured herself a
cup, adding sugar and cream before taking her first sip.
The caffeine was a welcome jolt to her jangled nerves,
and by the time she'd downed half a cup, she was feeling
almost human.

She dug through the refrigerator, chose a small cup
of yogurt to go with her coffee, then took her food
outside to eat on the terrace. Seen in the bright light of
day, this house was just as impressive as the one on the
coast of Georgia had been. It was a hacienda of elegant
proportions, sprawling across what would have been
four or five city lots. The walls were adobe, the color of
the desert in which it had been built. The roof was
covered in Spanish tiles the color of ochre, while the
brown shutters that could be closed over the windows
were open and lying flat against the outer walls.

It took her a moment to realize the chopper was now
engulfed in some kind of camouflage netting. She sat
down in a chair beside a black wrought-iron table, put
her coffee down, then propped her feet up on another
chair and began to eat her yogurt. She was licking the

spoon and thinking about finishing her coffee when she saw movement in the distance and realized it was John.

It reminded her of the morning back at his home in Georgia—how she'd watched him come out of the surf stark naked, then how he'd walked past her without explanation or apology. She couldn't help but wonder if this morning would be a repeat.

When he was less than a hundred yards from the house, she stood, unable to sit and wait. She walked to the edge of the terrace, marveling at the long, easy stride with which he ran. Thinking to herself that his body, except for the multitude of scars, was about as perfect as any she'd ever seen. There wasn't an extra ounce of fat on him, yet he gave the appearance of great strength.

To her surprise, he lifted a hand in greeting.

She waved back, then put her hands on her hips and waited for his arrival. He didn't slow down until he reached the terrace, and even then, he didn't stop. He went from his running stride to a jog, and then to a walk, allowing his muscles to cool down before going inside.

"You're a glutton for punishment, aren't you?" she said, smiling as she pointing to the sweat running down his body.

"It feels good," he countered. "Don't you like to feel good?"

She blinked, the smile suddenly frozen on her face. Was that a double entendre or an innocent question?

"Not unless I'm flat on my back when it happens," she fired back.

John threw back his head and laughed—long and loud. "Point taken," he said, still smiling as he paced the terrace. "Have you eaten?"

She pointed to the empty yogurt cup. "That and coffee, which I should thank you for. I'm not human until I've had a cup of coffee. How about you?"

"I like it, but I don't need it like you do, to wake up."

Alicia shook her head. "Yikes! A morning person."

"Guilty," John said. "I'm also a very sweaty person. If you will excuse me, I'd better shower off before we continue this conversation. Oh…and when I come back, be ready to eat breakfast. I'm starved."

"But I just had breakfast," she said, pointing to the yogurt cup. "Remember?"

"That's sissy food," John said. "You need to eat. I'll be right back."

"But what if I'm not hungry for anything more?"

He pointed toward the desert. "Then I suggest you work up an appetite."

"I'm not running, but I'll make a deal with you."

"Like what?"

She pointed to his scars. "You tell me how come you're still alive after all that, and then I'll eat."

He stared at her for a moment, trying to imagine what she would do if he told her the truth, then shook his head. "You wouldn't believe me if I told you. I'll be back in a few. Oh…if you see or hear a plane of any kind, get back inside the house."

Alicia followed him in, closing the door behind them. "After the dream I had, I don't think I want to stay out here without you anymore, now that you tell me that."

John paused, then turned and looked at her. "You had a bad dream?"

"The worst," she said, and shuddered in spite of herself.

"Tell me."

She sighed. "Well, considering all that's been happening, it's no wonder. But it was like all dreams. Part of it made sense. Part of it didn't. But the gist of it was, I was running through smoke, and I was bleeding. People were chasing me, and I was looking for you but I couldn't find you. Then suddenly someone grabbed me by the hair and yanked me down. I was on my back and fighting someone on top of me. I could see his face, but not clearly at first. When I realized it was my father, he was trying to strangle me with his bare hands."

John watched her, studying the trembling in her voice and the tension in her body, knowing she was reliving the nightmare during the telling. But he was an old friend of bad dreams. He knew that the more you kept them inside, the worse they got. Letting her spit it all out was the best thing he could do.

"Is that when you woke up?" John asked.

She shook her head. "No...it just kept getting worse. I think he knocked me out. When I came to, he cut my throat. I screamed your name, but knew I was dying." Alicia subconsciously rubbed her fingers along her throat, reassuring herself that she was still in one piece. "Anyway, in the dream I think I died. I was standing back, watching everything from a distance as you came running. You pulled my father off my body and killed him with your bare hands, but it was too late. You were holding me and crying and telling me that you were sorry."

She shuddered, then looked up at John and tried to grin. "Then I woke up. How's that for dreaming? I go all out, right down to weather, geography and dialogue—a beginning, a middle and an end. Maybe I missed my calling. Maybe I should have been a writer."

Bile rose at the back of John's throat, but he swallowed it down. He couldn't look at her—*wouldn't* look at her. He didn't know what this dream meant, but he knew dreams had their own meanings. Right now he was too shaken to delve into that nest of snakes.

He waved a hand, then walked out of the room without saying a word.

Alicia eyed his sexy backside, then shrugged and went to refill her coffee.

John's legs were shaking by the time he got in the shower, but he knew it had nothing to do with his morning run. Except for a few minor details, one of which being that he'd killed the person who attacked her, she could have been telling him about White Fawn's death.

He stood beneath the water, letting it beat down on his face until the worst of the memory was gone; then he grabbed a bar of soap and got down to business. A short while later he was back in the kitchen and digging through the refrigerator. He heard Alicia moving about within the house and knew she was probably exploring.

It didn't matter. There was nothing more here that would give him away than there had been at the house in Georgia. Still, it felt a little odd to know that he was sharing anything with a woman—even if it was nothing but breathing the same air.

Corbin Woodliff was on a mission. He'd made more than a dozen phone calls since his meeting with John and Alicia, and the more he'd delved into Richard Ponte's life, the more convinced he'd become that Alicia was telling the truth. The man had homes in half a dozen countries. He had connections in governments around the world and, as best as Corbin could tell, had more money than Croesus. Which begged the question, if he was so wealthy, why risk it all for more? But that was often the way of men like Ponte. It wasn't about the money. It was about the power.

After some fast talking, he was now en route to Boston with two federal agents riding in the seat behind him. He'd made enough phone calls to learn that Jacob Carruthers was reported to be at home and hadn't been seen at his art gallery in more than two days. Called in sick, they said. Corbin's read on that was that, if Alicia Ponte's story was on the up-and-up, he was worse than sick.

He turned and glanced over the seat back at the agents behind him. One was asleep. The other was reading. He arched an eyebrow when he saw the title, then wisely turned back around and returned to minding his own business. Still, he couldn't get past the notion that a big nothing-but-the-facts guy like Morris Joshua was reading one of those books about psychics.

A couple of hours later, they were pulling up to the security gates leading to the Carruthers estate. Corbin leaned out the window and pressed the call button. A disembodied voice answered.

"Yes?"

"Corbin Woodliff to see Mr. Carruthers."

"Do you have an appointment?"

"No, but—"

"I'm sorry, but Mr. Carruthers isn't taking visitors today."

Corbin rolled his eyes and then pressed the button again.

"Yes?"

"The Federal Bureau of Investigation wishes a few moments of Mr. Carruthers' time."

There was a long pause, then a question. "The FBI?"

"Yes, the FBI," Corbin said.

The gates opened.

Corbin took his foot off the brake. "I knew I brought you two along for a reason," he said.

"This better not be a wild-goose chase," Agent Joshua said. "This is my day off."

"I know," Corbin said as he drove toward the house. "And I do appreciate the company. If I'm right, you'll be glad you came along."

A few minutes later, they were in the foyer of the Carruthers mansion. There were footsteps on the grand staircase behind them. They turned as one. Jacob Carruthers was coming down the staircase with a look on his face that Corbin could only describe as looking like he'd seen a ghost.

The moment the butler told him the FBI was at the gate, Jacob's first instinct had been to throw up. When that didn't pan out, he tried to call Richard's cell, but to no avail. He didn't know what was happening, but it couldn't be good. Richard's secretary told him she hadn't heard from him but expected him in at any minute. None of that made sense. Richard's secretary always knew where he was. That was when he panicked. His first thought was that

Richard hadn't been able to stop Alicia from talking and had taken himself off to God knows where, leaving Jacob to face the questions. It wasn't like Richard not to let him know what was going down, but it was the first thing that popped into his head. Still, he didn't believe they could prove anything. All he had to do was stay calm and deny everything. He pasted a smile on his face and held out his hand in greeting as soon as his feet touched the floor.

"Why…Corbin Woodliff, I do believe. My man told me it was the FBI. How silly."

Corbin smiled. "Yes, Carruthers, it's me. Haven't seen you since the President's Christmas Ball a couple of years back." Then he moved aside and pointed to the men beside him. "I'd like to introduce my friends. Special Agent Joshua and Special Agent Morrow from the FBI."

Jacob's belly rolled. Shit. It was the FBI after all.

"So what can I do for you?" he asked.

"We're going to be needing some privacy," Corbin said. "Where do you suggest?"

Jacob felt the urge to pee. "How about the library?"

Corbin remembered Alicia Ponte telling him that her father's opinion of Carruthers was that the man had a tendency to panic. He decided to give him a push in that direction.

"Do the doors close?" Corbin asked.

Jacob froze momentarily, too shocked by the question to answer. Then he gathered himself and nodded.

"After you," Corbin said.

Jacob led the way. All the way to the library, he couldn't help thinking this might be his last walk down this hall. His heart was pounding so fast he feared he might have a heart attack on the spot, then that he wouldn't and would wind up in prison instead.

Corbin made a point of nodding to the agents as they sat, making sure Jacob knew they were completely involved. But Jacob wasn't as passive as Corbin hoped. As soon as they were all seated, he threw out the first question.

"So…forgive me if I'm a bit confused," Jacob said. "Is this an interview or an inquisition?"

Special Agent Joshua took a notepad out of his pocket and clicked his pen.

"Depends on how you answer Mr. Woodliff's questions," he said.

Jacob swallowed, but persevered. "I'm sorry. I'm just not following this. What are you talking about?"

Corbin began, using the voice he used when he was interviewed on-air to indicate the seriousness of the situation. "The reason I'm here and you're not already under arrest is because the information we were given was first presented to me rather than the authorities. The FBI has graciously allowed me to follow through because of my firsthand knowledge."

"Knowledge of what…and from whom?" Jacob asked.

"It's like this," Corbin said. "Alicia Ponte has informed us that you and her father are guilty of treason. That you have been selling weapons to the enemy with whom we are at war. She has firsthand information linking you and Richard Ponte to Osama bin Laden, to al Qaeda and to Mohammed al-Kazir, along with delivery dates." He paused. "Stop me if any of this rings a bell."

Jacob didn't know that his face had turned a faint shade of purple, but he did know he couldn't feel his feet. He had a flash of his entire life passing before his eyes and knew, in that moment, that despite everything he might say, this run was over.

"I don't know what you're talking about," he said, then stood abruptly, pointing angrily to each of them in turn. "What I do know is that it seems you've taken the word of a woman who has recently suffered a mental breakdown. I don't believe a single thing you've just said. I know for a fact that Alicia Ponte was kidnapped, so you couldn't have spoken to her—unless you're the kidnapper! Is this true? Gentlemen...I urge you to look into Mr. Woodliff's wild claims and question his morals, not mine."

"Sit down, Mr. Carruthers," Agent Joshua said.

It was the tone of voice that got to him. Jacob dropped.

Corbin scooted to the edge of his seat. "I assure you, Alicia Ponte has not been kidnapped, and the woman I spoke to only yesterday had every one of her faculties securely in place. The one thing she was disturbed about was that her father is obviously trying to have her killed. There's already been one attempt on her life. I can also assure you that if you continue to maintain your innocence and something *does* happen to Miss Ponte and her father is responsible, you'll not only be tried for treason, but there will be an added charge of murder to go with it."

"I don't know anything," Jacob said. "All I know is what I heard during Richard's press conference. Do I need to call my lawyer?"

Corbin ignored his questions and threw out another of his own. "So you haven't spoken to Ponte since the press conference?"

"No, I have not."

"Have you tried?"

Jacob's heart actually skipped several beats, and

when it picked back up, it was with a thud so hard it made him hiccup.

"Fuck," he muttered, and got up and poured himself a drink. He downed the first shot of bourbon, looked at the trio and poured and downed a second.

"That's enough," Agent Morrow said.

Corbin waved toward the chair Jacob had vacated. "Come sit back down and let's talk about this," he said.

"Talk about what?" Jacob asked.

"How we're going to work this out. I have it on good authority that if you cooperate in helping us with bringing Ponte to justice, your death sentence will be commuted to life. It's a pretty damn good deal, considering. Otherwise, you'll both be tried as traitors and you'll both fry. What's it to be? Wanna help us put a traitor out of business and regain a measure of your dignity?"

Jacob wanted to argue. He kept thinking that if he ignored them, they would eventually go away. He stared at the floor until his vision blurred and the bourbon he'd just downed was hanging at the back of his throat. He thought about calling his lawyer, but what difference would that make in the grand scheme of things? They'd already made him the only offer that would be on the table. He couldn't get out of what he'd done, but he could save his own life. Still, betraying Richard Ponte was dangerous. Suddenly the bourbon made a move.

"You'll have to excuse me a minute," he rasped. "I'm going to be sick."

"I'll go with you," Agent Joshua said, and followed Carruthers out of the room.

Corbin eyed Morrow. "What do you think?" he asked.

Special Agent Morrow grinned. "I think when he's

through puking, if he's got any guts left, he's going to spill 'em. I also think you're one lucky bastard that this fell in your lap and you're probably going to win yourself another Pulitzer."

"That may be," Corbin said. "But I can't help thinking of how many men and women in our armed forces are dead today because of what these two sons of bitches have been doing."

The smile on Morrow's face shifted. "I'd hate to be either one of these guys when the cons get a hold of them."

"How so?" Corbin asked.

"Even cons have their breaking points. Traitors to their country and child molesters don't get any breaks behind bars. It will be a miracle if Ponte makes it to trial and Carruthers makes it to Christmas."

Corbin looked up, then pulled his tape recorder out of his pocket and set it on the coffee table in front of him.

"Here they come, and from the look on Carruthers' face, I feel a story coming on."

Richard Ponte was signing a handful of letters that his secretary had laid on his desk, anxious to finish up this last lot of paperwork before he left for his lunch appointment. He'd turned the television on a couple of minutes ago, planning to catch the latest figures on the stock market, when he tuned in to the fact that a news bulletin was playing. He looked up, saw a familiar Washington, D.C., landmark hotel in the background and upped the volume.

"This just in from our news bureau. The body of a man has been found in the stairwell of the hotel behind me. He has been identified as Peter Wayne Joiner, also known as Shark Joiner. Joiner has long been suspected of being a hit man for hire. Authorities have no leads at this time, but theories run the gamut from a mob hit gone wrong to a message being sent to the people with whom Joiner was associated. We'll have more on this developing story on the evening news. And now, we return to our regular programming."

Richard sat staring at the screen for what seemed like an eternity while his mind raced, trying to sort through what the implications of this were for him. Obviously his latest plan to get to Alicia had failed.

Who the hell was this man she was with?

He'd put Dieter down, and now Shark—two of the best in the business. His lawyers were still working on getting the attempted murder charges dropped on Dieter, but as of now, he was still behind bars. Richard aimed the remote to turn off the TV and noticed his hands were trembling. Angry with himself for showing weakness, he slammed the remote down on the desk and willed himself to be calm.

At that moment there was a knock on the door and then his secretary came in.

"You wanted me to post those letters," she said, pointing to the papers he'd been signing.

"Yes, yes…I'm almost through," he said quickly, signed off on the last two and shoved them toward her.

A memo floated from his desk onto the floor. "Oh, you dropped something," she said as she picked it up and handed it back to him. "It's that message from Mr. Carruthers."

Richard's head began to pound. "What message? I didn't know Jacob called. Where was I?"

"It was before you came in, sir. I told him I expected that you were en route to the office, since he said you hadn't answered your cell. I left the message on top of your mail."

Richard cursed. He'd tossed the morning paper on top of his desk without looking at the mail.

"Thank you, that will be all," he said shortly, and was patting down his pockets for his cell phone when he realized it wasn't on him.

Frantic now, he began digging through his pockets again, unable to believe he'd left the house without it. All of a sudden he remembered that he'd been about to disconnect it from the charger when the maid had come in with a problem about the plumbing. By the time he'd dealt with that, he'd forgotten to get the phone.

"I'll have his heart on a stick if he's screwed anything up," Richard muttered as he grabbed the phone and quickly dialed Jacob's number.

The phone rang twice before the maid answered. "This is Richard. Get Jacob immediately."

"I'm sorry, Mr. Ponte, but Mr. Carruthers isn't here."

"Where is he?" Richard asked.

"I'm not sure. He left about an hour ago with that reporter and two federal agents. He didn't say when he'd be back. Do you want me to—"

Richard hung up the phone.

What the hell just happened? Obviously Alicia had spoken to someone, but why had they gone to Jacob instead of coming to him with Alicia's accusations?

Suddenly it hit him. Other than Alicia's word, they had no proof. He cursed beneath his breath. He'd underestimated his daughter. She'd pinpointed the crack in his empire: Jacob. Jacob the worrier. Jacob the whiner. Jacob the weak.

He glanced down at the photo on his desk, then tilted his head.

"First round to you, daughter dear," he said softly.

For a moment he allowed himself the luxury of looking around his perfectly appointed office one last time, knowing that he had a very small window of opportunity to get the hell out of the States. For all he knew, it might already be too late. In the back of his mind, he'd always known this might happen, but he'd never imagined it would be his daughter who brought him down. Even as he was emptying the office safe of all the cash he had on hand, he promised himself that, if it was the last thing he did, he would make her pay for what she'd done.

Eight

Richard's passport was in his pocket. All the cash he'd had in the safe was in his briefcase, as well as an untraceable phone. His heart was pounding as he took the back stairs out of his office and then the freight elevator to the ground floor. He exited in an alley, hailed a cab two streets over and told the driver to take him to the marina. As they drove, he called his bank and had two different accounts emptied and wired to his account in Geneva.

If Jacob was in custody, he would be next. They would undoubtedly be watching the airports. They would know he had a private jet and also a yacht. He couldn't use anything he owned without being traced. But he wasn't whipped. Not by a long shot. All during the cab ride, he was on the cell, tying up loose ends, issuing orders at his home, calling a residence he owned in East Germany and hiring a boat to take him north up the coast from Miami. His first step out of the FBI net was simply to get to South Carolina. Paulo Gianni, an old friend as well as a famous Hollywood actor, had a vacation home in Myrtle Beach. Richard knew for a fact that Paulo was in the States, and the man owed him a big favor. He was only a phone call away from making an escape. His fingers were flying as he punched in Paulo's number, smiling with satisfaction when he heard Paulo's voice, rather than his voice mail.

"Yes?"

"Paulo...it's Richard Ponte. How have you been?"

"Ricardo, my friend, I am fine, as always. I am so glad you called. I have learned of your daughter's kidnapping and am shocked. Do you know anything more?"

Richard relaxed. *Right into his hands.*

"There's nothing I can tell you without putting her life in danger, but I need a favor. I need to get to Italy without the press knowing. Is your jet there?"

Paulo reacted immediately, believing, as Richard intended, that Richard's need to get to Italy must involve his daughter. "They have taken her out of the country? Ah...my friend...but of course. Where are you now?"

"I'll be coming to your location oceanside."

"You know the hangar I always use?"

"Yes. I've landed there in the past myself."

"I'll call my pilot. He'll be waiting."

Richard sighed. One more piece falling into place. "I can't thank you enough," he said.

"No, no...it is my pleasure, and know that my prayers will be with you. When you next see your beautiful daughter, give her my love."

"Definitely," Richard said, and disconnected.

Moments later the cab driver pulled up on the side of the marina with boats for hire. Richard tossed a handful of bills into the front seat and got out on the run.

He stopped the first local he came to, who happened to be a man selling balloons.

"Can you tell me where the *Martini Mama* is berthed?"

"That way," the man said, pointing up the wharf. "It's a white boat with a naked woman holding a martini glass painted on the prow."

"Of course it is," Richard muttered, and headed off, trying not to think of his own perfectly appointed yacht less than a quarter of a mile away.

He found the boat with ease, and after locating the pilot, revised his disdain. The man was dressed to the nines in white, right down to a captain's nautical cap and the prerequisite white soft-soled shoes.

"Captain Roberts?" Richard asked.

"Call me Weed, and yes…for the obvious reason. But relax, it's a holdover from my hippie days." He held out a hand to Richard, easing his step from the wharf to the small gangplank leading to the boat. "So, Mr. Colt, is it?"

Richard nodded. "Yes, Paul Colt. Please call me Paul."

Weed smiled as he rubbed his hands together in a playful show of greed. "Shall we get the business end of this out of the way first?"

"You said five thousand?" Richard asked, counting out the money into Weed Roberts' hand.

The other man nodded. "Myrtle Beach, South Carolina, is quite a distance, and fuel is sky-high."

"It's fine," Richard said. "Can we start now?"

"Sure thing, Paul. Let me show you to your cabin."

"I'll find my own way," Richard said. "I'm just in a hurry to get started."

Weed pocketed the money and pointed to the stairwell.

"It's your call. First door on the left will be your cabin for the duration of the trip. The head is across the hall."

Richard went down below. Moments later, he heard the engine start up. Not until they were out of the bay and into open water did he relax.

At that point, he tried contacting Jacob one more time, but this time on his cell.

Jacob was sitting in an interrogation room in his lawyer's office, listening to his lawyer and the Feds working out the conditions under which he would agree to testify. He'd give them names, dates and delivery points of illegal sales for the past five years. He knew where Richard was banking that money, but he didn't know account numbers. It was everything he knew. If they wanted Richard Ponte, they had to take it.

He knew his life was basically over. His children were grown, but their conception of their father was a lie. He also knew that, because of him, their reputations would be tarnished, if not ruined. They would hate him, but not as much as he hated himself. The only positive part of this hell was that Delia was gone. He didn't think he would be able to bear the look in his wife's eyes, and for the first time since her passing, he was glad she was dead.

He was staring out the window, absently watching a pair of pigeons pecking at something on the window-sill, when his cell phone began to vibrate. He slipped it out of his jacket pocket, saw Richard's name on the caller ID and then laid the phone on the table.

"The man of the hour is on the phone," Jacob said. "Help yourself."

Corbin Woodliff leaned forward, then looked at Agent Joshua in surprise. "Why isn't he in custody?" he asked, knowing that agents were supposed to have picked him up that morning.

Joshua picked up the phone, then handed it to Jacob. "Answer it, but don't tell him where you are." Then he motioned for another agent to trace the call.

Jacob sighed. "I never could lie to him. He'll know something is wrong."

"Our men were supposed to have him in custody. Something must have happened. Ask him where he is," Agent Joshua said.

Jacob cleared his throat, then answered. "Richard…where on earth are you? I've been trying to call you all morning."

"Just answer my questions. Are you alone?"

"No, of course not," Jacob said.

"Are you with the Feds?"

"Yes…all morning. I left two or three messages on your cell. Why didn't you answer?"

Richard sighed. The first time he'd ever left home without that damned phone, and this was the result.

"Did you give me up? Don't lie to me. I'll know."

"I see, well, yes, and that's too bad," Jacob answered. "So…have you heard anything from the kidnappers yet? Have you talked to Alicia? Is she okay?"

"You did, didn't you? Damn you to hell, you sorry bastard. I thought you were my friend."

Jacob drew a slow, shuddering breath. "I did think the same, but I didn't get your invitation."

All of a sudden Richard began to understand Jacob's verbal shorthand. He was telling Richard in the only way he could that he thought Richard had run out on him first. That must have been what he was calling about earlier that morning. Poor Jacob. He never could run a bluff.

"It wasn't like that, my friend. All I did was forget my damn cell phone. It's still at home. This one is a disposable. I wouldn't have left you behind."

"But as it turned out, you did, didn't you, Richard?"

Silence.

Agent Joshua was making frantic hand gestures—wanting Jacob to ask Richard's location—but Jacob had said everything he intended to. He handed the phone to Joshua.

"You ask him."

By the time Joshua had the phone to his ear, the line was dead.

"Did you get that?" Joshua yelled to the agent tracing the call, who shook his head. "He hung up too fast."

"Damn it," Joshua muttered.

"What did he say?" Corbin asked.

"He knows I'm in custody. God only knows where he is, but asking would have been stupid. He's not going to tell me anything more…other than what he just said."

"What was that?" Corbin asked.

"To go to hell."

"That's enough," Jacob's lawyer said. "You get nothing more from him until we have all this in writing and signed by the attorney general." Then he pointed at Corbin Woodliff. "And *you*. Don't print a word of this."

"Sorry," Corbin said. "You can make deals with the government but not the press. The story came to me. It's mine to tell."

"At least wait until—"

Corbin held up his hand. "You and I aren't negotiating anything," he said. "And as far as I'm concerned, the sooner the American people know their sons and daughters are being shot and killed with their own countryman's weapons, the better."

Jacob put his head down on the table and wept.

Corbin glared at him, then at his lawyer. "Do we understand each other here?"

The lawyer looked at Jacob, then back at Corbin. "Think of his family…of his children and grandchildren."

"Why?" Corbin snapped. "He didn't think of the mothers and fathers who are burying *their* children and grandchildren, or the children and grandchildren who are being orphaned, because of the weapons these two sold to al Qaeda. It's over. The whole ugly scheme is over."

Then Jacob lifted his head. His eyes were swollen and brimming with tears, and he looked as if he'd aged ten years in the last two hours.

"Let it go," he said, speaking to his lawyer. "Just get the papers drawn up. I want this over with."

At that moment Agent Morrow entered. There were a half-dozen people behind him, one of whom Corbin recognized as the attorney general of the United States. Corbin was promptly escorted out of the room, but he didn't care. He had his story. The details could come later, in follow-up pieces. For now, he knew warrants had been issued for the arrest of Jacob Carruthers and Richard Ponte for treason against the United States of America, and why, and that was enough.

He pulled out a phone to call in the story. The piece had already been written while they'd been waiting for the AG to arrive. All he had to do was let the editor know, then e-mail it. Even though it was a coup for Corbin, it was a sad day for his country.

Alicia was sitting in the kitchen, waiting for John to come back from his shower, when she heard him call out her name. She raced into the living room just as he was turning on the television.

"You need to see this," he said as he aimed the remote. "I caught part of it in my room."

Alicia gasped when a live shot of Jacob Carruthers in handcuffs came onto the screen. The news anchor was talking over the footage in a highly excited voice. Then they flashed a photo of her father. Even though she'd known this was what would happen, the physical evidence was still shocking. She grabbed on to the back of the sofa as her knees went weak.

"Oh, Daddy," she whispered. "What have I done?"

John could have told her right then about the soul he'd been after. That with every incarnation, when the time to make choices had come, it had chosen the dark side every time. He could have told her that Richard Ponte's fall from grace had nothing to do with what she'd done and everything to do with something that had happened centuries ago. But she'd already suffered enough shocks. Dumping a revelation like that in her lap would have sent her straight over the edge.

"It wasn't you who committed the crimes, it was him," John said. "And don't forget, he was willing to kill you to keep himself safe. What kind of a father does that?"

Alicia turned, almost eye to eye with the man behind

her. "Obviously mine. The issue is…if he's that evil, then what does that make me?"

John's anger came out in his voice. "A victim. Nothing more."

"That's easy for you to say," Alicia said, but immediately wished she could take the words back when she saw the look on his face. It was then that she remembered his claim that her father was responsible for killing his wife, his entire family. "I'm sorry. That was a stupid, thoughtless remark. I wasn't thinking about your own losses. I'm sorry."

"Let it go," John said. "Again, it wasn't you who killed them. It was him."

"How?" she asked. "Were they in a war zone? Was it a bomb? Help me understand."

John's nostrils flared. "They died because of ignorance and greed. As for helping you understand, how can I do that when I don't understand it myself?"

Before she could answer, something the announcer was saying caught her attention. Alicia looked back at the television, then grabbed the remote from John's hand and increased the volume, catching the broadcast in the middle of a sentence.

"…is in custody as of an hour ago. They've been unable to locate Richard Ponte. Authorities have all the usual points of travel under surveillance, but with Ponte's international connections, there are rumors that he may already be out of the country. And here's an ironic twist that we've just learned. It was Ponte's own daughter, Alicia, who blew the whistle on him. We aren't sure what that press conference he called the other day was all about, but we have it on good authority that she was not kidnapped, nor has she suffered a mental break-down, although after this, one could hardly blame her. We have been given to understand that she is, at the moment, under tight security and in fear for her life."

Alicia's hands were shaking as she laid down the remote. "He got away. Oh my God…this still isn't over."

John felt sick. The man he'd been searching for had, once again, slipped past him.

"Where would he go?" he asked.

Alicia sat down before she fell down, then leaned back and covered her face with her hands.

"Anywhere he wants."

"Does he have a favorite—"

Alicia suddenly lost it. She bolted up from the sofa and turned on John. Her cheeks were flushed, and her eyes revealed all the panic and frustration she was feeling.

"Favorite? *Favorite?* You still don't get it. You don't get *him*. He's running, and he has the money to do it and the whole fucking world to hide in. He'll never be found, and *I'll* never be safe."

She strode out of the living room with her chin up and her hands curled into fists.

John cursed beneath his breath. He'd had his chance to get to the man, but he'd let it pass. He'd chosen to help his enemy's daughter and this country first. It had come at a high cost.

He put his head down and walked out of the living room, heading in the opposite direction from the one she'd taken. The last thing either of them needed was to argue with each other, but that was what it would come down to. He was mad at himself for the choice he'd made, and mad at Alicia for getting under his skin.

Alicia knew the minute she walked out that she was wrong. She shouldn't have lashed out at John. It was her father and the situation that had her in knots. She stood for a few minutes within the silence of her bedroom, gathering herself for the apology she needed to make.

John had gone straight to the room where most of his personal artifacts were hanging. It was all he had left of his people. Usually he felt their spirits here in this house where he had a measure of peace, but he now stood before them in mute apology for having failed them once again.

His gaze slid to a scrap of ancient leather with a bird painted on it that he'd mounted behind glass. It had once been part of his father's quiver, and he could remember watching his father, Red Eagle, paint it, as if it were yesterday. He'd pulled it out of Red Eagle's burning lodge after the massacre.

The trio of arrowheads framed on leather in a shadow box were his, and had been cut out of the men who'd attacked the village. From shards of pottery to fragile shells and tiny bone beads, everything in this room had once belonged to the Ah-ni-yv-wi-ya.

Then he turned to a painting hanging alone in the middle of the east wall. He'd commissioned it more than a hundred years ago. He'd sat beside the artist, watching while he sketched the face, describing every nuance of the woman's features. The warm brown shade of her skin, the slight flare of her nostrils at the end of her nose, perfect brows and lashes framing eyes so brown they could have passed for black, lips wide and full, a mouth that was nearly always laughing, the hair, thick, black and straight with a small blue feather tied near the crown of her head…

White Fawn.

He reached a hand toward the painting, then let it fall against his leg.

"I'm still here…without you." His voice was nothing but a whisper.

Alicia was standing in the doorway behind him and knew he had no idea she was there.

She didn't hear what he said. Once she'd seen the painting, she'd lost focus on everything but those eyes. The life within them was palpable. If the lips had parted and a voice had emerged, she wouldn't have been surprised.

"Oh Lord," she whispered, and backed out as quietly as she'd come.

By the time she got into the kitchen, she was bawling. Ugly gulping sobs that burned all the way down her throat. She'd heard his story. She understood what death meant, but it was seeing that beautiful, vital woman and knowing her father was responsible for the light going out in those eyes that did her in. It was a miracle in itself that John Nightwalker could even look at her. She felt shame and guilt—so much guilt—and yet John had said it himself. It wasn't her fault. She was a victim, too. And while she understood that, it didn't make the shock of seeing that woman's face go away.

She cried until her eyes were mere slits in her face, until she was numb from the inside out, then staggered to the sink and began sloshing her face with cold water.

"Oh God, oh God," she muttered as she continued to sluice her eyes and cheeks. If only her father's sins could wash away as easily.

As she was drying her face, she heard John's footsteps nearing the kitchen. She didn't want him to see her like this. Without thinking about the fact that she was barefoot, she headed for the back door and out onto the terrace.

She thought she heard John call her name, but she wouldn't turn around, and she wouldn't look back. She didn't think about anything except getting away until she'd regained her sense of self.

Her stride was quick and long as she bolted off the terrace and down onto the hot sand. Almost immediately, she realized she shouldn't be out there barefoot, but this wasn't the first time she'd done something she shouldn't, and it probably wouldn't be the last.

"Alicia! Wait!"

She flinched. Damn. He was already outside and headed her way. Without turning around, she waved him back.

"I'm fine," she said. "I just want some time alone."

"Not without shoes, damn it."

She stopped, her shoulders drooping, her chin slumped against her chest.

Please, she begged silently, *just let him go back inside.* "Okay, okay. Just go away. Please."

Silence. She waited until she heard the door open and close. Only then did she relax.

Thank God. She sighed, then turned around, only to find John still on the terrace. Her first instinct was to be pissed.

"You're not supposed to be here. You lied."

"I did not lie. I didn't say I was leaving. All you heard was the door open and close, and you know it. And you've been crying."

Alicia threw her arms up in the air as she started to weep all over again. "So what? It's not against the law.

Give me a break. I'm a woman. We cry when we're happy. We cry when we're sad. And sometimes we cry when we're mad. Right now I'm so mad at the situation and at my father that I can hardly think. So don't come out here with that look on your face and tell me I can't cry."

John sighed. Now she was crying all over again. Damn, but that ate through every defense he ever had.

"I never said you can't cry. I just pointed out that you're doing it."

Alicia choked on a sob as she swiped at the tears running down her face. "You're making me crazy," she said, and then kicked at the ground in frustration.

Sand flew in every direction as her toes cut through the loose grit; then she felt a sharp, burning pain and grabbed at her foot.

"Oh, oh…owww."

John leaped off the terrace as she dropped onto the sand. Within seconds he saw what had happened, and his heart sank. He ground the black scorpion she'd unearthed beneath his boot, then scooped her up in his arms and headed inside.

"It burns," she mumbled, and then licked at her lips, because they suddenly felt numb.

"Are you allergic?" John asked.

"I'm…"

John was running down the hall with her when he realized she hadn't finished her sentence. Every breath she was taking sounded like a whistle, which meant her throat was closing up. Not only that, but she was now unconscious.

"No!" he yelled, and clutched her tighter as he ran. "Don't you do this, woman. Don't you dare die on me."

His head was spinning as he laid her down on the bed, then made a run for his room. He had a first-aid kit, but he didn't know if there was anything in it that would counteract an allergic reaction.

"Sweet Lord…help me," he muttered as he tore through the contents of his medicine cabinet and the first-aid kit without success. Just when he thought all was lost, he heard something odd.

Through all the years that he'd owned this place, he'd never had an uninvited visitor, and yet the doorbell was ringing—over and over, as if someone was holding a finger on the bell.

He straightened abruptly and dashed back across the hall. Alicia was barely breathing, and what breaths she was taking were labored and shallow. It wouldn't matter how fast he could get the chopper up and running to get her into Sedona. She would be dead before they got there.

He dashed toward the front door and then flung it open. An old Indian man was on the doorstep with a small black bag in one hand and a wide-brimmed straw hat in the other. He was wearing bright blue shorts and a Grateful Dead T-shirt. His long gray braids had small turquoise beads interwoven between the strands, and there was an enormous turquoise ring on his right hand.

"Where is she?"

John looked past the man toward the yard. It was empty. No car. No horse. Not even a motorcycle.

"Who are you? Where did you come from?" John asked.

"I asked first," the old man said, and then pushed past John and headed toward Alicia's bedroom as if he'd been there before.

John slammed the door shut and then followed on the run. By the time he got back to Alicia, the old man already had his bag open and was in the act of giving her a shot.

"Epinephrine," he said shortly, then tossed the used syringe into his bag. "White man's medicine." Then he pulled out a thick bundle of twisted sage and struck a match. The sage caught. The old man let it burn for a few seconds, then blew out the blaze, leaving the tiny brush ends to smolder. "Indian medicine. Just covering all the bases," he added, then began waving it above Alicia's body as she lay motionless on the bed, chanting words John hadn't heard in centuries, speaking the old language of the Ah-ni-yv-wi-ya.

"Who are you?" John asked, his voice thick with tears.

"The answer to your prayers," the old man said, then pointed to a nearby chair. "You're messing with my vibe. Go sit."

John backed up without taking his eyes from the old man, but he sat and watched—and remembered such rites performed back in the village before the world as he'd known it had come to an end.

Time passed. Finally the old man stopped chanting. He turned, caught John's gaze and nodded.

John stood abruptly and moved toward the bed. Alicia's breathing was steady, but she was still unconscious.

"Is she going to be all right?"

The old man shrugged. "She has all the medicine she needs."

"Then why isn't she waking up?" John asked.

"She has not yet decided if she wants to live."

John felt as if someone had shoved a knife in his gut. "What do you mean?"

"I cured her illness, but someone else has broken her heart. That is out of my hands. She has to decide for herself if life is worth living." The old man shrugged again. "It is up to her. So I will go now," he said, and gathered up his things and headed out of the room.

John looked back at Alicia, afraid to leave her, but needing answers the old man wouldn't give. He followed him through the house, then out the front door.

"Where are you going?"

"Back where I came from," he said. "I know what you are, *time walker,* and I know why you are still here. You don't need me, but you need her. She's part of your path. I have done all that is necessary. The rest is up to her."

"But—"

"There are no buts. My job is done here. I go now."

John had known from the moment he heard the chanting that this man was one of the Old Ones. He didn't understand why the Old Ones had suddenly decided to interfere in his fate now. There had been countless times before when he could have used their help. Then he remembered what the old man had said. Alicia was part of his path. He needed her to fulfill his vow.

The old man put on his hat and stepped off the front steps. Within moments of clearing the yard, he disappeared.

John grunted as if someone had just kicked him in the gut, then remembered Alicia and hurried inside. She hadn't moved since he'd laid her on the bed. The only positive thing was that she was still breathing.

He stood for a moment, then went into the bathroom and came back out with a wet washcloth. He sat down beside her, then lifted her lifeless hand in his own. He knew her body was fragile, but he also knew her will was strong.

"Fight this, Alicia. I need to know you're going to survive this. I can't bury another woman I care about."

Before he thought about why, he lifted her hand, turned it palm up and kissed it. Her skin was soft and warm, and he could feel a faint pulse beneath his lips. Then he began to wash her face in a slow, gentle motion—not because it was doing her any good, but because he had to do something for her. He removed her clothes and began bathing her.

Dark shadows colored the skin beneath her lashes, evidence of how the scorpion's toxin had impacted her body. The rest of her face was colorless, her lips slightly parted. John brushed his fingers across the pulse at the base of her throat, taking comfort in the strong, steady beat. But she wouldn't wake up. It was a sickening thought to know she was so emotionally devastated that she might not want to come back.

He sat with her for hours, talking about things he would never have said aloud, starting with the massacre and the Spaniards who'd sailed into the bay, telling her about living in Europe, traveling through India by train, being at Little Big Horn, being in Mexico during the Spanish-American War and about being snowed in one winter in a desolate cabin in the Rockies. He told of watching great treasures being buried, only to come back generations later and claim them for himself. He'd lived through fires and plagues, earthquakes and floods, and more wars than history had recorded. It was a catharsis long overdue, unburdening himself of a truth no one would believe and of the aching loneliness of being the only one of his kind. And finally, when his throat was so dry it hurt to swallow, he stopped.

The sudden silence was frightening. It took a few moments for him to focus enough to realize that he could still hear her breathing. He nodded once, then wearily got up. He started to leave, then stopped, and leaned down until he could feel the breath from between her parted lips. He inhaled as she exhaled, taking in a moment's worth of her life force, knowing that forever after there would always be a tiny part of her within him. He thought about what he was about to do. Knowing it would be cheating, because he was the only one participating. But he'd lived all this time without bothering to follow the rules. Why start now?

His lips parted slightly, then he matched them both to hers, gently, coaxingly, silently pleading for her to wake and ask for more. But she didn't.

He walked away long enough to fix some food, eating for stamina only, then heated some chicken broth from a can, poured it into a cup and carried it back into her bedroom.

He sat down on the side of the bed with the soup, a drinking straw and a plan.

"Alicia…it's me, John. I know you're in there, but you've gone to a place where I can't help you. I can't hear your voice. I don't know where you are, but I'm out here. When you come back, I'll still be here…waiting for you. You don't know it yet, but I'm real good at waiting. In the meantime, I will feed your body while you heal your soul. When I put this straw to your lips, all you have to do is swallow."

A muscle jerked in his jaw as he waited for a sign that

she had heard and understood, but it didn't come. He dipped the straw into the cup, put his finger over the open end and siphoned off a small sip. Then he put the straw to her slightly parted lips and lifted his finger. A tiny drizzle of soup went into her mouth, but then ran out the corner of her lips.

He grabbed the washcloth and blotted the drips, then siphoned another sip. This time, when he put it to her lips, he was determined to make things work.

"Alicia! Swallow the damned soup." Then he let it flow.

To his surprise, he saw her throat working, and knew that some part of her consciousness had heard and obeyed.

His nostrils flared. "That's what I'm talking about," he muttered, and so they went until most of the soup was gone.

Satisfied that he'd done all he could for the moment, he covered her carefully and then closed the door behind him when he left. He needed to talk to Corbin and find out what the hell had gone wrong, and what the Feds were doing about it.

Alicia Ponte had checked out of the human race. She was still breathing, but she didn't know and didn't care. She'd gone deep into her subconscious, past the place where dreams begin to a tiny corner in her mind where memories from a hundred lifetimes had been stored. And there she hovered, lost between the present and the past. For all intents and purposes, she'd put herself on hold.

Nine

Richard was in Italy, but not for long. He'd entered the country under an assumed name, flashed the appropriate matching passport and identification papers and made his way to Naples. From there, he'd hired a car and headed south toward his next destination, which was Sicily, with the ultimate goal of reaching East Germany.

There were more direct routes to take, but Richard wasn't one for the obvious, and he was changing his appearance as fast as a chameleon changes colors. He'd long since dumped his Gucci shoes and Italian suits for workman's wear: loose denim pants, a little baggy in the rear; a faded blue, collarless shirt he left hanging outside his pants; and a fisherman's cap pulled low over a freshly shaved head and a two-day growth of beard, which was turning out to be gray. Not even his mother would have recognized him. This escape plan had been in place for years, although in truth, he'd never thought he would have to use it. He carried the papers that matched his new identity and his money in a workman's duffel bag slung over one shoulder, along with a couple of changes of clothes. Beyond that, he was still vulnerable. He needed to get back in control of his life and his money.

Paolo Gianni was probably furious. He would know by now that he'd been had. What Richard wasn't certain of was whether Paolo would tell the authorities and risk being arrested for aiding and abetting. Treason was an awful thing. Being accused of it in a foreign country would be even worse, and while Paolo Gianni was a big-deal actor in America, he was still an Italian citizen. If he caved and informed the authorities how he'd been duped, they would soon know that Richard had landed in Italy. But they had no way of knowing where he would go from there. His plan was perfect. All he needed was a little more time to see the rest of it through, and then he would, for all intents and purposes, have disappeared from the face of the earth.

After that, he would be able to focus on retribution. But he was going to need help Stateside, and the only man he trusted to follow through for him there was still in jail in Justice, Georgia.

He sat near the shore, waiting for the fishing boat he'd hired to arrive, and glanced around, making sure he was alone and unobserved. Then he pulled another disposable cell phone from his pocket, punched in a series of numbers and waited for the call to go through. A few moments later, he heard the cell begin to ring.

"Borden and Wheaton law offices."

"Put me through to Paul Borden."

"May I say who's calling?" the receptionist asked.

"No, you may not. Just put him on."

The receptionist had heard this voice too many times

in the past not to know who it was. And considering that their biggest client had been the talk of the office for the past twelve hours, she knew not to mess this up.

"One moment, please."

When the music came on, Richard cursed. It was an overseas call, for God's sake, and they'd put him on hold. Of course, they didn't know where he was, but he knew good and well that she'd recognized his voice. He could only imagine the hullabaloo that was going on there right now.

When the receptionist bolted from her desk and dashed into Paul Borden's office without knocking, he was in the middle of a consultation with a client and gave her a look that, ordinarily, would have sent her to clean out her desk. But when she laid the phone slip in front of him, he instantly understood.

"I'm sorry," he said quickly to the client on the other side of his desk. "Please excuse me for a moment. Family emergency. I must take this call."

He left the room, closing the door behind him, and then indicated his partner's office across the hall, which was, at the moment, empty.

"Put the call through in there," he told the receptionist. "And for God's sake, keep your mouth shut."

She nodded, then punched a button on her console. "Thank you for holding. Mr. Borden for you, sir." She punched another button, heard the call go through, then replaced the receiver.

Borden was shocked that the man still had the balls to call them. "You son of a bitch! I hope to hell you don't think we're still willing to represent your sorry ass, because we're done with you. Do you understand?"

This was exactly what Richard had expected. But he knew something Paul Borden didn't.

"What I understand is that a million dollars has recently been deposited into an account in the Cayman Islands payable to whomever shows up with the account number. All you have to do to get that number is get Dieter Bahn out of jail."

Borden was so angry he was shaking. "You've put a black mark on this that will take years to get off— if ever. The Feds have been here and confiscated all our files regarding anything we've ever done for you. We've lost three of our biggest clients since noon, just because they don't want to be associated with the law firm that did business with a traitor to his country, and the phones are still ringing."

"Then you're going to need that million dollars, aren't you, Paul?"

Borden swiped a hand across his face and dropped into his partner's chair. It was a good thing Wheaton was in court, because he would have ripped this phone out of the wall before he would have let Paul have this conversation.

"Why, Richard? Why did you do it? You didn't need the money. Was it just a game to you, or are you truly without a conscience?"

"It's none of your business. Are you going to do what I asked?"

Paul sighed. A million dollars. Damn his sorry soul to hell. Ponte probably knew he was in debt up to his neck.

"Answer me this."

"What?"

"When Wheaton's son died in Iraq last year, did that even register with you?"

"I sent flowers, didn't I?" Richard said.

Paul was so stunned by the callous answer that for a long moment he couldn't speak.

"Well…answer me, damn it," Richard said. "I know plenty of others who'll do a whole lot more than what I've asked you, and for a whole lot less money."

"Fuck you," Borden whispered. "I'll get him out, but that's it. After that, you're history here. Now what's the account number?"

"Not until Dieter is out."

"No way, you lying bastard. I have no reason to trust you. You either do this my way or you're on your own."

Richard cursed beneath his breath. He could find someone else to do it, but it would take time, and time was of the essence.

"Fine," he said. "But remember this. If you stab me in the back, I know where your kids go to school, where your wife gets her hair done and where you live."

Borden felt sick that he'd ever done business with this man—but sicker still that he'd just sold his soul to the devil for only a million dollars. Still, while he'd sold out, he wasn't going to be bullied. His voice was barely above a whisper, but the intent was evident.

"Don't threaten me. Ever. I know way too much about *you*, too, including some hidey-holes you may plan on accessing. Do we understand each other?"

Richard blinked. He hadn't expected Borden to fight back. "Okay…point taken. Got a pen and paper?"

"Talk."

Richard rattled off the name of the bank, the phone number and the account number. "One more thing… Give this number to Dieter." He recited the number of the phone he was using. "And don't even think about giving it to the authorities. Remember…I'll know if you try to take me down."

Richard started to say something else, but the line went dead in his ear. He frowned, then disconnected. He would know soon enough if Borden was going to come through. Just as he dropped the cell phone into his pocket, he heard someone call out. It took a few moments for him to recognize the name he was going by. He stood up and waved, then shouldered his bag and shuffled off to the pier, where a small boat had just moored.

He climbed aboard, and within half an hour, he and the little fishing boat were out of sight.

Paul Borden wasn't the only one of Richard Ponte's acquaintances who was in turmoil. Paolo Gianni was furious that he'd been duped and, at the same time, scared he would wind up being charged with aiding and abetting a traitor. He'd made a frantic call to his lawyer, who'd agreed that Paolo needed to make a big deal out of this and play the victim along with Ponte's daughter, Alicia. By the time the latest news of Ponte's actions had hit the airwaves, the CIA had become involved. Agents all over the world were on alert. Photos of Richard Ponte were circulating in every police department around the globe.

Paolo had used every ounce of acting chops he had to play the wronged friend, and it had worked. He'd cooperated fully with the authorities, bringing in his pilot and the flight plans for every stop along the way. His claim of being duped passed muster, in part because at the time of Richard's request, the world still thought that Alicia Ponte was a kidnap victim, and believing she'd been taken out of the country was logical.

Meanwhile, Paul Borden had taken several days' leave from the office and driven up the coast to Georgia. After a frustrating afternoon trying to get an audience with a county judge, he'd finally been able to make his case. Like Paolo, Borden played the ignorance card, insisting that Dieter Bahn had believed that his boss's daughter had been kidnapped. So when he'd located Alicia at Nightwalker's residence, he had been acting on the assumption that he was "saving" her, not endangering her life. Given everything the authorities now knew about Richard Ponte, the judge was convinced.

Paul was sick to his stomach at what he'd done. But, as he'd promised, he had one last thing to do for Richard Ponte. He was waiting outside the jail in Justice when Dieter was released from custody and rushed forward to shake Borden's hand.

Instead of returning the greeting, Borden slapped a piece of paper in Dieter's palm.

"Know this," he said. "As of this moment, all connections between Borden and Wheaton Law and the Ponte empire have been severed."

Dieter frowned as he looked down at the paper Borden had given him.

"What's this?" he asked.

"Ponte's number," Borden muttered. "But if I were you, I'd throw it away and run for my life."

Then he turned away and headed for his car.

"Hey. Wait. What about me?" Dieter said.

Paul looked back, then shrugged. "You're a big boy. Figure it out on your own."

Then he got in his car and headed back to Miami as fast as he could go.

Dieter cursed, then started walking down the street toward the impound yard. He knew where it was from the first time he'd been jailed in Justice. He glanced down at the phone number the lawyer had given him, then slipped it into his pocket. Right now, he needed to get out of this chickenshit town before something else happened. After that, he would decide if he wanted to ride this out with his boss or do as Borden had suggested and simply disappear. The only problem was, he knew his boss well enough to know that running away from someone like him was next to impossible.

Part of Jacob Carruthers' deal with the U.S. government was that he'd waived his right to trial and would be shipped straight to federal prison. He was, at the present moment, sitting in the county jail awaiting the U.S. marshals who were en route to escort him. He'd tried, through his lawyer, to contact his children, but they'd refused to speak to him. It was nothing more than what he'd expected.

For the past seven hours he'd been in this cell, listening to the catcalls from the other inmates, hearing their curses and jeers as they took turns telling him in colorful terms what would happen to him once he was inside.

Part of him felt betrayed by the way Richard had left him behind, but when he wanted to be indignant and self-righteous, he was reminded that he'd given up his rights to be any such thing. So he sat on the cot, staring at the bars before him and knowing he wasn't strong enough to survive this—knowing he didn't care enough to try.

"Hey, traitor…my cousin is in Iraq getting fucked over by what you did. Watch your back, 'cause when I get a chance, I'm gonna fuck *you*."

Jacob winced. The voice was harsh, the promise ugly. He felt the contents of his belly roll and knew he was going to be sick. He bolted up from the cot and made it to the toilet just in time.

The sounds of his retching could be heard up and down the cell block, which only increased the shouts and catcalls. By the time Jacob had puked himself to nothing but gagging, he managed to pull himself together and staggered back to his cot, where he threw himself down, belly first.

As he did, his pants caught on the corner of the metal frame. When he heard them rip, his first instinct was regret; then he remembered he wasn't wearing designer clothing anymore. The county had furnished these, and they probably had more.

He rolled over onto his back and closed his eyes, and as he did, an idea began to form. If the corner of his cot was sharp enough to tear fabric, flesh would be a no-brainer. He moved to a sitting position, then bent over to study the metal frame. The end had rusted, which had caused the mitered corner to separate, leaving two sharp edges. In the grand scheme of things, it was nothing much. But it wouldn't take much for what was going through his mind.

Without giving himself time to think, he got down on his knees and shoved his wrist back and forth across that point with every ounce of strength he had. The pain was staggering, but he bore it with stoic silence, determined to be the master of his fate.

As expected, the metal ripped through flesh and veins in short order. Blood gushed, then, with every beat of his heart, began to pulse from the wound. He shifted position and did the same thing with his other wrist, but by then an odd sense of euphoria had kicked in. He watched the blood flowing as freely from that wrist as it was from the other. All of a sudden, it dawned on him that if the blood ran out from beneath the bars, it would give away what he'd done. After all this, he didn't want to be saved.

He pulled himself up and crawled onto the bunk. He blocked out the pain as he rolled over on his belly, pinning his arms beneath himself and using the cot as a sponge to absorb the blood. Within a couple of minutes, he began to feel faint. Instead of fighting it, he just closed his eyes.

"God forgive me," he whispered.

The last thing he heard was an inmate cursing.

Corbin Woodliff was at the newspaper pounding out a follow-up piece on Ponte when his phone rang. He finished his sentence, then grabbed the phone and held it against his ear with his shoulder as he continued to type.

"Woodliff."

"Carruthers is dead."

Corbin dropped the phone as his fingers stumbled on the keys, leaving him with a whole line of typos. He grabbed the phone and repositioned it against his ear.

"Joshua?"

Special Agent Joshua affirmed Corbin's question. "Yes, it's me."

"What the hell happened?" Corbin asked, as he shuffled beneath the files stacked on his desk, searching for a pen and paper to take notes.

"Suicide in the county jail before he could be transported."

"Why wasn't he on suicide watch?" Corbin asked.

"I don't know that he wasn't," Joshua said. "Bottom line is, he ripped his wrists open on a corner of his cot and bled out. They found him about an hour ago."

"Will his testimony hold?"

"Oh yeah, although it might not be necessary. Without going into details, the files we've confiscated reveal way more than anything we've been told so far."

"You mean Ponte was stupid enough to keep records?"

"I know it's strange, but we often find that's the case. I think powerful men often believe they can't be brought down."

"This keeps getting weirder and weirder," Corbin said, then added, "Is any of this off the record?"

"If it was, I wouldn't have made the call."

"Anything else you can tell me?"

"No."

"Then I thank you," Corbin said, and hung up the phone before heading for his editor's office. He knocked, then entered. In two long strides, he was at his boss's desk.

"Boss…I've always wanted to say this."

Sam Frost looked up. "Say what?"

"Stop the presses."

Frost frowned. "They aren't running. Besides, I think you've said that before."

"Damn," Corbin said, then rubbed his hands together. "Are you ready for this?"

Frost's frown quickly switched to an expression of interest. "Talk to me."

"Jacob Carruthers committed suicide in his jail cell."

"Are you serious?"

Corbin nodded.

Frost picked up the phone and called down to printing. "We're running a new headline. You'll have the piece in…" He looked at Corbin, waiting for him to jump in with a timeline.

"An hour," Corbin said, thinking of all the research he was going to have to do to fill out the piece announcing the incongruous end of a powerful man's life.

"Forty-five minutes," Frost countered.

Corbin rolled his eyes, then headed back to his desk. He saved the story he'd been writing to be run another day, then picked up the phone and dialed the paper's morgue. Maggie Summers, the woman who was in charge of it, had been there almost longer than Corbin had been alive. She didn't cave in to threats or begging, but there was a crack in her armor. Maggie had a thing for chocolate. He knew this was going to cost him a big box of Godiva, but it would be worth it.

"Maggie…it's Corbin. I need everything you have on Jacob Carruthers…family, education, hometown, etcetera. You know the drill."

"When do you need it?" she asked.

"Now."

She laughed.

"I'm serious," he said.

"So am I," she fired back.

"Two pounds' worth," he offered, and felt like a bidder at an auction.

"Five, and make sure it's—"

"I know, I know. Godiva."

"Yessss," Maggie said, drawing out the word until it sounded like a hiss.

"You do know you're a chocolate whore."

Maggie snorted. "And you, at the moment, are my pimp. Now shut up and leave me alone. I'll have your info in fifteen minutes."

"Ten," Corbin bartered.

"Nuts only, no nougat centers. I don't like nougat," she countered.

He cursed.

She disconnected.

The deal was done.

John was in the kitchen making himself an omelet. He had the television turned on for background noise as he mixed, chopped and sautéed. He wasn't paying it much attention until he heard the announcement that a news bulletin was about to be broadcast.

He took the skillet off the burner and turned to face the screen as the news anchor came on.

"This just in…Jacob Carruthers, one of the men recently charged with treason, has been found dead in his jail cell. Early reports state he managed to cut his wrists on a jagged piece of metal and bled out before he was found. At this point, we have no new news on his partner and accomplice, Richard Ponte, who escaped the FBI's dragnet. In an ironic twist of fate, both men have managed to escape the justice system of the United States."

John turned off the burner and reached for the phone. He'd been planning to call Woodliff all evening, and now he had to. The phone rang four times before it was answered and when John heard Corbin's voice, he could tell the man was distracted.

"Corbin…it's John. What's going on?"

Corbin sighed. "Just what you would imagine."

"This is getting crazy. Ponte skipped, and now Carruthers is out of the picture, too. Please tell me the Feds didn't need Carruthers to confirm the charges against Ponte."

"No. They've got everything they need except the man himself. On another note…where are you? How is Miss Ponte holding up?"

"I heard the news earlier…that Paolo Gianni was conned and that's how Ponte got out of the country," John said.

Corbin sighed. Nightwalker wasn't going to answer his question. Under the circumstances, he could understand why.

"Yeah, well, Ponte must've conned someone else, too, because the last I heard, Dieter Bahn is out of jail."

John froze. "What? Why? Since when do they dismiss attempted murder charges so quickly and without a trial?"

"As I understand it, the case was made to the judge that Bahn was acting under the impression that his boss's daughter had been kidnapped, so when he found her, he believed you were the kidnapper and acted accordingly."

"That's bullshit! He knew Alicia was running, and he knew why."

"Yeah, well, some high-powered lawyer from Miami tap-danced around the story, and the judge bought it."

John had been worried before. This upped the ante. Ponte was out of the country, but his right-hand man was free.

"I don't suppose you're going to tell me what's going on at your end?" Corbin asked.

"I don't suppose," John said.

"Come on. You at least owe me the end of the story," Corbin finally said.

"There is no end of the story yet…may never be an end that she can live with."

"Is she okay?"

John hesitated, then thought about how far away from okay Alicia was.

"Without going into details, I would ask you to remember her when you pray."

Corbin's pulse jumped. "What's wrong?"

"About as much as could be wrong without buying her a burial plot."

"Christ Almighty, John. What happened?"

"According to the old man who treated her…she hasn't yet decided if she wants to live."

Now Corbin was sorry he'd been flippant. "My God. I'm sorry. Is there anything I can do from my end?"

"Just push them to find Richard Ponte. If he isn't brought into custody, even if she manages to survive, her life won't be worth living."

Twenty-four hours and several countries later, Richard Ponte had reached his final destination: a three-story chalet that looked like an oversize version of a

Black Forest cuckoo clock. It was in a part of East
Germany that would once have been out of bounds for
anyone who wasn't a citizen. But much had changed
since the Berlin Wall had come down. Richard Ponte's
contacts were on the western side of the border, but his
alter ego, Anton Schloss, had owned this chalet for just
over five years, even though he'd only been here twice.
The man and woman who lived on the premises now
had never met him in person, so when he arrived, they
were excited to show off all they'd accomplished.

"Herr Schloss…welcome," Helga said as she opened
the door to Richard's knock.

The fact that his head was shorn and he was growing
a beard meant nothing to her. For all she knew, he'd
always looked this way.

Richard nodded. "It is good to be here."

"I hope you will be staying for a while," she said.

"Indefinitely," Richard responded.

Helga beamed as her husband came hurrying into the
hall. "Gustav, carry Herr Schloss's bag to his room."

"No…there are some papers I want to put in the safe
first," Richard said. "But I *am* hungry."

Helga's smile widened. "But of course," she said. "I
made apple kuchen and bratwurst when you called to
say you were coming. You let me know when you are
ready to dine."

"A change of clothes and a wash, and I'll be down,"
Richard said.

Helga shooed her husband away and hurried to the
kitchen.

Richard didn't breathe easy until he'd unlocked the
wall safe, making sure the other set of identification

papers was still inside. And they *were*—just as he'd left them, with a single piece of white thread from the inside of the coat he'd been wearing lying on top of the stack, proof that no one had been in the safe since his last visit. He put his money and papers inside and locked them down, then turned to survey the room.

The place was pretty much as he remembered, with the repairs he'd requested well in place. The elaborate carvings in the ceiling were no longer covered in dust and spiderwebs, and although it wasn't the season for it, logs had been laid in the massive rock fireplace, ready to be lit at the master's whim. He inhaled slowly, smelling beeswax and lemon polish, and caught himself listening for the sound of his daughter's footsteps. Then he remembered and looked away. Richard Ponte's life was over because of his daughter. Anton Schloss had no children, and it was better that way.

Within the hour, he was in the dining room, supping on his favorite German beer, fresh rye bread, hot bratwurst and slices of white cheese dappled with caraway seeds. He ate with relish, while making sure he saved room for the apple kuchen Helga had left on the sideboard.

A short while later, he'd retired for the evening and was in his room readying for bed when his cell phone began to ring. His pulse leaped. The only person who could be calling would be either Paul Borden, telling him he'd failed, or Dieter Bahn, telling him he was out.

As he answered, it dawned on him that he was actually nervous as to who was on the other end of the line.

"Hello?"

"Boss, it's me."

A big smile began to spread across Richard's face. "Dieter. I knew you wouldn't let me down."

"No, sir."

"Where are you calling from?"

"A pay phone at a bus stop."

"Do you have any idea where Alicia is?" Richard asked.

"No, sir. But I do have some news."

"What?" Richard asked.

"Jacob Carruthers is dead."

Shock spread slowly, numbing Richard's tongue and thoughts to the point that he couldn't find the words to ask how. Luckily, Dieter was forthcoming on his own. "He committed suicide in his jail cell. But not before he made a statement. I heard on the news that he'd traded you for life in prison. Only that doesn't make sense, boss. Why would he make that deal and then kill himself?"

Richard felt sick and, for the first time, ashamed. He'd left Jacob behind, and this was what had happened. Everything was coming undone, and it was all Alicia's fault. If she had just listened, he could have made her understand. She didn't know what it was like to be poor—to be laughed at for the way you looked and the way you lived. He'd given her everything, and this was how she'd repaid him. Poor Jacob.

He swallowed past the knot in his throat and then took a deep breath. This only reinforced his intent. If it took the rest of his life, he was going to find Alicia. He wanted to hear her beg. He wanted her to admit she was wrong. And then he would render his own brand of justice.

"Get a pen and paper," he ordered.

"Okay, boss, just a minute," Dieter said, and began digging through his pockets.

Richard waited, thinking about what had to be done, and remembering where and how he'd learned it. Growing up on an Iowa hog farm, he'd watched his father sort through the new litters, culling out the sickly and deformed. He'd always claimed it was for the best, that only the strongest should survive. And no matter how distasteful a task it had been, he'd made Richard help him throw them into the boar's pen to be eaten alive. Always for the best, his father had said. Always for the best.

And now Richard had fathered an imperfect daughter, one who did not know the meaning of familial loyalty. One who was faulty, imperfect in Richard's eyes. Letting her get away with destroying him wasn't an option. But he had to do this the right way, and with Dieter's help, he would—as always—succeed.

"Okay, boss, I'm ready," Dieter said.

"Perfect," Richard said. "Here's what I want you to do first."

Dieter listened carefully, then began to write.

Ten

Alicia wasn't present anymore. Her body was right where John had put it, but who she was had gone into hiding, just as her father had done. The allergic reaction to the scorpion's sting had been the last shock she'd been able to take. She did not react to stimuli or sound or hunger. It had been twelve hours since the incident, but it might as well have been an eternity. She had no concept of the past or her present. She'd gone AWOL in the most literal sense, and the only person left on this earth who cared was her father's worst enemy.

The whale sounded, spewing through its blow-hole in a most spectacular way. The village children shrieked and pointed, laughing and squealing, then mimicking the action by spewing water at each other.

White Fawn watched the children's antics from her seat by the fire, all the while making sure the fish she was smoking wasn't too close to the flames. It was a constant heartache that she had not been able to give Night Walker any sons of his own. Every warrior wanted sons, but because of her, he had none. Despite the fact that he had never blamed her, or berated her for her failure, she felt the shame.

A spark popped out of the fire and onto her moccasin. She sighed as she absently brushed it away, unaware that her husband was watching her from the other side of the clearing.

He knew his woman as he knew himself. She was gentle to a fault, loving to all in the village, and held in high esteem for her sewing skills. Of all the warriors in the village, Night Walker's ceremonial garments were always the most striking. The skills with which she utilized porcupine quills, delicate shells and the tiny beads she fashioned from animal bones was unlike any other's. He loved her more than his own life and grieved for her sadness in her inability to bear a child. But he would not trade a night in her arms for a dozen sons. She was the reason he drew breath, the single thing that gave his life joy. He shook off the moment of contemplation as he continued readying for the hunt, and was about to leave with the other men who were gathering when he saw her throw her head back and laugh.

The sound pierced the sadness within him, causing him to look for the source of her joy. Then he saw that a young puppy, one of the village dogs, had stolen a huge bone from one of the older dogs that had wandered off to sleep. The puppy was trying to run with the big bone in its little mouth. But every time the puppy tried to run forward, the bone slipped and jammed itself into the ground, throwing the puppy backward to the point that it was losing more ground than it was gaining.

He grinned. It was a funny sight. But it was the smile on White Fawn's face that brought the joy to his heart. One of the other warriors called out to him. He was turning to leave when suddenly a gust of wind rose out of nowhere and blew smoke into his line of vision. He waited for it to pass, but it only seemed to grow thicker. He tried to step out of it, but everywhere he walked, it was there. He couldn't see White Fawn any longer, or anyone in the village, but he could still hear her voice—only she was no longer laughing. She was crying and calling his name. Even though he couldn't see where he was going, he began to run. But the faster he ran, the thicker the smoke became, and no matter how fast he moved, he couldn't seem to find his way out. Suddenly a huge gust of wind blew again, clearing the vista before him. In that moment, he felt a piece of himself die.

She was gone. The village was gone. The children, the puppy with the bone…gone. Night Walker was alone. Fear spread through him like a wave washing onto the shore, enveloping him in devastation. He turned in a circle, searching for a sign—praying that this was only a bad dream from which he would wake. He began shouting her

name, calling for White Fawn over and over, until
nothing came out but a scream.

The scream that came out of John's own mouth
was what woke him. He was out of his bed and halfway down the hall, stark naked, before he realized
he'd been dreaming—before he remembered that he
could run for eternity and never find her. He was now
the lost one.

He reached for the wall to steady himself, and as he
did, he heard a sound behind him.

He spun.

She was standing a few feet away, as naked as he was,
a dark silhouette in an even darker hall.

His heart hit a beat so hard that he lost his breath.

"John? What's wrong?"

He exhaled a slow, shaky breath. At least one woman
had returned to the land of the living. He moved toward
her on bare feet, wanting to test the temperature of her
skin, anxious to reassure himself that this wasn't just
another dream.

He slipped his hands beneath the thick fall of her hair,
pulling it away from her face and then cupping the back
of her neck.

"So…you decided to come back," he said softly.

The touch of his hands on her bare body was dis-
turbing enough, but it was the tone of his voice that
drew her in.

"What do you mean…I came back? I didn't go
anywhere."

Despite the fact that they were both without clothing,
he pulled her into his arms. For a moment he allowed

himself the luxury of the embrace, laying his cheek against her hair, then rubbing her back with slow, sensuous strokes.

"You went far, far away, Alicia. I didn't think you were coming back. I thought you would die."

Die? If he didn't turn her loose, she thought, she might die from a sudden attack of lust. Other than that, she didn't know what he was talking about.

Suddenly she remembered. "The scorpion!"

He nodded as he swept his fingers along the curve of her face and neck, feeling for signs of fever. There were none.

"I'm allergic," she said.

"Now you tell me," John said.

"How did you—"

"Don't ask," he said. "You wouldn't believe me anyway. Suffice it to say you scared the hell out of me."

"I seriously doubt that," she said, and then suddenly felt embarrassed, so she crossed her arms over her breasts in an effort to cover them.

"Are you okay? Are you hungry? Thirsty? I can—"

Alicia shook her head. "I'm okay. I feel sort of weird, but I'm okay."

John took her by the arm and led her back into her bedroom. "You need to lie down. I know you're still shaky, even if you won't admit it. You've been unconscious for over twelve hours."

Alicia let herself be tucked back into bed and then watched him as he moved around the room, fussing with her covers, adjusting the flow of the air conditioner, refilling her glass with water, until he was making her nuts.

"You aren't wearing any clothes," she muttered.

He was standing at the foot of her bed when she made her announcement.

"Neither are you."

Alicia decided to change the subject. "Why were you calling?"

"I just…I had a bad dream, that's all."

Alicia frowned, then shook her head. "I think I was dreaming before, too. What was yours about?"

He didn't try to explain himself. There was never a way to explain. But he was grateful for the sound of her voice as he listened to her talk, feeling thankful that she hadn't given up on living after all.

"You know how goofy dreams can be," Alicia said. "They always seem so real and logical while you're in them…but when you wake up, nothing about them makes sense." She put her hands beneath her head and then shifted to a more comfortable spot. "This one felt so real. I was sitting by a fire, cooking fish." She laughed once, so softly he almost didn't hear it. "Which proves it was a dream, because we both know I can't cook."

John was too shocked to speak. He kept staring at her face, watching the words come out of her mouth and telling himself that what she was saying meant nothing.

"In the dream, a puppy was playing with a bone that was too big for him, and I was laughing so hard. Then I heard you shouting. I called back, telling you that I was right there. But you kept shouting and shouting, as if you couldn't see or hear me. So I began to get up from the fire to go see what you wanted, but it felt like my legs wouldn't work."

John shuddered. He wanted her to stop talking. He couldn't think about this. She didn't belong in his dreams. They were all he had left.

"Finally, I managed to get up from the fire, and when I did, the dream was gone and it was just me getting up out of bed. You ran past my room shouting my name. So I came out to see what was wrong."

"You heard me…calling your name?"

She nodded.

"*Your* name?"

Alicia frowned, then suddenly pushed back the covers and sat up, unconscious of the fact that she'd just bared herself to him again.

"No. No. Actually, that wasn't what you were saying." She shoved her fingers through her hair, wishing for something to tie it back, because it was hot against her neck. "I guess I must have still been half-asleep when I got out of bed. You were calling a name, but not mine. I guess I got confused because it was me you were calling for in the dream. The dream me, not me in this bed. I told you dreams were crazy."

John needed to walk out of the room right now, but he couldn't leave without knowing.

"What do you mean, it was you in the dream, not you in the bed?"

She laughed.

His fingers curled around the bedposts. Their laughter was nothing alike. This meant nothing. He was making a big deal out of nothing.

"That did sound crazy, didn't it?" Alicia said. "What I meant was…in the dream, I wasn't me. My name wasn't Alicia. That's what I meant."

"What was your name?"

"Oh, something Indian. It's probably because of you and all the stuff in your house."

Something Indian. *Okay,* he told himself. *Let it go. Don't push. It doesn't mean anything. It can't. Yeah, right. Then why was she dreaming my dream?*

Even while John was giving himself the big let-it-go speech, his mouth was opening and the words were coming right on out.

"Exactly what 'something Indian' are we talking about?" he asked.

"I'm sorry. I didn't mean for that to sound condescending, I swear," Alicia said.

"Alicia, I'm very glad you're no longer unconscious. And I'm very glad that you didn't die. But I swear to your God, that if you don't answer my question, I am going to—"

Alicia threw up her hands. "White Fawn. For pity's sake…my name was White Fawn. Now go on. Laugh yourself silly. I know that sounds like a Hollywood version of the traditional Indian maiden bit, but I didn't make it up. In my dream, that was my name."

John reeled as if he'd been slapped, then backed away from her bed as if she'd turned into a witch.

"Go to sleep," he said.

She flopped back down and pulled up the covers, grumbling beneath her breath.

"Happy to oblige. But if you want people to be quiet, you need to look to yourself first. Running naked all over the place and yelling out crazy names."

John pulled himself together by sheer will and was almost out the door when she spoke again.

"Hey! Wait a minute!" she called. "Why were you shouting that name out in the hall?"

"I told you…I was having a bad dream," he said. "Go back to sleep."

Alicia frowned. "You were dreaming about a woman named White Fawn? The same woman *I* was dreaming about?"

He sighed. "Yes."

"That's a little weird," she said.

"Not to me," he replied.

"But…"

John gritted his teeth. "In the name of all that's holy, woman…let it go."

"Who is White Fawn?" Alicia pressed.

He looked away, wanting her to shut up and knowing she wouldn't until she got an answer. "The woman in the painting… She's the woman in the painting."

"But I thought that woman was your—"

One minute John Nightwalker had been in her doorway, and now he was gone. Alicia frowned. "For pity's sake," she complained. "You want all your questions answered ASAP, but just let me ask a question, and you go and pull the silent act on me. Fine."

She lay down again and pulled the covers back up, still fuming about the way he'd made his exit when it hit her. Yes, she'd seen the painting, but she hadn't known the woman's name. So how had she stumbled on that exact name in her dream?

She rolled over onto her side and closed her eyes. It was stupid trying to make sense of a dream. Besides, she'd probably heard him say the name before and just forgotten. Within a few minutes, she had fallen back to sleep.

For John, sleep was over.

As Alicia slept, he put on a pair of sweats and went into the kitchen. It was almost four in the morning. Might as well make some coffee.

The scent of the freshly ground beans permeated the room as he measured grounds and water and then slid the carafe onto the burner and punched Start. When the coffee began flowing into the carafe, he turned away and moved to the windows.

There was already a change in the density of the darkness toward the east. He didn't think about how many thousands of mornings he'd watched this happening. He was still trying to combat the shock of what Alicia had said. It had knocked him so far off center that his head was spinning. For all he knew, the Old Ones were messing with him. Suddenly he pivoted and strode quickly through his home, heading for the portrait. The house was dark, but he navigated it easily. He wanted—needed—to be near her. He had to see for himself that there was nothing about them that was alike.

The display light over the painting was the only light in the room. Entering in the dark to see her face—so alive that he could almost hear her breathing—was a physical pain. He stared at her from across the room, studying the shape of her eyes, the curve of her mouth, the widow's peak dip in her hairline, searching for anything that reminded him of Alicia Ponte. There was nothing.

Momentarily satisfied that he'd made a big deal out of nothing, he started to walk away when he remembered: Richard Ponte looked nothing like the Spaniard who'd destroyed his world, and yet he knew in his soul that they were one and the same.

He told himself that if he was able to feel the soul of his enemy, he would certainly also recognize the other half of his heart. Disgusted with himself and his flight of fancy, he stalked back to the kitchen, poured himself a cup of the freshly brewed coffee, disarmed the security system and walked out onto the terrace to wait for morning.

Richard had been waiting for a call from Dieter for more than twenty-four hours. He needed as much information as Dieter could get on the state of the case against him. He wanted details from the news and anything they reported about his daughter. He'd also put Dieter in contact with a man who could find just about anyone on the planet if they were still alive. One way or another, he would face his daughter one last time.

On top of everything else, he needed to get rid of this cell phone, but he couldn't discard it until he'd given Dieter the new number he wanted him to use, and he couldn't do *that* until the man called back.

At least the past twelve hours had been fruitful in another way. He'd reconnected with the business world in a big way. As Anton Schloss, he manufactured tires in Germany and was the absentee owner of a lucrative ski lodge in the Swiss Alps. His beard was longer now, and neatly clipped. He shaved his head daily, and had purchased a whole new wardrobe befitting his status.

In two days he would be traveling to Switzerland for reconstructive surgery. During the time of his convalescence, Richard Ponte was going to meet with a very violent and untimely death. After that, no one would be looking for him, and he would be able to move about the world with comfort and ease. And that was when payback would begin.

* * *

A day had passed since Alicia's awakening. She had recovered completely and was back to her old acerbic self, pushing at boundaries John didn't want breached, asking questions he had no intention of answering. She seemed determined to get to the bottom of what made him tick, and he was just as determined to ignore her.

He had been in his office for the better part of three hours. Twice she had found a reason to walk past, and each time, he'd either been online or talking on the phone. From the bits and pieces of conversations she'd overheard, it was business as usual for him. He was giving orders to import a new shipment of brass and copper pots from India, then bargaining with some middleman to double his order of Native American blankets and jewelry into Great Britain.

It gave her insight into where he got his money, but it didn't do anything for her peace of mind. And his work ethic only brought home to her how shallow her own life had been. Her social calendar had always been full of one event or another that she needed to attend— sometimes on her father's behalf, sometimes as a pet project of her own, but as she spent time with John, it had become painfully clear that without the auspices of her father's power and notoriety, her life had no meaning. She didn't have a job other than to play decorative hostess. She didn't have close friends, only acquaintances with whom she shared lunches and committees. And except for a college boyfriend, there'd been only one other man in her life, and that had been years ago. She'd had the occasional interlude, but nothing lasting beyond four or five dates. She'd never thought about why, but now the question kept coming back to haunt her.

John Nightwalker still grieved for the woman in the painting.

She wanted someone to love her like that.

She wanted John, but knowing her father had been responsible for his family's deaths made pursing a relationship with him an impossible dream. He would never see her as anything but the spawn of his own private devil.

Alicia awakened the next morning with a plan. It was time to rethink her existence, but living in this cocoon with a man who didn't like her was making it difficult to broaden the range of her skills. Still, she could start small, and one thing she could do was learn how to cook. Everyone needed to know how to feed themselves. It was embarrassing that she could not.

She prowled through the library looking for some kind of cookbook without success, then gave herself a mental thump on the head when she found several on a shelf in the kitchen. Where else should a cookbook be? She pulled a couple off the shelf, then took them and a soda to an easy chair in the living room. The terminology and preparations were mind-boggling. She wasn't even sure how to pronounce them, let alone perform them. But it wasn't long before she was completely absorbed.

It was the quiet that finally soaked into John's consciousness. Too much quiet. He glanced at his watch and tried to remember how long it had been since he'd seen or heard Alicia. Immediately, his instinct to protect went into gear. He saved his work, then got up and started his search.

The first place he went was her bedroom, but after knocking and receiving no answer, he looked in to find the room empty. He then went from the library to the living room. It wasn't until he'd paused there that he realized he could smell something cooking.

That in itself was shocking. He headed for the kitchen, trying not to run.

She was at the sink, her long hair pulled up in a ponytail, wearing white shorts and a simple yellow cotton shirt, untucked. Her feet and legs were bare. Steam was rising from a pot bubbling on the stove, and there were at least a half-dozen dirty bowls and pans scattered across the counter.

He knew what she looked like naked, but damned if she didn't look almost as good like this. That she was cooking was a shock. He didn't know what had prompted it, but he gave her a mental high-five for the effort.

"Hey," he said softly.

Alicia looked over her shoulder and grinned when she saw him. "I'm making dinner."

He glanced at his watch again. "It's ten after three in the afternoon."

"I know…but I didn't know how long it would take. I'm not exactly a pro at this, you know."

He stifled a smile as he walked up beside her, then noticed she'd suffered a few battle wounds in the process. One hand was sporting Band-Aids on three fingers, while her other had a Band-Aid on the thumb.

"What happened?" he asked, pointing.

"Um…" She nodded toward a bowl of potato peelings, which, when he looked closer, had a good quarter inch of potato on each spiral. "Peeling potatoes is harder than it looks."

He took the knife out of her hands, laid it aside and turned her hands palms up. She'd also managed to slice a thin flake of skin from the area above her left wrist. The blood had dried, but not before leaving a smear on her chin and another on the hem of her shirt.

"I know…it looks like I went to war, not the kitchen," she said, suddenly embarrassed by her lack of skill.

"Poor little fingers," he said softly, and couldn't help thinking of how adept White Fawn had been with nothing but a thin piece of flint. "But an A-plus for effort."

Alicia beamed.

Man…she did have her moments. That smile was a heartbreaker. "So…we're having potatoes."

"Oh…that's not all," she said. "I'm boiling eggs…and making toast."

He grinned, then glanced at the pot on the stove. There were four eggs on the boil, but with less than an inch of water in the pan.

"Er…uh…about how long do you think those eggs have been boiling?"

She frowned, then glanced up at the clock over the stove. "Maybe thirty minutes."

"They're done," he said, and turned the burner off under the pan.

"Oh…well…okay," Alicia said, and pointed to the potatoes she had chopped up in a bowl. They'd been there long enough that they were starting to turn a little brown, but he knew from experience that wouldn't change the flavor. And he wasn't going to complain about a thing. "I'm going to cook those next," she said.

He also wasn't going to point out that timing was all-important in a kitchen. So her hard-boiled eggs were probably going to be rubbery. There had been hundreds of times in his life when he would have killed for a rubbery egg.

"How are you going to cook the potatoes?" he asked.

She pointed to another pot. "In that." She dumped the chopped bits of raw potato into the pan, and then put it on the stove and fired up the burner.

"So…what are we going for here?" John asked. "Boiled or fried?"

She looked a little puzzled. "What difference does it make? What am I missing?"

"They'll need a little something to keep them from sticking. If you boil them, you'll need salted water. If you fry them, you'll need a skillet and some hot oil in the bottom first."

She frowned. "Oh. Well…what's your favorite?"

"I'm a big fan of fried anything."

"Then fried it is," she said, and took the pan off the stove, then looked up at the pot rack above the stove. "John?"

"Yeah?"

"Which one should I use?"

He reached up and took one down for her without moving a facial muscle. "Oil is in the pantry."

"Pantry. Right," she said, and turned in a circle without going anywhere.

"Want some help?" he asked.

"No…no…I've got it," she said.

"Then I'll leave you to it," he said, and started backing out when all he wanted to do was pick her up, put her gorgeous backside up on that counter and lose himself in the V between those long shapely legs.

"One last thing," Alicia said.

"Yeah?"

"Where's the pantry?"

He pointed to a door on the other side of the room.

"Right," she said, and waved him away with her bandaged fingers.

He couldn't watch any longer without giving himself away. All the way back to his office, he knew he was getting in trouble. Something had changed when he thought she was dying. The thought of never hearing her give him hell again had scared him. She was as aggravating as a woman could be, but she was beginning to grow on him. Even worse, he was starting to want more from her than her father's present location.

He bypassed his office and went outside, needing to put more than a few yards between them. He hadn't been outside for more than a few minutes when he began hearing a familiar sound. His house was in the direct flight line to Sedona, so planes often flew over, although usually high enough that he was only peripherally aware of them. This one sounded lower. He turned in a slow circle, searching the sky until he located it. It looked like an old crop duster, only there were no crops out here needing dusting. There was also the fact that it was too low to be following a normal flight plan. This felt like a scouting expedition.

John spun on one heel and ran for the house. He'd left the front door slightly ajar, and he hit it with the flat of his hand as he ran. It flew inward, hitting the wall with a thud as he ran to get his binoculars. He wanted a good look at that plane, and maybe even who was in it.

Alicia heard the commotion and came out of the kitchen, wiping her hands on a towel.

"What's going on?" she asked.

"Maybe nothing," John said. "But don't go outside, and stay away from the windows."

He hated putting fear back on her face, but staying alive often involved a whole lot of fear. He grabbed the binoculars from a hook on the inside of a closet door and then ran for the kitchen. The windows were smaller there, affording whoever was up there less of a view, but still large enough for his purpose.

Alicia had crouched down inside the hall with her hands over her head. He could hear her praying as he ran past but didn't have time to reassure her. He got to the window, lifted the binoculars and waited for the plane to go over. If it didn't mean anything, they would keep flying. But if they were looking for something—or someone—special, they would turn and circle back.

As expected, the plane buzzed the house, low enough to be able to distinguish the camo covering on the chopper. He watched as it continued on, still low, but still moving away. Then, just when he thought he'd made a big deal out of nothing, the plane suddenly banked.

He cursed beneath his breath.

"John? Are they gone?"

"They're coming back."

"Dear God," Alicia whispered.

"If I tell you to run, head for my room," he said. "There's a small door in the back of my closet. It leads to what amounts to a storm shelter. Get in there, and don't come out unless you hear my voice."

She didn't answer.

"Alicia…did you hear me?"

"I'm scared."

"I know, baby," he said.

It was the gentle tone of his voice and the tender word he'd said without thought that calmed her soul. Whatever was going to happen would happen. She was just thankful she didn't have to face it alone.

The plane was retracing its route exactly.

"So…you want a look at what's under that cover, don't you?" he muttered.

He adjusted the binocular sights. Just a little bit closer and he would be able to see their faces.

Eleven

There was a reason why Sam Watkins could set his own fees. He never failed.

When Dieter Bahn had called him about a job, he'd asked one question. "Who's the subject?"

"Alicia Ponte."

Sam considered himself a man who kept up with current events. After all, it was usually in his best interests to know what was going on, so when he heard the name Ponte, alarms went off all over. There was only one person who would want Alicia Ponte dead, and that was the man she'd given up to the Feds. For a moment Sam was speechless. He knew who Bahn worked for. He was still trying to wrap his mind around the fact that Richard Ponte wanted his own daughter done, when Dieter spoke up.

"There's a problem with this, though."

"There's always a problem," Sam countered. "Talk to me."

"A man named John Nightwalker has taken her underground. Last sighting was in a hotel in Washington, D.C. Nightwalker took out the hit man. Left him on a service cart in a storage room."

"I heard about a body being found, but no one said it was related to a hit on Ponte's daughter."

"That's because no one knows it but her, and for whatever reason, she's not talking."

Sam frowned. That didn't make sense. Why keep something like that a secret? It was something to consider before he decided whether to take the job.

"So…I never did hear the identity of the body they found. Who was it?" Sam asked.

"Joiner."

Sam's gut tightened. Besides himself, Shark Joiner was the best—or at least he *had* been. This meant Nightwalker was not to be underestimated.

"What do you know about Nightwalker?" Sam asked.

"He's Native American, tough as hell, and apparently unstoppable. The rest is your problem."

"Two million…all of it in my account before I take one step on his behalf."

Dieter hit the ceiling, cursing in German and English, and adding in the few Polish curse words he'd learned on the wharf as a young man. When he could talk without screaming, he lit into Sam.

"Don't fuck with me, Watkins. This is serious."

"Don't *you* fuck with *me*. I know who's calling this hit. I know what he's worth, and I know he's number one on America's most wanted list. If he wants his daughter dead, it's gonna cost him. You want the account number to send the money to or are we done?"

"Give me the number," Dieter asked, then wrote it down. "I'll call you back."

"You've got fifteen minutes. After that, I'm history. Do we understand each other?"

Dieter was still cursing when he disconnected. What was worse, now he had to deliver the news to the boss. He dialed the number, holding his breath that Richard would answer and not let the call go to voice mail. Time was of the essence. Even with the deadline looming, when Richard answered, Dieter felt a moment of panic. Revealing Watkins' ultimatum to a man who scared him shitless wasn't easy.

"Yes?" Richard said.

"Boss, I connected, but there's a hitch."

Richard frowned. "I don't like hitches."

"Yes, sir. I know, sir."

"So what is it?"

"He wants two mil or he's gone, and he gave me a fifteen-minute deadline."

"Hell no!" Richard yelled. "You tell him I said—"

"Boss, he's serious, and he's not dealing. It's that or no go."

Richard stifled a shriek of frustration. He was over the proverbial barrel, and the whole fucking world knew it. "Fine. Pay it. Then, when it's done, kill him."

Dieter gasped. "Boss!"

"You heard me," Richard said.

Dieter's gut knotted. "Yes, sir. I heard. Uh…he wants the money wired into his account. Said he won't start looking until it's there."

"What's the number?" Richard asked.

Dieter rattled it off as Richard wrote. He was still fuming when he gave Dieter his last instructions. "This phone number is no longer any good. I'm going to give you a new one. And after we disconnect, get rid of the phone you're using and get a throw-away. I don't want the Feds trying to get to me through you."

"Yes, sir," Dieter said, and took down the new number.

When the line went dead, Dieter flinched. This wasn't the first time he'd wished he'd given Paul Borden's advice more serious consideration. Borden had told him to throw away Ponte's number and run. He should have listened. Now it was too late.

He called Sam Watkins back.

Sam answered on the second ring. "Yeah?"

"Done. But if you fail, you're a dead man."

"I don't fail. Ever," Sam said, and hung up.

That had been two days ago, and now Sam was in the air in an old Piper Cub with a pilot who'd pissed him off within minutes of being airborne. When the plane banked, Sam had hiccuped, which led the pilot to ask if he got airsick and point out a barf bag. Sam had fired back with a none-of-your-fucking-business-just-fly-the-plane look, and thus the flight had begun.

This would be his third site check in two days, and the first he'd had to fly to get to so he could avoid calling too much attention to his presence. As they flew, he did a mental recount of his progress to pass the time.

The starting point for his search had been the hotel in D.C. It was where Alicia Ponte had last been seen in Nightwalker's company. Part of what made Sam Watkins good at what he did was his ability to find where his targets had gone to ground. He knew every trick in the book that involved hiding ownership within other companies: shell companies that didn't really exist, businesses registered in mothers' maiden names. You name it, he'd seen it.

Knowing John Nightwalker most likely owned the Georgia house gave him his first clue. According to county records, that property had belonged to several different corporations over a period of the last hundred years. What was really weird to Sam was that, for over a century, the same name kept cropping up in the corporate records. John Nightwalker.

Lots of families used the same first name, especially for their male children, but what surprised him was that a hundred years ago, there weren't a lot of Native Americans with the financial wherewithal to acquire such properties.

Running a check on one corporation had given him another lead, and then a third and a fourth, but the locations were scattered all over the place. Now he had to do some follow-up, and part of that involved on-site investigation. Because he was certain that if he could find Nightwalker, he would find Alicia Ponte.

"We're almost there," the pilot said, pointing out the window.

Sam could see the Spanish-tile roofline of a house below. Even from the air, it looked huge. Two long wings, one on either side of a large central area. The landscaping was desert-style, with cacti and the occasional large boulder placed in a pleasing alignment with the house. None of it was unusual for this part of the country.

He didn't see a car, but there were several outbuildings, at least one large enough to house a vehicle. He didn't see any people, but that wasn't an indicator of anything. They were long past the days when people would run out of their houses to watch a plane flying over.

"There's a helipad down there," the pilot said, pointing downward. "Got what looks like a chopper under that camo cover."

Sam swiveled in his seat. He knew Nightwalker owned a chopper. He and the Ponte woman had left Georgia for Washington, D.C., in one. His pulse accelerated. Something told him he'd just hit the jackpot.

"Do another flyover," he said.

The pilot nodded and, a few moments later, banked into a right turn for another sweep of the area. Coming at the house from this angle and this low, Sam could tell that the pilot had been right. There was a chopper under that cover.

He grinned to himself as he adjusted his binoculars.

"Gotcha," he said under his breath.

"What did you say?" the pilot asked.

"Nothing. Just take me back to the airport. I've seen all I need to see."

John had seen the pilot but had immediately discarded him as no one of interest. It was the man in the passenger seat who got his attention. The man was using binoculars, too, and seemed far too interested in the chopper. John cursed beneath his breath. Whoever the man was, he had done some serious digging to even know to look for them here. And finding a chopper on property he owned was, more than likely, the cherry on the sundae.

He watched them fly over, then ran to the front window to see if they came back again, but they didn't.

He watched until the plane disappeared beyond the horizon. It wasn't until he went to hang up the binoculars that he realized Alicia was still crouched in the hall.

"You can get up now," he said, and offered her a hand up.

She was shaking as he pulled her to her feet.

"Are they gone?"

"Yes."

"Thank God," she said, and then tried to make light of it. "Probably just sightseers, right?"

"Maybe," John said. It wasn't a lie. There was that thin possibility, although every instinct he had told him the man would be back—and soon.

"I guess I'd better finish dinner," Alicia said.

John grabbed her arm as she started to walk away.

Startled, she stopped, then looked back.

"What?"

"You should be proud of yourself today," he said, looking down at her hands and separating her fingers with his thumb, gently tracing the lifeline on her palm.

Alicia shivered. He was making her so crazy she couldn't think.

"Proud?"

"Yeah…you took on a whole meal by yourself, and that's nothing to ignore."

Alicia beamed in spite of herself. No one had ever praised her for such a simple task.

"Thanks. I just wanted to do my part, you know?"

Her emotions were there on her face for him to see. All he had to do was move and she would be in his arms. But something held him back. He didn't want her, not like this. Not when she was so distracted. If this happened—and he knew it was bound to—he wanted it to be on equal terms.

"So…how about those potatoes?" he asked.

Alicia shivered with sudden longing. Right now, cooking was the last thing on her mind, but his was obviously focused on food.

"Yes, coming right up," she mumbled, and headed for the kitchen. She looked as disappointed as he felt.

John started to follow her, but there were some things he needed to do before it got dark. Before whoever was in that plane had time to come back. And he *would* come back. Of that John was certain.

A short while later they sat down to fried potatoes drowning in grease, hard-boiled eggs so rubbery that if they'd dropped on the floor, he was pretty sure they would have bounced, and toast. It was the oddest meal he'd ever been served, and yet the one that had touched him most. Talk about a woman out of her element, and yet she'd tried.

"Looks great," he said as he seated her first. "I like butter on my toast. How about you?" he asked as he got some from the refrigerator.

"Oh. Yes. I should have thought of that," she said. "And jam. Do you have jam?"

"Coming up," he said, and got a small jar of blackberry preserves from a shelf in the refrigerator door.

As he set it on the table, he couldn't help but remember White Fawn picking blackberries until her fingertips were the same dark purple color, just so she could put them in the ground maize she cooked, knowing it was his favorite.

"I love blackberry," Alicia said. "It's my favorite!"

John was a little taken aback as he sat. He still hadn't forgotten their shared dream the other night. Still, he was convinced it was nothing more than the mysticism of Sedona messing with their minds.

Alicia was so taken with the fact that she'd cooked the food that she didn't seem to notice the excess grease and the chewiness of the eggs. She slathered her toast with butter and jam, licking bits off her bandaged fingers and smiling at him as he dug into the food on his plate.

"It's really good," John said, knowing he would be forgiven for the lie.

"Thanks," Alicia said, and for the first time in her life, she felt a huge glow of satisfaction for a job well done.

When they were finished eating, John started gathering up the dirty plates.

"You cooked. I'll clean up," he said.

Alicia wasn't going to argue. With the passage of time, the cuts on her fingers were beginning to hurt.

"Thanks. If you don't mind, I think I'm going to go lie down."

"Are you feeling okay?" he asked, thinking about how ill she'd been just a short time ago.

"I'm fine. It's just that I didn't sleep so well, remember?"

"Yes, I remember," he said. "Go to sleep, then. I won't be far."

She nodded, gave him a last, lingering look of what he read as regret, and then left him alone with a kitchen full of dirty dishes.

He sighed, surveying the mess, then began to clean up in a slow, methodical way. Once he was done, he went to check on her. She was rolled up in a ball on top of her bedspread. The air in the room was cool from the central air-conditioning. He covered her with an afghan and then made himself walk out instead of crawling in beneath the covers with her.

There was still the issue of setting a trap.

Richard zipped his suitcase shut, patted his pocket to make sure he had his papers, grabbed the bag and headed down the stairs. Helga was waiting below with his hat and coat. He put on the hat, then let her help him into the coat before heading for the front door.

"I'll be in touch," he said. "Just carry on with business as usual."

"We will take good care of everything, Herr Schloss. Have a safe trip."

"Yes, thank you," Richard said, knowing that when he came back the next time, he would have undergone yet another physical change. But this one would be permanent.

He nodded once more to the maid, then stepped aside as she opened the door for him.

Gustav was outside, waiting beside the car. He loaded the suitcase, then opened the door for his boss.

"We still have plenty of time to make your flight," Gustav said.

"Yes, but I don't like to arrive late," Richard said, then got in and settled comfortably into the backseat as Gustav got behind the wheel.

They drove to the airport without conversation, as was proper between a boss and employee. Upon arrival, Gustav carried Richard's suitcase to the curb.

"I'll call when I'm heading back so you can pick me up," Richard said.

"Yes, sir, and do have a safe trip."

Richard nodded, then headed for the gate. Within

the hour, the plane had begun to board. He made it through every security checkpoint without a hitch. By the time he was in his assigned seat in first class, he was riding a high at how easy it was to deceive.

The plane took off without incident, and before long, Richard was being served hot coffee and reading the international edition of the *New York Times,* which he'd purchased in the airport.

The headline and accompanying story were somewhat startling. Seeing not only his own face but his friend Jacob's picture, as well, only reinforced what he was planning to do. He couldn't believe how easily his world of privilege and power had toppled. It seemed impossible to believe that this time last week, he and Jacob were sharing a drink in his office, and now Jacob was dead by his own hand, and Richard was halfway across the world and on the run.

The approaching flight attendant caught his focus, but only for a moment.

"Would you care for more coffee?" she asked.

He nodded, smiling cordially as she topped off his cup and then moved along. He let the coffee cool as he continued to read. By the time he'd finished the article, the coffee was cool enough to drink. The dark, bitter German coffee was an acquired taste, but one he knew he was going to have to get used to.

When the attendant came back by, Richard stopped her.

"When do we land in Lucerne?" he asked.

"In about two hours," she said as she retrieved his empty cup.

"Thank you," he said, then laid the paper aside, leaned his seat back, closed his eyes and promptly fell asleep.

The snow was coming down thick and heavy. The flakes were huge, like down from a duck's back, but cold—so cold. Blood was oozing from both ears and from the corner of his mouth, and when he inhaled, the sound was like a rattle. He could feel the life force seeping out of him with every breath he took. He was going to die.

Just like before.

The memories were vague, but he knew, as well as he knew his own face that they were real. In other lifetimes, he kept dying early, always within sight of achieving greatness, yet failing at the hands of fate or the hands of those he should have been able to trust.

This time, it was the weather and twelve broken bones that were going to take him out. He was afraid. So very afraid.

"Don't leave me," he pleaded from inside his small tent, reaching out to the others, who had shifted their packs to accommodate what he'd been carrying.

"We'll send help," someone said, and then they were gone.

The others walked past his tiny tent without looking back—unable to look at the man they were leaving to die alone. But the leader, Trevor, stopped and squatted down and peered into the opening.

"Trevor, I thought you were my friend."

But Trevor just shook his head. "I am your friend, but I'm not God, and He's the only One who could fix what's wrong with you. You're all broken up inside, and you know it."

He choked, then exhaled, bringing up a fresh stream of blood that oozed from between his lips and down onto the sleeping bag they'd put him in.

They'd had no choice—and he'd taken the risk when he'd decided to attempt the climb. Everest was the Holy Grail of mountains. He'd come so close to achieving greatness. Now all was lost because of one misstep and a snowstorm.

"Don't leave me," he said again, but this time the words were sucked up and blown away by the wind.

"Sorry," Trevor said. "Maybe in another life-time, my friend."

He watched in horror as Trevor walked away, disappearing into the blowing wall of snow.

"No!" he screamed, then shuddered as a wave of unbearable pain shot through him like a bolt of lightning.

Once again he had been abandoned to his fate by people he'd believed he could trust.

Richard sat up with a gasp. His heart was thumping erratically, and he had the strangest urge to see if he could stand—but of course it was only a dream. His bones weren't broken. His body was solid and unharmed. Still, he shuddered. The dream had seemed so real.

A little nauseated, he leaned against the headrest and quietly closed his eyes. He'd had similar dreams his whole life, the theme always the same. He was teetering on the brink of greatness, only to fall short of his goal. And always he was defeated by those he'd thought he could trust.

Then the cabin light came on, and Richard heard

the flight attendant readying the passengers for landing. He smiled with satisfaction, more than ready for what lay ahead.

While Alicia slept, John spent the next few hours setting up an undetectable series of alarms. He positioned tiny solar-powered lasers that, when tripped by someone passing in front of the beam, would set off a small alarm inside John's bedroom. There would be no way for anyone to sneak up on the property undetected.

He had toyed with the idea of packing Alicia up and running again, but from the way things were going, there didn't seem to be a way to hide without being found. The bottom line was, Alicia was never going to be safe as long as her father was on the run.

He'd promised to help, and that meant keeping her alive in the process. He wouldn't let himself think of the consequences of putting Alicia and the nation's needs ahead of his own. He was weary of the passage of time, and the constant and fruitless hunt. He wanted it over. But once again, it seemed as if the man he sought might die at the hands of others, which did him no good whatsoever.

Finally he was satisfied that he'd done all he could with regard to security. He gathered up his tools and put them back in the storage shed, then retrieved the binoculars and circled the house, doing a 360-check of the horizon.

He was going up the steps of the back terrace when he caught a flash of light from the corner of his eye. He turned toward the distant mountains and watched, checking to see if it happened again or if it was just an anomaly. His curiosity was soon rewarded by a second flash, like sunlight reflecting off the windshield of a car—or a pair of binoculars. The only thing was, there were no other houses in that direction. No roads leading to Sedona. No reason for anyone to be out there—unless they didn't want to be seen.

"So…you're a little ahead of schedule," he said softly. "But take your time. When you get here, I'll be waiting."

"Who are you talking to?" Alicia asked.

John jumped, startled by the unexpected sound of her voice,

"Hey," he said. "I didn't know you were awake. Feel better?"

"Yes, thanks. So…who were you talking to?"

He glanced toward the mountains. Whoever was out there had moved.

"Just talking to myself. Comes from living alone."

Alicia shaded her eyes against the glare of the afternoon sun for a better look at his face. He was the epitome of stoic. Hard to read. Even harder to communicate with.

"Why do you?" she asked.

John frowned. "Do what?"

"Live alone."

He shrugged. "Because it suits me, I guess."

"I don't mean to pry…but how long has it been since… I mean, when was your family…" She sighed. "Crap. Forget it. That's prying. I'm sorry."

She strode back into the house, slamming the door shut behind her.

John looked toward the mountains. Nothing would happen until after dark, of that he was certain. Whoever was coming would want the element of surprise on his side, and there was no way in hell to come up on this house in daylight and not be seen from miles away. Satisfied that he had some time before all hell broke loose, he followed her inside.

She was taking a cold can of pop from the refrigerator.

"Want one?" she asked.

"Yeah, sure," he said, and set his binoculars on the counter.

Alicia eyed them as she poured the soda into glasses, then added some ice. She set one glass in front of him, then took hers to the table. She sat down, took a sip and then pointed to the binoculars.

"What aren't you telling me?"

John's eyes narrowed as he took the chair across from her. He wasn't fooling her one bit.

"That plane today…"

"They were looking for me…for *us,* weren't they?"

"I think so."

"What did you see out there just now?"

"Sunlight reflecting off something shiny, most likely glass."

"Maybe it was just a car on the road."

"There are no roads out there. There are no houses. Nothing leads to anything out there."

Her bandaged fingers curled around the glass. She was afraid to ask but needed to know.

"Was Dieter in that plane?"

"No. I didn't recognize either of them, but that means nothing. We didn't know the man who came at you in D.C., either, but he still found us."

"What's going to happen? Are we leaving here?"

"I thought about it," John said. "My instinct is to stay and fight."

She leaned back in her chair and let her gaze slide from feature to feature on his face. From that tiny silver feather in his ear to the jut of his chin, the high, chiseled cheekbones and those dark, flashing eyes. He didn't look like a man accustomed to backing down.

"I don't want to be responsible for your death," she said.

The urge to confess was strong. But how did a man admit he couldn't die and not sound like a madman? She was already scared half out of her head. He didn't want to push her the rest of the way.

"I've been around a very long time and survived some ugly stuff. I'm a hard man to kill."

She shivered, remembering the scars on his body and the way the gunshot wounds had closed up almost before her eyes.

"I've thought about that a lot," she said.

He grinned wryly. "I can imagine."

"So how do you do it, John? How does your body…you know…"

"I told someone once that I'd studied healing under the Dali Lama. Learned how to heal myself, how to control bleeding."

"Did that someone believe you?" she asked.

"I guess. The conversation ended."

She slid her glass around and around in a little circle on the table, leaving wet rings of condensation behind, then paused and looked John straight in the face.

"Is that the answer I'm going to get, as well?"

"Pretty much."

She sighed. "If I asked you something else…would you tell me the truth?"

He frowned. "Depends."

"Did you know about my father selling weapons illegally before we met?"

"No. Lord no. Why would you think that?"

"Well, you said he killed your wife…your family. I thought maybe it was because of the weapons he sold. That he was responsible in that way."

John looked away for a few moments, then took a deep breath and made himself face her.

"It was a long time ago. But I made a promise, a vow that I would find the man who killed them before I died. It's just taken longer than I imagined, that's all."

"But I don't understand…were they on foreign soil when—"

"No. He was the one who didn't belong. Look. Just let it be. You would never be able to understand." Then he sighed. "Hell. Sometimes I don't understand, either."

Alicia's fingers trembled. Her physical attraction to him was so strong that it made her ache. How ironic that she finally met a man she could see spending the rest of her life with and her father was responsible for destroying his family. She pushed her glass aside, then balled her hands in her lap and closed her eyes.

"It's going to be all right," he said. "I promise."

Alicia shook her head as she looked up. Her eyes were swimming with tears.

"No. It won't. The irony of it is that every day I wake up is one day less to live. Whether it's because I'm just going to grow old and die, or whether my loving father finally ends it for me, won't change the fact that I've gotten myself into a mess from which there is no escape."

"You're talking in riddles," he said.

She laughed, but it was not a funny sound. "You

should know," she said, and shoved her chair back from the table and walked out of the room.

John started to follow her, then stopped long enough to go back and set all the security alarms, including the ones he'd located along the outer perimeter of the property. He wasn't going to let their conversation end like that, but didn't want anyone interrupting them unannounced, either.

As soon as he was satisfied that they were safe, he went to find Alicia.

Twelve

Alicia felt sick. She could tell from what John wasn't saying that he fully expected them to be attacked. And since he wasn't, at the moment, in any kind of panic, she assumed it would be after dark. So what did that mean? Another night of fear? Another battle to be fought before they could find a safe place to hide for a while? Or was she kidding herself by believing she even had a future? She knew her father better than anyone. She'd seen him at his worst and barely remembered him at his best. Not since she was a small child had there been any tenderness between them, and whatever had been there had died when they buried her mother. It was as if whatever was good and gentle in Richard Ponte had ended with his wife's death. Afterward, he saw that Alicia was cared for, but he didn't bother himself with how it happened. It shouldn't have been surprising, then, that he'd been able to separate his emotions from his need for revenge. No one took down the king—not even the princess who'd sprung from his loins. She was sick and tired of men who kept secrets, and that included John Nightwalker. So when he finally caught up to her and called for her to wait, she snapped.

She paused in the hallway, then turned. Her hands were curled into fists, and her body was stiff, as if braced for battle. She lifted her chin and glared.

"Wait? For what? For the next hit man to come calling? Oh…I know. You expect me to wait around while you dangle me like a carrot in front of my father's flunkies in hopes that he'll get tired of their failures and come on his own."

Her accusation hit him like a slap in the face. He'd set aside his own agenda to keep her in one piece, and now this was what he got? He reacted without thinking and grabbed her by the shoulders, then yanked her forward until they were standing eye to eye.

If Alicia had known him better, she would have realized that the soft tone of his voice was deceptive, and that the grip he had on her shoulders was to keep himself from wringing her neck.

"I am not using you for bait, and you know it. I'd lay odds that your father isn't even on this continent, so there's no chance of him doing anything on his own. But if you're feeling all that misused and trapped…there's the door. Start walking. I won't stop you."

His breath was hot on her face. His eyes were blazing. She felt his anger. She should have been afraid, but all she could do was remember him naked and gentle, holding her in his arms. Her fingers uncurled. *Walk away—now—before you do something you'll regret,* she told herself. Instead, she reached toward him and cupped his face with her hands.

"John…"

He flinched, then grabbed her by both wrists. "Woman…"

Alicia heard the warning in his voice, but it didn't stop her. "I'm so tired of running. I'm tired of being afraid. I'm not asking you for anything permanent. I just want to forget…even if it's only for a while."

He wanted her. She knew enough about men to see that. But he didn't love her, and she wasn't going to waste her energy pining for a man who was locked in the past. But they could use each other for comfort, and right now that was all she wanted.

"Please," she whispered.

He grunted, as if she'd just punched him in the gut, but it was his only hesitation. Suddenly he was pulling her shirt over her head, popping the hook on her bra and yanking her panties and shorts down around her feet. Before she could react, she was in his arms.

The swift surge of lust that rose in response was painful. She couldn't remember ever wanting a man this much in her life. Her heart was beating so fast she couldn't think, and when he kicked open the door to his bedroom and took her inside, she was physically shaking.

"Hurry," she begged.

John was out of his clothes within seconds and left them where they fell. His erection was hard and aching. His only intention was to bury it deep inside her where she was tight and hot and wet. Then he crawled onto the bed.

"Let me in."

Her legs parted of their own accord as he slid a finger into the V between them, testing to see if she was ready.

She was.

Considering the situation, foreplay wasn't happening. He rose up, then moved over her, before slamming himself into her.

Going deep.

Falling fast.

Losing what was left of his control.

One long minute passed, then another and another, as Alicia rocked against him, taking everything he was willing to give. When she began to burn, she locked her legs around his waist and pulled him deeper, moaning softly as he rode her down. Over and over, thrust after thrust, mindless ecstasy built and built until there was nothing to do but burn out.

One moment Alicia was flying with the feeling, never wanting it to end. Then the climax hit—hard and fast—rolling through her body in waves that wouldn't stop. She threw her arms up over her head, grabbed hold of the headboard and screamed.

Her physical reaction to their lovemaking sent John over the edge into an animal lust for completion. When it came, the emotions that came with it shocked him. Even though he'd started this without any motivation other than lust, everything changed when he finally let go. Spilling his seed into her should have left him feeling sated. But it was just the reverse. For the first time in centuries, he felt as if he would never get enough. Even more, the lost, lonely feeling that he'd lived with for so long was no longer there. With Alicia's arms around his neck and her legs around his waist, he felt a sense of having come home. The muscles in his arms were trembling as he finally gave up and collapsed on top of her, burying his face against the curve of her neck as she quietly sobbed.

He didn't know if the crying was good or bad, but the sound killed him. He kissed the side of her cheek, then her eyes.

"Alicia...baby."

"Shh...please...don't talk...don't move. Give me this time, I beg you. Let me pretend that this mattered to you as much as it mattered to me."

He groaned, then rose up on one elbow and cupped her tearstained face with the palm of his hand.

"There was no pretense," he said softly, and brushed his lips across hers, nipping, pulling, then teasing them apart before starting all over again. "I didn't mean for this to happen, but you can't pretend it hasn't, and I don't want to forget."

Alicia's eyes widened. After all these years of thinking she would never find her soulmate, could John Nightwalker be the one? Right now it felt so, and she was too full of emotion to debate it.

She ran her fingers across his back, tracing the scars scattered here and there upon his body, all the while wondering how he had survived them. He seemed invincible. And because she was learning to trust him, he made her believe they might actually make this work.

Then he leaned down, whispered in her ear, and sent her right back to that place between heaven and earth where only lovers abide.

It was almost dark when John woke up. Alicia was wrapped around his body so tightly that he couldn't move without waking her up. He sighed, then slid his arm beneath her and pulled her even closer. To hell with staying still. He wanted her awake again. He wanted—

An alarm began to ring. As sounds went, it was small, but it was deadly. It was the only warning they were going to get that the perimeter had been breached.

"Alicia!" he said, and yanked her up into his arms before she was fully awake.

"What? What's happening?" she mumbled, startled by the sudden awakening, then scared by the look on his face.

"He's here," John said. He pulled the sheet off his bed, wrapped her up in it and headed for his closet.

"What are you doing? Wait!"

"Shut up and listen," he said swiftly as he pushed a rack of hangers aside and punched a switch at the back of the closet. A door swung open. "There's a light on your right, just inside the door. It's an old bomb shelter. It was here when I bought the land. I built the house over it. There's food and blankets, water and light. Get down there, and don't come up until I come for you."

He pushed her forward, watched until she found the light, then grabbed for his clothes.

They had time for one frantic look at each other, and then John slammed the closet door shut and her inside. As he was putting on clothes, Alicia was scrambling down the steps, still wrapped in the sheet, trying not to fall.

She got to the bottom step, raced across the cold concrete floor to the single bed and jumped up on it before pulling the sheet more tightly around her. It was cold and quiet—so quiet. How would she know what was going on up there if she couldn't hear? What if he never came back? What if she died down here? Scared half out of her mind, all she knew to do was pray.

John put on a pair of pants, slid his knife into his boot and managed to slip out the front door way ahead of the intruder's arrival. He'd set the perimeter alarms a good distance away so he would have time to reconnoiter on his own. And he'd coded the different beacons so that he would know from which direction the perimeter had been breached.

He allowed himself one last thought for the woman in the middle of this hell, then crouched down and began to move silently through the night. Once he was a good distance away from the house, he began to circle. A few moments later, he caught a glimpse of moonlight reflecting off metal and guessed it was a gun. He paused, watching, waiting for a silhouette to separate itself from the rest of the shadows. When the shadow took shape, he palmed his knife. Now he was the one on the hunt.

Sam Watkins was still riding the high of having located his target so quickly. He'd already made up his mind that this windfall was going to be the kickoff to his retirement. Two million dollars in Mexico was like twenty million in the States. He planned to head for the coast, maybe Puerto Vallarta, maybe Cozumel, and find himself a little hacienda and a pretty senorita to warm his bed and cook his food. He would be set for life.

All he had to do was this one last job.

Something moved off to his right. He paused long enough to identify the sound, as he'd done off and on since he'd left his vehicle miles away. His trek to the house had flushed out a half-dozen desert denizens, including a coyote, a lizard and a night owl. His only concern was making sure he hadn't stirred up a rattlesnake. Confident that all he'd disturbed was another ranging coyote, he shifted his focus back to the house in the near distance.

He could see what appeared to be a small glow from one set of back windows, which was most likely a light shining from a room on the other side of the house.

He grinned. Either they were already asleep or they were otherwise engaged. This was going to be a piece of cake. He touched the butt of the semiautomatic in his shoulder holster out of habit, then shifted focus. He would check for a security system, disarm it if there was one, then pop right in.

The last thing he expected was a touch on his shoulder. He spun, then caught a glimpse of a shadow between him and the mountains behind him. Suddenly the gun was no longer in his holster and he was spitting bits of desert out of his mouth.

"You're trespassing," John said softly, and rested the point of his knife against the back of the man's neck as he held him facedown in the sand.

"Listen," Sam started to say, hoping he could talk his way out of this.

"No, *you* listen. I need the answers to two questions or I shove this knife right through your third and fourth vertebrae, at which time you will still be alive, but you'll never move a muscle below your jaw for the rest of your natural life."

"Jesus…Jesus…don't, mister, don't."

John applied a fraction more pressure to emphasis his seriousness. "I find it ironic that you decide to call upon your God to spare your life when you came here with every intention of taking one."

Sam shuddered. The lack of emotion in the man's voice was genuinely frightening.

"I'll talk. Just don't cut me."

"I know you're here to kill Alicia Ponte. Who hired you?"

"Her old man."

Up until now, they'd been operating on assumptions, but hearing the truth from the hit man's mouth was shocking.

"How much?"

"Two mil."

"Shame you're not going to get to spend it," John said, then hit the man on the back of the head with the butt of his knife. The moment Sam went limp, John pulled his cell phone out of his pocket and made one call. He waited, listening as it rang once, then twice, then three times. Just as he was afraid that his call was going to go to voice mail, it was answered.

"Damn it, John, do you know what time it is here?"

"It's not that late, old man, so wake up and listen to me. Ponte sent another hit man."

Corbin was already grabbing for his glasses as he was crawling out of bed. "Are you two okay? Where are you? Do you need—"

"I have everything under control," John said.

Corbin sighed. "Of course you do. What do you need?"

"I think it's time we called in the Feds, which is where you come in. There is a possibility that this man knows details that might lead them to Ponte."

"Fantastic! Tell me where you are and how to get there. I'll make the necessary calls."

"I own a place in the desert north of Sedona."

"Give me directions," Corbin said, writing quickly as John rattled them off, then added a phone number.

"It'll probably take at least a couple of hours to get everything together and get there. Are you going to be all right until then?"

"Yes."

"John?"

"What?"

"Don't kill him."

"You don't have to tell me that. If I wanted him dead, I wouldn't be talking to you."

"Yeah, right. Okay. I'm making the calls now."

"We'll be waiting," John said, then pocketed the phone and the semiautomatic, grabbed the man's heels, rolled him over on his back and started dragging him toward the house.

Alicia was so scared she was sick to her stomach. She didn't know how much time had passed. She couldn't hear anything. She had to trust what John had told her and remember the fierceness with which he'd kept her alive so far. Now was not the time to doubt him.

And then there was the passion with which they'd made love. It had forever changed her life. She was never going to be the same—never going to be satisfied with the status quo again. She wanted a life with John Nightwalker in every way a woman could want a man. During the good times and the bad. In joy and in sorrow. But she couldn't get past the memory of how he'd stood before the painting of his dead wife's face, fearing that he would never love her the way he'd loved White Fawn. She would gladly take second best. She didn't care if he didn't love her enough. She could love enough for the both of them. She just didn't know if he would be willing to go that far.

She didn't know how much time had passed when she realized she was hearing footsteps running through the room above. The breath caught in the back of her throat. Was it John? Or was it her killer?

Then a door slammed loudly. She looked up. John was coming down the stairs on the run. She bolted up from the bed, the sheet falling to the floor as she threw herself into his arms.

"Are you all right?" she asked, running her hands across his face, checking for bruising, then examining his clothing for blood.

"I'm okay," he said quickly, then grabbed the sheet and wrapped it back around her. "You're freezing, baby."

"Is it over?"

"Not yet," he said. "But it soon will be. You're going to want to get dressed. We're going to have company in a while."

"Company?"

"The Feds. Come with me. I don't want to leave our…visitor alone any longer than I have to."

Alicia's eyes widened in disbelief as he pulled her up the steps and then back into his bedroom. She paused at the foot of his bed, watching as he began digging through a dresser. "You brought him here? The man who was going to kill me?"

"He's tied up out on the back terrace. Get dressed and meet me out there," John said, then stopped long enough to slide an arm around her waist and pull her against him. He kissed her then—hard and fast, but with a silent reminder there was more where that came from—and left the room on the run.

Alicia stumbled out of his bedroom, pausing long enough to gather up her clothes, which were still lying in the middle of the hall, then ran into her room to get dressed.

Sam Watkins came to consciousness staring straight up at the night sky. It took him a few moments to realize he was lying on the patio of the house he'd been planning to invade. His hands and feet were bound so tightly that they felt numb, and he could see the silhouette of someone sitting in a chair about ten feet away.

"So you took two million dollars to end my life? How much would you charge to kill my father?"

Hearing a woman's voice was surprising, but not as shocking as what she'd just asked. Suddenly he realized he was in the presence of the woman he'd been sent to kill. There was a moment of excitement when he wondered if he was going to get out of this after all, a moment when he believed he could make a deal with the intended victim and double-cross his employer.

"I'd do him for the same as what he paid me to do you," he said.

"And what amount was that again?"

"Two."

"Million?"

"Yeah. I mean…he's got the—"

Alicia interrupted. "I know what he's got. What I want to know now is…John, did you get that confession on tape?"

"Every bit of it," John said.

Sam Watkins arched his back and looked behind him,

saw the same silhouette he'd seen out in the desert, and realized he'd been had.

"Son of a bitch," he swore.

"You certainly are," Alicia said, then suddenly pointed upward. "John! I hear a helicopter. There…see the lights. Is that them?"

"Looks like it," John said, and picked up a remote from the table beside him and aimed it toward a box on the back of the house.

Suddenly the whole place was flooded with light, along with a good hundred yards of land at the back of the property. Sam closed his eyes against the glare, wondering where it had all gone wrong. Part of it was his own greed. He would admit to that. But part of it was most likely complacency. He'd begun to believe his own PR. He couldn't be caught. He didn't fail.

But that was before he'd walked into the wrong territory and underestimated the enemy. He had time for one moment of regret, thinking about the two million dollars that would never be spent, and then he watched a helicopter land, and a half-dozen men spill out and come running. At that point, the rest of his carefully laid plans fell down around his ears.

"The money was wired into Watkins' account from a numbered bank account in Switzerland, which tells us nothing about Ponte's location. But it does add to the charges piling up around him. Treason. Attempted murder. And the county judge down in Georgia who let Dieter Bahn go is in hot water, too. With Watkins' statement implicating Bahn as the go-between for the hit on Alicia Ponte, Bahn can no longer claim any kind of innocence as to his employer's intent. Unfortunately he, too, has disappeared. If I were guessing, I'd say Bahn, like his boss, is most likely out of the country."

Alicia sat without moving, listening to the phone conversation between John and Special Agent Joshua on speakerphone as the FBI man filled them in on the latest details. Most of them she already knew, and her mind began to wander.

It had been two days since they'd taken Watkins into custody. Two days during which she and John had tiptoed around the obvious. They'd made love. But where did they go from there? When this was over—if she was still alive to tell the tale—was that also going to be the end of the line for their relationship? Even worse, was she kidding herself by calling what they shared a relationship? He made love to her, but the word *love* never crossed his lips.

Then her reverie ended as she suddenly focused on something John asked.

"Do you think the threat to Alicia's life is as high as it was?"

Joshua paused for a moment before he answered. "It's hard to say. I mean, it's obvious this has become personal to Ponte. He knows we have the goods on him, so it's not as if we need her testimony for anything. In fact, she didn't actually give us anything we could have used in a trial, although she's the one who set the ball rolling. If she hadn't told us what she did, it's unlikely he would ever have been caught. Everything we needed for trial came from Jacob Carruthers. Even though he's dead now, thanks to his sworn statements, we had probable cause to confiscate everything we could have hoped for, and it was all there. Both in Carruthers' office and in Ponte's computer records. So Ponte's agenda regarding his daughter is obviously personal. I can't say this won't happen again. And if it does, we have no way of knowing who he'll hire next. People will do a lot of wrong things for the right amount of money."

John glanced toward Alicia, then realized she was upset. But who wouldn't be? He'd learned all he could from Joshua; it was time to wrap up the call.

"Yes, you're right, of course. I was just asking on her behalf."

"So what are your plans?" Joshua asked.

John glanced over at Alicia. She shrugged, then looked away.

"We're not sure," he said. "But if we leave this location, I'll be sure and let you know. Oh…and when you see Woodliff again, tell him thanks for getting you guys out here so fast the other night."

Joshua snorted softly, but there was humor in his voice. "Yeah, if he gets any more involved in this case than he already is, we'll have to put him on the payroll."

John laughed. "Knowing Woodliff, he'd turn down the offer."

"You think? Why so?" Joshua asked, feeling slightly insulted.

"Because you guys have too many rules, and Woodliff doesn't always play by the rules."

Joshua laughed then, relieved they hadn't been dissed. "You're right about that. Later."

The line went dead.

John hung up the receiver, turned to Alicia, crossed his arms over his chest and fixed her with a steady gaze.

"Talk to me."

"About what?" she asked, then turned away.

"Don't look away from me," he said shortly.

She frowned. "Don't tell me what to do."

"There's something about me you need to know," John said.

Her frown deepened. "I'm listening."

"I don't play games, Alicia. If there is ever going to be anything between us, you deal with that now or call it quits."

She went still. "If? As in you're willing for there to be something between us?"

"Ah…" he said softly. "Now I understand."

Alicia inhaled a shaky breath. "Good for you. Enlighten me, please, and then we'll both get the joke."

In three strides he was standing in front of her. He reached down and took her by the hands, pulling gently until she was standing up.

"Do you see me laughing?"

She shook her head.

"Then pay attention, because I haven't said this to a woman in a real long time. Something happened between us when we made love. Something I don't want to lose. I know we've got a hell of a fight ahead of us, but when it's over—and it *will* be over, I promise you— I'm going to ask you a question."

Alicia was beginning to tremble. This was so far beyond anything she'd hoped for that she was afraid she was dreaming. He could be infuriating and formidable and damned bossy, but she was so falling in love.

"What's the question?" she asked.

He grinned. "You weren't paying attention."

"I was…am…paying attention," she muttered.

"Is this mess over with yet?"

"Oh. No, I don't guess so."

"Then it's not yet time for me to ask the question."

She doubled up her fist and thumped him lightly on the chest. "You make me crazy."

Then she saw his eyes darken as the smile slid off his face.

"You make me forget promises I made. Promises that have to be kept."

"You mean what my father did to—"

He suddenly pressed two fingers across her mouth, stopping the words before they were spoken. The tone of his voice softened until it was hardly more than a whisper as he said, "Know this, and know it now. What that man did to my family was done long, long ago…before you existed. You hold no part in it. No guilt in it. You are as much a victim as they were."

She sighed as her vision blurred. "Oh, John," she said softly, then slid her arms around his neck and kissed the hollow at the base of his throat.

John flinched as if he'd been shot. He wrapped his arms around her, resting his chin on the crown of her head, and tried not to think of White Fawn, but it was an impossible task. That was the way she used to show him that she wanted to make love.

Alicia paused. She could feel the tension in his body. She'd done something wrong, but she didn't know what.

"John?"

He groaned, then picked her up in his arms. "I want to make love to you. I *need* to make love to you. Now."

Alicia sighed. Everything was all right. She'd just been imagining things.

"Then what are you waiting for?" she asked softly.

He turned around and laid her down on the Navajo rug in front of the fireplace.

"Here?" she asked as he began to undress her.

"Too far to the bed," he answered.

She laughed, and began pulling off her clothes and pointing at him. "You're so overdressed."

The shock of her kiss slid away. "You are so right," he fired back, and peeled off his clothes in record time.

Alicia paused for a moment, allowing herself to look her fill.

The scars that had first shocked her were hardly noticeable now. And she couldn't understand where the term "red man" had ever come from, because his skin was a beautiful shade of brown. Then he was lying beside her, exploring her body with those long, supple fingers, teasing every pulse point to a maddening ache. She reached for him, encircling his erection with her fingers, then stroked slowly, steadily.

He groaned. "Don't stop," he said hoarsely, and gave himself up to her touch.

Learning that she had the power to make a man like Nightwalker weak with longing was heady stuff, but when he began to return the favor, she lost her sense of self. Suddenly nothing mattered but the moment when he would bury himself so deep inside her that the separation between man and woman ceased to exist.

"No more playing," she begged. "Take me now."

He slid between her legs, pausing a heartbeat longer before burying himself inside her.

And then he began the dance.

Alicia wrapped her arms around his neck, then closed

her eyes and rode the rhythm with him until they were both half out of their minds. Seconds turned to minutes, minutes to mindless pleasure.

When Alicia began to climax, the tremors of her body were the ultimate aphrodisiac. Knowing he'd given her that joy was an exhilaration that pushed John past the limit of his control. With a final thrust he went deep, then let go, spilling his seed in her womb until there was nothing left but aftershocks.

Alicia was shaking from exhaustion, but she'd never been this happy. She couldn't keep what she was feeling inside. She was stroking his back in a slow, gentle motion as she kissed the side of his face.

"You make me feel so loved."

John rose up on his elbows to gaze down at her face. "It isn't me. It's us. I cherish you, Licia…more than you can know."

Alicia sighed as she looked up at him. His expression was fierce, but his touch was gentle. His husky words of love stroked her ragged senses.

Cherish. Such an old-fashioned word, and one with a wealth of meaning.

"Love you, John," she said softly, then parted her lips just enough for the kiss she saw coming.

Thirteen

Dieter was in New York City, in a hotel he'd chosen for its unassuming appearance and its proximity to a subway station, chewing a bite of hamburger and channel surfing when he caught the tail end of a newscast that startled him.

He swallowed before he was ready and choked, then dropped the burger back into the wrapper as he upped the volume.

"What the hell?" he muttered, staring in disbelief at the screen, listening as the newscaster spoke over the stock footage.

"Samuel Todd Watkins, a man long associated with organized crime, was taken into custody yesterday after a failed attempt on missing heiress Alicia Ponte's life. A spokesperson for the Federal Bureau of Investigation lists Watkins' arrest as the latest event in the unfolding drama of the hunt for Richard Ponte, the multibillionaire munitions magnate who's been charged with treason against the United States of America. At this time, there are no new leads into Ponte's whereabouts, but it remains obvious to the authorities that Ponte's desire to end his daughter's life, in retaliation for turning him in, continues. Rumors abound that Watkins has made a deal with the federal prosecutor in exchange for a reduction of charges, although reports are that he will still spend the rest of his life behind bars. According to authorities, additional arrests are pending."

Dieter's belly rolled with panic as he bolted up from the bed and grabbed his suitcase and began tossing in his belongings. He started to leave, then ran to the window instead. He didn't see anything out of place, but that didn't mean he wasn't already made and marked.

"Damn, damn, damn," he muttered as he threw the room key on the bed and headed out the door. He paused in the hallway long enough to locate the stairwell, then started walking, making it down seven flights in record time before exiting into an alley. By the time he got to the sidewalk, he was shaking. In his haste, he bumped into a pedestrian and got a cursing for his carelessness.

"Sorry," he said quickly, put his head down and headed for the subway stop.

Every step he took, he felt a thousand eyes on him. Every sound he heard became amplified a hundredfold, until he was at the point of panic. Suddenly someone grabbed his shoulder.

He spun, his eyes wide with shock.

"What? What?"

A well-dressed man pointed toward the street. "The light, man. It's red. You need to pay attention or you'll get yourself run over."

"Oh. Yes. Thank you," Dieter said.

The moment the light changed, he was across the street and running down the steps into the subway, where he promptly disappeared into the crowd.

The Newbury Clinic and Hospital in Lucerne had once been the private home of a deposed duke. Now, it was a world-renowned center for gender-changing surgery, as well as state-of-the-art techniques in facial reconstruction—and all in the strictest confidentiality. Over the seventy-five years they'd been in practice, many well-known celebrities from all over the world had availed themselves of the Newbury's discreet services.

When Richard arrived, he was just another patient. He had asked, and paid dearly, for an entire facial reconstruction, as well as chest implants, giving him the physique of a bodybuilder without any of the work and training. But he'd had one more request that had given the doctors pause for thought. Over the years, the staff had received many bizarre requests, but no one had ever asked for what amounted to a doggy bag of the removed bits and pieces. When Richard was ready to leave the hospital, he had requested that all the tissue, bone and skin removed from his face and body be ready to go with him. The surgeons didn't ask why. For an added fee, Richard's request was met. Everything they removed from him would be cryogenically frozen and awaiting transport upon his release.

He'd been in surgery for more than eleven hours, then in recovery for two. The nurse had been monitoring her latest patient's vitals carefully, noting that he had been in and out of consciousness for some time. Everything seemed to be stable, but his surgery had been major, and the danger of infection or blood clots was high. And if a clot did form and break loose, at the least he could suffer a stroke. At the worst, he could have a fatal heart attack.

She checked the drip on his IV, then upped the dosage of painkillers as per the doctor's instructions, before taking another blood pressure and pulse check. Satisfied with the stats, she said, "Mr. Schloss…Mr. Schloss. Can you hear me?"

Richard groaned.

"You are out of surgery and doing well."

"Um."

"Good, good. Are you in pain?"

He blinked.

"I've increased your pain medications. You should be feeling relief any moment."

He grunted, counting every heartbeat until the narcotics kicked in. When the sounds and voices began to fade, he sank into blessed oblivion.

"You're a coldhearted bastard. You promised me a shilling. I could get more, you know. You're worth a whole lot more to the crown."

He ignored the prostitute as he continued to button up his trousers, but he didn't like her tone. And what she'd said had sounded vaguely like a threat. He tossed tuppence on the floor at her feet and had turned to leave when the sudden sound of a disturbance outside caught his attention. He ran to the window. Something wasn't right. The king's guards were everywhere!

He spun around. The woman he'd just bedded was on her way out the door.

"What have you done?" he yelled.

Suddenly the door flew inward as more guards spilled into the room.

"Grab him!" someone shouted as he flung himself toward the window.

He'd been in a London prison once before and barely survived. He wasn't going back again.

The mullion-paned window shattered on impact as he went through it headfirst. He fell in a shower of sunlight and glass, only vaguely aware of the screams and shouts above him. All his life he'd fought to be in control. Never trusting anyone. Always wanting more than the seventeenth century deemed a man of his status might have. And now gravity was in charge of the few seconds he had left of his life.

"Bugger them all!" he cried.

Then everything went black.

Richard was gasping, drawing one deep, bone-jarring breath into his body after another as he came to. The pain it caused racked him from head to toe. He clawed at his face, but nothing felt right. Before he fell, he'd had a full head of hair and a beard. He felt the bandages and realized in horror that he hadn't died from the fall after all.

God, oh God. I can't go back to gaol.

Suddenly people were grabbing his hands to keep them from his face, talking to him in urgent tones, beseeching him to calm down.

"Mr. Schloss. Mr. Schloss. You're in hospital. You had surgery…remember?" a woman said. "Please, you must calm down."

A man's voice rose above the woman's, issuing orders that made no sense.

Who the hell was Mr. Schloss, he wondered, and why were they putting him under? Under what?

Confusion ended with the new dose of narcotic that slipped into his veins and sent him back into unconsciousness.

Dieter was in Houston, Texas. Not because he knew the city so well, but because it was big enough that he figured he could lose himself there. And it was a seaport, which enhanced the possibility of slipping out of the country on a ship leaving the docks.

In his youth, he'd worked for a Greek shipping line for a while, so passing himself off as a sailor would be a cinch. What he needed were the papers to back it up. But he didn't know who to contact or have the money to make it happen. He was as fucked as a man could be without ever having had a moment of the pleasure. He'd tried to call Richard off and on for the better part of two days, but without any success. All he could do now was lie low and wait for the man to call back. If he didn't, it was as good as over for him.

Damn Richard Ponte. Damn himself for not abandoning a sinking ship. Damn the whole world to holy hell.

The western sky over John's house was a wash of reds, oranges and yellows, a display of heavenly fireworks the human hand could never reproduce. The sight always moved him, but at the same time it reminded him of how very, very long he'd been on this earth.

He stood silently, watching as the sun continued to sink, until there was nothing left but the glow below the horizon. A coyote howled somewhere in the distance. The sound spoke to everything he was: wild at heart. He'd learned to live within the rules of the twenty-first century, but he would forever be a warrior of the Ah-ni-yv-wi-ya.

"John?"

He turned. Alicia was standing in the doorway with a hesitant expression on her face.

"Yes, baby?"

The endearment should have reassured her, but it didn't.

"I wish I could take away that look in your eyes," she said.

Startled that she'd learned to see through him, he tried to deny it.

"What look?"

She sighed. "At least have the decency not to lie to me."

As he lifted his chin in challenge, the last of the evening light turned him into a dark silhouette. Now his features were as vague as the little bit of himself he showed to the world.

"I did not lie."

She shrugged. "There's such a thing as a sin of omission."

Once again, she was on target. "So what do you want to know?"

She crossed the terrace, then stopped before him and lifted her hands to his face. The hard angles were becoming as familiar to her as her own features.

"It breaks my heart to see the sadness in your eyes and know a member of my family is responsible. I know what you said…that I'm a victim, too. But it's not the same thing, John. It's not."

She put her arms around his waist and then laid her cheek against his chest. His heartbeat was strong and steady, just like the man. But it was the scars on his body and in his heart that told the true story. She didn't know how it had happened and he wouldn't talk about it, but he was alone in the world—all that was left of an entire family—and it was her father's fault.

John sighed. This woman deserved more than he was able to give, but he wasn't man enough to walk away. He wanted her. She'd started out as part of the problem, and now she was becoming the solution to his lonely existence. But it would be at her expense. She was right. He hadn't been honest with her. Only, he didn't know how to explain what he was or if explaining was even the right thing to do.

"Let it be. Time has a way of working out the knots in almost every problem. All we need is more time."

She nodded. It wasn't what she wanted to hear, but knowing John, it was all she was going to get.

"Come inside?"

He nodded. "Yes. I'm hungry. How about you?"

"If you're cooking," she said.

He grinned. "Yes, I'll feed you."

And another day passed.

The hallucinations Richard had been having for the last week were driving him crazy. Every time they gave him something to sleep or the pain meds put him out, he slipped right into another wild dream. The dreams were so real—meticulous in detail, including historically correct clothing, speech and food. What was even stranger was the fact that sometimes the locations no longer existed or had been renamed from one century to the next. History had never interested him, so it wasn't as if he was just dreaming about people and places he'd studied. And it kept him in a state of constant stress, always dreaming about dying. It led him to the fear that he was getting some sublime message from God, that he was being prepared mentally for imminent doom. Even though the doctors seemed to think he was healing properly, he was well aware of the possibility that anything could happen.

He was also getting nervous because he hadn't talked to Dieter since before his surgery. When he'd finally felt well enough to dig out his cell phone, he'd been horrified to see that Dieter had been trying to contact him for more than a week. The only problem was, Dieter had left no messages other than that he needed help. When Richard had returned a call, he'd been put through to voice mail, which pissed him off. He couldn't leave his name for fear the phone might fall into the wrong hands—or, even worse, that Dieter had been taken into custody, like Jacob. So now he was playing a waiting game of his own, hoping Dieter called him back before long.

He kept the phone on the small table beside his hospital bed. Following hospital policy, he had it turned to vibrate, and when it started a little dance across the surface, he grabbed it anxiously.

"Hello?"

"Thank God," Dieter said. "I've been trying to contact you for days."

"So we're talking now," Richard said. "What's happened?"

"Watkins failed. The Indian took him down and turned him over to the Feds. According to the latest news, he agreed to testify in return for a lighter sentence."

"No," Richard said, and closed his eyes against the news.

This was bad—very, very bad. Once again, he'd been defeated by this Indian. He was beginning to believe the man was some kind of CIA spook. It was the only thing that made sense. As for Alicia, the fact that she continued to elude his justice was infuriating. Logic told him that this was the moment when he should make the choice to stop, to let it go and live out what was left of his life under his new identity. But he was too wrapped up in the lust for revenge to heed the inner whisper of warning.

"Watkins gave me up," Dieter said. "And they immediately linked me to you, so I've been in hiding since the arrest. I need money for new papers to get out of the country."

Richard cursed.

Dieter flinched. Did this mean he was becoming collateral damage? "I'm sorry," he said. "Watkins was the best. Who knew he'd fail?"

"It's not your fault," Richard muttered. "It's Alicia. It's that Indian. It's my fucking life coming apart at the seams." Then he sighed. "I can't have money deposited in an account under your real name. They'll be watching for that."

"I know," Dieter said.

Richard's mind was racing as he ran through the names of people who owed him favors. It had to be someone who was already on the wrong side of the law. Suddenly he realized he didn't even know what city Dieter was in.

"Where are you?" he asked.

"Houston."

Richard smiled to himself, then winced beneath the bandages on his face. At last, some good news. "I think I have a contact for you there. Keep your phone at the ready. If you're contacted by a woman calling herself Isis, take the call. Once you're out of the country, call me again. By that time, I'll have a task for you."

"Yes, sir."

"Next time you call, I want good news," Richard said.

Dieter struggled not to fire back with the comment that it was Richard's fault the news was all bad to begin with. "Yes, sir," he said.

The line went dead in his ear. He dropped his cell phone in his pocket, then picked up the phone book in his motel room and began leafing through the restaurant pages. Now that there was a plan in motion, he was suddenly starving.

Richard had disconnected just as his doctor entered the room. "Good morning, Mr. Schloss," the doctor said. "How are you feeling this morning?"

"Fine," Richard said.

"Good! Good! So, are you ready for today?"

"What's happening today?" Richard asked.

"How would you like to get those bandages off?"

Richard's pulse skyrocketed. "Yes!"

"Fine," the doctor said, then motioned to a nurse, who had come in behind him and was carrying a covered tray. "Set it there," he said.

The nurse put the tray down on a small table, then removed the cover, revealing an assortment of small surgical implements.

"The scissors, please," the doctor said as he pulled on a pair of surgical gloves, then proceeded to snip away at the outer bandages covering Richard's face.

Richard was motionless, anxious to see what the doctor's skill had wrought, trying to judge by the expression on the man's face if the surgery had been a success. Layer by layer, the bandages came off, until Richard could tell by the feel of air against his skin that they were finally gone.

"Let me see!" he demanded.

"Just a moment," the doctor said as he swabbed at Richard's neck with antiseptic-soaked cotton.

"A mirror. Let me have a mirror," Richard said.

The doctor smiled, then nodded to his nurse. "Pass it over, please. Mr. Schloss wants to see his new look. And, Anton, I think you're going to be pleasantly surprised. Keep in mind there is some bruising and, of course, swelling, but all of that is temporary. All in all, I am very pleased with the results."

Richard took the mirror, then turned it around. Within seconds, he felt as if he'd stepped into a twilight zone. There was a moment when he wondered if he was in the middle of another one of those crazy dreams. Then he focused on the eyes. Green, with short stubbly lashes.

He felt the world return to center. There he was. But the rest…it was like night and day.

"Amazing," he mumbled.

"Yes, isn't it?" the doctor agreed. "As you can see, the cheek and chin implants changed the rounded shape of your face and created a more chiseled countenance. Of course, the wrinkles and extra flesh are also gone. We removed the bulbous tip from the end of your nose and reshaped the width of your nostrils. The bump on your nose was also removed, as were the bags under your eyes. I know you can't see that quite yet for the bruising, but I promise you're going to be very pleased."

"I already am," Richard said as he gingerly felt his face, ears and neck. "My ears are flat to my head now, and my double chin is gone."

The doctor laughed. "That's a good thing, yes?"

"Yes," Richard echoed.

"So…now we remove the bandages from your chest and arms," the doctor said.

Richard handed over the mirror and leaned back as they cut away the bandages from his torso, as well. The implants in his chest and biceps were remarkable.

"Looks good," the doctor muttered as he checked incisions and drain tubes. "Nurse…come closer with that pan. I'm going to remove the drain tubes now."

She scooted closer, holding out a small, shallow pan.

A few places ended up rewrapped, but with lighter bandages. The rest were left open to the air. Richard felt as if he were a good twenty pounds lighter. The mental stress he'd been under was almost over. Now that the doctor was gone, he was free to finish his quest to get Dieter out of trouble.

The call to Isis was going to take finesse, but that was something Richard had plenty of. He picked up his cell phone and punched in the number.

"Isis, phone for you."

"Get the fuck out of my face. Can't you see I'm busy, boy?"

The man standing with the phone in his hand didn't budge. Given that he was seven inches over six feet tall, only a woman like Isis could get away with calling him *boy*. That and the fact that she liked the way he made her feel in bed.

"You're gonna wanna take this call," he said, then took a step backward, just in case.

Isis rolled her head from one side to the other, then took a deep breath to calm herself. Her shrink kept telling her she was going to burst a blood vessel if she didn't learn how to let off steam without hurting someone. But for a six-foot-tall black woman who'd been born into a world where standing out could get a person noticed by all the right people or get her killed, she'd decided to be the one in charge of choosing which it was going to be.

She could have been a model, with her rail-thin body and the stunning Egyptian cast of her features. But no one had told her she was pretty enough or smart enough, so she'd learned how to be mean enough to do what she needed to do to get respect. Now she ran all the prostitutes between Houston and Galveston, controlled most of the drugs, ran guns into Colombia and wasn't above anything else that might net her a profit.

It was through guns that she and Richard Ponte had

become acquaintances. But Richard had wanted more from her than the sale of a cache or two of the newest automatic weapons or a truckload of hollow-point ammo for one of her drug cartels. He'd been somewhat mesmerized by her beauty, but more so by the power she wielded. She didn't consider him her lover, but when he was in the area, she did take to the way he treated her. The wining and dining, the jewelry, the flowers, the elegant style with which he chose their food, and their wines—it was all part of a world where she would never belong. She'd heard about his recent misfortunes, but she wasn't one to judge. She had plenty of her own sins to worry about. Still, she'd been somewhat uneasy that their prior "moments" together might have garnered the notice of the Feds, who seemed to be hauling all the skeletons out of Richard Ponte's closet. When it seemed their attention wasn't going to turn her way, she'd begun breathing easy.

Now she was giving the evil eye to the man on the other side of her desk.

"Are you still here, fool?"

He handed her the phone and walked out.

She hit Save on her laptop, then slapped the phone to her ear.

"Yeah?"

"Isis."

Her breath caught at the back of her throat as her gut knotted. Then she exhaled slowly.

"You are one gutsy fucker," she said softly.

"Miss you, too," Richard said.

"Why are you calling me?"

"I need a favor."

"Hell no."

Richard flinched. He'd been afraid this would happen, but he was desperate.

"It's not for me…exactly."

"Exactly who *is* it for?"

"Dieter."

She snorted beneath her breath. "That gay pretty boy? I can't give him what he needs. I don't swing that way."

Richard frowned. It was the first time he'd ever given a thought to Dieter's sexual preferences, and while it was somewhat startling to hear her say it, it also didn't surprise him.

"He needs money and a new identity to leave the country."

"I'll just bet he does," she said. "Why you think I'd go and mix myself up in your messed-up business? I'm not some stupid cunt you can pay to do your dirty work."

"That's not fair," Richard said softly. "I never called you that. I never treated you like that. I treated you with honor and respect…because I honor and respect you. No one will ever know you helped."

"I'm sorry, but that's not the way the justice system works. It's called aiding and abetting, and I'm not going to prison for aiding and abetting anyone accused of treason. You get me?"

"I get you, my beauty. I've always gotten you. And I never intended to play this card, but you've given me no choice."

Isis stiffened, then stood abruptly and started to pace.

"Damn you. Damn you. You swore you'd never talk about that."

"I'm still not talking about it. But I'm asking you to reconsider my request."

Isis was so mad she was shaking. The one time—the only time—she'd ever shown the chink in her armor had been to this man. Yes, he'd been good to her in the past, but that was because it suited him. She'd never been deceived into believing he cared about her. He'd used her just as much as she'd used him. He'd wanted to fuck a black woman, and she'd known it. And she'd let it happen for the glimpses he'd given her into a world in which she would never belong.

But he knew about Gabriel. He knew about her son— her beautiful, ten-year-old son. She'd known from the moment she'd gotten pregnant that she wasn't going to abort the fetus, and she'd known on the day she'd felt the first kick that she would not bring the child up in this world in which she'd chosen to live. And she'd known the moment she'd seen his innocent little face that he must never know where he came from or who his mother was.

At the least, it would ruin his life. At the most, it could get him killed. So she'd hand-picked his parents from an ad in a newspaper, an African-American couple unable to have children of their own and anxious to adopt a same-race child of one year or younger.

She'd considered it a sign from God. He was an up-and-coming young lawyer, his wife a pediatrician at Houston General. The kind of parents she wished had been hers. So she'd hardened her heart and given away her baby boy. But she knew where he was and what he looked like, and what kind of grades he made in school. She knew he was into *Star Wars* and liked computer games. She knew he was afraid of the dark and that his favorite flavor of ice cream was strawberry. It didn't matter how she knew all that, but it did matter that he never know about her.

If Richard Ponte had been standing before her right now, she would have killed him herself. But he wasn't, and he could bring down her carefully built house of cards.

"If I could, I would slit your throat for this," she growled.

"I know. I'm sorry. Really."

"You lie. You lie. You *lie.*" Then she drew a deep, shaky breath, and grabbed a pen and paper. "Give me the damned phone number. I'll do this one thing—and then I swear to God, if you ever threaten me like this again, I'll find you. And I'll cut off your balls and stuff them down your miserable throat."

Richard shuddered. He knew her well enough to know she meant it. He read off Dieter's phone number, repeated it again, and was rewarded with a dial tone humming in his ear.

Dieter was in the mall looking for some laborer's clothing when his cell phone rang. He glanced at caller ID, then frowned. All the screen said was Private Caller, but it had to be her. Besides Richard, she was the only person who would have this number.

"Hello?"

"Listen to me, you little worm, because I will not repeat myself. There is a Mexican restaurant down near the water called Mamacita's. Be there at eleven o'clock tonight. You'll get what you need. And when you see your boss again, tell him for me if he ever shows his face back in Houston again, he's a dead man."

Dieter stiffened. Was this the woman who was going to help, or was this a warning that everything was getting worse?

"Mamacita's. Right," Dieter repeated.

Like Richard, he, too, was rewarded with a dial tone. But he didn't care. He was out of options. He had to take a chance that this would work out. He paid for the three pairs of denim pants he'd picked out and left the store on the run. He needed to get back to his motel, pack and find that Mexican restaurant. The worst thing that could happen right now was being too late and missing his chance to escape.

Fourteen

John was in his office, running through e-mail and talking to his broker, when Alicia walked past the doorway. He saw the slump in her shoulders. When she didn't even look his way, he knew he needed to do something to get her out of her depression.

He'd been considering a trip into Sedona for a couple of days, and now seemed like a good time. He was going to put a smile on Alicia's face today or know the reason why.

Alicia was standing in the hallway outside what she called John's "memorial room," staring at the painting of White Fawn, when she heard footsteps behind her. She sighed. Damn. He'd caught her.

"Hey, baby…come away from there."

Alicia wouldn't turn around. She didn't want him to know she was jealous, and she figured he would see it on her face.

"I was just…uh…"

"Wanna go for a ride?"

She turned before she thought. "In the helicopter?"

"No. There is a Jeep out back. We can drive."

"Really? Is it safe?"

He scooped her up in his arms and kissed her soundly on the lips before he set her back down.

"Yes, really. And who the hell knows?" he said as he gave her shoulders a gentle squeeze. "We need some groceries, and I want to show you my favorite art gallery while we're there."

"Fantastic!" Alicia said as she clapped her hands. "You know what? This will be our first real date."

The right corner of his mouth tilted slightly.

"I'd say it was about time to show you a good time."

She grinned. "You'll have to work hard to surpass your own benchmark, Nightwalker."

"How so?"

"The best times I've ever had in my life were in bed with you. I can't think of anything you can do to top that, but I'm all for giving it a go."

A smile broke across John's face, then spread all the way to his eyes. Alicia saw them glitter and knew he was pleased by what she'd said. When he took her into his arms and kissed her again, this time slower and longer, she shivered with sudden longing.

He heard her sigh. The temptation to take her to bed and forget the trip to Sedona was strong, but he'd promised. Besides, there was always tonight.

"So put on your going-to-town duds and some comfortable shoes. I'll be in the kitchen making a list of things we need."

"I won't be long," Alicia said, and hurried away.

John watched her go, then hesitated before glancing

into the room—straight to the woman in the painting. He stood for a long, silent moment, waiting for a sound to come out of that beautiful smiling mouth, even though he knew better.

"You would like her," he said softly, then turned and walked away.

John drove with the windows down, letting the hot wind blow in and out at will, a smile on his face and the accelerator all the way to the floor. If he had a vice, it was speed. Alicia glanced over at him as they drove, eyeing his silver earring bouncing and swaying with the airflow, and thought to herself that, at that moment, he looked every inch an untamed male.

Sensing her gaze on him, he looked at her and winked, which made her want him all over again.

"You're a madman, aren't you?"

He threw his head back and laughed. "Not mad…just a little bit uncivilized."

She just shook her head, grabbed hold of the seat belt and held on.

They reached the outskirts of Sedona a short while later. John took her straight to the art gallery and introduced her to the owner, a woman he'd known for years named Sasha Macklin.

Sasha had started out trying to earn a living as a painter years ago but quickly came to the conclusion that she would make more money selling other people's art, rather than her own. She'd had the business for almost thirty years now and loved what she did.

She'd met John twenty-five years ago, when she was a size eight and her long red hair was thick and wavy.

Now her hair was short and gray, and her eight had turned into eighteen, although she didn't really care. She always laughed, claiming she'd earned every gray hair and every pound she was carrying, and was proud of them.

But when John Nightwalker walked into her gallery, the first thing she thought was that she was seeing a ghost. It had been almost fifteen years since she'd seen him, although they talked now and then on the phone. But looking at him coming in the door with a tall, dark-haired woman on his arm gave her a twinge of regret. The woman was probably somewhere between twenty-five and thirty. Just the age she'd been when they met.

John saw her eyes widen and could only imagine what she was thinking. Still, there was no getting around the obvious.

"Hey, lady…I'm looking for a good deal."

Sasha pushed herself up from behind her desk, opened her arms and hugged him.

"You crazy Indian…are you still driving like a bat out of hell?"

Alicia grinned. The woman obviously knew him well.

"Sasha, I want you to meet someone. A—Lisa, this is Sasha Macklin. Sasha…Lisa."

Alicia realized immediately why he hadn't called her by her name. The name Alicia Ponte was something of a lightning rod these days. No need to let the whole world know where she was.

"Sasha, I'm so pleased to meet you. John told me you had the best art gallery in Sedona. I can't wait to see the displays."

Sasha beamed. Praise for her first love always made her happy.

"It's the truth, if I say so myself. Look your fill, Lisa."

Alicia nodded, then slipped off for a closer look at a grouping of small sculptures, giving John some alone time with a woman who was obviously an old friend.

Sasha eyed John up and down, as if she were judging a piece of art, then shrugged.

"I don't know how you do it, Nightwalker, but you haven't aged a day since we met."

John just shook his head and hugged her again. "You're being too kind," he said. "So tell me, what's been happening with you?"

Sasha snorted. "Nothing is what's happening, but that's okay with me. Men are too much trouble to mess with these days."

He laughed. "Never thought I'd hear you say that."

Her eyes narrowed thoughtfully as she looked at him again. Impulsively, she put her hand on his face, feeling the taut muscles beneath his skin.

"Seriously…how do you do it?"

"Would you believe I'm immortal?"

She rolled her eyes and punched him on the arm. "Just like a man. Ask a serious question, get a bullshit answer."

He smiled. "What can I say?"

She sighed. "So let's go join your lady friend—who, by the way, looks suspiciously like the pictures I saw of that Ponte woman."

John's smile slipped.

"Don't worry," Sasha said quickly. "I learned a long time ago how to keep my mouth shut. She's in a hell of a fix, isn't she…having her father turn out to be a traitor and all? I don't know if I'd have the guts to do what she did."

John looked at Alicia, who was moving slowly along

the length of one wall while gazing at the paintings Sasha had hung there.

"She's a constant source of amazement," he said softly.

Sasha sighed. She was too old to feel jealous, but there had been a time in her life when she would have killed to have him look at her the way he was looking at Alicia.

"You're in love with her, aren't you?"

John was a little startled to hear it said outside of his own thoughts. Then he shrugged.

"It's beginning to feel like it."

Sasha patted him on the arm. "Even if she's a little young for you, I wish you the best."

John grinned. Young? Sasha had no idea how right she was.

"Let's go join her," John said, and pulled Sasha along as he hurried to Alicia's side.

John slid an arm around Alicia's shoulders. "See anything you like?"

She looked up at him, then smiled. "Easier to ask if there's anything here I *don't* like. Everything is amazing." Then she pointed to a painting to her right. "That one is stunning," she said.

Sasha smiled. "Good eye, my dear. That piece was painted by one of my most successful artists. His name is Troy Anderson. He's Cherokee, and a native of Oklahoma. I have some more of his work in another room. Want to see?"

"Please," Alicia said, then slipped her hand beneath John's elbow. "Do you mind?"

"Hey…we came here to see art. So let's see all there is to see, okay?"

"Okay," Alicia said, and followed along, listening and sometimes adding to the conversation between John and Sasha as they did a walk-through of the gallery.

They were almost back to the front gallery when Alicia saw a set of photos hanging on a wall just inside what appeared to be an office. Almost immediately, she realized John was in one of them.

"Hey!" she said. "That's you, isn't it?" She pointed toward the photo as she stepped inside the room.

"Wait!" John said, but it was too late. She was already there.

Sasha frowned at him, then followed them in. She didn't see what the big deal was. The woman could hardly be jealous. The picture had been taken the weekend she and John met, which was probably before Alicia Ponte had even been born.

Alicia was standing before the photo, frowning. Something was out of kilter about it, but she couldn't figure out what it was. Then all of a sudden, it hit her. The hair and clothes. They were seriously out of style. She pointed to the photo, smiling.

"Hey, John, what was the occasion? A costume party?"

Sasha burst out laughing. "No, honey. That was the height of fashion in the eighties. I distinctly remembered shopping for hours before I settled on that minidress. As for my hair...what can I say? I had myself a real Farrah Fawcett flip going on, didn't I?"

Alicia stared at the photo, trying to make sense of what Sasha had just said. "I'm sorry. Are you in the picture, too?"

Sasha pointed. "I know I've changed, but hey...it's been twenty-five years."

Alicia's heart began to beat so hard and fast that she felt dizzy. This couldn't be right. That pretty redhead in the photo was Sasha—twenty-five years ago?

She turned to John, unaware of the look of shock on her face.

He held his breath, not sure what to expect.

Alicia looked from Sasha to John, then back at the photo, before suddenly turning around and walking out of the office.

John frowned. This wasn't good. He glanced at Sasha, who shrugged, as if to say, *How can you blame her?* and hurried after her.

"Alicia…baby?"

She stopped and turned around. "Yes?"

The expression on her face was calm. He didn't know what to make of it.

"Uh, you just walked out so quickly, I thought you were upset."

"Who? Me? Upset? Why would I be upset?" she asked, unaware that her voice was rising with each word she spoke.

John flinched. Damn. "You tell me," he said.

She doubled up her fists, resisting the urge to slug him. "I don't know what to say, what to think, what to do. Have I fallen in love with a gorgeous sixty-something…or do you have another big round of bullshit to explain this away, as well? Oh, wait. Let me guess. That same Tibetan monk who taught you how to heal yourself also gave you the secret to eternal youth."

"This date isn't going as well as I expected."

She rolled her eyes and then spied Sasha standing in the hall behind them. She shifted gears so fast that

John's head was spinning as she stepped past him and retraced her steps with her hand outstretched.

"Sasha...I have to say that you have a wonderful array of Native American and Southwestern art. And, it's been a pleasure to meet you. However, we have a couple of errands to run before we head back home, so I know you'll understand that we need to go now."

"It was a pleasure meeting you, too," Sasha said, then gave the younger woman an impulsive hug. "I don't know why I did that," she said as she gave her a quick pat and let her go. "You just looked like you could do with a hug."

Alicia smiled. "Thank you. A person can never get too many hugs." Then she turned around and walked past John without speaking.

He sighed. So much for a change of pace. They were right back to square one, with distrust and anger.

"It was good to see you again," he told Sasha.

"It was good to see you, too." Then she added, "Better take care of that one. I think she's a keeper."

John nodded and hurried on out to the Jeep. When he got there, Alicia was already buckled up and waiting. She wouldn't look at him, and he didn't know what to say to make things better.

"Are you hungry?" he asked.

She looked at him as if he'd just lost his mind, then burst out laughing.

"Actually, man of mystery, I am. So feed me something hot and spicy. Then we'll buy our groceries and head for home."

Now he knew he was out of his league. This woman kept blindsiding him time and time again.

"I know this really good Mexican place…."

"Works for me," she said, then added, "Just so you know, you have not slipped by this. I just chose not to discuss the fact that I've fallen in love with a man my father's age and didn't know it. And…the big deal is not your real age. It's that you didn't tell me."

"Fair enough," he said, and backed the Jeep out of its parking place and headed down the street.

The meal had gone down well. The errands had been run. Groceries were on the back floorboard of the Jeep, and, to keep them from spoiling, John had rolled up the windows and turned on the air conditioner for the ride home.

This leg of the journey wasn't as carefree as the first half had been, but even considering everything that had happened, he was still fairly confident of the outcome.

Alicia was reading a story from one of the several newspapers they'd picked up when John suddenly hit the brakes and began slowing down. That brought her attention from the paper to the reason they were no longer driving at warp speed.

"What's happening?" she asked as she looked out the window.

"That car up ahead. It just swerved completely off the highway into the ditch, then back onto the road again. I think the driver is either falling asleep, drunk or sick. Impossible to tell which."

"Oh, no!" Alicia said, and then gasped as the car began a repeat version of what John had just witnessed.

This time, though, the driver didn't pull back onto the

road or even slow down. The car sailed over the ditch, hit a large boulder a few yards away from the road and then rolled end over end until it came to rest upside down.

"Damn it!" John said.

Seconds later they reached the place where the car had left the highway. He slammed the car into Park and handed Alicia his cell phone.

"We just passed southbound mile marker 123 a few moments ago. Call 911!"

Alicia's hands were shaking as she punched in the numbers, while John jumped out of the Jeep, leaped the ditch and started running.

"Nine-one-one. What is your emergency?" a dispatcher asked.

"We just saw a car go off the road, southbound on the highway out of Sedona. We're just past mile marker 123. I don't know how many people are in the car, but it rolled over twice before landing upside down."

"Is the highway blocked?" the dispatcher asked.

"No. But hurry," Alicia begged. "The car is starting to smoke." Then she gasped. "Dear God. It just burst into flames."

"I'm dispatching fire and rescue services as we speak. Stay on the line."

But Alicia was already out of her seat and digging through the back of the Jeep. She'd seen a fire extinguisher in there when they were loading up the groceries in Sedona. Shoving sacks aside right and left, she finally found it. Her heart was in her throat as she ran, because just before the car had started burning, she'd seen John crawl inside. Now the flames were blazing from beneath the hood. Smoke was everywhere, and she couldn't see John.

"John!" she screamed. "John! Where are you? Get out! *Get out!*"

The moment John reached the wreck, he saw the driver. The window was broken out on that side, so he dropped to his belly and began crawling inside. He was halfway in when he realized the driver was a woman with short dark hair. She was unconscious, and bleeding from a large number of cuts on her face and arms. She was also dangling upside down, still strapped in by her seat belt.

"Lady! Lady! Can you hear me?" he yelled, but she didn't answer. He began pulling at the seat belt, trying to undo it, but the latch wouldn't give.

He could already smell smoke. There was no time to waste. He pulled the knife out of his boot and slashed the strap in two. The moment she was free, she dropped upside down into his arms. He put the knife blade between his teeth and began backing out, pulling her with him. Suddenly he heard something pop. Within seconds, smoke began coming out from under the hood and sifting through the dash in huge, sweeping billows.

John grunted and kept on pulling. He kept telling himself not to think about what was happening, just to keep moving. Inch by inch, ignoring pain and fire, he pulled them both backward. Blood was dripping in his eyes, fire licking at his skin and clothing as he dragged her through fire and glass. With mere seconds to go before they were both engulfed, he suddenly felt her slide free.

Before he could move, they were engulfed in a new kind of smoke. But this time, instead of burning them, it was putting out the flames. The knife fell from his mouth as he rolled over on his back, still holding the woman in his arms. Then he saw Alicia standing over them, holding a fire extinguisher. He groaned aloud, violently shuddering from pain.

Then, from behind him, he heard a whoosh, followed by a hiss.

"Run!" he yelled as he got to his feet, then picked the woman back up. "It's going to explode!"

Alicia gave him a wild-eyed look, then turned and ran, taking comfort in the sound of his footsteps right behind her. They were about fifty feet from the wreck when it blew, knocking them facedown on the ground. When Alicia could think straight again, she rolled over, then got up.

John and the woman were a few feet away. The woman wasn't moving, and John was sitting beside her, holding his arms away from his body. His shirt was charred in so many places that she could barely tell what it had looked like before, and his hands and arms… Dear Lord, they were horribly burned.

"John! Oh my God…John!" she screamed, and rushed to his side.

He was shaking so hard he could barely speak. He knew it would pass, but for now, the agony was almost unbearable. He knew Alicia was panicked, but he was in too much pain to reassure her that it was temporary. When she reached toward him, he quickly withdrew.

"Don't touch me," he said, then put his head down on his knees, trying to bring the world back into focus. "The woman…see if she's breathing."

Alicia didn't want to leave his side, but she knew he

was right. She crawled on her hands and knees to the woman, then put her fingers on the pulse point at the side of her neck. There was a faint but persistent beat.

"Her heart's still beating," she said, eyeing the woman's injuries, which were too severe for any on-site first aid she might have tried. "There's some water in the Jeep. I'll be right back," she said, and ran as fast as she could across the ditch and up to the side of the road where the Jeep was parked. It wasn't until she began hunting for water that she realized the engine was still running. She turned it off and pocketed the keys before grabbing a newly bought plastic-wrapped case of bottled water and starting back to John's side.

When she got there, he was on his knees beside the woman. He'd undone her blouse and unbuckled her belt, revealing a huge, ugly bruise that was quickly forming in the middle of her abdomen.

"She may have internal injuries," he said, and then grabbed a bottle of water from Alicia and started pouring it on the woman's face in a small trickle, washing away the grit and blood from her face and eyes, then pouring it on the places where she'd been burned, as well.

Alicia was staring at John as if she were looking at a ghost. She couldn't move. She couldn't speak.

"Hand me another," he ordered. "She's only got a couple of small burns. I shielded most of her body with mine after the car started to burn."

When Alicia didn't respond, he turned to see what was wrong. Her lips were slightly parted, as if she'd been running hard. Her face was dirt-streaked and sweaty, and there was a smear of blood on her arm. But it was the look in her eyes that got his attention.

"Alicia?"

"Your burns."

Damn.

He ignored her. "Hand me another bottle of water, please."

"They're almost gone."

"Alicia, the water. Please!"

She blinked as her focus shifted to the task at hand, pulled another bottle out from under the torn plastic wrap and handed it over.

"Open some more… Hurry, baby," he said.

The urgency of his request finally sank in, so she continued to twist off the caps and hand the bottles over as quickly as he emptied them onto the woman's burns.

It seemed like forever, but they finally began hearing the faint sounds of sirens.

"I think I hear them," John said suddenly.

"Thank God," Alicia breathed.

Minutes later, the scene was swarming with firemen and rescue vehicles. Paramedics were working on the unconscious woman, trying to stabilize her for transport. John had moved aside but was telling them all he knew.

"We saw her swerve off onto the shoulder once, then get back on the highway. A few seconds later she did it again, and that time she kept going. She flew over the ditch, hit that boulder, and then went end over end twice before landing upside down. I think she was unconscious before she wrecked. Why she was out of it is your call. She was either asleep, ill or drunk. I looked for a medical alert bracelet but didn't find one."

The highway patrolman was taking notes as John talked. As John paused, he asked a question.

"Did you see a purse?" he asked.

"No, but then, I wasn't looking for one at the time."

The patrolman nodded, then eyed John's clothing. "You need to get yourself checked out before the paramedics leave."

"I'm okay," John said. "It was just my clothes. Lisa used my fire extinguisher on the both of us before much damage could be done."

The highway patrolman glanced at Alicia, noted the shock in her eyes and thought nothing of it. It was a typical reaction to witnessing a wreck.

"Way to go," he said.

Alicia nodded, but she couldn't quit shaking. If it hadn't been for seeing John's burns disappear before her eyes, she would have blamed her shock on nothing more than an adrenaline crash. But she *had* seen them, and now she was scared—scared out of her mind.

She didn't want to hear any more about Tibetan monks. There was something going on with John Nightwalker that made no sense. She'd heard of men who carried their age well, but not to the degree that he did. And she knew there were people who healed quickly, but not like this. She'd never believed in UFOs or aliens before, but she was beginning to wonder if she'd been wrong.

"Okay," the patrolman finally said. "I think we've covered everything. You two are free to go. And I'll tell you now, I don't know what's wrong with that lady, but she's sure lucky you two were behind her when this happened."

"Glad we could help," John said, and then reached for Alicia's arm. But when she flinched and pulled back, he knew his troubles weren't over yet. "Come on, baby," he said softly. "We can go now."

Alicia stared at him, wondering if she had the guts to get back in that Jeep with him and drive away. But there was an expression in his eyes that broke her heart—as if he was expecting to be shunned. She sighed, then pulled the car keys out of her pocket and dropped them in his hand.

John reached for her hand, waiting for her touch. When she finally threaded her fingers through his, she felt him shiver. They walked to the Jeep together. John opened the door for her, then waited until she was safely inside before seating himself. He started the engine and drove away—well under the speed limit.

Fifteen

The house was quiet when they walked inside. Alicia was carrying an armful of grocery sacks, as was John. They set them on the kitchen counters, then quietly went about the business of putting things away.

John felt the distance between them and hated it, but it was his own fault. There was a reason why he'd never indulged in a serious relationship before, and this was it. Sex for the sake of it was one thing, but staying with one person for a long period of time meant explaining the reality that was his life. And that was impossible. Yet here he was, faced with the inevitable result of his own foolish actions. He should never have let himself care about her, but he had. He wished he didn't love her, but he did.

Once they were done, there was a long moment of uneasy silence. John took a deep breath, and then decided the confrontation had been delayed long enough.

"Alicia…I—"

"I'll bet you're wanting a shower and a fresh change of clothes," she said. "I know I sure am."

John sighed. So she wasn't ready for a discussion yet. He couldn't blame her.

"Yes, I would. But when I'm done, we talk. Okay?"

She shrugged.

John frowned. "What's that supposed to mean?"

"I feel like I've already heard all you have to say. I'm not up for any more bullshit, and I'm sure you can understand why."

John's chin jutted angrily. "You go do whatever it is you need to do, but I'll be back in the living room in exactly fifteen minutes, at which time I will expect you there. If you're not, I'll come looking for you, and I'm sure *you* can understand why."

He walked out of the kitchen without looking back, leaving Alicia with the feeling that she'd been the one in the wrong, which wasn't fair. *She* hadn't lied about her age, and she wasn't the one who'd turned out to be some damn chameleon, changing skins and colors on a whim. But she'd seen the look in his eyes, and she knew he was pissed, and she didn't want to be on the receiving end of that anger again. So she headed for her room, trying not to run.

All during his shower, John kept playing one scenario after another through his mind, trying to figure out where to start and how to explain, which always seemed futile. He still didn't know how it had happened. It just had, and he was what he was. He'd learned his skills and weaknesses through accident and error. The Old Ones hadn't sent instructions along with their gift. They'd simply given him his wish, leaving him to figure out the rest.

By the time he dried off and dressed, he was sick to his stomach. He'd seen the gamut of expressions on

Alicia's face. Everything from intense fear to intense passion. He didn't know if he could survive seeing derision or disgust. He dressed without care, choosing a pair of jeans, leaving the rest of himself bare. He wasn't doing it to try to distract her. It was just that it was the closest to how he was most comfortable, and he needed all his wits to pull this off.

True to this word, he was in the living room, awaiting her arrival, twelve minutes later. Just when he thought he was going to have to make good on his threat, he heard her coming down the hall. He stood with his feet apart, his hands on his hips and his chin up, bracing himself for the possibility of an emotional blow.

And that was how Alicia saw him when she walked into the room. *Perfect,* she thought. *I have to get past that body to the task at hand.* Then she sighed. *I suppose I should be thankful he isn't completely naked.*

At first glance, he appeared defensive and angry. But she saw past that to the fear in his eyes and felt a sense of relief. If he was scared, then it was okay to let her own fear show.

"I'm here," she said hesitantly.

"As am I."

"Now what?"

This was where it got scary, but John had already decided to let her call the shots. He pointed to the sofa. "Maybe we could get comfortable? I don't know about you, but after being deep-fried this afternoon, I'm beat."

The memory of his skin charred and blistered and hanging in strips made her shudder, as did the fact that the horror was now nothing but a memory.

John sat in a chair opposite her when she took a seat on the sofa, then leaned forward.

"I'm going to swear to you now, by everything that's holy to me, that I will give you an honest answer to every question you ask. I will not lie or try to deceive you. Whether you believe me or not will be your choice, and yours alone."

Alicia felt a sense of elation. Finally she would understand.

"Thank you, John."

"What do you want to know?"

"I guess I'm going to start with the most recent of your revelations. Exactly how old are you?"

He groaned. Nothing like starting with the hardest thing to explain.

"We didn't keep a strict sense of time then the way we do now, but at my best guess, I'm about five hundred and twenty-nine years old."

Alicia's lips parted. Her heart started hammering so hard she thought it would burst. She jumped to her feet.

"Damn you! Damn you to hell and back, Night-walker! I am done with this. You keep treating me like some blithering idiot. Do I look like an idiot to you?" By now she was screaming. "Why did I think you would be honest? Why did I set myself up for this again?"

John sat without moving, waiting for her to run through her rage. Either she would get it over with or she would be gone. There was nothing he could do to change the outcome. But he couldn't stop his own reaction. Alicia's face had become a blur.

She was so lost in her fury that she didn't notice John wasn't moving—that he wasn't defending his statement or trying to explain why he'd said it. And when she finally did look at him, she was shocked. Right between one angry breath and the next, she spun, her finger pointed at his face with a curse on the verge of being born, and realized he hadn't moved.

Then she stopped. Were those tears in his eyes? She took another breath and shifted her stance, rearranging her thoughts in preparation for another angry round, when a tear rolled down his cheek.

The breath went out of her so fast it felt as if she'd been sucker punched. She paced back and forth in front of him, muttering to herself, then stopping and starting a half-dozen different sentences, until finally she sat back down and stared.

"John."

"What?"

"You don't expect me to believe that."

"Was that a statement or a question?" he asked.

"You expect me to believe you are five hundred and twenty-nine years old?"

"It was a faint hope, but an obviously misplaced one."

She leaned back on the sofa, exhausted from her rant, and confused beyond belief.

"You were serious?"

He nodded.

"Have you ever talked to anyone about this…delusion?"

The corner of his mouth twitched, then turned down. "You talking about a shrink, baby?"

"Well, there's nothing wrong with seeing one. Mental illness isn't anything to be ashamed of."

"You think I'm nuts."

"What would you have me believe?"

"That I told you the truth."

"Oh, for the Lord's sake," Alicia sputtered.

"Ask me something else," John said.

"I don't know if I dare," she said.

He waited.

"Okay…old man… If you're so old, and you claim my father is the man who killed your family, then I'm assuming you want me to believe my father is also an immortal."

"Not exactly."

"Then what—exactly—is it? Did he kill your family, or didn't he?"

"Do you believe in reincarnation?"

She swiped her hands across her face in frustration. "I asked you a question. You don't get to ask me one back until you've answered mine."

"I can't answer unless you tell me. Do you believe in reincarnation?"

"I don't think so."

"Then we're back up shit creek here, baby, because what I'm going to say hinges on that being a fact."

"Just spit it out," Alicia said. "I'll reserve judgment."

"It's a long story."

"I'm free for the evening. Do continue."

"My village…the village in which I was also born, was on the coast of what is now Georgia. The house where I first took you is built on the bluff that overlooked our village. The village of the Ah-ni-yv-wi-ya, also known as The People. I had seen twenty-nine summers and had taken White Fawn for my woman years before. We'd been together for fifteen of your years when I began to have visions. You would call them dreams. In the dreams, I kept seeing everything in flames, with blood all around and White Fawn dead at my feet. It's a dream that still returns from time to time."

Alicia shuddered. It was so close to what she'd dreamed after being stung by the scorpion. How was that possible? Had she somehow locked into his nightmares as he'd slept?

"I was second chief and felt the burdens of my duties strongly. And because of my visions and fear for my people, I began to stand watch over the village from the bluff. One day a storm began to approach, and as it came, it also brought strangers to our shore. I know now that they were Spaniards, but you can imagine my shock, seeing this huge canoe with what looked like great white wings, and seeing men with white skin and hair on their faces. Seeing their bodies covered in strange garments, some of them metal, although we had never seen anything like that before, so I didn't know what it was at the time. They came ashore, and I still don't know why they did what they did. We had nothing of what I now know would have been of value, but they came anyway, led by a man of great greed and evil. That same man's soul is now in your father, Richard Ponte."

Alicia covered her face. She was in love with a madman. "You blame my father for something that happened five hundred years ago?"

John felt her panic, but he couldn't help her. All he could do was explain himself.

"A man dies, but a soul lives on…and sometimes it's reborn. Sometimes quickly. Sometimes not for many decades. I always know when his soul has been reborn.

When that happens, I live with what amounts to a constant physical pain. The closer I am to the soul's incarnation, the worse the pain. I have chased his soul across the continents and the centuries, yearning for revenge, needing to find my rest."

Alicia felt sick. This was crazy, but she had to ask. "What happens if you finally find his soul?"

"Nothing—unless I'm the one who ends its current body's life."

Her head was throbbing. This was beyond ridiculous, yet she heard herself asking yet another question. "And if you ever did kill the body in which the soul resides…do you die then, too?"

He shrugged. "Obviously I don't know, because it hasn't happened. But I do know that no matter how many times I've been hurt or wounded, I heal almost immediately. You've seen that for yourself. I can't die until I've avenged my people."

She closed her eyes momentarily, trying to regain her sense of self, then remembered she'd interrupted him in the middle of his tale.

"So what happened after the ship sailed into the bay?"

"I sensed this was the danger that I'd been dreaming about and started running back down the bluff, trying to get to the village. I could hear screaming and war cries. I heard what I thought was thunder from the incoming storm, but later I learned it was gunshots. I smelled smoke mingling with the wind and the rain. By the time I got to the village, it was burning, and the Ah-ni-yv-wi-ya were dead…all of them. Including White Fawn."

Alicia didn't know what to believe, but the drama of the story had gotten to her. When he mentioned White

Fawn, she went still. What was most telling was the tremble in John's voice and the tears now running freely down his face. Whatever torture John believed was happening, it was hurting him badly. She tuned back in, listening as he spoke.

"There was a man standing over her. He had her medicine pouch in his hand." Then he paused, sensing she would need an explanation. "A medicine pouch was something each of us wore. It contained things sacred only to us. No one else knew what we chose, but it was vital to our lives. And he'd taken it from her without care for her soul or her life." He shuddered, then cleared his throat softly before the next words would come out of his mouth.

"He'd cut her throat."

At that point he stopped and scrubbed his hands across his face, as if trying to wipe the images from his mind. He took a deep breath, then began to talk again, and this time the emotion was gone from his voice.

"I tried to kill them all. Such a rage was in me that I can't even explain. I can tell you now what happened, but then, I didn't understand it. They tried to shoot at me, but their powder got wet from the rain. They were no match for me in hand-to-hand combat. I killed them as I came to them. Sending my arrows into their bodies, picking up a dropped spear and putting it through a man's chest. Any weapon I found as I ran, I used. Even their own weapons I used against them. When they saw they couldn't stop me, they began to run back to shore, then into their boats. They rowed away into the bay before I could get to them. I was alone on the shore. I was all that was left of The People. I couldn't live with the knowledge that I'd failed to avenge them. I didn't want to live without White Fawn. I began cursing and screaming, telling my people that I would not die until I'd achieved justice for the deaths. I said it over and over in a fever of a rage. Then suddenly there was this great light, and I thought it was lightning from the storm. Now I would die. Now I would join my people. But it wasn't to be. Instead, I was bathed in a light from the Old Ones and given what I'd asked for. I was told I would not die until I had avenged the deaths of my people."

He sighed, then shoved his fingers through his hair. "Who knew it would be so hard to find just one man? I've always sensed his soul and come close to catching up to him a couple of times, but it's never happened." Then he shrugged. "I always know when the body dies again. Then I'm left to wait until I feel the soul has been reborn before I can hope again."

"So you're saying my father has that soul?"

"Over sixty years ago, I felt it happen…that it had been reborn. Then I felt the connection again when we first met. In fact, at first I thought it was you."

Alicia suddenly shivered. "You mean if I was that soul, you would have killed me?"

"Right where you stood, in front of that fancy little BMW, beside Marv's Gas and Guzzle, without batting an eye."

The blood ran out of her face so fast John thought she would faint. He regretted her reaction, but not his answer. He'd sworn to tell the truth. And so he waited.

Nearly five minutes passed before Alicia could speak. When she did, he knew he was lost.

"Is that all of it?"

"Pretty much."

"Bottom line…you're five hundred and twenty-nine

years old, on a quest through eternity to find the reincarnated soul of the man who killed your people and your wife, and you're telling me that's my father. You also can't age, and you can't die. Is that about it?"

He nodded.

Alicia struggled to maintain a semblance of calm. She took a deep breath and almost managed a smile.

"John…I have to tell you…you are an amazing man. You have saved my life more than once. I've witnessed your bravery on behalf of others and at risk to your own well-being. I don't understand how your body heals itself, but I do know that you make love to me like a god. For the first time in my life, I was truly happy, despite the fact that my father still wants me dead."

He watched her, waiting for the "but" he sensed was coming, and he wasn't wrong.

"But…it has come to my attention that, while you are still all of the things I just mentioned, you are also, my darling, as mad as a hatter. You need help. Lots of help, from someone who knows more about mental illness than I do. I'll stick by you. I'll go with you. I'll do anything you want or need to help you get well."

John's heart sank. While she hadn't run away, she had still withdrawn. She thought he was crazy, and he couldn't blame her. But it didn't change the fact that the bond that had been between them was gone.

He nodded once, then slapped his legs lightly, as if to say that was that, and stood.

"Where are you going?" she asked.

He paused. "I won't run out on you, but I don't think I want to be around you anymore…at least for now."

He walked out without looking back, and Alicia was

shocked that he somehow maintained an air of having been betrayed. The longer she sat, the guiltier she felt.

"It's not my fault," she muttered. "He's the one who's nuts."

But the silence ate at her, until she finally got up and went to find him, shocked to realize that night had come unannounced.

She looked through all the rooms before trying the terrace. She walked out into the darkness, didn't see him and was about to go back inside when she saw motion from the corner of her eye and looked up.

It was a falling star.

She paused, thinking to herself that she hadn't seen one of those in ages. She stared at it for a moment, watching—waiting for it to burn out. But when it didn't and instead kept flying through space, coming closer and closer, her interest turned to shock, then disbelief. This must be a meteor—and if it didn't stop, it looked like it would hit out in the desert.

"John!" she cried, wanting him to see this. But he didn't answer and didn't come. "John! John! You have to come see this!" she cried. But she was still alone.

The light continued to come closer and closer until it was so bright it lit up the desert. At that point Alicia realized John was standing at the far end of the yard, watching it, too. She started to go to him, but then the light was upon them. It centered on John, bathing him in a glow so bright that she lost sight of him. The more time that passed, the more convinced she became that she, too, was losing her mind. She didn't realize she was holding her breath until the light suddenly shifted and started toward her.

She tried to run, but her feet wouldn't move. Fear unlike anything she'd ever known swept through her, and when she tried to scream, found herself unable to make a sound. And so she stood, expecting to die in flames.

The light was on her, then in her. What she thought would kill her instead left her calmed—waiting for what she knew would be a message. It came in the form of an old Indian man with braids so long they dragged on the ground, wearing a robe of rainbow-hued feathers that fluttered in a breeze she didn't feel.

When he smiled at her, she wanted to fall at his feet, but he reached for her instead. He didn't speak, but she understood she was to hold out her hand. This had to be a dream. Any moment she would wake up, and find herself back inside and in bed. But she didn't wake up, and when she held out her hand, she felt him drop something in it. She wanted to look down, but her gaze was locked onto his face.

Then he spoke only one word.

"Believe."

He closed her fingers over the object he handed her, and right before her eyes, he disappeared. Between one blink and the next, the light and the dream and everything she thought she'd been seeing was gone.

"Wow. That was weird," she said in a voice she hardly recognized.

As she spoke, John walked out of the darkness and up onto the terrace. He walked past without even looking at her and went on into the house. He'd been out there the whole time, and he must have heard her calling, but he hadn't answered. Hadn't cared. The ache in her heart was growing with each passing minute. She started to follow him into the house, when she realized there was something in her fist.

The hair rose on the back of her neck.

Impossible.

That old Indian had been a dream, and so had the thing he'd put in her hand. So if it had been a dream, what was she holding?

She ran into the house, slamming the door behind her, and turned on the lights. Everything in the kitchen looked the same. The same stainless-steel appliances. The same turquoise-colored dishes in the cupboard. John's sunglasses lying on the counter beneath the phone.

She closed her eyes and took a slow, shuddering breath, then slowly opened her fingers and looked down.

For a moment she couldn't think. Didn't know why the object looked so familiar. Then she remembered and let it fall onto the table as she screamed and jumped backward in disbelief.

Suddenly John was in the doorway. She pointed at the table. Her voice was shaking; her eyes were rounded in shock.

"Where did that come from?" she cried.

John walked over to the table and picked it up. "What is it?"

"My mother's brooch. Sweet Jesus…my mother's brooch."

She kept hearing the old man's voice, telling her to believe. But how could she believe something this impossible?

"Pretty," John said. "But what's the big deal?"

The big deal? Alicia wanted to laugh but was afraid if she let loose it would come out as a scream.

"The big deal is…I gave her the brooch the Mother's Day before she died. And I pinned that same brooch on her dress the day of her funeral. It was buried with her. It's supposed to be six feet underground in a Boston cemetery."

"So?"

This time she did scream. "But it's not!"

"What did the old man tell you?" John asked.

Her eyes narrowed. "How do you know about the old man? How do you *know?* Are we dreaming the same dreams again?"

"It wasn't a dream. And he always comes in a light, and he always comes with a message."

She was hearing his words and trying to deal with the fact that what she'd seen outside hadn't been a dream. It had been real. There really had been an old Indian who'd given her the brooch.

"What did he say to you?" John repeated.

"'Believe.' He said for me to believe."

John waited. "And still you do not. What is there left to say?"

"I don't know. *I don't know.* This isn't right. It isn't real. This can't be happening."

He sighed. "You sound like a broken record, Alicia. Get out or get over it."

Even though they hurt, the words were the slap in the face she needed. "He talked with you first."

"Yes."

"And he always brings a message?"

"Yes."

"What did he tell you?"

"It doesn't matter."

"That's not fair!" she cried. "You told me you would answer any question I asked."

"Yet you have rejected me and my answers. Why should I waste my time?"

"John. Please. I'm sorry."

"You're not. But I suppose it doesn't matter." He started to walk out again, then something seemed to occur to him, and he stopped and turned. "Alicia…do you believe in God?"

"Well, yes, of course."

"Not 'of course.' Many people don't."

"Okay…sorry. Yes, I do believe in God."

"Do you believe in angels?"

Her answer was a bit slower in coming, but still as positive. "Yes. Why?"

"*Why?* Yet another question. But I'll tell you why. If you believe in God and angels, why won't you consider the possibility that angels appear to mortals in many forms?"

"I didn't say that," she argued. "I just said I believe in angels…although I've never seen one."

"But you did. You saw one tonight and immediately rejected him with your own mind."

Suddenly she realized where he was going with this. "That old Indian man was a hallucination…or something. He was not an angel."

"You doubt my word, *and* you're prejudiced. You may have learned things about me tonight you didn't like, but it works both ways. I'm learning things about you, as well, that disappoint me greatly."

"That's not fair. I'm not trying to make you believe outrageous things. And just because I won't accept your crazy story, that doesn't make me prejudiced."

"You *are* prejudiced, Alicia. You rejected what you saw just because it didn't appear as some glorious being dressed in white, with huge white wings and a ridiculous gold halo over its head."

His words were more powerful than any slap to the face might have been. What if he was right? What if she *had* experienced a miracle tonight? She dropped into a chair, staring at him without speaking. Her thoughts were spinning. Her heart ached for this horrible ugly wall that was now between them. Then she remembered that he'd ignored her question. If this was true, what message had he been given?

She got up and moved toward him, stopping when they were close enough to touch.

"If I ask you one more question, would you answer it?"

He shrugged. "It appears that where you're concerned, I've become a glutton for punishment…so why not? Ask away."

"You said the…uh, angel in the light always brings a message."

"Yes."

"So if my message was to believe, what was the message he gave to you?"

He laughed. It was a short bitter sound that struck at the core of all she was.

"He told me that you would break my heart. So take comfort in his words, because my message has already come true."

He glanced down at the brooch one last time, then walked out of the room.

The pain in his voice had been sickening. Knowing

she was the cause of it was even worse. But how could she reconcile herself to this madness?

She picked up the brooch, clutching it to her heart as she stumbled to her room. By the time she reached the bed, she was sobbing. She crawled up onto the mattress, rolled herself up in a tight ball of misery and cried herself to sleep.

Dieter was in Austria. A simple walk down familiar streets, hearing the language he'd learned first at his mother's knees, made him weak with relief. He'd done it. Escaped the FBI's net, thanks to an angry woman named Isis and a set of fake papers that got him a berth on a Russian ship. It had taken the better part of a week to get here, but now that he'd arrived, he was anxious to reconnect with the boss. The sooner they began a new life, the better.

He'd rented a room in a small bed-and-breakfast, and paid for a week, hoping it would take no longer than that to finish the work Richard wanted of him, so then they could settle down in their new life. But for now, he was just looking for the nearest bar. He wanted a good, dark German beer and some kielbasa on rye. Maybe with a big smear of sharp, whole-grain mustard on the rye, and a big dill pickle on the side. Just the thought of it made his mouth water.

His new persona put a swagger in his walk, and when he turned the corner and saw a colorful sign swinging over a doorway that had a beer stein painted on it, he patted his pocket, making sure his wallet was inside, and headed in that direction.

* * *

Another week had come and gone since the bandages had been removed from Richard's face. During that time, he'd taken another step in his plan to change his identity by notifying Helga and Gustav that he'd suffered a serious accident while he'd been gone that had resulted in the need for plastic surgery to repair his face. They'd been horrified by the news of his situation, and expressed their good wishes for his speedy recovery and return. He'd also spent long hours on the phone, dealing with getting a new photo for his passport by offering the same explanation he'd given Helga and Gustav. With his doctor's sworn statement that he had indeed done surgery on Anton Schloss, the powers that be had accepted the reason, and his passport had been updated to reflect his new look.

Yesterday he'd been released from the hospital, and after spending the night in a hotel near the airport, awaiting his flight back to East Germany, he was now sitting at the gate with his new passport, awaiting departure.

It wasn't going to be a comfortable flight, but he had pain pills and the knowledge that he could rest all he liked once he was back home eating Helga's good cooking. He was even starting to get excited about his businesses. There were a couple of small manufacturing places near Bonn that he'd been looking at as possible locations for expansion.

It didn't seem odd to think of himself as Anton Schloss anymore, because the man he saw when he looked in the mirror was certainly not Richard Ponte. He was conditioning himself to be someone new—a he-man with a straight nose and strong features. A man with a slim waist and big chest. A man known as Anton Schloss.

Finally the announcement he'd been waiting for came over the loudspeaker. They were ready to board his flight. He picked up his bag and then his cane. All the people needing extra time to board were invited to enter first. He moved to the head of the line.

Sixteen

It was raining when the cab pulled up to Richard's East German residence. He tossed some euros over the seat, then had started to get out when the door to his home opened abruptly and Gustav came out on the run, carrying an umbrella.

He smiled to himself. Good help really was so hard to find, but when you got it, you really appreciated its worth.

"Thank you," he said as Gustav extended a hand to help him out.

"Welcome home, Herr Schloss. We were so sorry to hear of your accident but most pleased to learn you have healed quite well. I'm sorry you did not call me to come and get you, and that you took a cab instead."

"My flights were delayed due to the weather. It would have been impossible to tell you when to pick me up, because I did not know when I would be arriving."

Gustav nodded, making sympathetic noises, while the cab driver set the luggage, along with a small metal box, on the door stoop, then drove away. With Gustav holding the large black umbrella over his head, Richard made his way carefully up the walk and then into the house, sniffing appreciatively at the homey smells pervading the foyer.

"Helga must be baking. The house smells wonderful," he said.

"*Ja*...for you, Herr Schloss. She bakes for you."

"I will sample some of it later," Richard said. "For now, bring my bags and help me up to my room. After that long flight, I need to rest."

Gustav balanced the biggest bag and the metal box under one arm, then took Richard by the elbow and led him to the stairs. When they reached the landing, Richard was winded.

"I'm still not at my best," he said. "But I soon will be. Just put my things in my room. Helga can unpack for me later. I'm going to nap. If I'm not awake by dinnertime, you may wake me. I shouldn't miss a meal, as I'm trying to regain my strength."

Gustav nodded, then closed the door behind him as he left, leaving Richard in the quiet of his own elegance and hurried off, no doubt to fill Helga in on the news, Richard thought.

Richard looked around his bedroom with a studied glance, taking note of the fresh flowers, the highly polished wood, the gleaming floors, and trying not to think of his bedroom back in Miami. He'd always enjoyed the floor-to-ceiling windows overlooking the ocean and the sea breezes that blew through as he sunned out on the deck beyond his bedroom. He didn't know for certain what would happen to everything he owned under the name of Ponte, but he was determined that Alicia would not live to enjoy what she'd taken away from him.

Then he remembered the small metal box beside his suitcase.

"Ah yes, my ace in the hole," he muttered as he picked it up, checking to make sure the seal had not been broken.

Satisfied that all was well, he tucked it up high on a shelf in his closet and shoved a pair of extra pillows in front of it. He didn't care how macabre it had been of him to demand all the skin and flesh that had been removed from his body. No one could have imagined the future plans he had for it.

He kicked off his shoes as he walked into the bathroom, then turned on the light before going to stand before the mirror.

He smiled, watching the way his lips curved, then noticing the new lines the smile made on his face. They had put a different arch in his brows. The cheek and chin implants, as well as his new nose, gave his face a Slavic appearance. Coupled with that and the bald head he still maintained, he didn't even know himself. He patted his chest, feeling the outlines of his new physique, then turned sideways, admiring the toned appearance of his body.

He might even give thought to getting himself a new woman. But nothing serious. He didn't intend to marry again—ever. And not because he still held any love for his dead wife. He just didn't want to share his property and wealth with anyone ever again. He didn't know how he was going to manage the feat, but when he died, he intended to take it all with him.

A short while later, he'd freshened up and was

readying for his nap when his cell phone began to ring. He glanced at caller ID and then smiled. Even though no name appeared in the window, he recognized the number.

"Hello."

"Boss, it's me."

"Where are you?" Richard asked.

"Austria. I rented a room here, but I can relocate to wherever you need me to be."

Richard smiled again, as he sat down on the side of the bed. "Isis came through for you, I see."

Dieter hesitated. He didn't know whether to relay the message she'd given him or not. But Richard could tell by Dieter's silence that he hadn't been completely forthcoming.

"Talk to me," Richard said.

"She said to tell you that if you ever set foot in Houston again, you're a dead man."

"That seems fair," he said shortly. "However, she wouldn't know it if I did."

"What do you mean?" Dieter asked.

"You will see for yourself when we next meet."

"And when will that be?" Dieter asked.

"I've been a bit under the weather," Richard said. "When I feel better, I'll give you a call. How are you fixed for money?"

"I have plenty for now. She was generous with that, as well as my new papers."

"That reminds me. To whom am I now speaking?"

Dieter grinned. "Lars Vintner, a citizen of the U.S, born and raised in Wisconsin, but with familial ties to Austria."

"Nice to meet you, Vintner," Richard said. "And you

may call me Herr Anton Schloss, or continue with 'boss,' if you so choose."

Dicter felt like shouting. "This is great, boss. You did it. You've escaped them all. I'm looking forward to living this new life."

"Yes. Well. I still have a few kinks to iron out of the old one before I'm ready to celebrate," Richard said, then added, "I'll call when it's time to begin."

Two miserable days had passed since what Alicia privately referred to as "the night of John's angel." John wasn't exactly ignoring her. He continued to see to her comfort and safety, and patiently answered when spoken to, but he didn't initiate anything. She might as well have been a shadow on the wall. The emotional connection between them was gone. He rarely looked at her, and when he did, his expression was distant, as if he were looking at a stranger. She was devastated by what had happened, but at a loss as how to get back to where they had been.

She'd gone over and over everything he'd told her so many times that she'd made herself crazy. She no longer knew what was real and what wasn't. All she knew was that she'd lost the most important thing she'd ever had: John's love.

She cried herself to sleep every night, and woke up with a pounding headache and swollen eyes. It was obvious what was happening to her. But it was also obvious that John Nightwalker no longer gave a damn.

Her mother's brooch was lying on the table beside her bed. She looked at it a dozen times a day, touching it, feeling the weight of it in her hand, trying to figure out if it was a copy or the real thing. But the only thing she had for evidence was the message she'd received. Either she believed or she didn't. Just like John's story: she either believed him or not.

She wanted to. God knew how badly she wanted to. But what did that make her if she gave in and gave up? As crazy as John—or a woman in the middle of an eternal cycle of revenge?

Either way, she was screwed.

Every day that John kept Alicia at a distance was another day that seemed like dying. He hadn't felt this sad and empty since the day White Fawn and his people had been butchered. He wanted to hate her. He wanted to replace this pain with rage. But she was too deeply embedded in his soul for him to be able to distinguish where he ended and she began. It was the purest sort of irony that the only person to whom he'd revealed the real truth about his life had not only rejected what he'd told her but *him*, as well.

He knew she was suffering, too. He saw her swollen face and red-rimmed eyes each morning at the breakfast table. He felt her gaze on him a hundred times a day, but he was done with trying to make her understand. It was like the old man had told her. Either she believed or she did not.

And so their silent war continued through yet another day.

John's cell phone rang as he was getting ready for bed. He answered before he thought to look at caller ID.

"Is this John Nightwalker?"

"Yes."

"This is Officer Belmont. I worked that wreck you witnessed the other day."

"Oh. Yes, Officer. How can I help you?"

"I just thought you might like to know that the woman finally regained consciousness this afternoon. They diagnosed her problem as epilepsy. She'd suffered a seizure and passed out. By the time you got to her, the seizure had passed, but she had a serious concussion, as well as some broken ribs and a broken jaw. You saved her life."

"Glad I could help," John said. "But it was just a case of being in the right place at the right time."

"She would have burned to death if you hadn't pulled her out. The family wanted your name and phone number. I think they want to thank you personally, but I told them I'd run it by you first."

John sighed. "Please tell them I'm very happy she survived and that I was able to help, but there's stuff going on in my life right now that makes it better for all concerned if I maintain a low profile."

"I thought that might be the case. I knew your name was familiar when I was working the wreck, but it wasn't until I got back to headquarters that I made the connection. I suppose the young woman who was with you is Alicia Ponte, right?"

"Officer Belmont, I would be very grateful if you'd keep all this to yourself. Right now, her life and welfare depend on staying out of the spotlight."

"Absolutely," Belmont said. "And would you tell Miss Ponte for me that as an officer of the law, as well as the brother of a marine who is now fighting in Iraq, I'm grateful for what she did. I know it wasn't easy."

"I'll pass along your message," John said.

"And I'll pass yours along to the woman's family."

"So…we're even, right?" John asked.

"Okay."

"Thanks for calling," John said.

"Take care."

John laid the phone back down and started to get undressed, then thought of the message he'd promised to pass on to Alicia. Facing her again was the last thing he wanted, but he had to do it sometime. Better now than later.

He walked across the hall and knocked on her door.

Alicia was sitting in the middle of her bed, staring at the television, but deaf to what was on the screen. She'd been crying for so long her eyes were swollen and her nose was running steadily. She shuddered on a sob, then reached across her pillow for another tissue as the knock sounded on her door. At first she thought it was the program, but when it sounded again, she realized it was John.

She hit the mute button on the remote and then blew her nose one more time.

"What do you want?" she yelled.

John was a little taken aback. He'd expected her to answer the door, not yell at him.

"May I come in?" he asked.

Alicia knew what she looked like. The last thing she wanted was for him to see her in this condition.

"No."

John put a hand in the middle of her door, then leaned his head against his arm and closed his eyes.

Damn. All he seemed to do was make her cry. Her voice was so hoarse she sounded sick. He wanted to walk away. She'd brought this all on herself. But even though she'd hurt him to the core, he couldn't bear to think of her in the same kind of misery.

"I have something to tell you. It's something you'll want to hear."

Alicia rolled her eyes, wadded the tissue into a ball and tossed it toward the wastebasket where she'd thrown the others. She missed, as she had several times before. But she didn't care. She rolled off the bed, stomped to the door and yanked it open.

"What?" she demanded, well aware of how rude she was being.

"You've been crying," he said accusingly, then thought how stupid that sounded. She was obviously aware of her own condition, as well as who had caused it. Him.

"No shit, Sherlock," she snapped. "So, is that the something you came to tell me? Because if it is, I have news for you. I already knew it."

She slammed the door in his face.

He bit his lip to keep from shouting back and knocked again.

"What?" she yelled again.

"I wasn't through."

"Well, I am," she returned. "I'm through with my father. I'm through with you. In fact, I'm through with men in general. All they ever do is lie to me and hurt me."

That was the wrong thing to say.

John opened the door with a shove, slamming it against the inside wall as he strode in.

Alicia's eyes widened, and her heart skipped a beat. Oops. Maybe she'd overdone the indignation a bit. John Nightwalker looked beyond pissed.

He walked up to her until there were mere inches between their bodies, then poked a finger at her chest, using it to drive home every word he spoke.

"I did *not* lie to you. You just didn't believe me. You're wallowing in your own misery. I didn't cause it. You can wallow all you like, but do *not* blame me for it."

"Ow," she complained, rubbing at the spot above her right breast where he'd poked as he spoke. "That hurt."

"Good," he shot back.

She sighed. "What did you come to tell me?"

"The highway patrolman from the wreck called. He said the woman regained consciousness and is going to live. She has epilepsy. That's what caused her to crash. The officer also recognized my name and put two and two together. He knows who you are. He said not to worry, he won't give us up, but he wanted me to tell you something. He said he knew it must have been really tough for you to give your father up, but he wanted to thank you for it. He has a brother who's in Iraq with the marines."

Then he turned around and left, slamming the door shut as loudly as he'd swung it open.

Alicia sniffed, then grabbed another tissue and blew again. "That went well," she mumbled, then picked up the scattered tissues and tossed them into the wastebasket, before leaving the room.

She expected John to be in his bedroom, ignoring her existence, as she stomped toward the kitchen. She wanted something cold to drink, and considering the fact that she'd sulked her way through dinner, she was still hungry.

She fixed herself a cold Pepsi and was in the act of making a sandwich when John appeared in the doorway.

His first thought was that she'd come a long way

from the woman who'd never made herself a meal, becoming someone at home with a fully loaded refrigerator. "I didn't know you were in here," he said. "Sorry."

She shrugged. "It's your house," she said, and continued to smear mayonnaise on the bread.

He started to say something, then knew it would just turn into another brawl, and turned and walked away.

Alicia felt a little bit guilty, but she kept on making her food. Instead of taking it to her room, she sat down at the kitchen table and proceeded to eat.

A few minutes later, John reappeared in the doorway.

"Sorry," he repeated. "I thought you were back in your room."

She licked a swipe of mayonnaise off her finger, then sighed.

"John. Shut up, would you? Stop apologizing for walking around your own house. I'm the interloper here, and obviously an unwanted one. Granted, I'm hurt, and I feel bent all to hell and back, but I've learned that I don't break. Go about your business and leave me to stew in the mess of my own creation, okay?"

The last thing she expected was to hear him laugh. When she looked up, he was already gone, but she could hear him laughing all the way down the hall.

"Happy to have supplied the humor for the day," she muttered, then got up and carried her dishes to the dishwasher, too preoccupied to realize that she'd been the one to put the first big crack in the wall between them.

John was still grinning when he got to his office. Granted, there were huge hurdles to get back to where they'd been before his big reveal, but this was the first exchange between them that had made him believe there might be hope for them yet. He had to give her credit where credit was due. She was one hell of a woman, and she'd been right on all counts. She could be hurt, but it would obviously take more than what he and her father had dished out to put her under.

When she'd told him to shut up in such a tired, disgusted voice, he'd wanted to kiss her. She was the most aggravating, hardheaded, single-minded, defiant woman he'd ever known. Not even White Fawn had been able to stand up to his authority as a second chief. But it was quite obvious to him now that Alicia Ponte was not impressed with his status or with him—or, as she'd so succinctly stated, with men in general.

He chuckled again and turned on his computer. It would be impossible for him to sleep now. And it was just breaking day across the world. It was always time somewhere to do a little business through the World Wide Web. As he waited for his computer to boot up, it was not lost upon him what vast strides mankind had taken since the day he'd first drawn breath. His father would have called him crazy if he'd tried to explain televisions and telephones, not to mention the fact that men had walked on the moon.

Then his hands went limp as the truth of that hit him square in the face. His father would have reacted no differently than Alicia had. He would have thought his son was crazy. He would have had the shaman perform a cleansing ceremony, then send him off to renew his spirit with a vision quest. He sighed, then scrubbed his hands across his face.

Damn it if he didn't owe her an apology. Maybe not for everything, but an apology nonetheless.

He got back up and headed for the kitchen. She was probably going to hit the ceiling if she saw his face again, but this had to be said. When he got there, though, she was nowhere in sight.

"Great. She's probably back in her bedroom, and I already know how the first try at talking to her there went."

"John."

He turned abruptly, startled by her voice.

"What?"

"You're talking to yourself."

"I know that," he said, and found himself knocked off center by her attitude.

Alicia shrugged. "All right, but I just thought I'd point that out, because people who talk to themselves are often considered—"

"Crazy?" he offered.

"Um, maybe 'eccentric' is a better word."

He tilted his head questioningly, then held out his hand. "Truce?"

Alicia almost choked. Truce? There *was* a God. "Yes, thank you."

John pulled her into his arms and kissed the top of her head, then the side of her face, then her cheek, then her lips. Over and over. And over. Until they were both breathless.

"I had a small revelation a few minutes ago," he said softly. "Made me realize I owed you an apology."

Alicia was so grateful he was talking to her that she was having problems concentrating on what he was saying. "How so?" she asked.

"I was booting up my computer, and as I sat there, watching this small thing called a laptop connecting me to any place I wanted to talk to in the world, I thought what a difficult time I would have had trying to explain all the technology that we now take for granted to my father."

Alicia wanted to ask whether he was talking about his "real" father, who he seemed not to remember or discuss, or about his five-hundred-plus-year-old father whom he surely didn't have. She decided to wait and let him surprise her.

"And?" she urged.

"And it occurred to me that he would tell me I was crazy. He would have had the shaman perform a healing ceremony on me. He would have been embarrassed before The People that his son was making such crazy statements." He stopped to cup her face in his hands. "In other words…he would have reacted to what I said the same way you did. But I wouldn't have cast him out of my life. So I should not have cast you out, either. Does that make sense?"

She sighed. So he was still persisting in the belief that he was ancient. But so what? He was alive and vital and loved her. And he was smart and generous and brave. If she put that "quirk" into perspective, it was almost unimportant. Almost.

She put her hands over his, feeling the warmth of his blood pushing through his veins and seeing the reflection of herself in his eyes.

"John, right now I'm so happy you're not angry with me anymore that I'd agree to almost anything you said. The operative word being *almost*. Does *that* make sense to *you?*"

He heard the slight hesitance in her tone and understood it. Like him, she was reserving the right to disagree. Beyond that, they were pretty much back on the same wavelength.

"Enough to live with," he said.

"Me, too," she agreed, and hugged him fiercely. She didn't care if he was crazy. She was at the point of wanting to go crazy with him rather than live another minute with him angry at her.

"So where do we go from here?" John asked.

"To bed?"

He growled beneath his breath and picked her up in his arms.

"I thought you'd never ask," he said as he carried her down the hall.

They undressed without speaking, tearing at their clothes in hasty, jerking motions. John finished first and then reached for her, helping her out of the last bits. As she stepped out of her panties, he swooped her up in his arms. And for a moment, time seemed to stop.

He paused, taking in the satiny feel of her skin against his body, feeling the heat of her against the palms of his hands, seeing the love and the desire in her eyes and knowing he was feeling all the same things.

"Alicia…"

"Make love to me, Nightwalker. I've been missing you…missing this…."

Blood pounded through his body as he put her on his bed. *Take her. Take her. Take her.* His pulse rocked with the rhythm looping in his brain. *Love her. Love her. Love her.*

So he did.

He began with her mouth, kissing those lush, sensual lips until they were pink and swollen from the pressure, stroking every inch of her with his fingers and his tongue until every pulse point on her body was throbbing. He heard her whispers and promises, and answered back with the old words, making love to Alicia in the tongue of the Ah-ni-yv-wi-ya. Healing his heart along with his soul. And when she took him into her body, it was, for John, a sense of having come home.

Alicia couldn't get enough of his kisses—of his touch. The passion in his greed to take more and more of what she gave heightened her senses. Every muscle in her body was focused on the fire building low in her belly. She wanted more, pulled him deeper and harder and faster until they were moving in sync.

Her climax came suddenly, an urgent and nearly painful demand, sweeping what was left of her senses straight out of her mind.

John felt the sudden onset of her climax, but it was the low, guttural moan near his ear that made him lose all control. The unexpected ejaculation of his seed into her womb came with all the force of a blow to the back of his head. His body was on autopilot as he thrust once, then again, then a third time, before he fell on top of her with a deep groan of satisfaction. His muscles were shaking from the exertion he'd put them through, and once again, instead of feeling empty and used up, he felt renewed.

"Alicia…Alicia…" Then he rolled, taking her with him until she was lying on top of him, still clasped tight within his embrace.

For a few quiet moments they just lay there, savoring the afterglow and the closeness. But when Alicia started to move, John slid his fingers through her hair, winding the long dark lengths around his wrists, then sighed and closed his eyes.

Alicia was hovering on the verge between consciousness and sleep when she thought she heard him whisper one word.

"Mine."

She sighed. It was true. For better or for worse, she'd given her heart to this man.

Seventeen

Dieter was sitting at a sidewalk café, having his morning croissant and a cup of cinnamon roast coffee, when his cell phone rang. It had been over two weeks since he'd settled in at his Austrian bed-and-breakfast, and he was developing a routine that suited him just fine. But hearing that ring quickly put an end to his peace of mind. He pushed his coffee aside, dusted the croissant crumbs from his hands and answered.

"Hello, boss."

"I was beginning to think you weren't going to answer," Richard said shortly.

"Sorry," Dieter said. "I was eating breakfast. Had a mouthful of food I needed to swallow."

Richard still needed someone to bring the last of his plans to fruition and didn't want to antagonize Dieter into quitting on him when it mattered most. "Yes, well…all right," Richard said. "I suppose I'm just impatient to put all this to rest."

That sounded positive, which pleased Dieter. "As am I," he said.

"You will be receiving a FedEx packet at your residence today. In it will be some instructions and a plane ticket."

"Where am I going?" Dieter asked.

"Correct that to 'Where are *we* going?'"

"You're coming along?"

"I will be meeting you in the Bahamas."

"That's marvelous!" Dieter said.

"It's not exactly a vacation," Richard reminded him.

"Yes, of course, boss. I didn't mean—"

"Never mind. Just follow my instructions to the letter and don't miss your flight."

"Yes, sir. I mean, no, sir. I'll be there. How long do you plan to be there?"

"Until the job is done," Richard snapped, then hung up.

Dieter sighed, dropped his phone back in his pocket and retrieved what was left of his croissant. Then he lifted his hand to signal a waiter and had his coffee refilled, determined to enjoy what might be his last peaceful day for a while.

Corbin Woodliff was in the middle of an exposé regarding a doctor and a welfare scam when his phone rang. He answered absently, but when he recognized his caller, his attention sharpened.

"John! Long time no word," Corbin said. "What's been happening?"

"That's what I called to ask you," John said. "I've been thinking of going back to Georgia, but I'm not sure where the Feds are with their search for Ponte. What can you tell me that I don't already know?"

"No much, I'm afraid. There was a flurry of investigations in the Balkans a couple of days ago that proved to be dead end. It's as if he dropped off the face of the earth."

John frowned. It wasn't what he wanted to hear, but they weren't really any safer in Arizona than they had been in Georgia. Both places had been located and infiltrated. The fact that Alicia was still alive was mostly due to timing and planning, and he could arrange that there as well as here.

He hadn't spoken with Alicia about the idea yet, but he knew she was feeling the pressure of being stranded in the middle of nowhere. They wouldn't exactly be returning to a social scene, but the ambience and comfort of the Georgia house were more suited to good vibes than the severity of this desert hideaway. This was where John came to heal when he needed peace in his life. When he had brought Alicia here to hide, he'd had no idea that they would end up healing each other.

When John didn't comment immediately, Corbin followed up.

"So what are you going to do?"

"I'm not sure. I'm going to run it by Alicia first. If we make a move, I'll let you know. And if you get any information that would help, give me a call."

"Absolutely," Corbin said, then added, "And don't forget, when this is over, the whole story is mine."

"Yeah, sure," John said, and hung up. But he already knew Corbin wasn't ever going to get the whole story. Corbin could have whatever Alicia chose to tell him about her end of it, but that was where it stopped.

He looked down at the computer screen, noted that

one of his stocks was starting to plummet and picked up the phone and called his broker.

John made arrangements to sell and hung up, then scanned the stocks for a few more minutes. After that he checked his e-mail, answered what he needed to and deleted the rest before pushing back from his desk to go look for Alicia. She'd made herself scarce right after breakfast, and he wasn't sure why, or what she was doing.

Alicia stepped out of the shower and reached for a towel. As she dried herself off, she kept glancing out the arched window by the shower door. The day was clear. By noon the sun would be scorching. But she felt stifled. She'd never been inside this long in her life, unless she counted the winter she'd broken her leg on the ski slopes and been laid up for almost six weeks.

She dressed slowly, thinking about how she used to spend her days. If she died today, no one but John would really care. Oh, there would most likely be a media circus made out of the actual funeral, but no one would cry for her. No one would remember for long that she'd even lived. She felt the lack of conscience with which she'd lived her life. Why hadn't she done more, like volunteering in places that really needed help? God knew she had the time and money to do it.

She paused, then leaned her elbows on the windowsill and looked at the vastness of the landscape. Mountains, desert, cacti and scrub brush abounded, and while she knew it came with its own set of wildlife, there were no other people in sight. On the surface, this place was a mirror image of her life: barren and empty.

She ran her fingers through the thick, wet length of

her hair and then wrapped a towel around it to catch the drips before going to dress. Even then, she was still caught up in retrospection. Maybe her life would have been different if her mother hadn't died when she was so young. Maybe her father would have turned out to be a different kind of man.

She sighed.

Thinking about what-ifs and maybes got her nowhere. And she wasn't going to allow her father any excuse for what he'd done—what he was still trying to do. Some males in the animal world killed their own offspring to get to what they wanted. Her father was no better, and she was sick and tired of being scared.

She went back into the bathroom to use the hair dryer, then changed her mind, picked up a hairbrush, pocketed a scrunchie and headed for the terrace.

With the scorpion sting foremost in her mind, she kept her eyes on the flat, sun-bleached tiles as she walked outside. The sun was up. The sky was clear, and there were no creepy crawlers in sight. She chose a seat near the patio table, unwrapped the towel from around her head and draped it over the back of another chair. Then she unloaded the scrunchie from her pocket, turned her back to the sun and began to finger comb her hair.

As it began to dry, Alicia alternated her fingers with the brush, working with the long, silky length until it was smooth and shining. She slipped the scrunchie over her wrist to have it at the ready, then began to gather her hair into a ponytail. Just as she began, a turkey buzzard flew into her line of sight. She watched it circling overhead, slowly widening each loop to cover more territory in search of prey. Distracted by the scavenger's hunt, her mind lost focus as her fingers continued to weave the thick strands of her hair not into a ponytail but into a single long four-stranded braid.

John had been through the entire house without a sign of Alicia, but when he got to the dining room and looked out through the terrace doors, he saw her. His anxiety settled as he started toward her. Then he focused on her hands and what she was doing with her hair. And he forgot to breathe.

All of a sudden he was back in his village watching White Fawn braiding her hair. Instead of separating her hair into three separate lengths, she separated it into four, ending up with a flat plait instead of a fat braid, all without being able to see what she was doing. She was the envy of many women for that simple ability and had been quietly proud of it.

But that was White Fawn's skill, not Alicia's.

His heart was pounding so hard he could barely think as he started out the door. Was this really happening, or was this yet another hopeless dream from which he would wake? He walked up behind her just as she slipped the scrunchie off her wrist onto the end of her braid, wrapping it around over and over until it was securely fastened, then let the braid fall. Just as she was about to get up, she saw John's shadow coming up from behind her.

"Hey...I was just about to come inside." She turned toward him with a smile.

John cupped the side of her face, tracing her smile with a thumb, then touched the crown of her head, his fingers trembling as he ran them down the length of her braid. There was a knot in his throat as he lifted her hair in his hand.

"Alicia…baby…how did you do that?"

"Do what?" she asked as she stood up and began gathering her things to take back inside.

"Fix your hair like that."

"It's just a ponytail. My hair is heavy, and it keeps it off the back of my neck. Why? Is it a mess? Did I miss some bits?"

She reached for the back of her neck, searching for loose strands, only to discover something wasn't right.

"What on earth?" she mumbled, and then pulled her hair over her shoulder. She gasped, then slung it back behind her as if it were a snake.

"I didn't do that. I don't know how to do that," she whispered, and then touched the braid again, unable to believe what she'd done.

John took her face in his hands, staring at each feature as if he'd never seen her before. She looked frightened, and he felt as if he was sleepwalking.

Alicia's voice was shaking. "What just happened? Is this another one of those Sedona moments I'm not supposed to understand?" She tried to pull away, but he wouldn't let go.

"Look at me, Alicia. Look. At. Me."

She stopped. Something was going on that she didn't understand.

"I *am* looking. I see you," she said.

"Is it you…is it you, my love?" John whispered, letting his fingers trace the shape of her face—the curve of her hairline, the breadth of her brow, the cut of her cheekbones—then down her face all the way to her chin.

Alicia was beginning to get scared. What the hell was going on?

"John? What's wrong? Please. Talk to me."

He shook his head as if coming out of a trance, then leaned forward and pressed his forehead against hers. For a few silent moments they were nose to nose, breath mingling, hearts pounding with shared uncertainty over what had happened.

Finally he just wrapped his arms around her shoulders and pulled her close against his heartbeat.

"Did I do something wrong?" she asked.

"No. I think you just did something right. Something you've been trying to tell me ever since the day we met, but I couldn't see it for the hate in my heart. I'm sorry. I'm sorry. I'm sorry."

"I don't understand," Alicia said.

He looked down at the plait lying across his arms and then hugged her. "It doesn't matter. Nothing matters but that you're here."

Alicia frowned. "You're not making sense. Of course I'm here." Then she pulled out of his arms and looked up at him with her hands on her hips. "Are you about to freak out on me? If you are, just tell me now, so I can figure out how to help you. I've already come to terms with your…uh…shall we call them…beliefs. It's okay with me if you want to be five or five hundred. I just don't want to lose you."

John leaned down and kissed her. He was so shaken by what had transpired that he could hardly think. There was no way he was going to try to explain this to her, too.

"You aren't going to lose me, baby," he said softly. "And I am not going to lose you. Ever again. Okay?"

"Okay," she said, and then ran her fingers over her braid again. "What on earth is this, anyway? I wasn't really paying attention. I was watching that buzzard. I probably couldn't do this again in a million years."

"Probably not," John said, and then took her by the shoulders. "Hey. I've got an idea."

Interest lit her expression. "Tell me."

"What do you say we go home?"

She frowned, then pointed over his shoulder. "Uh, John…sweetheart…turn around. We *are* home."

"No. I mean back to the ocean…to Georgia."

She gasped. "Can we? I mean…this place is beautiful, but it's so…so…"

"Far?" he offered.

She smiled. "Yes. Far. It's far. Very far. From everything."

"Well, initially, that was the reason we came, remember? But I'll keep you safe, no matter where we are."

"You think?" she asked, suddenly nervous.

"I *know*," John said. "The Old Ones didn't send you back to me only for me to lose you again."

She frowned. Here they went again. "The Old Ones?"

"Never mind," he said.

It sounded like a good idea to her. "Right. I'm going to pack. When can we leave?"

"I need to refuel the chopper. In the morning we'll fly into Sedona, refuel there and then head east, okay?"

"Definitely okay," she said, and then she lifted her arms above her head and did a little victory dance before heading back into the house.

John watched her go, the long black plait flying out

behind her, just like it used to do when she'd been small and brown and worn a bluebird feather in her hair.

Richard was standing at baggage claim in the Nassau airport, wearing white shorts and a blue polo shirt tucked in at the waist. For shade to protect his bald head and nearly healed face, he'd chosen a wide-brimmed Panama hat and aviator sunglasses. He looked like a well-to-do businessman on holiday.

He checked his watch, as he had every few moments since his arrival. This was where he and Dieter were to meet. Dieter's plane had been on time, which was good. He hated waiting.

Richard had arrived yesterday, giving him time to settle in. He had yet to recover his full physical stamina, so the extra time had been a good idea. He hadn't wanted to fly with his precious metal box, so he'd shipped it earlier to the Nassau hotel, with a fresh supply of dry ice to keep the contents safe and instructions that it was to be held there until his arrival. He'd had a few nervous moments after he'd arrived, while the hotel staff searched their mail room before it was finally located. After that, Richard tipped them handsomely, carried it to his room and secreted it at the back of the closet.

Tomorrow, or maybe the day after, Richard Ponte's death would become a fact. He would make sure it hit the worldwide news. It was important that the authorities have access to whatever it took in the way of DNA for them to believe his death was real. He thought himself a genius for having come up with the plan, and wished he had someone besides Dieter with whom he could share it. Unfortunately for his ego, this was one coup that would have to stay secret.

As he waited, a flurry of travelers began coming into baggage claim. Finally, he thought, and quickly turned his attention to the newcomers' faces. He didn't have long to wait and recognized Dieter within seconds of his appearance.

Dieter had dyed his hair to match his new identity papers, and he'd grown a mustache, which looked a bit affected, but it didn't matter. As long as their identities passed muster, he didn't give a damn if the man opted to dress in drag.

Richard started to wave, then decided to wait until Dieter retrieved his luggage and see if he could recognize Richard on his own before he made himself known.

Dieter was travel-weary and dealing with a two-hour headache when he reached baggage claim. He quickly located the correct carousel and looked around for a place to sit. As usual, there was none. He swiped a hand across his forehead, quietly wishing he'd chosen different ent clothing. It was hotter than he'd expected, and he wanted something cold to drink.

He looked around to see if he could spot Richard, then realized he would also be in disguise. Still, he should be able to recognize him. He'd worked for him for almost fifteen years. He knew the coldhearted bastard as well as he knew himself, but after a couple of minutes of searching, decided he had yet to arrive.

"Carry your bags, sir?"

Dieter turned at the question to find a dark-skinned

porter in a starched white shirt and shorts pushing a small empty cart, obviously hoping for a few quick bucks.

"No, I only have one bag, but thank you," he said, and smiled to soften the blow.

The man nodded cordially and moved along to the next passenger.

Dieter glanced at his watch, then scanned the crowd again. Still no one in sight who fit the bill, and when the carousel started to move, he began weaving his way through the crowd to retrieve his bag.

To his disgust, it was the next to last one to appear. He pulled it off the conveyor with a grunt, then popped up the handle and began wheeling it toward the exit, hoping Richard was waiting for him outside with a taxi.

"Aren't you going to say hello?"

Dieter stared at the man who'd stepped in front of him. The voice was familiar, but that was all.

"Boss?"

Richard grinned. If he could fool Dieter, who'd known him longer than anyone except for Jacob and Alicia, he was home free. He dipped his head slightly.

"Anton Schloss. I believe you've been expecting me."

Dieter's mouth was agape, and he kept staring at the man in disbelief.

"Boss? Is that really you?"

Richard laughed out loud.

Dieter shuddered. He knew that laugh, but God in heaven, what had happened to the rest of him?

"Are you, uh…?"

"Oh, for the love of God, Lars, get hold of yourself and follow me. I have a taxi waiting outside."

Dieter stumbled, then shifted his bag from one hand to the other and hurried after the stranger in the Panama hat.

Once inside the cab, Richard put a finger to his lips, indicating that they needed to maintain their deception in front of the driver, then began to point out places of interest as they rode to their destination.

The hotel was five-star, which Dieter expected. Richard Ponte might be in disguise, but there were some spots that a leopard never changed, and first-rate food and accommodations would have been where Richard drew the line.

They strode through the lobby, mingling with the tourists coming and going, and then straight to the elevators. Once on, Richard swiped a card that took them to an executive level of suites, then handed it to Dieter.

"Put that in your pocket," he said. "We're in Suite 812. I have one just like it."

Dieter did as he was told, then followed Richard off the elevator and down the short hall to their door. Richard swiped a card through the keyless entry box, then opened the door.

"Home sweet home," he said, and walked in first, once again leaving his errand boy to follow behind.

The moment the door closed behind them, Dieter dropped his bag and opened his mouth.

"What happened to you?"

"A nip here, a tuck there, some enhancement procedures and...*voila,* you have Anton Schloss, East German businessman on holiday in the Bahamas."

"You had plastic surgery? On your face?"

"On my whole body," Richard said, then took off the hat and sunglasses. "How do I look?"

"Scary…I mean…scary good. Honestly, boss, you look so different it takes my breath away."

Richard couldn't have been more pleased. "Good. Good. So, I'm sure you're tired. Why don't you rest a bit, say for an hour or so? Then we'll have some dinner and scout out a few local businesses down by the shore."

"Why? Are you looking to do some deep-sea fishing?"

Richard grinned. "Why, Lars, how astute of you. I want a shark. Doesn't have to be a huge one, but I need one that's a good size."

"You want a shark?"

Richard's smile slipped. "Do stop repeating everything I say," he grumbled. "It's annoying."

"Sorry, boss, but I don't understand."

Richard sighed. "Of course you don't. Okay. Here's the deal. I need a shark, but I want it to be one that's freshly caught. Hopefully you can procure one tomorrow. If not, you'll just have to wait for one to show up on the docks."

"They're not very good for eating," Dieter offered.

Richard grinned. "Oh, I don't want to eat the shark. I want the *shark* to eat *me*."

It was nearing sunset as John circled above the helipad outside his cliffside home. The water was dark and choppy, typical of the Atlantic, but just the sight of it after so much mountain and sand lifted his spirits.

"We're here," he said, although the announcement was unnecessary.

As before, Alicia had not enjoyed the flight as much as she would have liked and had been counting off the minutes until their arrival, although she had not suffered from motion sickness this time, thanks to a good dose of Dramamine.

"Does everything look safe?" she asked.

John gave her a quick glance, realizing that she was afraid someone was lying in wait.

"Everything looks fine. I have more security around this place than I did at Sedona. Believe me, if it had been breeched, I would have been notified. The local police department in Justice knows about my alarm system, as does the county sheriff."

"Why don't you have staff who live at your different residences year-round? It would make keeping everything safe a lot easier."

"I do have someone who stays in Sedona when I'm not there, but I don't want anyone here, and I don't need to be taken care of."

"But who cleans?"

He grinned. "Don't worry. That job isn't going to fall to you. I manage to pick up after myself just fine, and I get help in when I need it."

She grinned. "Oh. Well…good. I mean…I would be glad to do my part, but I'm just getting the hang of learning how to cook."

He refrained from mentioning that making sandwiches and pouring milk on cereal wasn't really cooking, although there was that one effort she'd made, though he hadn't quite recovered from that yet. The truth was, he was so grateful for her presence, he didn't care if she never lifted her hand to cook again.

Then he turned his attention to landing, and within a few minutes of sighting the house, they were on the ground.

"Wait here until the rotors have stopped turning," he said. "I'm going to tie her down, and then we'll go into the house together."

"Her?"

He grinned. "All ships and planes are female. You know that."

"I wonder why," she said.

His grin widened. "I would venture to guess it's because men were always the ones at the helm, so they liked the idea of a woman being subservient."

"Humph. I wonder how in control they felt when the engine quit running or the ship sprang a leak?"

"Probably blamed it on the woman for being too weak to hold up."

"That's sick," Alicia objected.

"Naw…that's just the fragile male ego afraid to admit any fault."

She laughed. "So go tie down this broad. Nothing personal, but I'm anxious to get out of her."

John was still smiling as he exited the chopper. He made short work of stabilizing the metal bird, then went back to get Alicia. He opened the door and held up his arms. She leaned out and down, letting him brace her until her feet were on firm ground.

"I have never been so glad to stand in dirt."

He started to get their bags, then paused, took her in his arms and kissed her instead.

"Welcome home, baby," he said softly, then reached in again to get the luggage.

A strong gust slapped her hair across her face, but she just laughed and turned to face the wind. The view across the water was never-ending. She remembered what the sunrise would be like and couldn't wait to witness it again.

"Are you ready?" John asked.

She turned, about to answer, then her thoughts momentarily turned to mud. He was standing beside the chopper. The wind was whipping at his clothes, flirting with the collar of his red polo, delineating every muscle on his upper body, while the tight fit of his Levi's did the same for his backside and legs. He was, in her opinion, magnificent, but she also accepted that she was strongly prejudiced in John Nightwalker's favor.

"I'm ready," she said.

Together they crossed the short distance from the helipad to the back of the house. John set down the bags long enough to get out his keys, then unlocked the door. He stepped inside to disarm the security system, then came back out to get her.

"Come in out of the wind," he urged, tugging her by the hand.

"It feels good," she said. "Different from the wind in Arizona."

She paused in the doorway, then turned toward the ocean once more and inhaled deeply. "I've always loved the smell of sea air. I guess that's why I always stayed in Miami when Daddy chose to stay away for such long periods of time. I didn't want to get so far from home."

"You're pretty far from Miami here," John said.

She frowned. "I guess, but it doesn't feel like it. For some odd reason, this has the same feel."

John was struck by the innocence of her answer. It occurred to him that she might never know she'd been with him before, and if she didn't come to that conclusion on her own, he wasn't going to shove it down her throat. It was enough that *he* knew. He picked up the bags and carried them inside as she closed the door behind them.

The house seemed a little stuffy, but that would soon be remedied. As soon as he had their bags in their room, he was going to open up the doors and windows and let the air blow through. Like Alicia, no matter where else he stayed or how many properties he owned, this was the place he called home.

Eighteen

The first part of the plan hinged on blowing up Richard's favorite yacht. He hated to do it. He loved this yacht more than the one in Miami, even though he kept it berthed in Nassau most of the time. About once a year he and Alicia would vacation on it, but those days were over. He knew the Feds had probably staked out the yacht, as well as every other personal possession he owned. The captain took it out weekly, as per Richard's orders, and he had no reason to assume he would stop just because Richard was persona non grata.

Last night Dieter had put on a wet suit and swum out to where the yacht was anchored. Within a short time he'd fastened a bomb beneath the hull and set the timer to blow in ten hours. By that time, it would be out to sea. There would be no witnesses as to who was on board, but when Richard brought the shark in later, the explosion would explain the bits of Richard Ponte that would be found inside the animal's belly.

Richard was sitting on the dock that morning with a

cup of coffee, ostensibly watching the boats, when the captain raised anchor and started out to sea. There was something to be said for habit and routine. Richard glanced at his watch. One hour to detonation.

He got up from his seat and strolled back to the car where Dieter was waiting.

"I'm going to get breakfast. You stay here and wait for the catch of the day," he said, then grinned at his own wit.

"Yes, boss," Dieter said, muttering beneath his breath as he watched Richard stroll off toward one of the local cafés. He would have enjoyed some breakfast, too, but that wasn't going to happen.

Richard had sent Dieter down to the docks yesterday with a message for the local fishermen. Whoever was the first to bring in a decent-size shark would get a thousand dollars. Since it was crucial that there was no connection between Richard and Dieter when the shark was brought in, that left Dieter to wait for the day's catch on his own.

He'd been there about an hour when there was a flurry of activity on the docks. A siren sounded, and Dieter saw a helicopter take off from somewhere farther down on the shore. A half-dozen boats started up their engines and quickly set out to sea.

"Hey, what's going on?" he asked as a man came hurrying past.

"Just got an SOS call from some fisherman. Said someone's yacht blew up about an hour south of here."

"Good Lord!" Dieter said. "Are there any survivors?"

"They don't think so. Said the yacht sank before they could get close enough to help."

"That's terrible," Dieter said.

The man nodded, then hurried on. As soon as the coast was clear, Dieter called Richard. "It blew."

"What a pity," Richard drawled. "Any survivors?"

"Doesn't seem to be."

"Call me when the shipment comes in."

"Yes, boss," Dieter said.

Four long hours later, his shark came in. Within minutes of its arrival, he had the shark loaded and was on his way to an empty building Richard had rented.

The shark wasn't a great white, but it was large enough for their purposes. The precious contents of the metal box that Richard had hauled halfway around the world were finally going to be put to use. Richard had brought the box from the hotel, and now he calmly dumped the contents out into a small tub filled with salt water. With Richard watching and directing the preparations, Dieter carefully destroyed every cleanly cut edge on the bits of skin and flesh. Nothing could be left to give away the fact that they'd been surgically removed. Once that was finished, the bits were dumped into another bin of sea water, along with Richard's wallet, some pieces torn from a pair of his slacks, and a piece of bloody shirtsleeve with a button on it. After everything had soaked for at least an hour, Dieter put on a fresh pair of surgical gloves and began forcing the salty mess down the throat of the dead shark, while Richard held the mouth agape.

Once the contents were down, Dieter flushed seawater down the throat, and at Richard's bidding, he also wedged some leftover pieces of flesh between the razor-sharp teeth.

Richard was beside himself with glee.

On the other hand, by the time he finished, Dieter was of the opinion that he might never eat seafood again.

"I think that's it, boss."

Richard checked the carcass, making sure there was no trace of what they'd done. Then he took out his phone and made another call.

"Landis Taxidermy."

"This is Anton Schloss," Richard said, lowering the timber of his voice and assuming a German accent. "I called you yesterday for a quote on what you'd charge to mount my catch."

"Oh, yes, yes, of course, Mr. Schloss. I assume you've caught your shark?"

"I have. It was a very lucky morning for me."

"Congratulations. I have everything ready. Do you know where I'm located?"

"Yes. I asked at my hotel. They gave me directions."

"Super. Then I'll see you soon?"

"Yes. I have the shark on a trailer behind my car. I'll be right there."

Within the hour, George Landis had the shark lying on its side on his worktable, while Richard stood by with his video camera. He'd insisted on filming the first steps in the taxidermy process, although George hadn't seemed all that happy about the request until Richard handed over an extra five hundred dollars, which smoothed away any further objections.

The fact that Richard's video was intended to wind up on TV around the world was the ultimate in-your-face snub for those who'd tried to take him down. They would have no idea who he was, other than the poor slob who'd landed the shark that ate Richard Ponte.

He was well aware that the bits and pieces would most likely have gone unnoticed, but for the torn pieces of his clothes, to show that the shark's last meal had been human, and his wallet, complete with driver's license, four credit cards and over a thousand dollars in cash, to show who that last meal had been. Just to put a little icing on the cake, he'd dug up an old snapshot of himself and Alicia at some charity event and put that in the wallet, too. He hoped it gave her nightmares.

"Are you ready, George?"

George nodded.

Richard turned on the camera, focusing on the man's hand as he made a careful cut along the belly in a place that would be invisible once the shark was mounted.

"Ugh," Richard said as the contents of the belly spilled out, and it wasn't a fake reaction. The smell was disgusting.

He moved closer, continuing to film, making sure the camera lens was centered on what the man's hands were doing. When the wallet suddenly appeared among the offal, he cried out, "What's that?"

George paused. "I'll be damned," he said, and then started poking through the rest of the stomach contents. "Oh sweet Lord," he breathed.

"What?" Richard asked.

"I think this here is a piece of skin…human skin." George opened the wallet. "There's an American driver's license for a man named Richard Pont."

Richard rolled his eyes. No one ever said his last

name right. He moved closer, focusing the camera right on the license photo.

"I think that's pronounced Ponti," he offered.

George frowned. "I've heard that name before. And here are some credit cards and... Holy Moses, look at all that cash. Wowie, Mr. Schloss. You sure landed yourself an expensive fish."

"I think we should call the authorities," Richard suggested.

George looked startled. "Oh. Yeah, of course." He quickly washed his hands and ran to the phone. Richard could hear the excitement in his voice as he relayed his find to the police.

"You won't believe this. I just opened up a shark, and I think I found a dead man."

Richard played his part to the hilt, right up to willingly giving up the video to the local authorities, along with all his rights to the shark. They never noticed that he'd wiped down the video cassette before he handed it over. He wasn't stupid. He wasn't going to take a chance on someone running the prints, even though there was no earthly reason why they should.

"Yes, yes, I will be at my hotel for a day or so longer, then I must return home," he said as the officer took down Richard's information. "Needless to say, my taste for game fishing is gone. Poor man. Poor, poor man."

The officer handed Richard back his passport, thanked him for his service and apologized that his vacation had been ruined.

"Oh...it is nothing on my part," Richard said. "It is this Richard Ponte who is the unfortunate one." Then he shuddered. "I cannot imagine a worse fate than to be torn to shreds and eaten by such a fearsome creature."

Within minutes, he was in a taxi and on his way back to the hotel.

"How did it go?" Dieter asked, wishing he could have been present to see their faces. But they couldn't have chanced it. Not after he'd been the one down on the docks buying a shark earlier in the day.

"They swallowed the whole story," Richard said, smirking at the analogy, and then folded his arms across his chest and announced, "I'm feeling a little hungry. I think I could eat a whale."

They laughed and headed down to the restaurant.

John and Alicia had been back in Georgia for two days. They'd slept late this morning, eaten brunch, and just after one o'clock, Alicia had opted for a little tanning session. She'd gone out on the second-floor balcony off John's bedroom, stretched out on her belly on a chaise lounge without a stitch of clothes and blamed her dwindling lack of decorum on John, who would happily stay naked if society would allow it. He'd gone inside to see if he could find some sunscreen, although it wasn't something he ever used. He finally found some body lotion with an SPF factor in it that he guessed would serve the purpose and was on his way back outside when the phone rang.

He paused, glanced longingly through the sliding glass doors to where Alicia was lying, admiring her long, toned legs and that beautiful backside. The phone rang again. He started to let it go to voice mail, then noticed the caller ID, and quickly backtracked.

"Hello?"

"John Nightwalker?"

"Yes."

"This is Special Agent Joshua of the Federal Bureau of Investigation. Corbin Woodliff gave me this number."

"What's wrong?" John asked.

"Is Miss Ponte still with you?"

"Yes."

"I'm going to have to ask you to bring her to Savannah."

"Not until you tell me what's wrong," John fired back.

"Richard Ponte's yacht exploded and sank off Nassau in the Bahamas a couple of days ago. A few hours later, a tourist brought in a shark to a local taxidermist. They found a wallet, some bits of clothing and some human flesh inside the shark's belly. The wallet belonged to Ponte. We're running DNA testing on the flesh, and we need to compare it to his daughter."

"It wasn't him," John said.

Joshua frowned. "What the hell do you mean, it wasn't him? What do you know that we don't?"

"Nothing. I'm sorry. That came out wrong. I meant it couldn't have been him. You know…that it's too simple." He couldn't explain how he knew with every fiber of his being that Richard Ponte's soul was still on Earth.

"Oh. Yeah. I see what you mean," Joshua said. "Anyway, can you bring her in, or should we send a car to pick her up?"

"No. No. I'll bring her. Tomorrow okay?"

"Yes. Got a pen and paper? I'll tell you when and where, and who you'll be meeting."

"Go ahead," John said, writing down the info and trying to stay calm, when he was screaming inside.

After they disconnected, John headed back to Alicia, trying to figure out how to give her the news. They didn't discuss the immortal business anymore, so he wasn't sure how she was going to take the fact that he was certain the Feds were wrong.

Alicia heard the sliding door open, then close.

"I thought you'd forgotten me," she said.

John sat down beside her, then squeezed a little of the lotion into his palm and began applying it to her skin.

"Never," he said, rubbing the lotion in a smooth, circular motion. Then he paused, looking down at her. His throat tightened with unspoken emotion. She might never know, and he was never going to tell her, how bonded they really were.

"I thought I heard the phone ringing," she said.

"Yes. It was Joshua, one of the Feds who arrested Carruthers."

Alicia rose up on her elbows, then gave him a side-ways glance. She could tell by the look on his face that something was wrong.

"Talk to me," she said.

"Does your father keep a yacht in Nassau?"

"Yes. Why?"

"They said it blew up. A few hours later some fish-erman brought in a shark. When they cut it open, they found some human flesh, bits of clothing and a wallet."

Alicia rolled over, then sat up on the side of the lounge and pulled her knees up to her chest, as if bracing herself for what was coming.

John saw her eyes shimmer with the sudden onset of tears, but her voice was calm when she asked, "And?"

"The wallet belonged to your father. They want you

to come to Savannah for a DNA test so they can compare it to the flesh that was found."

"Oh my God," she said, and then put her head down on her knees. "Oh God…oh God."

John sighed. Did he tell her what he knew, or leave her to grieve unnecessarily? He laid a hand on her shoulder. It had to be said. Then she could do with it what she chose.

"Alicia."

She looked up. "He tried to kill me. Why am I crying?" When John didn't answer, something told her there was more. "What aren't you telling me?"

"You won't like it."

She reached for the beach towel at the end of the chaise, then stood up, wrapping it around herself sarong-style before facing him.

"There are a lot of things I don't like, but you're not one of them, so say what you need to say."

"You remember when I told you that I could sense when the Spaniard's soul was reborn?"

Alicia nodded warily. "Yes, I remember you telling me that."

"And do you remember that I also said I knew when the soul's current body was dead? That I felt an emptiness inside me?"

She nodded again, even more warily.

"I don't care what the DNA test shows. I don't care what the Feds say. I am telling you now that your father is not dead."

Alicia wanted to argue. But to do that was to call John crazy or a liar, and she couldn't bring herself to do that. Not anymore.

"Maybe the DNA tests will prove you're right," she offered.

John shook his head. "I doubt it. I don't know how he did it, but I can guarantee that your father ran a scam. We'll go take the test. And the Feds will tell you whatever they tell you. But he's not dead, and you're still not safe. Just know that, and know that I won't let him hurt you."

Alicia wanted to cry, but this time for John. Instead, she wrapped her arms around him and just held on.

"I love you, Nightwalker," she said softly. "So much. So much."

He knew she didn't buy his story, but at least she wasn't going to fight him on it. For now, it was the best he could hope for.

"When do we have to go to Savannah?" she asked.

"I told Joshua I'd have you there by 1:00 p.m. tomorrow. There will be someone from the agency at the hospital to take the sample. I guess they don't trust the regular channels on this one."

"I'm sorry," she said.

"For what?" John asked. "You've done nothing wrong."

"I know, but as long as you're stuck with me, you keep having to deal with this kind of mess."

"You still don't get it, do you, baby? I'm not stuck with you. You're the one who's stuck with me. You couldn't lose me if you tried."

She smiled, but it wasn't a happy smile. "Unfortunately, our homecoming celebration has been sidetracked."

"Not for long. We'll go to Savannah, then be back here before you know it."

"I know. And I know I have you to thank for so much.

But if my father is dead, at least we won't have to worry about him trying to have me killed anymore."

John didn't comment. No need repeating what he'd already said. She obviously hadn't believed him the first time. Saying it again wouldn't change her reaction. But it didn't matter. Richard Ponte might have fooled the Feds, but John Nightwalker was the one person who would always know the truth.

They'd had dinner served en suite. Richard waited until they were finished and the dishes had been removed before he broke the news of his next plan. He went to a drawer, took out a ticket and handed it to Dieter.

"Pack your suitcase before you go to bed tonight. Our flight leaves at ten-fifteen tomorrow."

"Great," Dieter said. "I'm ready to get back to Austria."

"We're not going back to Europe just yet."

"Why not?" Dieter asked. "I thought once this was over, we'd return to our new identities."

"That's what you get for thinking," Richard snapped.

"Then where are we going?"

"The States."

"Hell no!" Dieter said, and leaped to his feet, threw down the ticket and glared at Richard as if he'd lost his mind.

"Sit down and *calm* down!" Richard ordered.

"I'm not sitting, and I'm sure as hell not calm. If you aren't willing to pay for my ticket back to Austria, I'll buy it myself."

Richard strode forward until he was only inches away. He was so pissed, his voice was shaking. "Remember who you are," he growled. "You do not threaten me."

"I know who I am. I also know who *you* are. You might just as well shoot me now, get rid of your last witness and save the Feds the trouble."

Richard was stunned. He hadn't considered that Dieter might balk like this. He'd *always* obeyed.

"I'm not going to shoot you, for God's sake, so stop being so dramatic."

Dieter glared. "I'm not being dramatic. I'm being serious."

"What would it take to make you take the risk?" Richard said.

Dieter shook his head. "Not until you tell me why you're going."

"Revenge."

"Revenge? On who?" Then it hit him. "Not only no, but hell no. I'm not going to kill your daughter. I'm not even going to try. I've met the Indian, remember? You, on the other hand, are blithely oblivious of how deadly he is, but there's no amount of money you can pay me, because I wouldn't live long enough to spend it."

"Five million."

Dieter grunted, then scrubbed his hands across his face in frustration. "You bastard."

Richard grinned. He had him. All he needed to do was reel him in.

"What, exactly, are you asking me to do?" Dieter asked.

"I want you to help me find out where she is. I'll do the rest. But I need a driver. Someone who'll be waiting in the wings, so to speak, to get me out of the vicinity quickly."

Dieter began to pace.

"Look," Richard said. "The authorities are already of

the opinion that I'm dead. You won't be on anyone's watch list anymore. Besides, you have clean papers and a completely new look. I don't see a problem."

"That's because *you* don't *have* a problem being recognized. *I'm* the one with the problem, damn it. That Indian *will* kill me."

Richard sighed.

"Six million."

Dieter stared at Richard in disbelief. "You are insane. First, because you're willing to kill your own flesh and blood, and second, because you're willing to pay me six million dollars just to find out where she is and drive a fucking car."

"Ten."

Dieter sank down onto the sofa. "You no longer have access to the Ponte wealth. Does Anton Schloss have that kind of money?"

Richard was insulted. "Of course I have money. I'll always have money."

"How the hell would I know?" Dieter objected.

"Will you do it?"

"Only if the money is in my account before we leave this damn hotel."

"Get your laptop," Richard said.

Dieter dragged his feet all the way across the suite to his bedroom. He had a bad, bad feeling about what he'd just done, but at least he'd learned something about himself. He'd always heard that, no matter what someone was asked to do, if the price was right, they would do it. Now he knew it was true—and he knew his price. His only saving grace, if there was such a thing, was that he hadn't sold himself cheap.

A few minutes later he watched the money go into his account, then stared at it in disbelief. It didn't even look real. But he'd done it. Now he was committed.

The next morning, Dieter's demeanor was cool, even distant, but Richard didn't care. He'd gotten what he wanted. They'd breakfasted early and called down for a bellman to get the bags. Now they were just waiting for one to arrive.

Soon there was a knock on the door of the suite.

"That'll be the bellman," Richard said. "Take your bag and get out of sight until we're out of the room, then you can follow. From now on, we no longer appear together in public unless it looks like a coincidence."

Dieter nodded, then stepped into his bedroom as Richard let the bellman in.

"There are four of them," Richard said, pointing to the bags beside the door. "I'll be needing a cab to the airport, as well."

"Yes, sir. There will be one waiting for you outside," the bellman said as he loaded Richard's bags on the cart.

Richard followed him down, leaving Dieter to come on his own, carrying his own suitcase. Even though there'd been no backlash regarding the shark incident, this was not the time to become lax.

Outside, as the cab pulled up, Richard turned to Dieter. "Excuse me, sir, but are you by any chance on your way to the airport?"

"Yes, I am."

"Would you care to share my taxi?"

"Yes, thank you," Dieter said.

Richard waved to the bellman. "Put all the bags in my cab," he said.

Two hours later, they were in the air and, to Dieter's regret, on the way back to Miami.

Nineteen

John hadn't been back to Savannah since getting caught up in the attempted bank robbery. He loved the old city, and wished they were going there for fun and not a meeting with the Feds. Alicia was tense, fidgeting through the entire drive north, but it was an emotion he understood. She was facing the possibility of being told her father's death was a reality. Even though he knew that wasn't so, he expected the DNA to match. He didn't underestimate Ponte for a moment. The man was obviously capable of anything and had the money to make it happen.

The big problem was going to come when the Feds made Ponte's death official. That was when the search would be called off. After that, the man would be free to roam the world at will. If he was smart, he would quietly disappear and live out his life in whatever guise he'd chosen, but something told John this wasn't over. Ponte wasn't a man who failed, and he'd tried and failed twice to end his daughter's life. That had to be eating at him in a major way.

John reached across the seat and took Alicia's hand, giving it a gentle squeeze.

"We can do this," he said.

"I know," she said. "And you know why?"

"Why, baby?"

"Because you make me believe anything is possible."

John tightened his grip on her hand. "Since you came into my life, I'm beginning to believe the same thing."

She leaned back against the seat and closed her eyes, letting the hum of the wheels on the pavement and the sound of passing traffic lull her into a brief but welcome sense of calm.

By the time they reached the Savannah city limits, she was ready to get out of the car and get this over with.

John wanted to stop by his bank but decided to use the drive-through instead of going inside. The fewer people who could speak to their whereabouts, the safer Alicia would be.

Alicia woke up as John made a sharp turn into a bank drive-through. She could tell by the way the teller was talking to him that she knew him. As he drove on, it became even more obvious to Alicia as they wound through the streets to the hospital that John was very much at home in Savannah. He navigated the route with ease.

"You know something? I'm beginning to wonder if you really *are* some kind of superman."

He smiled. "Why?"

"I hear you talking to your business partners on the phone. I see you scanning e-mail and stock market reports. You buy and sell all over the world. You fly helicopters, and you seem to cope with everything with such ease. Do you ever get lost?"

He grinned. "Hey, baby, you know a man's never going to admit it if he does." Then he pointed to the dash GPS. "There's also technology, just in case."

She laughed. "Lord. He's gorgeous and honest. What's a girl to do?"

"Forgive me for my weaknesses and love me in spite of them?"

"Only if you grant me the same favor."

"Done and done. And by the way, we're here."

The smile slid off her face as she saw the imposing edifice of Savannah Memorial. All of a sudden they were back in the real world.

"Oh Lord."

"Don't let it get to you," John said.

He was right. She took a deep breath and let the butterflies settle. All they wanted was a DNA sample. She could deal with the results later.

It took a week for the Federal government to make their official announcement that Richard Ponte, the man wanted for treason against the United States of America, was in fact dead. After factoring in the explosion of his personal yacht in Nassau, then the DNA from the flesh found inside the shark, which was a match for Alicia Ponte's, they considered this the end of the story.

Alicia was officially an orphan. Since there was nothing left of Ponte to bury, she was spared the business of a funeral. She'd moped around the house until one night John decided he'd had enough. The next morning he went looking for her and found her, as usual, on his balcony overlooking the bay.

"I have a surprise for you," he said, tugging her up from the chaise longue.

"What is it?" she asked with a noticeable lack of enthusiasm.

He shook his head. "If I tell you, then it won't be a surprise."

She managed a wan grin, then let herself be led across the hall to the room that had once been her bedroom. One that she'd begun to use as her own little nook. She had a stack of books by the chair near the window. There was a photo of her mother that she'd brought with her when she'd first run away. As she entered the room, she noticed a second frame now sitting beside the first.

"What's that?" she asked as she pointed across the room.

"It's your surprise. If you don't like it, you can get rid of it, but I thought it would be a nice way to remember that one night in Sedona, you had a heavenly visitor."

Immediately, she knew what it was, but even so, she was anxious to see what he'd done.

The frame was small but elegant. He'd chosen black, with a black velvet backing to best display her mother's gold-and-ruby brooch.

"Oh, John. I love it," she said, running her fingers over the surface of the piece.

She tilted it to the light, watching the tiny red stones as they winked from the reflection.

"Do you ever think about that?" he asked.

Alicia nodded. "All the time."

"And do you *believe,* the way he told you to?"

She sighed, then set down the frame and put her hands on his chest.

"Someday, when I'm teaching my children about God, and the subject of angels and miracles arises, I will tell them that once upon a time I was visited by an angel, and that I know they are real."

"What do you think about me...about what I told you?"

"I believe you do not lie."

He sighed. She was skirting the issue. She didn't say she believed he was immortal. She'd just said he didn't lie. That left all kinds of room for the insanity theory, but he wasn't about to go there.

He smiled instead. "I can live with that," he said softly, then kissed her.

"As long as you live with *me,* too, we're good to go," Alicia said.

He kissed her again, and when she moved from his lips to the hollow at the base of his throat, he picked her up in his arms and carried her to bed.

The law firm representing the Ponte empire had contacted her soon after the announcement of her father's death, requesting her attendance for a reading of his will. She'd declined, and hired her own attorney to see to the legalities. She already knew she was his heir. What the rest of the world had yet to learn was that she didn't want his fortune. She'd inherited her mother's money, which was more than she would ever need. She could never have spent a penny of what she considered blood money.

When she announced her decision, through the auspices of her attorney, to sell the munitions part of her father's empire, it stirred excitement all over the business world. But when she further stated that all the monies resulting from the sale were going to the families of the American soldiers who'd been killed in Iraq, as well as to the ones who'd come home too damaged ever to work again, the media began calling her a modern-day Mother Theresa. The money would be in the billions. It wouldn't pay for lost lives, but it might keep the surviving families from losing everything else.

Every talk-show host in the nation wanted her. Publishers were offering huge sums for a book deal, and Hollywood came back with a slew of similar offers for the rights to her story. She refused them all. She didn't want to be a celebrity. She wanted to forget she'd ever been born to a man she considered a conscienceless demon.

John knew she was suffering a combination of grief and shame, but there was nothing he could say that hadn't already been said. He also knew, with every fiber of his being, that Ponte was not only still alive but back in the States. The physical pain that was his clue was a dull and constant ache. It triggered an ongoing barrage of dreams about the massacre, ending, as always, just as the Spanish galleon sailed out of sight.

When John wasn't sleeping with Alicia wrapped in his arms, he was on the balcony off his bedroom, keeping watch toward the ocean, just as he'd done so many centuries ago. He could no more explain his feelings of dread to Alicia than he'd been able to convince Chief Red Hawk of the approaching danger to the village.

Alicia knew he was unsettled, but no matter what he thought, she knew her father was dead. The DNA proved it—just not to Nightwalker. And she knew when the nightmares overtook him. She'd pretended sleep more than once as he'd wakened with a soft, muffled sob at the back of his throat. She'd seen him slip out of bed to go stand on the balcony, staring out at the ocean in the dark. And the days were no better. He let his work slide in order to stand watch. Once she'd tried to kid him out of it, only to realize the depths of his concern.

"Hey, John…what time does the guard change? We're out of milk and butter."

He turned toward the sound of her voice, saw the laughter in her eyes, and was struck by how swiftly her joy could fade if he let her father get to her.

"Sorry. I knew that this morning and forgot about it," he said. He put down his binoculars, picked up a rifle from the corner of the balcony and carried it back into the bedroom.

It was impossible to ignore the elephant in the room. "When did you break out the gun?"

"It's always been around," he said in an offhand manner. "Do you want to change clothes before we go to Justice?"

Her slacks were still clean, but she brushed at the crease, then picked a piece of lint off her shirt and ran her fingers through her hair. She'd begun going barefoot when they were home, and the thought of putting on shoes was unwelcome. It made her realize how easily she could fall into John's habit of wearing less, not more, clothing.

"I'll get my shoes, and then I'm ready," she said.

He watched her fly across the hall, then started to follow her, when an inner alarm gave a jangle. He turned toward the ocean, giving the horizon one last sweeping glance, then locked the sliding doors, pocketed his wallet and met her in the hall as she was coming out.

She put her hand through his elbow, chattering happily as they walked down the hall toward the front door, while the knot in his belly continued to tighten.

"That bitch is giving it away!"

Richard was so angry that the veins in his neck were bulging. A fleck of spittle hung at the corner of his lips. His face was awash in bloody fury.

"Did you hear that?" He pointed to the television screen. "She's put the munitions factories up for sale, and she's donating the entire proceeds to the fucking soldiers! She can't do that! I spent my life building all that, and she just throws it away? What kind of child does that to her own father?"

"Obviously one whose father has been trying to kill her."

Richard was so shocked by the fact that Dieter had dared to make such a comment that he was momentarily mute.

Dieter couldn't have cared less. He'd already figured out that the man he'd sold his soul to for the tidy sum of ten million dollars was the devil. This just proved it. How could Richard rant about his child and what she was doing with her inheritance when he wanted her dead?

Richard's fingers curled into fists as he stared at the man he considered hired help.

The urge to watch him die was so strong he was shaking.

"I won't let her get away with this," he vowed.

"You can't stop the sale. You're dead, remember?" Dieter said, and then turned his back on Richard and walked to the window overlooking Miami.

He was so tired of doing this crazy man's dirty work and living on the cusp of arrest that he'd actually considered the notion of killing the bastard for real himself.

Richard flinched as if he'd been slapped. No one turned their back on him and walked away when he was talking. Ever. His gaze landed on a plaster bust of Aristotle displayed on an antique pedestal, and he actually took a step toward it before sanity surfaced. He paused, then took a deep breath. He couldn't kill Dieter. He needed him.

Dieter turned around just as the killing look passed over Richard's face.

"You want me dead? Do it."

Richard didn't answer.

Dieter sneered. "You don't have the guts to do it yourself. I've had enough of this. I'm going out. I have my phone. Call me when you're on to your next mad moment."

"If you walk out that door, don't bother coming back," Richard said.

That option was more appealing than Richard had intended.

"Really?" Dieter asked.

Richard cursed. The interest in Dieter's voice was not the result he'd hoped for when he'd made the threat, so he chose to ignore it and threw another question at him instead.

"Did you rent that speedboat yet?"

"Yes."

"When can we get it?"

"Anytime after seven tomorrow morning. It's ours for the day. If you want it longer, you can tell him when we pick it up. He wants cash, and a deposit."

"Fine, fine," Richard muttered. "I want to be on the water by 8:00 a.m." Then he ran his hand over his freshly shaved head, trying to reconnect with his purpose. "She thinks she's safe now, coming out of hiding and moving in with that Indian. But we know where he lives."

"You can't get to him from land. He's got the perfect setup for privacy. I hot-wired that gate once, and it still set off alarms."

"Thus the reason for coming at them from the water," Richard said sarcastically.

Dieter no longer cringed at Richard's voice. He'd become impervious, although there had been a time when that tone would have made the hair stand up on the back of his neck.

"It's a long trip up the coast in such a small boat."

"I'm down to one yacht. Even though it's berthed in Miami, we can hardly use it now, can we? Besides, it's not that far, and I'm assuming you don't have a prior engagement," Richard pointed out, then waved his hand. "Go do whatever it is you were planning to do. Just be back here by dinnertime."

"Yes, Mother," Dieter said, then let the door slam behind him as he left.

Richard picked up a water glass and threw it against the wall. It shattered forcefully, scattering hundreds of tiny shards all over the carpet; then he grabbed his hat and sunglasses, and left the room, as well. He had a sudden urge to drive by his Miami home one last time.

* * *

Nightwalker. Nightwalker. Wake up.

John sat up with a jerk, his heart pounding and his body covered in sweat. The room was bathed in shadows, with moonlight dappling the walls and floors. He looked at Alicia. She was still asleep. He combed his fingers through his hair, then rolled out of bed and strode through the open doors to the balcony, welcoming the ocean breeze on his heated flesh.

The moon was full to bursting, spilling its pale glow over the water and delineating the crevices in the rocks along the bluff. Something broke the surface of the water, then quickly disappeared below. Nothing looked out of place. But he'd heard the voice, urging him to wake up. Even the Old Ones were anxious, which didn't bode well for anyone.

Just when he was thinking about going back inside, he heard the soft pad of Alicia's footsteps on the balcony behind him. He turned to face her, then took a slow, deep breath, thinking, as she moved, *She is mine.*

She was magnificent in the moonlight, bare to the world into which she'd been born, with her dark hair tousled and her eyelids still heavy with sleep. Her breasts swayed slightly as she came toward him, taunting him to touch. So he did.

She walked into his arms and gave him a hug.

"Another bad dream?"

He sighed. He should have known he wasn't fooling her.

"It's gone now," he said, and laid his cheek against the crown of her head.

"I'm still here," she said.

"I know, baby. I'm sorry if I disturbed you."

"It doesn't matter," she said, taking both comfort and pleasure in being with him like this.

But there was something that mattered that she hadn't yet told him. Something that had been on her mind for days now. Seven, to be exact. Somewhere between the time they'd met in Justice and their time together in Sedona, she'd changed her sense of direction as to what was important in life. The two failed attempts to kill her had given her a different way of looking at the world. Suddenly there were more important things than keeping a hair appointment or getting her nails done. From the time she'd fallen in love with John Nightwalker to right now, when she'd awakened alone in their bed, she'd decided to live life without stoplights and blinders. It had been life affirming and, at the same time, life changing. She'd hesitated to broach the subject because of all his bad dreams and distractions. But maybe now was the time. Maybe this would be what it took to make him happy again.

She leaned back in his arms, looking at his face in the moonlight. He was magnificent, her hero—but a hero who lived with too many demons.

"John…"

"Yes, baby?" he said softly as he fingered a loose strand of hair away from her eyes, then kissed the side of her face.

"We haven't talked a lot about the future."

He kissed the other side of her face before he answered. "You're in mine. Am I in yours?"

She smiled. He couldn't have given her a better

opening if she'd drafted it herself. She took his hand and laid it in the middle of her belly.

"You are so very in me, Nightwalker, and will be for the next eight months or so."

John heard the words yet was afraid to believe what she was saying. Her belly was flat, her skin warm to the touch.

"Alicia...what are you saying?"

She took his other hand and put it on her stomach.

"There's a baby in there. I'm going to have your baby."

A look of awe swept across his face as he thought of what was growing beneath his palms. He tried to talk, but the words wouldn't come. When her face became a blur, he shook his head and dropped to his knees, holding her close with his face pressed against her belly. This was something he'd only dreamed of. A dream that had ended with White Fawn's death. Not only had she come back to him, but she'd come back with the one ability she didn't have before. The ability to bear children. His imagination was already running wild, imagining what the baby would look like—what he or she might grow up to be.

A little startled by his reaction, Alicia dug her fingers through his hair, then stroked the back of his neck. "I take it you're okay with this."

She saw the shine of tears on his cheeks.

"John...sweetheart..."

He stood abruptly, then looked down at her, unashamed of his emotions.

"You have made me so happy...happier than you could ever know. Thank you, Alicia...thank you for loving me and for carrying our child."

John cupped her face, kissing her lips, then her nose,

then hugging her over and over again until Alicia got it. He was seriously happy. She smiled.

Then he paused and stepped back, unaware that he was gathering his courage.

"Do you remember when I told you that when this was all over, there was a question I was going to ask you?"

"Yes," she said.

"Well, I may be jumping the gun a little bit here, but hey…this baby changes the odds."

"The odds of what?" she asked.

"Of you telling me yes if I asked you to marry me."

Laughter bubbled. "Was a proposal going to be the question?"

"It was."

"And now you think you have me over the proverbial barrel because you got me with child?"

He grinned. "I was hoping for just such an assumption, yes."

"Then I say yes. To your proposal *and* the assumption, and to the fact that I'm beyond ecstatic to be having your child."

The innocence of his joy overwhelmed her. She wrapped her arms around his neck, and just as she lifted her lips to his, the moonlight caught the tiny feather in his ear. It seemed to wink, as if at some secret they shared. Then she told herself she was just being fanciful and gave herself up to his kiss.

They left Miami without looking back, Richard sitting in one of the chairs at the prow of the boat, feeling the sea spray against his face and the sun beaming down on his shaven head. At first he'd been fidgety, anticipating what he was going to say to her, wanting her to understand his sense of betrayal before her broke her damn neck. But one hour passed, and then another, and the sun got hotter, and the sea went on forever, and Richard felt a constant sense of déjà vu that made no sense.

Dieter steered without speaking, lost in his own morbid thoughts. Wondering what it was in him that made him so weak. Wondering why he was still here. It couldn't be for the money. That was already in his bank. He could have skipped out, and there wouldn't have been a thing Ponte could have done about the money. But he'd stayed. And not because he'd been afraid Richard would come after him and kill him. He felt a sickening sense of destiny, as if this had all been preordained before any of them had been born.

And so they sped over the water, bouncing with the waves that slapped hard against the underside when he steered too far into the wind. Jarring them in every way possible, except into the good sense they needed to turn back.

Richard got bored and came back to stand beside Dieter, urging him to go faster. Constantly asking how much longer it would be.

Finally Dieter turned, pointed and shouted in his face, "Look there! That's it. That big house on the bluff belongs to John Nightwalker."

For the first time in weeks, John woke up happy, remembering the news Alicia had given him during the night. He could hear her in the shower, singing what they called a golden oldie. He heard something about a pale moon rising, and then "the writing on the wall."

He hoped it wasn't a portent of things to come, and chalked it up to nerves as he went into the bathroom and joined her in the shower.

Later, after they'd shared breakfast and the dishes, he went into the office to catch up on some work. Alicia kissed him goodbye, mentioning something about going to the library to look for a book to read. A couple of hours passed as he worked. Once she walked by the open doorway and waved her fingers at him. The second time she went by she was wearing sunglasses. He assumed she was going out to sunbathe. Another thirty minutes passed before he finally glanced up at the clock. As he did, he realized the house felt empty.

He pushed back from the desk and began searching the downstairs, but there was no sign of Alicia. He took the steps up to the second floor two at a time and glanced into his bedroom, then out to the terrace. There was no one there.

He thought back, trying to remember if she'd been carrying anything when he last saw her, then remembered the sunglasses. He dashed out to the balcony to search the grounds below. And then he saw her down below, walking on the beach with her shoes in her hands, wading in the shallows as the water ebbed and flowed against her ankles.

Another sickening sense of déjà vu swept over him as he remembered standing here before, watching the village in what had once been a clearing, trying to catch a glimpse of White Fawn.

He looked out to the horizon, then beyond, and as he did, realized he was hearing a motor, although nothing was in sight.

It was just like before.

The same sense of dread.

The knowledge that evil was coming and he couldn't stop it. His heart was pounding, his body bathed in pain. The soul of the Spaniard was closer than it had ever been. He did not miss the irony of the Old Ones' ways. He'd searched the world for five hundred years without finding his enemy, and now the Spaniard was coming to him—back to the scene of the crime.

John tried to get Alicia's attention by calling, but she didn't seem to hear. He knew the sounds of the ocean were probably drowning out his voice. If only she weren't so far away. He was about to leave the balcony when a speedboat rounded the promontory far up the beach. But instead of passing by, it swerved and started toward the shore.

Struck by a hopeless sense of doom, John began calling out her name, frantic to gain her attention.

Alicia had gotten bored, but rather than bother John, she'd opted for a walk on the beach. In deference to her newly pregnant state, she'd taken the long way around rather than walk the steep, uncertain steps down the side of the bluff. It was the first time she'd gone down this way, but the farther she got from the house, the more certain she was that she'd been here before.

The terrain of the area felt familiar, and walking through the marsh grass and then up and down the small dunes, she felt at home in a way that made no sense. The day had gotten hotter, and the cool water of the Atlantic beckoned. As soon as she reached the water's edge, she pulled off her shoes and started meandering, letting the waves break against her ankles while watching for the occasional seashell to emerge from beneath the sand.

She didn't know how long she'd been down there when she realized she was hearing an engine. She paused, shading her eyes against the sun as she stared out into the bay. All of a sudden a speedboat come flying around the finger of land up the coast.

She was watching the rooster tail of spray shooting out behind it when she thought she heard John shout. Then the shout turned to a scream.

She turned toward the house to see him waving frantically. Something was terribly wrong. Then one word carried clearly. *Run.*

She spun toward the ocean. The speedboat was bearing down on the shore, directly toward where she was standing.

"Oh my God!"

She dropped her shoes and began to run, flying over the dunes, leaping the clumps of grass, so caught up in escaping to see that she was only vaguely aware of John on his way down the side of the bluff with his knife in his boot and his rifle in his hands.

As she was racing back toward John, the house and safety, something strange began to happen. Odd, disjointed scenes began to flash before her eyes.

She was still running, but through an ancient village where all the huts were on fire. There was smoke in her eyes, up her nose. Suddenly the smoke disappeared as a storm front swept through, bringing wind and the rain. She heard screams of fear and pain, then an Indian war cry.

The wind grabbed her hair, slapping it into her eyes and across her face, and then she couldn't see John anymore, and her terror increased a thousandfold.

Alicia was caught between the present and the past, running for her life now as she'd done once before—in the same place, toward the same man—while the devil and his demons surged at her heels. In her mind, a figure loomed over her, and as he did, she stumbled and fell. Then her throat began to burn. When her hands came away covered in blood, she began screaming, a never-ending shriek that came echoing down the centuries.

Screaming Nightwalker's name.

Richard saw the house rising up from the bluff, a huge edifice of wood and glass, like a giant crystal half-unearthed from the womb of Mother Earth. The house was magnificent, but it was just a house. It was the bluff looking out over the bay and the curve of the shoreline that seemed familiar. An odd sensation of having been here before swept through him, but he shook it away, telling himself that he was just anxious.

Suddenly he saw movement on the beach and recognized the tall, slender figure of his daughter. He grabbed Dieter by the shoulder, pointing, as he shouted into his ear.

"There! Look! Down on the shore! Delivered right into my lap, by God!" Then his anxiety level rose. "Damn it! She's seen us. She's running. Faster! Don't let her get away!"

The throttle was open as far it would go. The closer

they got to shore, the more certain Dieter was that he wouldn't leave here alive.

"Run it aground!" Richard shouted, so Dieter did. The engine stopped on its own as the boat beached itself on the sand. Then Richard grabbed Dieter's arm. "She's running! Catch her!"

Dieter spun on him then, snarling back in his face. "You said you only wanted me to drive."

Richard pulled out a gun and put it to Dieter's head. "Run or die. Your choice."

Dieter's eyes went wild. He slapped the gun away, then leaped from the boat. Richard picked up the gun and followed, clumsily splashing through the shallows to get to firm ground.

Dieter's legs were longer and younger than Richard's, and he soon made up the distance between himself and Alicia Ponte. She was only yards away when she suddenly stumbled and fell. Now he had her.

He never saw John Nightwalker come over the dunes, but he heard the gunshot a heartbeat before the bullet went into his right eye and blew out the back of his head.

He was dead before he hit the ground.

Richard was a good thirty yards away when the shot rang out. When a spray of blood suddenly flew out of the back of Dieter's head and then he dropped to the ground, Richard hesitated. What now? Run or die? When he realized Alicia was no longer running, he made the choice.

Alicia staggered to her feet and struggled toward Dieter's body, unaware that anyone was coming until Richard caught her in a flying tackle. They fell to the ground, rolling and kicking. The gun popped out of his hands as he rolled on top and then straddled her waist. As soon as he had her pinned, he put his hands around her neck, pressing tighter and tighter against her windpipe.

"You destroyed me! You destroyed everything I worked for! What kind of a daughter does that?" he shouted as his fury raged.

He didn't feel her pummeling his body or scratching at his neck and face, trying to reach his eyes. She was fighting for her life, and he was trying to end it. For Richard, there was no moment of familial recognition. No sense of wrong for what he was about to do. In his mind, he was destroying the enemy.

"You bitch! You unholy bitch! Not only have you destroyed everything I ever worked for, you went and gave it away. How does it feel to know you're going to die?"

Alicia couldn't believe what she was hearing. The man on top of her was a stranger, but his voice was one she'd known all her life. John had been right. Her father wasn't dead. And she wasn't going to be, either. She wasn't about to die, not when she had so much to live for.

While she still had the breath to do it, she screamed John's name, all the while fighting back, kicking harder, scratching deeper. Kneeing him when she could and pummeling him with her fists.

When Alicia raked her fingernails down the side of his face, the pain was so sudden and intense that Richard lost focus. Without remembering that he wanted her conscious as he killed her, he doubled up his fist and hit her on the side of the jaw.

Her eyes rolled back in her head as she went limp.

Richard's chest was heaving from the exertion. He was streaked with dirt and sweat. At least now he had time to find the gun, he thought. Then he heard the sound of someone running, remembered the Indian and frantically looked up.

Nightwalker was still coming, and he was less than fifty yards away. In a fresh wave of panic, Richard rolled off Alicia and began digging through the loose sand in a frantic effort to arm himself. He looked up again. Nightwalker was almost on him, coming with a cry on his lips so wild it rattled Richard's senses, and the gun was still nowhere to be found.

Then all of a sudden the air shifted and he felt the sting of cold rain on his face. The stench of burning flesh was in his nose, and his clothes were covered in blood. Men in strange clothing were running amok, slashing and burning and laughing wildly. And all the while it was as if he were standing outside his own body, watching the scene from afar.

There were savages all around, but most lay injured or dying, their wounds being washed clean by the storm that was upon them. And in the midst of it all, another savage appeared—a savage with the same face as John Nightwalker. He came out of the trees on the run with a bow and arrow in his hands, and a war cry on his lips. It sent a chill up Richard's spine as he watched the Indian slay his men one by one—slashing and stabbing and disemboweling one after the other, until there was no one left standing between them.

When Nightwalker pointed at him, Richard knew he was next. Then the savage was upon him, screaming words he couldn't hear in a language he didn't understand.

Everything around John seemed to be moving in slow motion. He couldn't distinguish between the energy of the spirits that haunted this place and the ones who'd just beached themselves on the shore. All he could hear was Alicia screaming his name. He came out of the trees and over a dune just as Dieter Bahn was about to grab her. Insanity was upon him. Not again. *Not again.*

He didn't even break stride. He shot from his hip, downing Dieter with one bullet, and kept on running. Then he turned his attention to the man with Bahn. Although he no longer wore Richard Ponte's face, John still knew him. He ran with the pain of recognition, feeling the blood pumping through the stranger's body, hearing the thunder of his heartbeat, tasting the fear boiling in his belly. The dark soul had returned to the scene of the crime.

John lifted the rifle over his head and let out a war cry that shattered the air. Then he put the rifle to his shoulder. Just as he was about to fire, Alicia suddenly staggered into his line of vision, blocking the shot.

"No! No!" he screamed. "Alicia, get down!"

She kept going, apparently unable to hear him.

His heart sank. He couldn't risk a shot at this angle, and the bastard was going to get to Alicia before he did.

John saw the man leap, taking Alicia down in a flying tackle. He thought of the baby she was carrying, and a white rage spilled through him as he kept on running. But five hundred years had changed a lot of things. Now the sand was deep and shifting beneath him, slowing his progress, hindering his speed.

As he topped another dune, he saw that Ponte had already taken her down and was now on top of her. As Ponte wrapped his fingers around her neck, John suddenly gave out a great roar of rage.

John saw him double up his fist and knock her out. When Alicia went limp, it gave John the clear shot he needed.

The first bullet hit Ponte in the arm. A second grazed his forehead.

Ponte went down screaming as blood pumped out of his wounds and soaked into the sand.

John tried for another shot, but with them both on the ground, Alicia was once more in the line of fire. He leaped a piece of driftwood and kept on running.

Suddenly Ponte came up with a gun and started firing.

The first two bullets went wild, but the third bullet went through John's shoulder, ripping through flesh with a hot, burning pain.

John staggered, then lifted his rifle to jack another round into the chamber. Just as he realized it was empty, Ponte swung his gun toward Alicia.

"No!" John screamed, then pulled the knife out of his boot and threw it.

He saw Ponte grunt as the knife buried itself in his chest all the way to the hilt.

Ponte looked down at the protruding handle and then back up at John Nightwalker. For a fraction of a second he thought he saw a half-naked Indian coming at him with a spear, and he felt a sense of relief that it was finally going to be over. Then the world went dark as he fell on top of his daughter's body.

Blocking out the pain in his shoulder, John ran the last few yards, grabbed Ponte by the back of the shirt and dragged him off Alicia. She was covered in blood as John fell to his knees beside her.

"Please let it be his, please let it be his," he mumbled

as he felt her neck, trying to find a pulse. His face was streaked with tears. He could hear his own heartbeat pounding against his eardrums, but he couldn't feel hers.

"No," he groaned. "Please, please…no."

Then suddenly it was there, steady and strong beneath his fingers.

"Thank you, God," he said softly, then pulled her into his arms and just held her.

His rage had been spent with Richard Ponte's last gasp. And so, apparently, had his immortality. Blood was still flowing from his shoulder, running down his arm and onto Alicia.

"So be it," he muttered, realizing what had happened, as he pulled his knife out of Ponte's chest, then stabbed it into the sand a few time to clean it, before sliding it back in his boot.

Then he staggered to his feet, gritted his teeth against the pain rocketing through his body and picked Alicia up. He carried her away from the carnage, into the shade beneath a stand of small trees that were bent and stunted from years of salt spray and wind. Once there, he leaned against a tree trunk, then, using it for a brace, slid downward, still holding her in his lap. When they were safely on the ground, he got his cell phone, shifted Alicia to a more comfortable place in his lap and made a call.

The phone rang twice, and then a man answered.

"Corbin Woodliff."

"Corbin, it's John Nightwalker. I have that story I promised you. But I need you to make a call for me first."

"What now? Where are you?" Corbin asked.

"Back at my beach house in Georgia. You need to call the Feds. It's about a cleanup job."

Corbin frowned. "What the hell are you talking about?"

"There are two dead men on the beach below my house. One of them is a man named Dieter Bahn. The other is Richard Ponte."

"You're out of your mind, man. Ponte is dead."

"Well, yes, he is now. Ask the FBI if they want first dibs on breaking the story, or do I call the locals and let them be the ones to break the news to the nation that Richard Ponte pulled a fast one on the U.S. government with a fancy plastic surgery job and some of his own DNA planted in a big fish."

"You're serious, aren't you?" Corbin said.

Alicia moaned. She was regaining consciousness just as he was close to losing it. He needed to get both of them some medical help.

"I've got to call an ambulance now. The bodies are on the beach. Tell the Feds to come and get them, or the tide will."

He hung up the phone, then dialed another number. This time the call was local, and he not only knew the dispatcher, he also knew the EMTs.

"Nine-one-one. What is your emergency?"

"Sandy, this is John Nightwalker."

"Why, hi there, John. Are you all right?"

"No, ma'am, I'm not. I've got a bullet hole in my shoulder and an unconscious woman in my lap. Do you suppose you could send Mark and Penny out this way? We're down on the beach below the house."

"Oh good Lord! Yes. Hang on, John, I'll have help out there before you know it."

"Thanks, Sandy."

"Who shot you? Do you need the police, too?"

"Might as well send someone on out, although you could warn him ahead of time that the FBI is already on the way."

"Sakes alive," the dispatcher said. "Hang on, honey. Help's coming."

John leaned back against the tree trunk, then looked down at Alicia. Bruises were already beginning to appear on her face, but her eyelids were fluttering. When he heard her moan, the relief within him was so overwhelming he could hardly move. Then something happened— something so fleeting that he almost missed it. As he was looking at her, her features seemed to fade, and just for a moment he saw the fleeting image of darker skin, a wider nose and a mouth always curved in laughter.

"I see you," he said softly, then tightened his hold on Alicia and closed his eyes.

Alicia came to with a pain in her jaw and a scream on her lips, only to find herself lying safe and sound in John's arms. When she saw the blood on his shoulder and the ashen cast of his skin, she quickly forgot her own pain as she crawled out of his lap.

"John? John!"

When he didn't answer, she panicked. She pulled his shirt aside, expecting to see a healed wound. To her horror, it was still open and freely bleeding.

"Help me, God," she whispered as she pulled her shirt over her head, folded it up into a thick pad and slid it underneath his shirt, arranging it over his shoulder so that it was over both the entry and exit wounds. When she began to apply pressure, he groaned.

"John… Oh God…sweetheart, it's Alicia. John, are you okay?"

He groaned again, then opened his eyes and gave her a half smile. "No, I'm not okay. I have a bullet hole in my shoulder."

"But why didn't it heal? You always heal yourself when you're hurt. Do it again. Hurry. You're losing too much blood."

"I never healed myself. It always happened before because I couldn't die. Now I can. You should be happy." He grunted as he shifted to a more comfortable position.

It was then that she remembered. Her father. Dieter. They were here! Still on her hands and knees, she looked over her shoulder, checking to see if they were alone. When she saw the bodies down the beach, a few yards apart, she felt an odd sense of relief. Her father was dead, and she was glad. What kind of a world had this turned out to be?

She turned to John. Her eyes were welling, her voice was starting to shake as the horror of what she'd seen and what she'd endured finally hit.

"John…you were right all along. My father wasn't dead. He tried to kill me. He really tried to kill me."

Then she started to cry, huge, quiet tears that hurt his heart, tears made more poignant by the silence with which they fell. John pulled her close, then lifted her hand to his lips. He kissed the cuts and the bruises that her father had put there, making promises between each kiss.

"It won't happen again. No one's ever going to touch you like that again. I made sure of that." Then he moaned beneath his breath and shifted again as the sun began to bounce before his eyes. That couldn't be good. He hoped to hell the ambulance got here soon.

Alicia felt shame for what John had gone through

on her behalf. "Who shot you, sweetheart? Was it Dad or Dieter?"

John frowned. Didn't she remember what had happened? How could she forget Dieter dropping dead at her feet? Then he let it slide. The more of this hell she forgot, the better.

"Your father shot me, but I'll heal eventually."

Then they both heard the sounds of sirens.

"Finally," John muttered as Alicia looked up to the top of the bluff. Within a few moments they saw a police cruiser pull up, and then an ambulance. She got to her feet and began waving to show them their location. Once they saw her, she knelt back at John's side.

"Help is coming, sweetheart. It's going to be all right."

John took her hand. "Help me up, baby."

"I think you should wait for the EMTs," she said, then steadied him as he ignored her and pulled himself up.

"I've been waiting too long as it is," he said. "No more waiting for us. We already made a baby. It's time we make a new life."

Epilogue

A tiny squeal, then a shriek of little-girl laughter, spilled through the doorway as John got out of the car. His heart leaped with joy, as it always did when he saw his family, no matter how long he'd been gone, which today had amounted to a little less than two hours running errands and picking up the mail at the post office in Justice.

"Daddy! Daddy!"

He grinned at his daughter, Annie, noticing that she'd already shed all but her pink Cinderella panties again. No matter how many times they dressed her during the day, if they turned their backs, she was naked, running with her little brown legs pumping and a small black ponytail flying out behind.

He quickly put the mail beneath his arm as Annie came leaping off the front steps.

"Hey, baby girl," he said as he caught her on the run. He kissed the side of her cheek, then gave her ponytail a quick tug. "Were you good for Mama?"

"Yes, Daddy…I good. Did you bwing me sumpin?"

"Look in my pocket," he said, laughing as she thrust a tiny hand in his shirt pocket and pulled out a little pack of gummy bears.

"Gummies! Gummies! I loves gummies."

She wiggled to be put down, and he reluctantly did so. He was still smiling when he saw Alicia coming out the door. Four years ago she had walked into his life and he'd never been the same. There were no words for how much he loved her and the babies she kept giving him. His gaze moved to the fat little boy perched on her hip. His eyes were black as coal, his copper skin an echo of his daddy's. His baby hair was the color of a raven's wings, and no amount of water and combing could make it lie flat. It stood straight up on his head like grass. A drop of drool hung at the corner of his mouth, and as he spied his father, he clapped his hands and then laughed aloud.

"And was the little man good for Mama, too?" he asked as he gave them both a hug.

"No," Alicia said, and rolled her eyes.

John laughed, then scrubbed the funny hair on his son's head in a gentle, playful way.

"Way to go, buddy," he said, then leaned forward and kissed Alicia square on the mouth.

She groaned beneath his lips, then pulled back far enough for him to see the twinkle in her eye.

"So…Nightwalker…did you bring *me* something, too?"

Passion surged, and he knew he would never get enough of the woman who held his heart.

"Oh yes, ma'am. I brought you something I know

you'll enjoy…if you don't mind waiting until night-time to get it."

Alicia sighed. Four years, and he could still make her toes curl.

"I feel like I've waited forever for you to show up in my life. I think I can wait a couple hours longer," she said, then took her daughter's hand. "Come on, Annie. Let's go open those gummy bears and let Daddy put his things in the office."

She gave him a wink and a smile before they walked away.

He was so full of emotion that, for a few quiet seconds, he couldn't breathe. Suddenly, anxious to be with them, he took off his coat, hung it in the closet and followed the sound of their laughter.

AN INTENSE NEW THRILLER FROM
JOSEPH TELLER

One phone call changed Jaywalker's life forever....

Criminal defense attorney Harrison J. Walker, better known as Jaywalker, receives a call from a desperate mother. Her son, Darren, has been arrested for raping five white women in a long-forgotten corner of the Bronx.

A young black man, Darren is positively identified by four of the victims as the fifth prepares to do the same. Everyone sees this as an open-and-shut case—everyone except Jaywalker.

As he looks deep into the characters involved in the crime and the character of our society, what he finds will haunt him for the rest of his career.

BRONX JUSTICE

Available wherever books are sold.

MIRA®

www.MIRABooks.com

MJT2635

REQUEST YOUR
FREE BOOKS!

2 FREE NOVELS
FROM THE ROMANCE/SUSPENSE
COLLECTION PLUS 2 FREE GIFTS!

YES! Please send me 2 FREE novels from the Romance/Suspense Collection
and my 2 FREE gifts (gifts are worth about $10). After receiving them, if I don't wish
to receive any more books, I can return the shipping statement marked "cancel." If I
don't cancel, I will receive 4 brand-new novels every month and be billed just $5.49
per book in the U.S. or $5.99 per book in Canada, plus 25¢ shipping and handling
per book plus applicable taxes, if any*. That's a savings of at least 20% off the cover
price! I understand that accepting the 2 free books and gifts places me under no
obligation to buy anything. I can always return a shipment and cancel at any time.
Even if I never buy another book from the Reader Service, the two free books and
gifts are mine to keep forever.

185 MDN EF5Y   385 MDN EF6C

Name _____ (PLEASE PRINT) _____

Address _____ Apt. # _____

City _____ State/Prov. _____ Zip/Postal Code _____

Signature (if under 18, a parent or guardian must sign)

Mail to **The Reader Service:**
IN U.S.A.: P.O. Box 1867, Buffalo, NY 14240-1867
IN CANADA: P.O. Box 609, Fort Erie, Ontario L2A 5X3

Not valid to current subscribers to the Romance Collection,
the Suspense Collection or the Romance/Suspense Collection.

Want to try two free books from another line?
Call 1-800-873-8635 or visit www.morefreebooks.com.

* Terms and prices subject to change without notice. N.Y. residents add applicable sales tax.
Canadian residents will be charged applicable provincial taxes and GST. Offer not valid in Quebec.
This offer is limited to one order per household. All orders subject to approval. Credit or debit
balances in a customer's account(s) may be offset by any other outstanding balance owed by or to
the customer. Please allow 4 to 6 weeks for delivery. Offer available while quantities last.

Your Privacy: Harlequin is committed to protecting your privacy. Our Privacy
Policy is available online at www.eHarlequin.com or upon request from the Reader
Service. From time to time we make our lists of customers available to reputable
third parties who may have a product or service of interest to you. If you
would prefer we not share your name and address, please check here. ☐

BOB08R

SN61812

SHARON SALA

32596 BAD PENNY	___ $7.99 U.S.	___ $7.99 CAN.
32544 THE HEALER	___ $7.99 U.S.	___ $7.99 CAN.
32507 CUT THROAT	___ $7.99 U.S.	___ $9.50 CAN.
32352 NINE LIVES	___ $7.99 U.S.	___ $9.50 CAN.
66967 REMEMBER ME	___ $6.50 U.S.	___ $7.99 CAN.
66966 REUNION	___ $6.50 U.S.	___ $7.99 CAN.

(limited quantities available)

TOTAL AMOUNT	$ _____
POSTAGE & HANDLING	$ _____
($1.00 FOR 1 BOOK, 50¢ for each additional)	
APPLICABLE TAXES*	$ _____
TOTAL PAYABLE	$ _____

(check or money order—please do not send cash)

To order, complete this form and send it, along with a check or money order for the total above, payable to MIRA Books, to: **In the U.S.:** 3010 Walden Avenue, P.O. Box 9077, Buffalo, NY 14269-9077; **In Canada:** P.O. Box 636, Fort Erie, Ontario, L2A 5X3.

Name: _____
Address: _____ City: _____
State/Prov.: _____ Zip/Postal Code: _____
Account Number (if applicable): _____

075 CSAS

*New York residents remit applicable sales taxes.
*Canadian residents remit applicable GST and provincial taxes.

MIRA®

www.MIRABooks.com

MSS0409BL